D1551301

DEDICATION

When we authors are remarkably lucky, we find ourselves in writers' groups, best known as Critique Groups. If we are amazingly lucky, the people in our critique group connect, and it becomes a support group, which becomes a team. We keep each other motivated. We know someone cares that we've written anything at all! We keep going.

I have become incredibly lucky. In the early stages of writing *Invisible Wounds*, I was invited to join Phoenix Hall Writers, a critique group that's still going strong and so am I. After many years, Bill Stong, John Marvin and I still review, critique and support each other.

Bill opened a special account to save my revisions and keep my story secured as I was writing.

Angels can be men, you know. Mine is John Marvin, who protected my manuscript through all its many iterations. He kept it on a flash drive and a duplicate on his computer to make sure it was safe. Because he knew it was important to me, it was important to him. In the background of northern California fires, John took it on himself to put a final copy of *Invisible Wounds* in his safety deposit box for extra protection. I didn't ask, he just did it. You are my guardian angel, John.

From that original group, I lost my staunchest cheerleader, Jack Drory, who made me promise to finish my story. Jack believed in me. He would adamantly say, "This is a story of great substance and magnitude." Those were Jack's words. "Promise me, Lyn. Promise you'll finish. This story is too important." And here we are, Jack, publishing without you. We miss you.

I am forever grateful for those magnificent men.

If we're doubly lucky, we end up in a second Critique Group. More perspective!

From Camille Minichino's writing class evolved a courageous group of people who simply wanted support with their writing, and by learning and working, reviewing and revising, we became a Tribe. These writers are generous, inclusive, fearless and occasionally a bit unhinged. We care about each other. We support each other. We joke about not wanting to miss our therapy sessions every Monday.

We share our writing, our troubles and our lives with each other. We became more than a critique group, we became a family. Thank you, Camille, for bringing this crazy bunch together and letting us loose to learn good writing by listening to each other.

Then, along came Coronavirus, and it could have shattered us. Instead, we're all back together again, meeting on Zoom. We're still learning and sharing our writing with Camille and each other.

But with Covid-19 came fear, at least for me. Fear that I'd get sick before I finished, fear that my story would never get published. Fear that the book publishing industry had gone underground, and no one was getting published. The only solution was to take control and do it myself. Jo Mele shepherded me through the process and helped me pull it all together. I am forever grateful, Jo.

Don't wait. Do it while you can. And so, I have.

Is there such a thing as doubly, doubly lucky? I think so. I discovered the amazing talent of Brian Shea, who must have intuitively understood this novel, and visually created the remarkable cover. He then designed the inside pages, while working with complicated text and a variety of font styles. Thank you, Brian, for your patience and appreciation for my story and for your remarkable creativity.

Ann Damaschino, the Editors' Editor, offered her expertise from the beginning. Your support means everything, Ann. Thank you.

These people have been my rock. I am grateful.

In no particular order, I thank this very special critique group:

Ann Damaschino, Billie Dupree, Jo Mele, David Flower, Nancy Hurwitz Kors, Judith Overmier, Charles McFadden, Brian Shea, Donna Darling, Roger Chapin, Susan Lawson, Ellen Aubry, Ginny Estabrook, and especially Camille Minichino, who brought us together, kept teaching and kept caring – about our writing, and about us.

How do you express enough gratitude for someone who is always there for you – and happens to be an amazing copy editor, who finds those tiny errors that are so easy to miss? To my chosen sister, Ellen Barrons, I offer a huge thank you. I appreciate your kindness, your support and your skills. You were always willing to help, every time I needed it.

And most notably to my brilliant, loving brother, Don Chaffee, who had the fortitude and expertise to read my not-so-final manuscript – twice.

In Praise of
INVISIBLE WOUNDS

In *Invisible Wounds*, author, Lyn Roberts, has created a compelling page-turner and has painted a dramatic and inspiring picture of a man fighting to regain his life after suffering trauma.

Chuck McFadden, Author of *Trailblazer: A Biography of Jerry Brown*

When Steven, a medic, returns from Vietnam a broken man, he discovers a cache of Civil War letters written by a doctor, equally broken. The letters provide Steven with a path to redemption, a guidepost for him to reject the doctor's mistakes, and to connect with new friends. As he regains confidence in himself, he's able to love, and to rebuild his family connections.

Ann Damaschino, Author, Poet and Editor

Invisible Wounds is a story for all of us. We have all been wounded at one time in our lives. It's what we do about it that counts.

Jo Mele, Author of *The Odd Grandmothers, The Travel Mystery Series: Bullets in Bolivia, Homicide in Havana, Mystery in Monte Carlo, Burglary in Belgium*

I was completely pulled into this novel. I cared about Steven and I wanted to read more about his journey.

Billie Dupree, Author of *Still Kicking But Not High*

You can't see Steven's wounds, but his efforts to heal them will touch you.

Judith Overmier, Author of poetry, short stories, and creative non-fiction

Lyn Roberts has written a gripping life journey. Steven, a Vietnam medic, discovers letters from a Civil War soldier that change his life. The letters offer tantalizing clues as to what happened to the other soldier more than a hundred years ago. Two men, two wars, two lives. Steven's quest to understand what had happened to another family a century before allows him to put his life back together.

Bill Stong, Author of *God Help Us, Volume I*

In this intriguing story, Roberts exquisitely captures the recovery of a Vietnam medic after discovering the letters from a Civil War doctor written 100 years earlier.

David Flower, Author of a thriller called, *Urges*, and 50 short stories in a collection called *The Book of David*

In searching for understanding of his own life, Vietnam vet and medic Steven seeks insight into the life of a Civil War veteran and physician. While seeking to understand a stranger's experiences, Steven comes to greater insight into his own life, his father's anger, and his new friends' troubles. An excellent, thoughtful read.

John Marvin, Author of *Second Opinion* and *The Stained-Glass Door*

This story is not only powerful, but credible. The reader is right there in the scene with the characters. Great descriptions. We feel sympathy for Steven and want the best for him. As you read, it keeps getting better and better.

Nancy Hurwitz Kors, Ph.D., Author of *I'll Give You My Baby if: Three Adoption Stories.*

Invisible Wounds is a fascinating story of two men in different eras, facing similar traumas. Letters written by a man from the Civil War are discovered by Steven, a Vietnam vet, 100 years later. Steven learns from the letters how to come to grips with how to live his life now in a world where war's aftermath won't let go.

Ellen Aubry, MA., Author of *The Great Fiction Book Proposal: Make it Happen*

Lyn Roberts' timely novel of a Vietnam veteran stands out from others because of her use of actual letters from a Union doctor in the American Civil War which Steven reads and compares to his own experiences. Traumatized by his life at home and in Vietnam, Steven finds reasons to move forward.

Susan Lawson, former Community College professor

Letter from Jack Drory, M.D. 2012

Hi Lyn,

May I share some thoughts with you about your novel?

This is an important book.

Your two main characters, two vets, one from the Civil War and the other from the Vietnam War, 100 years apart, deal with the same existential human issues that will never cease to exist. War issues are depicted, along with the sheer beastly inhumanity visited upon each other as opposed to peace, harmony and resolving issues between people.

And in this sea of human turbulence and mayhem, aspirations for justice and compassion, and the after affects visited upon each individual, whether a fighter, a civilian or helpless bystander, are all present and revealed.

Remember, all man-made dilemmas can be solved!

More power to you and may your writing be blessed.

Love,

Jack

The

Beginning

Northern California, 1987

The letter. His secret. His discovery. He had to find the letter. Was it still there, hidden inside the old medical certificate after twenty-five years? No one else knew it was there.

The old hardwood floor moaned with each step Steven took down the ancient hallway of his father's house – as if it knew an insult was coming. He stepped into the study, yearning for a moment of peace before the old man returned.

Get away, escape his toxic venom.

Even as a kid, Steven had been fascinated by the faded medical diploma hanging on the wall behind his father's desk. It was conferred on Lt. David R. Lane. Who was this man? Curiosity had overcome Steven. His child's inquisitiveness had to see the medical certificate up close. Not tall enough to touch it, he'd dragged the desk chair closer to the wall to reach the certificate and lifted it off the wall. His small hands couldn't grasp the wide frame and it slid along the wall to the floor. The wood frame was bent, but not broken and the paper backing was ripped but not ruined. And there it was. A yellowing paper had fluttered to the ground – a letter.

Steven had read the words over and over, then tucked it in the frame's backing, sealing the rip with tape. He lived in fear that one day his father would discover the repair, so he had never again touched the certificate. He had wondered and worried about the letter's meaning since that day he had found it as a boy. The medical certificate and the letter were dated 1868, three years after the Civil War. He couldn't forget the words. Years went by and Steven still wondered: who was this man? Why does it matter to me? Why can't I tuck him away the same way I left the letter hidden? Every instinct told him this was more than a simple medical certificate, and the letter held special meaning – for him. Somehow, there was a connection. All these years, and he'd never forgotten the letter that quietly waited in the back of the frame. His secret. His message. His letter.

Steven had been a medic in Vietnam and wondered why David Lane would become a doctor, having witnessed the unbearable conditions during the Civil War. Steven's homecoming from *his* war had not only deepened his despair but destroyed any faith he once had in the goodness of men. From the final day of the Civil War in 1865, it looked as if David Lane had left the battlefield and immediately entered medical school. Why would any man do that? Why would he choose a life of more pain and death?

Steven now cautiously lifted the antique certificate off the wall in search of the letter. Was it still there? Had he secured it to the backing well enough? He began to tremble.

He lowered the certificate to the desk, gently slit the backing, reached inside and with two shaking fingers, touched the paper, as it revealed itself to him once again. He tenderly pulled the letter out of its hiding place, returned the certificate to its home on the wall and read:

June 1868

My Dear David,
Congratulations! Your accomplishments have been realized.

You are now legitimate, a true and real doctor. I am proud of your tenacity and your wish to turn your life around. Put the past behind you and discover the answers you have been seeking.

What is that part of the oath? "First do no harm." And now you can make amends, my friend. You are ready to begin your new life. You will be a great doctor; you have already proven that to be true.

My best wishes to you, my friend
Dr. Robert James

Steven jumped when he heard the kitchen door slam.

Damn!

Hands shaking, he quickly slipped the letter inside his shirt pocket and returned the certificate to its hook on the wall. He took a deep breath, bracing for the explosion he had experienced so often. His father pounded down the hallway, every footfall an angry refrain. The floor groaned its painful response.

Go easy on the antique wood old man. It can't take your abuse much longer. Me either.

His father turned into the door of the office, brushed by Steven as if he were a ghost, plopped into the wooden desk chair, and finally looked up at his son.

"What the hell are you doing in here?"

Steven gritted his teeth. Keep an even footing. Stay calm.

"Taking another look. You know I've always been curious about that," Steven said as he indicated David Lane's medical certificate hanging above his father's head. Steven held his breath. He realized he hadn't hung it straight on the wall and casually walked behind the desk as if to take a better look. He moved the corner of the frame and quickly straightened the certificate.

"It's David Lane I'm curious about. Have you remembered where it came from? How you found it?"

After asking the question, Steven focused on his father's fists, as they tightened and clenched. Then the old man's spine straightened, menacing, as Steven recognized the familiar, rigid hostility. "I don't know – damn it, I already told you. Has your memory gone, too? I think I found it in some old pawn shop. A medical degree, from a hundred years ago. Pretty

4

impressive, I'd say. More than *you* ever accomplished. What the hell, Steven! Couldn't even finish med school. You had to leave school to fight in that godforsaken war. Lower yourself to Medic status and came back a crazy man. Maybe I kept the damn thing because I thought you would model yourself after this brave soldier. David Lane got his degree. And what did you do? You came back a drunk, a misfit, a crazed..."

"Easy, Dad," Steven said, as he strained to keep an even tone. His fingernails pressed into the palms of his hands. He tried to deflect the fury directed at him. "I'm curious. The horror of what he must have witnessed...he's...he's familiar to me. I don't know how, but I have to find the connection."

I know this man. His suffering is mine.

"Just get on with your life, you idiot. You're never going to achieve what David Lane accomplished."

Steven stepped closer and leaned across the desk. "Listen to me. The war may be over, but even after so many years, it's the torment. It haunts me. I don't believe it's possible to heal soldiers who survive war; we're permanently wounded in ways you can't imagine."

"Cut the crap, Steven. You remind me of a homeless bum. Have you looked in the mirror lately? You're a mess. What happened to your hair? It used to be the color of wheat, now it looks like you're turning gray, long and stringy. I'll bet you haven't washed it in a week. Get a haircut. And your eyes – used to be bright blue, now they've turned a dull gray. Matches your skin."

Steven cringed – declined to defend himself.

His father piled it on. "Maybe you're still in there somewhere, underneath all that grime. Go take a bath. Wash this obsession out of your system. Why the hell would you want to wade into somebody else's garbage – do something about your own mess. What happened is *over*, you fool."

Steven took a step back from the desk. "Try to understand. My war has never ended. It still plays out in my head every day."

"Look at you. You weren't even injured. So, what is this really about?" His father leapt out of his chair. "Oh, I know! This is about all the soldiers who were your patients – the wounds you couldn't fix. The soldiers *you* couldn't save. All the ones you failed." Venom poured from his tongue. "That's it, isn't it?" He plopped back into his chair, panting.

Steven leaned into his father's taunts and shook with rage as he rounded the corner of the desk and drew back his fist, ready to pound the old man. Resisting, he stopped abruptly, choked down the rage, and swallowed his urge to strike back.

He took a step back, scrutinizing his father, then quietly asked, "What happened to you? What made you so cruel? You've been punishing me my whole life. I don't remember you any other way." Red-faced and gasping for air, his father started to rise from his chair, then sank back as Steven turned to leave.

Steven took a ragged breath as something broke in him. He spun back at his father and let his pain spill out. "Can't you see? It's never over. Not for me. It eats at me and burns me up." Fury crept in as he shot back, "And what would you know anyway? You can't possibly comprehend what you haven't experienced, can you? I'll bet you never even saw combat.

Arizona? Isn't that right? Tough duty. You fought World War II in Arizona! That's *your* ugly truth, isn't it, old man."

His father turned white as he leapt from his chair and staggered back against the wall. "How dare you...you've no right...you're not...not even..."

Steven realized that any understanding was hopeless and didn't care to comprehend what his father was trying to say. Later, he'd face it later. He placed his hand over his heart and felt the letter. *First do no harm.*

Get away.

This was how it felt when he was a little boy. Punishing. Nothing had changed.

Get out. Save yourself.

He turned his back on his father and charged out of the house.

Chapter

2

And now you can make amends... First do no harm...

Steven stumbled down the front steps to the street.

What did his father know? No more than the shrinks knew. They didn't understand. What is wrong with us?

They haven't been where we've been – seen what we've seen. From war, we bring home pain and agony and guilt.

It didn't matter which war, whether it was an 1853 musket or an AK 47 rifle – it's still a gun to your head. Fear feels the same in any battle.

Time to walk it out. Steven was determined to reject the temptation to head for his old watering hole for just one shot, followed by just one beer. Nope. Breathe in – breathe out. The letter – "First do no harm..."

~   ~   ~

Keep moving.

He forced himself into a casual saunter – with attitude.

Spine straight, shoulders back – that's it – feign confidence.

Enjoy the fresh breeze on your face – be glad the smell of napalm isn't in the air.

Ahh! Let in the light.

Feel gratitude – there's no sound of gunfire.

No one's screaming for a medic. No one's in pain.

Be in the moment.

What crap!

Steven tried to tamp down his anger as he stomped down the street, away from his father's toxic words. As he walked out the tension, he ignored the bright, crisp Northern California day, aching instead for his 'go-to' place. He longed for one of those trusty, deserted tunnels he used to crawl into, embracing it as his sanctuary. First, he'd clear out the bodies, and check for anyone with a pulse.

Darkness. Quiet. Safety. No one to question you. No one to find fault.

Here he was again, fleeing his father's house, running away from the same confrontation, trying to quell the rage boiling in him. During medical school, dependence on his father had become oppressive. He needed a way out. He wanted the ability to pay for his schooling himself, on his own terms. With a college degree, he would be an officer in the army. He could save his salary and pay his own way. It was his first chance to flee his father's abuse and he had eagerly joined the war effort. Steven had survived an ugly war, only to confront an uglier battle when he returned home. His father saw him as a damaged and disappointing son.

"Shake it off," Steven said to himself. He threw back his head and howled aloud to the sky, "Listen to your father. He sees me as tortured and tormented. Crazy." That's me all right, he thought. "He'd take me in, then throw me back on the street," he muttered bitterly.

Suddenly uneasy, Steven jolted to a stop. He was being watched. A woman cautiously walked toward him, then crossed to the other side of the street. He realized she observed him with alarm; her face expressed fear and apprehension. He forced a polite smile, then nodded to reassure her and continued walking.

How pathetic he must look. His unruly hair hadn't been cut in weeks and he couldn't remember when he had last washed it. He looked down at his wrinkled shirt and saw he had forgotten to change the jeans with holes in the knees. He couldn't deny there were advantages to living in a house with a warm bed at night and a hot shower he ignored each morning. But at what price? His father's scorn was relentless and reflected the bitter resentment they felt toward one another.

I can only imagine how that woman must see me.

Some deranged thug on the loose. She sees a disheveled, angry weirdo stomping down the street, babbling to himself.

Steven flashed back to the day he had joined the Army as a college graduate, all crisp and clean, eager to serve.

"Quite a resume you've got here," the admiring recruiter had said. "Med school, huh? You left in the middle of medical school to join? Why not go to officer's training?"

"I just want Medic training, Sir. I want to learn how to heal people, then finish Med school."

"Impressive. Go serve your country, young man. You could be our poster boy with those good looks. Stay safe."

Steven knew the war had damaged him, but the fear in the woman's eyes as she passed him reflected the full extent of his torment. He had paid a heavy price for coming home in one piece.

Better to have arrived in a box.

Maybe the old man had it right. Here he was, obsessed with some ancient letter and a 100-year-old medical certificate. Yet, he felt there was a connection. He was sure of it. Something compelled him to discover the answer.

And so it had begun. A quest for answers. For what purpose, he didn't know. Nor did he care. It seemed better than listening to his father berate him and he had nothing better to do. He couldn't manage to hold down a job. Keeping to a schedule didn't work with a hangover.

The search would be a good distraction and would get him out of the judgmental, toxic atmosphere that he currently called home.

~   ~   ~

Steven's decision to start at the library would take him on a journey he could not have imagined for himself. As he walked in the direction of downtown, he decided to begin with basic research on the Civil War. He could at least try to understand David Lane's war. He would never understand his own.

He wondered what it must have been like for those poor soldiers. From what little he knew, it was a bloody, ugly war. So was his. But then, weren't they all?

He obsessed over how the medical degree came to exist. What would induce this man to become a doctor? Was Lane some kind of medic during the war? How did Civil War doctors mend the injured?

Saving soldiers in war – what a joke.

We didn't do such a great job in Nam either. What was the point of saving those poor souls?

We're all still suffering – as if we walked out of that swamp yesterday. Look at what we became – a bunch of drug-induced misfits. We came home to people protesting – against us – against their own soldiers!

He stopped and leaned over to catch his breath. Hands on his knees, he studied the holes in his jeans and decided they reflected his ruined life.

Could they be repaired? Can I?

He needed to stop the anger, stop the self-loathing. Forget his war and focus on the Civil War. David Lane's war. His thoughts returned to the apprehensive face of the woman on the street.

Would she have been in the crowd as they spat at us? No empathy in her eyes - only fear.

Chapter

3

... Put the past behind you and discover the answers you have been seeking...

Steven felt the tension melt into a sense of wonder as he walked through the massive double doors of the city library. He was struck by a glorious sense of peace and enchantment. Filtered light streamed into the building's entrance, allowing the sun to illuminate the sheen of the brass door knobs, creating an array of dancing rainbows as it sprayed across the entrance. He stopped and allowed himself to relish this single moment. His frozen heart made every effort to recognize a sense of pure joy.

Hopeful was the word it inspired, or maybe a sense of restoration, although he was fairly sure it was too late to mend his wounds. He hadn't taken the time to change into clean clothes or get a haircut and didn't much care, except he should show some respect for this venerable building. He hoped they wouldn't think he was some homeless bum looking for a warm place to sleep, although he knew he looked like one.

This feels safe. Let's see where it takes me, he thought.

An older woman sat enveloped behind a huge desk at the entrance, watching everyone who entered. Her alert eyes followed his every move. Steven nodded. She cocked her head. He moved on.

He wandered through the stacks of books, getting acclimated to the library, then paused to enjoy the sense of calm it brought to his senses. Letting his hand drift along rows of books, he wondered why he hadn't tried this before. History. Answers. Retracing his path through the maze of library books, Steven found his way back to an official looking desk. The sign said 'Research.' He stood quietly, enjoying the unfamiliar serenity, unsure how to begin his search. The desk looked deserted, so he waited, embracing the quiet.

Suddenly, from under the desk, up popped a living replica of Little Mary Sunshine. Steven could barely maintain a straight face in his astonishment. Mary Sunshine all right. Fresh off that box of raisins. Crisp, clean, and oh, so sweet. He could almost taste the sweetness. Was it apples or pears?

'Mary' cocked her head as she struggled to climb out from under the desk. He watched her carefully. Maybe not *The* Mary Sunshine, but mighty close. Scrambling to stand up, she faced him fully to reveal a polished, freshly scrubbed young woman all soft and smiling, with long auburn curls, highlighted with copper that tumbled about her face. Artists who paint portraits believe there is a perfect shape to a face that is the very definition of beauty. Steven could only gaze in wonder at the face before him. Leonardo would have loved painting her, he thought.

Too virtuous, he decided. Too refined. Out of my league. Anyway – it would end badly like all the rest.

He wondered how he must appear to her – a homeless bum off the street? He decided it didn't matter. Who cared what he looked like? Bathing was overrated.

"Hello," she said warily. "Awfully sorry. Didn't mean to startle you. I've spilled my stack of pamphlets for the lecture tonight." She reached below the chair for the remaining papers. She came up with a smile, but never took her eyes off him. He watched her steady gaze and realized she was afraid. She took a step back and said, "May I help you?"

He met her gaze and shrugged in an attempt to appear non-threatening. "Don't know. Are you a librarian?"

"Yes, I'm the library's research, history and genealogy specialist. May I help you find something?"

Steven forced himself to lessen what he knew was a stupid grin, unaccustomed to the stretch of his cheeks across his bemused mouth. Trying to equal her professional demeanor, he replied, "Yes, if you can direct me to the history books."

"Sure can," she said. "What era – which country?"

"The American Civil War."

"The Civil War? That's the lecture I'll be giving next week." She stretched across the desk and leaned toward Steven to offer a pamphlet. He froze, then took a cautionary step backward.

Not this time. Stay vigilant. No attachments.

"Nope. I don't know about the lecture, just looking for the best books to research."

She appeared not to notice his reticence and continued. "Any particular information? You could camp out here for days exploring all the books written about the Civil War."

He took another step back. "I know I must look like it, but I don't need a place to camp out, thank you, ma'am."

"No, I didn't mean..." She blushed.

Do I smell bad?

"Never mind," he said sharply. "Look, maybe you could just help me get started and it will give me some direction. I don't know for sure what I'm looking for. I don't even know why," he admitted. "I'm just exploring."

She looked at him squarely and he wondered if she felt revulsion. He studied her as she pulled herself out of his gaze and gestured for Steven to follow, then turned and began walking toward the stacks of books. He realized how conflicted he felt. He would gladly follow wherever she led him.

Just not too close.

He ignored his bewildered desire to meet her stride-for-stride and walked slightly behind. Exactly where he belonged. Did he really smell apples in her hair or was he imagining it?

"Well, maybe something that could tell me about doctors and medicine during the Civil War," Steven suggested.

She turned toward him. "Medicine? During the Civil War? It could hardly be called medicine. Their brand of medicine was barbaric. Are you sure you want to delve into that brutal practice? It's not pretty, I warn you."

"I discovered a medical certificate dated three years after the war, and it's become a challenge to me. I'm trying to understand if it has significance."

"Interesting...you have a medical certificate from the Civil War era?"

He nodded, trying to appear serious and scholarly.

Directing Steven along two full stacks of books, she said, "Here you are. Have at it. If you're back tomorrow, come say hello. My name is Lindsay. Good hunting."

So – Mary Sunshine is named Lindsay. And she smells so good. Watch yourself, Stevie-boy.

Turning to walk away, she said, "If you get interested in tracing your genealogy during your research, let me know. That's the subject of my lecture tonight."

"Civil War genealogy?"

"No, that's next week. Tonight, will be the American Revolution. Lots of people can trace their families back to the Civil War and before. They're curious about the past, about their ancestors. It's quite normal to wonder who came before us."

Normal, he almost blurted aloud. Did she say 'normal' – go tell my father it's normal, would you? Tell him I'm not so crazy after all.

Maybe that's it, Steven thought. Maybe David Lane is my ancestor. Maybe he's in my blood. Maybe we're both a couple of misfits. Does a trait like that pass through your bloodline? Or maybe we're a couple of nut cases...

He shook off the tingle of anticipation. "Thanks for your help, Lindsay. I'll let you know how it goes."

Steven watched her walk away with regret.

If I could only hold her for a moment – feel the warmth of her body.

Nope. Stay away. You don't deserve this one.

He turned to face the daunting task of making sense of the Civil War and how it could have resulted in the medical degree in his father's study, with David Lane's name prominent in the center.

~   ~   ~

As he read, Steven discovered that medical practices during the war had no basis in science but were entrenched with ignorance and incompetence. Most of those working with medical teams in the fields of battle were country doctors with little or no training in treating injuries or wound care. Disinfectants had not been discovered; surgical instruments were germ-infested, and wounds became easily infected.

Science failed those who were trying to save wounded soldiers. Little was known about the actual cause of infection, while even less was understood about hygiene and cleanliness and the deadly cost of ignorance. The tragic consequence resulted in minor wounds that easily became infected and made amputation the only solution. The humid, damp conditions in the South were like Vietnam, he realized. Neither was conducive to healing wounds.

Doctors were often referred to as 'Sawbones,' describing the common practice of amputating limbs, which for many, caused a more serious infection. 'Saving a soldier' often resulted in mutilation, but death was caused from infection.

They had limited knowledge of the deadly diseases that spread through hundreds of army camps. Infectious diseases were rampant: cholera, malaria, smallpox, measles, scurvy and tuberculosis. Dysentery ravaged most of the soldiers, with no knowledge of how to treat it. He read that the Civil War era was known as the 'the medical Middle Ages.' The discovery of the causes of most diseases was years away.

Steven discovered that the common vehicle used to retrieve the wounded from a battlefield during the Civil War was a makeshift ambulance that consisted of a 4-wheel or 2-wheel cart pulled by one or two men, although stretchers and mule litters were also used. The injured were hauled to medical tents close to the battlefield. Surgical procedures were often performed in the open air, when tents became too crowded to house them.

At least we had helicopters to rescue our soldiers, Steven thought. Better than a mule. At least we had a fighting chance to save lives. We performed the same procedures, didn't we? Cutting off limbs to save lives. Maybe we had better training and our surgical instruments were cleaner and we had anesthesia, but still – how many poor souls did we mutilate?

He flashed on Lindsay's warning – 'A brutal war.'

And so was ours, he silently cried. *So was ours.*

Chapter

4

... Your new life can now begin ...

Steven couldn't believe his good fortune. He'd found David Lane's living, breathing granddaughter.

Despite his reluctance to get too close to Lindsay, he had finally asked for her guidance – strictly business. She had taught him how to trace the genealogy of the Lane family, where he hoped to find some of David's living relatives. Within days, he had found Anna Lane, David's granddaughter. He couldn't wait. He had called her from the library's pay phone. After he explained his quest, she had allowed him to visit. He was amazed that she would trust a stranger.

As he drove down her street, he was relieved to see that the neighborhood wasn't posh, just average working class. Although her house was just short of shabby, it communicated a sense of warmth and welcome. He had washed his hair and scrubbed his body clean – fresh start.

Steven had walked with caution toward the front door, where he spied three sets of eyes peering out at him from behind the sheer front curtain, one pair human, two feline. Before he had a chance to ring the bell, the door was opened. He stood face-to-face with David Lane's granddaughter. Anna Lane was an elderly woman with gray, curly hair. Savvy intelligence blazed in her bright blue eyes.

He stood respectfully on the porch, waiting for her to feel comfortable with this stranger at her door. Although they had spoken on the phone, he realized she was probably not prepared for the unshaven vagrant-looking man standing on her doorstep.

What was I thinking? I should have at least ironed a shirt and shaved – make a presentable appearance.

"I guess you must think I look like some kind of low-life," he said, as he ran his hands down his worn shirt trying to smooth out the wrinkles.

She raised a hand to stop his apology. From her other hand she slowly revealed a baseball bat. She rolled it from back to front, to make it more visible. With a knowing grin she raised it in the air and said, "And I know how to use this. We're used to hardship around here, but I still take precautions. Can't be too careful. There's a soup kitchen down the street with families and veterans in need of help. I've learned to discern who I can trust and how to identify dishonorable people." She looked directly into his eyes. "After our talk on the phone, you seemed trustworthy, young man. I've lived long enough to know a good person when I listen to one, and now I see one."

Steven dropped his head and decided it was best not to

tell her that she was, in fact, looking at the reflection of a very confused mind inside an equally disheveled body. At least he had bathed and combed his hair, although she would surely notice he hadn't been seen by a barber in months.

Anna seemed satisfied, set down the bat and invited Steven into her little house. Without hesitation, she headed into the kitchen and indicated for Steven to follow. She opened a door that he could see led to a dark abyss. "Let's start our search right away. Is it possible we've all missed something after so many years? Maybe we'll finally discover answers to what became of my grandfather." She spoke in a whisper as if her ancestors were at the bottom of the stairs and knew there were secrets still hidden.

"My family has searched for clues to the past, and we know something terrible happened, but after his marriage, there's no documented trace of David Lane. Even his children – my father George and his sister, Aunt Mary, didn't seem to know much about their own father." She took Steven's arm. "You'll have to help me down the stairway to the basement, it's a little tricky getting to the bottom. I know better than to try this by myself."

He nodded, and held her tight, eager to begin.

Down to the basement – reminds me of my dark, trusty bunker. Feels right at home.

Chatting happily as she steadied herself on the first step, Anna explained, "All the old family papers are down there. This is our best bet to find answers. Come on, let's find David Lane. He's down there somewhere." Steven shivered with anticipation.

She took him by the hand, handed him a flashlight and led him down the rickety, wooden staircase as he steadied her. It seemed sturdy enough, despite the creaking groan produced by each step. Steven realized the sound was distinctly different from the moans generated by his father's wooden floor. Anna's stairs echoed disuse, almost as if they resented being ignored. Steven hesitated and smiled as he glimpsed stacks of old papers and piles of documents in the dim light. Their descent became a precarious journey. Dust floated above the piles of boxes as they passed more cartons along the edge of each step. The musty scent of timeworn paper rose up to greet them. He held her arm to steady her steps, as she apologized for the increasing chaos while they navigated the littered staircase.

"Don't worry," she giggled. "I don't think there are any critters down here, just piles and piles of stuff I should have gone through years ago." His foot hit cement, and Steven saw they were safely at the bottom. He adjusted his eyes to the dark basement, moved the beam of the flashlight along the walls, found the switch for the overhead light and realized the magnitude of her remark. Not piles of junk, but a treasure trove of letters, documents and yellowing newspapers, which he imagined had been handed down through generations of the Lane family. He stared in disbelief and admiration.

"This is incredible, Mrs. Lane," Steven said.

"How far back does your family's history go?"

"Who knows? There's stuff from the Revolutionary War, so I know we have Civil War documents, too. I thought we had some of David's letters, but they've never been found. With all the questions about what happened to him," she said with a hint of conspiracy, "you'd think something would be down here. The family legend was that he turned into a bad man, but no one knows why. We've never found any proof." She sighed and began opening boxes. "See, look here. This box is labeled 'Civil War' but there's nothing inside but history books." She continued rummaging in the boxes, pulled out more and threw them back. An hour of searching revealed nothing but dust and empty files. "Shine your light over there, Steven. No, that's not it. Maybe we're chasing rainbows."

Steven barely heard her. He refused to give up and moved from box to crate to an old desk, empty of everything but cobwebs. He focused his flashlight on an old dresser. "Okay if I look in here?"

"Sure. Explore all you want. We've all searched down here at one time or another. It's almost as if the family didn't want to know – couldn't confront the truth – stopped looking."

Steven dug into each drawer, shining the light on every document. Underneath a pile of old newspapers, his light hit upon on a weathered, dusty briefcase. "What's in here?"

Anna leaned over. "I don't think I've ever seen this before. Looks like it's been hidden under those old papers. And initials – look at the letters - DRL – David R. Lane?" She clapped her hands. "This has to be it! Take it out, let's look."

Steven's heart began to beat against his chest. He opened the case and pulled out a handful of yellowed envelopes, bound with a blue silk ribbon. He slipped one out of the pack and focused the flashlight on the envelope. The postmark revealed the date – March 1889. "Look at all these letters. A hundred year's old. Can we take them upstairs where there's better light?"

"Oh, Steven, this is so exciting! Could this be it? Maybe you'll be the one to solve the mystery. Will this tell us what happened to David Lane? My own father, George, would never discuss his father. If he knew anything, he took it to his grave. But whatever happened sure made my father an angry man. Maybe we'll find out. And then, there's his daughter, Mary. Oh well, you want to know about David Lane, not his children. Okay, take it upstairs. Let's see."

She fumbled through more papers. Steven stood back, resisting the urge to dig into the pile of letters. He was aching to ask more about David's children, but decided to save that story for another day. Steven was elated. Could he solve the puzzle of David Lane's medical degree, or was the mystery only in his imagination?

Steven hauled the case up the stairs, bracing himself against the railing to help Anna, while she gingerly navigated the staircase and finally stepped safely into the kitchen. As he dropped the heavy, leather briefcase on the kitchen table, her cats scattered from their post at the front window.

Steven chuckled. "Your cats don't seem to like me much."

"It's not you, Steven. Cats are a lot like some people I know. Wary and shy at first. You have to let them come to you. Just sit back quietly until they get to know you. See, they're watching. They'll learn to trust you."

"They're an interesting pair. They must be a comfort to you."

28

"Oh, yes indeed. We all need solace, don't you think?" He blinked and nodded. "Sometimes a warm, furry kitty cuddle is the best we can ask for. See, look under the chair, they aren't hiding from you any longer. Meet Tom and Jerry. They know I've accepted you, so eventually they will too. Just give it time."

Steven stood quietly so the cats wouldn't run away. He marveled at their good instincts.

"Come on, Steven. I can't stand it. Let's take a quick look. We should make sure this is what you're looking for." She gently pulled one of the envelopes out of the case and held it up to the light. He could see carefully sculpted handwriting and deciphered the word, 'soldier.' A chill slid down his spine.

"I think this is it. This is what we're searching for. And look, some of the letters are more like a draft. See the crossed-out words? And there's David Lane's name. Some of these must be first drafts of letters he sent, as if he was trying to get perfect wording."

"Oh Steven. What a gift. You may have found the answer."

"I don't have a clue what I'm looking for, Ms. Lane. We'll just fumble through this together."

"No more formalities, Steven. If I am going to entrust these letters into your care, you had best call me Anna."

To explain his quest without sounding desperate, Steven told Anna of his interest in the medical certificate conferred to her grandfather, David Lane. He was reluctant to admit he didn't understand his obsession, as his father called it, or why he felt such a strong connection to this man who had lived 100 years ago. Not wanting to seem paranoid, he suggested that, yes – maybe there was a connection way down the family tree somewhere. He went on to explain that he had been a medic in Vietnam and was curious about doctors during the Civil War era.

"Okay, here's my offer, Steven. I assume you are not living in that car parked out in front. So, you must have a place to live." He nodded, embarrassed by her observation and grateful she didn't ask where. "You may take the letters and documents with you, make copies and return the originals to me within 24 hours." She gently set them back inside the briefcase. "As we've discussed, you've brought your Honorable Discharge document to prove to me that you're a good guy. You will leave it with me until you return my letters. I imagine it's quite valuable to you. I'm taking a big leap of faith to trust you, young man. I need to know I can count on you."

He nodded, gave a little dip of his head and handed her the document.

"I'll allow you to make copies of everything and study them to your heart's content – but on one condition."

"Anything," Steven said, elated with the offer.

"I would like you to keep me informed of any interesting information you find about my grandfather. I doubt there is anyone more curious about him than you seem to be. So, it's on your shoulders, Steven. I want answers. It's been a mystery in our family for ages.

Fathers – not such a proud legacy, David.

Steven shuddered and shook off the memory, wondering what kind of devastation David Lane might have caused. "That's an offer I gladly accept, Anna. I'll be back on this very porch in less than 24 hours, I promise."

As he departed he gave Anna a grateful, steady look of thanks and resisted the urge to dance down the front walk. At the street, he turned to wave and gave a deep bow as she waved in return. Many years had gone by since Steven had felt so hopeful. He was elated that this gracious, kind woman would trust him.

He felt almost giddy and didn't stop to examine why his heart seemed to have lightened.

Chapter

5

June 11, 1881

Old Soldiers and Sailors Home
Sandusky, Ohio

My Dear Girl,
I am pained by your letter and wish
I could properly reply. Please, please
do not assume the worst about me.
Remember that things are not always
what they seem in times of war. The
information you think you know as true,
is not so. It is but a fabricated story,
told by an angry, vindictive woman.
She uses her tongue as a weapon.

It is true, we soldiers were not always so noble, but for the most part we fought honorably. It is not possible for a young, naïve girl to understand the complexities of war or conditions of battle, which occurred long before you were born. What was experienced by the common soldier during that horrible war is too brutal to share with such a tender soul. Much time has passed, with opportunity to make amends. My hope is to do just that.

With kindest regards,
David R. Lane

Girl? What girl? Steven flopped back against the library chair. What was David trying to tell her?

As he leafed through the stacks of documents, he wondered what David meant by that horrible war. Weren't they all? And who was the angry woman?

The letter spoke volumes but revealed little. Someone had been aware of David's war secrets, and *she* was out for blood. More digging required.

When he had returned to the library after leaving Anna's house, Steven read the first letter that fell into his hands. Too irresistible – couldn't wait. He'd look at just one before making copies. This first letter had been intriguing. He read it a second time and recognized Lane's sentiment. 'Things are not always what they seem in times of war.'

Now, as he pondered the letter, Steven was overwhelmed with more questions than answers. Steven read the letter again, with little insight. He understood 'complexities of battle' and conditions of war. At least he knew *his* war. But he didn't understand David's war. We were taught the Civil War was a noble war where soldiers fought for a grand cause, right? Maybe the soldiers weren't all so honorable, but the letter implied that David Lane did something terrible, and it had come back to haunt him. He must have had his own demons, Steven thought.

Don't we all.

Steven realized that understanding the realities of Civil War soldiers might give him clues. That much he could find. *But why do I care?* He gave up trying to understand his 'obsession,' as his father would say. Just go with it, he decided.

As he pulled books off the shelves, he thought he would at least gain some appreciation for what war was like for soldiers during the Civil War. His research revealed more than he could have imagined. The opening preface of the first book struck a chord in Steven's conscience as he took a deep breath and read,

War is not the fine adventure it is represented to be by novelists and historians, but a dirty bloody mess.

unworthy of people who claim to be civilized.

George A. Gibbs, Private, 18th Mississippi Infantry

"Amen," sighed Steven aloud.

Whoever said we were civilized?

Cowards, criminals and drug addicts. Psychos.

That's what my war produced. Nothing noble about it.

No adventure. No honorable sacrifice.

Steven was disillusioned by what he discovered. History revealed that many of the common soldiers who fought in the Civil War were children, just boys - fifteen and sixteen. "Maybe they thought it would be an adventure," he snarled. "Some had already lost their father in the war and some had no family left at home."

Steven was shocked to learn that young boys were told it was their sacred duty to fight for God and country, North or South, their war was considered a holy war, an honorable war. They were too young to resist, too scared to stay home, too ignorant to run away.

He read that over 600,000 soldiers died in the Civil War. Most never lived beyond their early twenties. 600,000! Steven slammed the book closed as he jumped to his feet, pacing along the stacks of books.

Children. They recruited children. Of course, all teenagers think they're tough. Think they're invincible. How naïve we all were. Human fodder. That's all we were.

"For God and country," he spat aloud. Flushed and clammy, he sat and continued to read. It got worse.

The horrifying truth he discovered was that hundreds of thousands died, not on the battlefield, but from disease, dysentery and starvation. Malnutrition was common. Few soldiers had families at home with the means or ability to send food packages to supplement their meager camp diet.

The more he read, the more his rage increased. Bile rose in his throat. He needed to sort it out. It was hard to absorb. Who would care what he felt? Not his father, for sure. He would accuse Steven of obsessing about a war that happened 100 years ago. What did he know about war, anyway? He looked around the library for Lindsay, maybe she would understand. No, not Lindsay.

Stay away.

Anna, he thought. She would care, I know it.

He resisted the urge to call her and continued reading. He discovered that most soldiers at that time had wives at home alone, or with small children, laboring to harvest the crops and maintain their farms. Their only help in the field was from the children too young to be recruited into the army.

Steven was struck by the plight of the soldiers' wives, imagining what it must have been like trying to care for small children and survive the backbreaking labor of harvesting their crops to stay alive. He wondered about Lane's wife, where was she during the war? Was she the angry, vindictive woman in the letter? He couldn't resist his impulse and went to find the pay phone and called Anna.

"Hi Anna. These letters are going to tell us a lot, I think. Do you know anything about your grandmother during the war?"

"Take a breath, Steven. Slow down. Tell me what you found."

"I'm reading about what happened to the wives of soldiers during the Civil War. One of David Lane's letters talks about an angry woman who was out for revenge. Do you know anything about his wife?"

"I think he was married after his medical training, after the war."

"It's unimaginable what most women had to endure. Families starved because there were no men at home to tend the fields and harvest the crops. Do you have a minute?" Steven didn't wait for her to answer. "Listen to this. The women and children left at home were starving. It drove women to violence. Soldiers' wives rioted at the train depots demanding goods and foodstuffs of rice and corn. And they found out food was being sent to the officers, not to the common soldier. I read this story about fifty women carrying axes, who stormed a supply depot demanding food. When the agent refused, they forced their way into the station and stole bags of flour. In another town, women by the hundreds rioted against town officials, begging them to discharge their husbands."

"At least they had the courage to fight," Anna said.

"And there's another story about soldiers who discovered their families were starving and deserted to try to save them. Here, listen to this; it says that both Southern and Northern soldiers had to make the agonizing decision of desertion or the firing squad if they were caught. Thousands deserted rather than allow their families to suffer. Many never made it home, either dying in an attempt to escape, or they were tracked down and forced to return to the battlefield in chains."

So much for that noble war.

Steven went silent, his mind racing, trying to imagine the dilemma the Civil War soldiers faced. But at least they had someplace to go, he thought, and someone was waiting at home. At least they had a fighting chance. They could walk home if they managed to escape. They weren't thousands of miles from home with oceans separating them from their families.

At least they weren't in the middle of some godforsaken swamp with no way out. Much of the fighting took place in Georgia and South Carolina. Walking distance. At least there was someone who would welcome them home.

"Steven, Steven are you still there?" The alarm in Anna's voice brought him back.

"I have to go, Anna. I'll bring your letters back tomorrow."

Chapter

6

May 10, 1888

To: Old Soldiers and Sailors Home
Sandusky, Ohio

My Dear Dr. Lane,
We were so very pleased to receive your
letter and to know your ordeal has not
defeated you. It saddens me to realize
you must reach out to neighbors to hear
news of your children.

In answer to your question, Mrs. S
told me to assure you that your daughter
and son are with their mother. Both are
lovely children, although your daughter
can hardly be called a child, she is

almost a young lady. We receive letters from Mary and have her photograph.

I haven't the least doubt a letter from you would be very welcome. I cannot say the same for their mother. She would still make every effort to separate you from your children. I suggest you do not contact your children directly.

We were glad to hear that you are getting along nicely.

Mr. Paul and I will always remain your friends,

Mrs. Franklin Paul

The next morning, Steven bounded up the steps to Anna's door. She accepted David Lane's original letters and documents that Steven ceremoniously placed in her hands. Steven brightened with anticipation. "Can't wait to show you this letter, Anna."

"Come on in and sit down. Let's see what you've found."

He raised the letter in the air. "I'm not sure what it means, but your father is mentioned during the time he was a boy. From the letter, we know that in 1889, David's son and daughter were living with their mother, and David had not communicated with either of his children for – I don't know how long. It doesn't say. But the implication is that your grandfather had done something to cause the family's separation."

Pushing her glasses further up her nose, Anna settled into her chair as Steven passed her the letter. "This proves what we thought, Steven. My grandfather, David, was estranged from his children. I wonder how much they knew about him. The mystery has always been – why? David must have been an elderly, sick man living in some old soldier's home when this letter was written to him. This is dated 20 years after the war. I think this 'home' must have been the beginning of what we know today as a veteran's hospital. In those days, there wasn't much they could do for sick old soldiers, just took them in and cared for them until they died. At least now we have a better support system for our veterans."

Steven snapped his head up and looked at her squarely. "You really think so?" He asked, revealing an edge to his voice. "I wouldn't bet on it. I sure haven't found much evidence of support. Not the kind of care most of us need, anyway." He jumped up and the cats scattered as he began pacing around the small room, back and forth, into the kitchen, in and out. Hesitating at the door to the basement he looked down the stairwell, tempted to descend into the darkness. *Back to my bunker.* He stood, then paced back to the living room. His distress increased with each step. He abruptly stopped in front of Anna's chair. Taking a deep breath, he crouched on his heels in front of her and grabbed the arms of her chair to make sure they were at eye level and spoke hesitantly.

"I want you to understand, Anna. My father thinks I've

gone completely 'off the rails,' as he calls it, over this obsession with your grandfather, David Lane. He would probably commit me to one of those veteran's mental hospitals if he had the chance. I don't know, maybe he's right. It's just an old medical certificate, why should I care? And the truth is, I can't find a single reason why I'm doing this, and I haven't discovered any connection between your family and mine."

He stood up abruptly, worried that he'd revealed too much, then plopped down on the sofa, defeated and confused.

"Steven, stop worrying about why you feel this burning need to figure out David Lane and his medical degree. I'm glad! Sometimes, we have to take a leap of faith and believe that, for whatever reason, this is what we need to be doing – right now. Try to forget your father's criticism, keep digging. There's no doubt in my mind you'll discover what you need to know. Believe in your instincts. There has to be a reason – a connection of some sort."

Steven gazed at her with gratitude. "Thank you for your trust, Anna. I know there's a reason. I can feel it." He jumped to his feet. "I get so furious with my father sometimes and wonder why he takes such pleasure in tormenting me. It scares me and I get so filled with rage. I want to pound him into the ground. All he does is criticize me. I can feel his disdain in the pit of my stomach. He doesn't understand at all. He wants me to erase the past and become the sweet, obedient son I was before the war. Well, that boy is gone forever, never to return."

"Yet, the soul of that boy is still in you, Steven. I've seen him."

"Well, I haven't. That boy died on a rice paddy somewhere in Vietnam."

"Steven, listen to me. That boy has been disillusioned and hurt and wounded, but he's still in you. I know it. I wouldn't have allowed you to step through my door if I hadn't seen the real you. It doesn't mean you have to become a compliant child again to please your father. You are not required to be the son *he* wants you to be. You only have to be true to yourself, and honest with the person you really are, as the man you are today."

"Are you serious? You don't know the real me, Anna. My truth is ugly and painful. *My* truth is...what I really want..." Steven paused, taking in air, not sure he wanted her to know. Almost in a whisper, he said, "The truth is, I wish I could go down to that dark hole of a basement and hide. I want to create my own bunker where I feel safe. I want to stay in the dark and try to deny any knowledge of who I've become. I want to get away from all the cruelty and suffering in this world. That's what I want." He plopped onto the sofa, grabbed a pillow and held it to his chest.

"I understand, Steven. I really do. Sometimes I wish I could too. It's cool and dark and there's no one to bother you or question you. No one to attack you. Unfortunately, I can't. It's not so safe for me to navigate those stairs on my own anymore," she chuckled. "So, I stay up here and find solace from my friends, my charity and my cats. Maybe that's what you're doing. You're trying to find relief too, only your comfort will come through knowledge and understanding. Maybe David's pain is your pain. When you appreciate his suffering, you'll understand your own. You seem to have found some kind of connection..."

He jumped to his feet and began pacing again. "Yeah, well this isn't about me. It's about your grandfather, David. Let's see what we can learn from this letter."

"All right, Steven. I won't push. Let's look at the letter again. I've got all kinds of questions. Why doesn't David know anything about his own children? We don't know why they're with their mother and why David's family has been removed from his life. We don't have any answers as to why he was in the Old Soldier's Home. Was he sick? Was he broke? Something may have happened to him during the war that left him with a disability, or over the years some illness might have taken a heavy toll on his health. Has your research told you anything about disease and illness during that time?"

"That's it! That's what I need to figure out first. Thanks, Anna. Now I know what I should do. I need to get right back to the library and see what more I can learn. I'll call you later or maybe come back. Is that okay?" She nodded. Giving her a hug of gratitude, he hurried out the door, thinking in amazement that he might just have found himself a friend.

~   ~   ~

Three hours later he was back on her doorstep. "Anna, this is unbelievable. May I come in and read some of this to you? I've got answers to our questions."

"Sure. Come in. Come sit down. Oh look! Tom didn't try to run from you this time. He's getting comfortable with your feet at least. Lean down a bit, and you can see Jerry peeking out from under the sofa. See, just give them time. Okay, I want to concentrate. This is going to be good."

"Just listen, Anna, and help me understand. I wonder

how much of this affected your grandfather." He consulted his notes. "Okay, here goes..."

He leafed through the book. "You were right. There were all kinds of diseases during the Civil War and we don't know which ones may have weakened David Lane. This book says they didn't know much about germs; disease would spread through entire camps just because the soldiers were in close quarters with each other. At the beginning of the war there was a measles outbreak, the epidemic spread, killing thousands of men.

"Then I read a medical history of the relationship between malnutrition and disease. During the Civil War, food was dangerously scarce. Failing crops or a confiscated harvest led to starvation and contributed to illness and disease for both the families at home and soldiers in battle. To combat starvation, they concocted this cracker called hardtack. Ever heard of it?"

"Just the name makes it sound awful. Probably resembled cardboard."

"I'll bet you're right. Hardtack was the main staple in the Union Army. It contained little nutrition, but was given to the soldiers because the rats wouldn't steal it."

"Ugh! Imagine how it must have tasted if even the rats didn't want it," Anna said.

He laughed, and said, "Well, at least they didn't have snakes trying to steal their food like we did. That's what we got in my war. Anyway, the Confederate soldiers baked cornbread, which quickly found its way into the stomachs of rats instead. What little meat they received went rotten because it wasn't properly cured. Fruits and vegetables were non-existent for the regular soldiers. Once in a while they'd find a lone vegetable in a field, but it was rare. The soldiers became desperate for food and raided the fields on farms when they marched through, sometimes stealing from farmers on their own side. Animals were stolen or slaughtered on the spot. Imagine the poor farmers, who were mostly women trying to maintain the farm. Nothing was left for them to eat."

"It's a wonder anyone survived."

"I think you're right, listen to this. 'Their other important food was called 'salt junk.' It was pork and was usually infested with worms, or bacon that was eaten raw when there was no time to cook. Imagine being so hungry, you'd eat raw bacon. Whenever cooking was possible, the meat was fried in rancid grease, which gave the soldiers dysentery and sometimes they died from it. In the South, most of the plantations had grown more cotton and tobacco than food products, so the Confederate armies often lived at starvation levels.'"

"How could they even lift those heavy muskets? They must have been desperate."

"Sounds familiar," Steven confessed to Anna. "I was close to starving once and awfully tempted to eat a rat. Couldn't go through with it, though."

She gasped in horror. Steven grimaced at the memory.

"The soldiers in the Civil War weren't so lucky. Or maybe they were just desperate. Each camp had designated soldiers who took turns being on rat patrol, using the rancid bacon scraps for bait, then they would divvy up the day's catch, and each soldier was allowed to prepare his ration any way he wished: fried, stewed or baked rat. Nasty way to get protein."

Anna squirmed.

"Here it is. 'Malnutrition led to deadly diseases, killing twice as many men as those who died in combat.' I couldn't believe it, so I did more research. Remember I told you historians document that 600,000 people died in the Civil War? I wonder how many died of disease, and not in battle. 600,000! I read that number more than once. And to make it worse, there was bad weather. It shows that bad weather along with lack of proper nutrition and clean drinking water left soldiers susceptible to pneumonia, malaria and lung diseases. I wonder if that's why David ended up in a veteran's home. Something like tuberculosis can infect a person's lungs and untreated will eventually kill you. I learned that much when I trained as a medic."

"Even today, there's a lot we don't know," Anna said.

"You're right. The soldiers in Vietnam were exposed to all kinds of diseases, too. Tuberculosis, dysentery, dengue fever and even leprosy. The difference was that in my war we had medicine to help the soldiers. Do you know what disease had the most cases?" Anna shook her head. "Malaria! But, by then there were ways to combat it. But still, there were 40,000 cases of malaria during the Vietnam War. And, most people know about the horrors of Agent Orange. I'm not sure how well those poor soldiers have been helped.

How could they do it? Permanent injuries to our own soldiers.

"At least they had cures for most diseases, didn't they?" Anna asked.

Steven nodded. "Yeah, I'm sure we had better care than the Civil War grunts. I found more about what caused diseases in all my research. The army camps were filthy. Here it is, listen, 'Sanitation in the camps was mostly ignored, inviting an infestation of flies and rats that contributed to the spread of bacteria and disease.'

"Those poor guys didn't stand a chance. Imagine living like that. I'm quoting, 'Little was understood about the importance of hygiene, and it was impossible to maintain. Soldiers lived in the stench and filth of camp life, unable to clean themselves for weeks. They carried misery and hunger from camp to camp.'"

"It's a wonder that anyone survived," Steven mused. "And here's another story about hunger. It tells about bands of soldiers who not only stole food from farmers, they stole from their own government's army supplies. They discovered when the trains would be coming through and would intercept the supply trains, making off with an entire cargo of bacon, flour and meal. Now that's ingenuity. Hot damn!" Steven shouted. "That's what I like to hear. Fight back!"

Anna laughed. "Well, I guess you could hardly blame them."

"I'm quoting again. 'At several camps, rumors circulated about food that was kept hidden from soldiers. They raided commissaries on their own army posts where they discovered warehouses filled with food and realized how much had been held back by the elite officers and not rationed to the common soldier. They found casks of brandy, whisky and piles of ample foodstuffs.' It had been reserved only for the officers. Common soldiers were starving..."

"How despicable. How could they do that to their fellow soldiers?" Anna asked.

"War can easily blur the lines between right and wrong. In Vietnam we had fragging, and it happened more than they admitted."

"What was it? I've never heard of it."

"It was called fragging when an enlisted man killed a despised superior officer, with a hand grenade. It happened fairly often in Vietnam. I wonder if common soldiers shot their own officers as far back as the Civil War?"

Chapter

7

June 15, 1890

To: Old Soldiers and Sailors Home
Sandusky, Ohio
Hon. John Sherman:

Respected Sir:
In my sore need, I turn to you for
help, although I have hesitated to
bother you about a matter so trifling
when compared with the objects of your
everyday activity. I was a soldier and
served in the 62nd Regiment P A
Infantry from July 1, 1861 to July 13,

1861; served 3 years and was discharged because of expiration of term of service.

I had my variations of fortune and health, but over three years ago had to avail myself of the comforts of the Old Soldiers' and Sailors' Home because of heart disease and chronic bronchitis. I put in a claim for a pension under the Act of June 21, 1890 acting as my own attorney. I have not received a response. I, therefore, as a last resort, ask you to use your influence to have my claim settled soon, as the weather here is most dangerous to my health.

I am a Republican casting my vote for Lincoln in November 1860. This information will do me no good probably, but with you, cannot do me harm.

Earnestly hoping that you may see your way clear to help me.

Most respectfully yours,
Dr. David R. Lane

"Jackpot!" Steven rejoiced. The next day he had discovered the letter and wondered if this John Sherman was the same man as the original author of the *Sherman Anti-Trust Act*. Why did David's letter sound so desperate? And why was receipt of his pension taking so long?

The letter was a goldmine. He was beginning to feel like a history detective.

Damn, this feels good.

Gives me just what I need - purpose.

The letter confirmed that David Lane had served as an infantryman in the Civil War.

It showed he was from Ohio – and fought as a Union soldier. Steven wondered if David ended up in those godforsaken swamps throughout the South.

Was it the same for David? Slogging through swamps. What a damn cesspool.

Steven sought to right himself.

David's war. Concentrate.

What did he experience? He had researched enough to know it was an ugly, violent war. Tore the country apart.

Sound familiar?

At least there were no protests in David's war, right? From his research, Steven understood that in the Civil War each side had a defined cause. No ambiguity. You either fought to preserve the Union or you fought for secession with the Confederates. Soldiers understood what they were fighting for. Soldiers believed in their war. No confusion. No duplicity. Deception was in *my* war. They lied to us and deceived us. The Civil War was straightforward. North and South. Isn't that what they taught us in the history books?

Steven tried to sort out the information revealed in David's letter to Sherman. Did men just sign up because they believed in the cause? How were soldiers recruited or was there a draft? There must have been some sort of conscription in those days. He had begun more research. He was surprised by the amount of time he was spending at the library. Was research the only reason? He occasionally ran into Lindsay, but reluctantly kept it neutral.

Keep your distance. Too tempting.

Steven had passed by a glass display case at the library one day and didn't recognize his own reflection.

What a bum I've become. No wonder there's fear in her eyes.

Stay focused! David's war – forget Lindsay.

He began digging through more history books and discovered information he could barely fathom. Agitated and yet exuberant, he longed for his gentle mentor. Despite his reluctance to depend on anyone, he realized he was eager for Anna's acceptance. Amazed by his willingness to connect with this wise old woman he decided to take a chance. The phone booth at the library had become his private communication tool and the nearby table was his office. He made the call, and Anna eagerly invited him to come back.

"Pick up some fresh bread on your way. I've just finished cooking a gigantic pot of soup for the Open Heart lunch we're having down the street, but there's still plenty for you and me. Come when you can." Steven eagerly loaded up the books and headed for the door.

~ ~ ~

When Anna greeted him, Steven smelled the welcoming aroma of soup simmering on the stove.

The simple warmth of a cozy kitchen – how I've longed for this.

The sensations almost got the best of him, then he straightened his soldier-spine, handed Anna the loaf of bread, gave her a shy hug and dashed toward her old stove for a better look.

"Welcome to my kitchen, Steven," she laughed with obvious delight. "Hope you like vegetable soup, it's my specialty. I made enough to feed an army, which is where most of it will go tomorrow. It feels mighty good to help those poor folks. Maybe you could help transport it for me."

"A homeless shelter in your neighborhood?" Steven drew back trying to hide his fear, uncertain he was ready to commit.

"No...it's not..."

Damn, not a place like that. Not again. Oh yeah, I know what to expect. I've seen plenty...

"Steven?"

Stop being such a baby.

"We'll see, Anna. I may have another commitment," and despised himself the moment the words left his mouth.

What is wrong with you? You don't have to live there. You're just delivering some fuckin' soup. Can't you even commit to that?

Walking past him to stir the soup, Anna looked puzzled and said, "Oh well, we'll see what tomorrow brings. Come test my concoction – kitchen sink soup."

"I'd eat it any day – straight out of the sink if I had to," Steven said.

After lunch Anna said, "Let's see what you found that was so interesting. I can't wait to hear. Read on!"

Steven shuffled through the papers looking for the Sherman letter as they both plopped down on opposite chairs in the living room to face each other. He marveled at the sense of calm and comfort that enveloped him, being with this good woman. Anna laughed as her cat, Tom, leapt into Steven's lap, scattering the papers and settling into a contented purr.

"Looks like you found a friend, Steven. He's a rescue cat. Very discerning in the company he keeps."

He gently placed a hand on the cat and felt the warmth, startled at the rumble of his purr.

Maybe that's what I need. Maybe she'll rescue me, too.

Gingerly stroking the happy cat, he gave Anna a rare smile and replied, "Good thing these aren't the original letters."

Not to be outdone, Jerry the second cat, jumped into Anna's lap as Steven leaned to the floor and scooped up the fallen papers. He read the Sherman letter to her. He proposed the same questions that had been roiling around in his head. "Why would David be so desperate for his pension? Was he broke? Could he have lost all his savings even though he had become a doctor?"

"Ever hear of the financial crisis called the Panic of 1873? I read somewhere it resulted in bank failures and a depression. I wonder if David was ruined financially. Could that be it?" Anna asked?

Without answers and unable to speculate, Anna listened to Steven's ramblings. "The more I study this, the more curious it gets. Maybe he tried to avoid the war. Did you know they ended up with a draft, just like my war? I never knew there were violent protests against recruitment during the

Civil War."

Finding his research papers, Steven continued, "It's crazy what they did!" He read from his notes. "Protests during the Civil War were rampant on both sides. As the war progressed, wives and families became desperate, most having no means of income without their men at home."

He looked up at Anna then continued reading. "In protest to forced recruitment, angry mobs smashed shops and burned the mansions of the rich, looting and destroying property." He looked up with mixed emotions. "Think of the chaos they created."

Almost gleeful at the idea of citizens pushing back against authority, Steven referred to his notes. "As the war raged on, and more soldiers were needed, groups of women banded together and took up arms, seeking vengeance against recruiters who arrived in their towns to draft their men into service. Anti-war meetings grew, and religious groups gathered in protest, believing this was unjust. Many of the poor complained that this was a rich man's war. They believed only the wealthy would benefit. And this may be the most despicable of all," Steven said. "With enough money, conscription could be paid off to avoid going to war. The rich could avoid doing service! For three hundred dollars, a man could buy his way out of the draft. Or he could pay a poor man to take his place and fight for him. Unbelievable!"

Truth be told...What I would have given...anything to get out of that hell-hole...too late now, the damage is done.

He looked up at Anna and added with disgust, "Sounds like history keeps repeating itself. With enough money, you could buy your way out of any war – David's war – my war.

Get a deferment, get a medical excuse, figure out a reason to be 4F. Maybe back then they took any man with a pulse who couldn't afford to buy his way out."

"Wars seems to have an awful lot of similarities."

"And it gets even worse. Here it says that medical exemptions were bought off. It says that many men feigned lameness or blindness, even resorted to self-inflicted wounds to avoid being sent to war. Draft opposition became violent as riots broke out and people died before ever seeing a battlefield. And listen to this – it says recruitment officers were ambushed and murdered before reaching the town where they were headed. Now that was a clever solution for draft dodgers," Steven said. "Just kill them before they find you. Kill them before they ruin your life. Too bad we didn't use that tactic." He stopped abruptly, overwhelmed by his true feelings. "Sorry Anna, it's not a very noble approach." He dropped his head.

Damn, I like their style. This was more vicious than my war. No running off to Canada for these folks – just stand firm and fight back.

Without giving Anna an opportunity to respond, Steven continued reading. "Recruitment didn't provide enough soldiers, and many men were falling ill from disease or were dying in battle faster than they could be replaced. Forced recruitment followed."

Well, there it is again...human fodder. That's all we were.

"It seems that a draft during the Civil War became inevitable because the antiwar sentiment was so strong and the attrition rate was so high." He looked up at Anna, wondering. "Maybe that's what the letter meant. The letter says he was old and sick, needed money to move out of the Old Soldiers Home. Had he tried to deceive the Army? Was he a deserter?"

Maybe that's it! Get the hell out of that damn war. Just disappear!

He scanned the letter again and realized his fantasy couldn't be right, yet lost himself in wishful speculation. David could have walked home. Soldiers tried it often. Some made it. The letter gave Steven the dates of service and the assumption that David Lane was honorably discharged. Yet, he was in poor health in 1889 – thirty years after the Civil War. In those days, he was considered an old man.

"What happened during those years?" he wondered aloud.

Anna answered with more questions. "Why wasn't there any family nearby to comfort him? It sounds like his only option was to be in that Old Soldier's Home. Was there no one to care for him? Why did he become so isolated? Families took care of each other in those days. Didn't they?"

Not my family.

We came back from an ugly war and got a cruel 'welcome.' Fighting in that God-awful swamp was bad enough, but facing the reception we got was... Family, what family? Even my own father didn't try to understand. Kept saying I wasn't the same, just a hard, cynical loser. Thought I must have gone over the edge. Yeah, well maybe I did. Who didn't? Carry your demons with you. Just don't let on. Hide them in the pit of your stomach.

Anna interrupted his thoughts. "Something awful must have happened to my grandfather. Something went terribly wrong. A doctor. How could he be broke and begging for his pension? That's the big question you should try to unravel, Steven. If you learn the answer to that, you might discover the mystery of David Lane."

"Looks like I've got more digging to do." Steven gathered the letters and headed for the door.

"Let me know if you can help tomorrow," Anna reminded him.

"I'll do my best to be here...bye, Anna."

Get the hell out of here...don't want anything to do with homeless shelters.

Chapter

8

In my sore need, I turn to you for help...

Terror gripped him in the pit of his stomach.

Nausea. The bats were back, attacking from the inside.

Fear – delivered to his throat, threatening to choke the breath out of him. He could taste the acid rising from his gut.

Reminds me of napalm. Same revulsion. Nope – don't go there. Just keep moving, he pleaded to his reluctant legs.

Okay, try deep breaths. Deeeeep breaths – in and out. Easy does it.

Shit!

What are you so afraid of, anyway?

He knew it didn't do any good to re-live the humiliation of hunger and handouts.

A little fear won't kill you, will it?

Steven wondered why he had promised to help Anna deliver her soup to the shelter. How could he refuse this kind woman? She had given him the gift of trust and friendship. Yet, the moment he walked out the door he regretted his commitment. Facing the reality of another homeless shelter was his own private agony. He decided to ease the way and do a simple drive-by. Test it out.

It might make it easier if he did a practice run. Just take a quick look.

He drove toward the shelter, determined to test his resolve.

Slowly, slowly. Not too close to the curb. Keep moving forward.

Shit! Can't do it.

He stopped abruptly, slammed on the brake and leapt out of the car, gasping for air, unable to continue. He swallowed hard to keep the nausea from reaching his throat and began to tremble.

Look at yourself! I'll be helping. Isn't that what she said? This time I'm not taking food, I'm bringing food.

Maybe I can just walk by. That's it – casually walk by and take a look at the same time.

~   ~   ~

Forcing himself to take one step at a time, Steven's legs betrayed him. His knees buckled and he struggled to stay upright.

Oh great, now someone's going to see me and think I'm this drunk, staggering along in the neighborhood. I could laugh at myself if I weren't so pathetic.

Okay, try again – head up, shoulders square, spine straight.

64

Walk. Keep moving.

And he did.

Walking with as much strength as he could muster, Steven forced himself to move, one step at a time, one foot then the other, cautiously and purposefully.

Okay, maybe I can do this.

Looking straight ahead, he saw the shelter getting closer. He panicked. The bats took charge as fear crept through him, slowing his gait to a shuffle.

Nope, not anymore. Not this time. Face it. This time you're not taking a handout, you're providing one. Keep going. Walk, you fool.

Determined to move forward, Steven continued walking briskly, proud of his steady gait, when he suddenly saw someone heading toward him. He was terrified the guy might know him. There were so many who suffered a similar fate and they all seemed to end up in shelters like this. In desperation, wounded vets would gather in silent understanding.

How pitiful we are. We were supposed to be the warriors, not the ones who continued to stumble.

He wondered if anyone came out on the other side of war with their soul intact. Did every war manage to spit out damaged men?

Lost in despair, Steven failed to see that the man was almost upon him as they walked toward each other. He forced himself to keep moving, afraid to look up, afraid to acknowledge him. At the last minute, as they passed one another he looked up, startled to confront the compassionate face of a kindred spirit. The man nodded in recognition and kept walking. Steven saluted him with silent acknowledgment and continued moving forward, grateful he had triumphed over his fears – at least this time.

~   ~   ~

The next morning he showed up early, arriving at Anna's door determined to help with the soup delivery. He wanted to explain his fear of the shelter, but he wasn't sure she could understand his humiliation. He had to try.

"You're just in time for breakfast." Anna greeted him with a warm smile, trailed by the welcome aroma of hot coffee and bacon sizzling on the stove.

"Anna, you're my savior. I didn't know how hungry I was, don't think I ate last night." She flipped two eggs onto a plate with a pile of bacon and gestured for Steven to pour himself a cup of coffee.

"Dig in," she said, as she joined him at the table. Suddenly famished, Steven did as he was told, grateful for her kindness. "How does someone forget to eat," she asked, rising to retrieve the rolls from the oven. "Did you find more information in the letters?"

"No, it was a different kind of search." He hesitated, stopped chewing and plunged ahead. "I owe you an apology. I hope you can understand my reluctance to help you take the soup to the shelter. You see..." He hesitated, not sure how to explain.

"It's alright, Steven. You don't have to explain a thing to me."

"But I want to. You've been so kind to me. Your generous heart seems limitless." His eyes glistened. "And here I am, dreading to do this one simple thing you asked of me. You see...well...uh...you see, I once lived in a shelter like the one where you volunteer. I was the one needing help in places like that. It was awful, Anna. There I was, a decorated veteran, begging for handouts. It was humiliating." His voice trailed off as sorrow overtook his courage to continue and he hung his head, unable to say more.

"Oh Steven, I am so, so sorry. You don't have to explain, and you don't have to do this. I have a neighbor down the street who can help…"

"No. Here's the good part. I forced myself to walk there yesterday. And I proved to myself that I could do it. So, whenever you're ready, so am I."

"Well then, let's finish breakfast while it's hot and get going." They ate in silence, and she quickly washed the breakfast dishes, as Steven hauled the pots of soup into her old pickup. As she drove the short distance to the soup kitchen, Anna smiled at him. "You're a brave man, Steven. Just remember, I'm right by your side."

He smiled in gratitude and nodded, hoping he would not humiliate himself. He still feared he would bolt.

As they approached the building, Steven was not surprised to see a long line of shabby men waiting for the doors to open, knowing in his gut exactly how it felt to be one of them. As they drove to the entrance, anxiety overcame him. His stomach did a backflip and nausea rose in his throat. He grabbed the door handle, ready to jump from the moving truck until, to his amazement, he saw that they were quickly surrounded by children jumping up and down, waving and laughing. His anxiety mellowed as he absorbed the joy of their happy little faces.

He was not surprised to see the familiar scruffy veterans,

but many of the families with children looked so painfully lean and hungry. Yet his astonishment was surpassed by the crowd's response as the truck stopped. The people erupted in a roar of greeting and applause as Anna stepped from the pickup.

He gave her a nod of appreciation and jumped from the truck, lifted out a pot of soup and set it down until someone could tell him where he was to take it. He silently rejoiced.

I have prevailed.

Several men stepped forward to help Steven carry the soup pots as he followed them into a huge kitchen and dining hall. While the soup was warming, veterans and families respectfully sat on benches, waiting to be served. Anna walked among the tables greeting many by name, each one offering a nod or a shy hug. Steven was left to face his own private struggle as he stirred the soup and silently watched in wonder at the gracious ritual of giving. He realized this was not the kind of shelter he was dreading, but more like a family soup kitchen. Stirring the pots of soup gave him comfort as they warmed on an ancient industrial stove housed in the make-shift kitchen. Volunteers were slicing bread and tossing a huge batch of salad greens.

"Salad," he said aloud. "This is amazing." He turned to one of the volunteers and asked, "Where do you get all the lettuce and vegetables?"

"We grow most of it ourselves," a man replied. "Come look out our back window. We have a community garden where we grow vegetables, and lettuce in the summer. The people who benefit also help tend the garden. We teach them how to plant, hoe and harvest. We provide the seeds and teach them how to garden. You know the old saying about 'teaching a man to fish' – same idea. It works wonders, and the kids get healthy meals. Most of these people aren't homeless, although we do know some who live in their cars. You are looking at the working poor – never enough to cover the cost of food. We do the best we can for them."

"I'm very impressed," Steven said.

"There's our master gardener – always helping us produce the best crops."

He walked out the back door to the lush garden to see what was in season, watching with admiration as someone in oversized coveralls and a baseball cap expertly harvested a row of carrots.

"This looks like a lot of work," he called out. As the baseball cap fell away and copper curls tumbled down her shoulders, her face revealed the one person he least expected to find digging in the dirt.

"Steven," Lindsay said. "What are you doing here? Looking for a free meal?"

His face turned to chalk, as the memories and humiliation came roaring back. He bolted for the door, raised a hand to Anna and fled to the exit.

~   ~   ~

His heart raced as he made his way down the street, fleeing Lindsay's mocking voice and his heightened sense of dishonor.

How could she think that, he wondered? 'Looking for a free meal,' I'm sure that's what she said. Do I look like such a bum? Does she see me as just another low-life veteran?

Reaching his car, still parked in front of Anna's house, he leapt into the driver's seat and sped off without looking back.

Lost in thought, Steven was startled to find himself in front of his father's house, driving on instinct, not realizing where he had taken himself. His father's house. He had never thought of it as his home – this was his father's control tower.

Steven slipped in the front door and walked quickly to his small office, where he grabbed a handful of David's letters.

"Can't even say hello?"

Steven whirled around, facing his father, anger roiling up to his head. "I'm in a hurry. This isn't a good time."

"Am I so repugnant to be around? Come on, boy. Let's talk. You are clearly agitated again. What is it this time?"

Fearing another ugly confrontation, Steven pushed past his father. "Not now," he said, and rushed out the door.

Seeking the one place that might offer sanctuary, Steven drove to the library, holding his packet of letters as if they were a lifeline, gripping them with his right hand, steering with his left. He felt confident that Lindsay wouldn't be there. She had to complete her gardening duties at the shelter.

Damn do-gooders – so smug and sanctimonious.

I should introduce Lindsay to my father.

Chapter

9

September 9, 1890

Old Soldiers and Sailors Home
Sandusky, Ohio

My Dear Dr. James,

It has been some time since we last corresponded, and I hope this letter will somehow find its way to you. We have now become old men, and while the war is many years in the past, it seems to rage anew in our hearts and souls. Can you explain to me what happens to such men in times of war? Does the agony never leave us?

Cannot our dreadful deeds be expunged from our hearts so that we can go to our Maker, forgiven of our sins? Must the fear and self-loathing haunt us forever? Can you offer any insight? I fear I need counsel soon.

Your fellow soldier and friend,
David Lane

Steven sat upright, dumbfounded. There he was – Dr. James! It had to be the same Dr. James who'd written the letter he discovered in the medical certificate – the letter of congratulations. He would check as soon as he returned to his father's house.

He could have written this same letter today, 100 years later. Oh, how he ached for answers to the very same questions.

Ours were distinct wars, yet the toll it took was the same.

Not such a "civil" war was it?

No research necessary to understand this letter, Steven realized. "I'm right there with you, David," he said to the library walls.

It wasn't so different – what our wars did to us. Not so different at all.

Steven wondered what he meant by 'dreadful deeds?' What went so wrong for him? Nothing he couldn't relate to.

72

Nope, don't go down that road, Stevie boy. Don't remember. Put it behind you.

Guilt. It was the agonizing guilt. Why couldn't he have done more? Saved more lives. Couldn't always save limbs, but by God, we sure saved what we could. So, why did I survive? Does anyone come away from war unbroken, unscathed?

It's war itself that drives soldiers crazy. Sounds like David lived with the same misery.

I've seen what it does to men. I've lived it.

Isn't there some way out of this? Will I ever feel joy – know the happiness of one good day?

Leaving the library, he stumbled down the staircase to the street. Time for another attempt to walk it out. He tossed the research books in his car, then laid one hand on the stack of letters as if to bless them. He believed the letters would be his salvation.

Somewhere behind him a car blasted its horn. Steven ducked for cover and in a panic started to run, crouching low to shield himself. The car horn followed him up the street as he turned the corner to escape the noise, hands over his ears, then over his head to protect himself from the bullets that would inevitably rain down. He tore around another corner, almost knocking down the old man walking toward him, then slowed his pace as the air in his lungs gave out. Leaning over, hands on knees, Steven fought to catch his breath.

"Hey, you okay?" the man asked. Steven dropped his head, gasping for breath, unable to speak and shook his head.

The old man put one gentle hand on Steven's back as his chest heaved, unable to take in air. "Just give yourself a minute, young man. You'll be alright. Try to breathe deeply.

That's it. Okay, now stand up straight and let air into your lungs. You're not helping yourself all hunched over like that. Come on, stand up. Look at me."

Steven stood straight and looked into the man's warm, intelligent eyes.

"Come along. Let's sit in this café a minute. I'll get you something to drink." The man took him by the arm and walked him into the coffee shop. Steven realized the horn had stopped and took another deep breath. Sitting down at a small table, the old man ordered two lemonades, as he watched Steven recover.

"What set you off?" He asked.

Steven blanched in fear of revealing himself, staying silent.

"It's okay, I understand those triggers. Lots of my patients reacted the same way. They call it hyper vigilance. It is the result of fear or panic."

Baffled and humiliated, Steven cocked his head and looked at the old man with the unspoken question, 'How did you know?'

"I'm a doctor. Used to treat war veterans. I retired, but hell, I'm not too old to observe – to help. My brain still works. My name is Robbins. Dr. Samuel Robbins. They call me Doc." He stuck out his hand and shook Steven's, who sat silent, attempting to shut himself off. "Worked at the Veterans Hospital for 40 years. Tragic, really. All those poor souls, suffering from war trauma."

Steven jumped out of his seat, knocking over the chair, preparing to bolt.

Oh no! Not another one. Get me out of here. No more analysis. Spare me the psycho-babble.

Sam stood, seeming to be aware of Steven's discomfort. "Are you feeling better? Looks like there's color in your cheeks now." Sam pulled out a card and pressed it into his hand. "I really might be able to help, young man," then he smiled warmly and walked out of the café.

Steven stood in rigid silence looking down at the card. As a waiter walked up to take his order, he bolted for the door.

Chapter

10

September 20, 1890

Dr. Robert James
Columbus, Ohio

My Dear Dr. Lane,
It was with great sadness that
I received your letter and humbly
sympathize with your despair and regret.
I too continue to relive the War after
all these years, tormenting myself with
the errors we made, the scarce number of
souls we saved and the devastating limits
to our healing abilities. The shattering

truth is – we didn't know how to help those poor souls much of the time.

Yet, I can attest to your effort my friend, under the most difficult of circumstances and despite the lack of an authentic license, I knew you to be a skilled and caring healer.

If I compare you to many I encountered in the field, you were by far superior to the many inept, fraudulent doctors who were practicing medicine in name only; they often caused more suffering than healing. At the least, we stayed away from drink most of the time, and did not succumb to the addictions that cursed so many in the medical field.

Remember David, after the war you righted your wrong and obtained your medical degree. No one was the wiser, and many a soldier benefited from your ministering. I suppose it is foolish to be putting this secret in writing, but much *time has passed and who will fault old men such as we?*

It is now time to heal thyself, my friend.

Your friend,
Dr. Robert James

Steven sat back, eyes wide. "Whoa!" he hollered to the empty house. "Dr. James again. And David Lane was practicing medicine without a license."

Now I get it, Steven thought. That's why his medical degree was dated after the war. He was covering his tracks, getting a degree as soon as possible. And there's the reference to 'inept, fraudulent physicians.' What does that mean? And the implication that Civil War doctors became addicted to drugs.

Welcome to my war, David! Not so different after all.

He almost laughed out loud at the irony, as he recognized the similarities of David's war and his. Drugs and War. The realization hit him like a brick – *were we so much the same?* Refusing to resurrect his own history, he zeroed in on David Lane's. The letter implied that Dr. James and David Lane survived the war unscathed by the temptations of alcohol, which must have been readily available to medical officers during the Civil War.

Yet something didn't feel right to Steven. Despite Dr. James' assurance in his letter, something happened that ruined David Lane. Years later, he was still tormented. The early letters implied his family had abandoned him. Why?

~   ~   ~

Steven could hardly wait to return to the library to unearth answers to this new revelation. Ignoring his reluctance to run into Lindsay, Steven sped back to his sanctuary. A smile stretched across his face as he entered. He nodded to the librarian sitting at the main desk but didn't slow down to see if she responded. He somberly made his way to the familiar Civil War section, looking for clues by expanding his search to include medical practices and doctors who were recruited to the battlefields during that period.

In the archives he found original letters from soldiers and intriguing anecdotes from Civil War doctors. He discovered evidence that spoke of ignorance and antiquated medical practices, physicians who were severely limited in their ability to heal wounds and combat infection. He found stories of soldiers who had suffered under the incompetent, inebriated doctors entrusted to treat their wounds, who wrote home pleading for help. The letters were wrenching. Suffering was often made worse by carelessness and neglect, by doctors who became addicted to alcohol and other drugs.

And I understand what drove them to it, he thought.

After a battle, there was often only one surgeon on site, one doctor was expected to treat hundreds of wounded soldiers. Steven found a quote from one disgruntled surgeon who fumed, "I am tired of this inhumane incompetence, this neglect and folly, which leaves me alone with all these soldiers on my hands, five hundred of whom will die before daybreak unless they have attention and I with no light but a five-inch candle."

He read of widespread callousness among Civil War doctors. Neglect of care for the wounded was the prevailing attitude among military officers as well. One officer wrote, "The business of war is to tear the body, not mend it."

No shit!

Then he found a statement that turned his stomach. 'There were never enough attendants assigned to help all the wounded and never enough ambulance wagons to carry them. Despite complaints from doctors, what ambulances they had were often diverted to carry the personal baggage of high-ranking officers.'

So, besides our helicopters in Vietnam, we had a strong dose of compassion for our wounded, Steven thought. We eased their suffering the best we could and sent them off for further medical care in the fastest time possible. Medical science had made significant advances in 100 years. Saved lots of lives that way. He was heartened to find something about *his* war that reflected better methods and better treatment.

Next, he discovered Mary Walker, the only woman doctor who practiced medicine on the battlefield during the Civil War. She cautioned against the overuse and unnecessary practice of amputation. She was ignored by her male counterparts, who viewed her as inferior, a female. In her diary she wrote about secret examinations with soldiers slated for amputation, teaching them it was their right to refuse surgery when not essential, and how it might cause more harm than good. She knew how many times the procedure led to infection and death.

He stood and leaned against the table, then straightened his spine, as if to honor Mary Walker.

It was the women who became saviors.

He dug further along the library stacks and found stories about the thousands of Civil War female nurses, called the 'angels of the battlefield,' who volunteered at military hospitals, comforting the wounded. Defying the rules of proper conduct for women in that era, Clara Barton was able to break through to the battlefields and served as a volunteer nurse on the front lines. Her efforts changed the face of nursing forever. Hundreds of young women defiantly opposed the dictates of family and society to volunteer as nurses during the war. It was considered scandalous to have any contact with a stranger of the opposite sex, regardless of their pure motives to care for the wounded.

"Leave it to the women to save the world," Steven said aloud, pressing the book to his chest as he rose – then bowed in a simple gesture of admiration.

"Of course, it's the women. Who are you talking to, Steven?" Lindsay poked her head around the corner, grinning at his noble performance as she returned his bow with a deep curtsy. Startled and embarrassed to be discovered bowing to a phantom, he straightened to military attention.

"Don't mock me, Lindsay," Steven demanded.

Without thinking, and with as much dignity as he could muster, Steven grabbed his letters and slammed the books into his bag. As he stalked out of the room, Steven could hear

Lindsay call after him, "It was just in fun. I didn't mean to..."
Her voice trailed off as he walked out.

~ ~ ~

Confused by his own abrasive reaction and angered by his renewed humiliation, Steven raised his book bag chest-high and ramrodded his way through the front door of the library, forcing fresh air into his lungs to calm the fury. Throwing himself into the front seat of his car, he slumped forward, tears of shame draining his rage.

His knee-jerk backup plan was isolation.

Hide out, find your bunker, be safe. Get a grip you idiot. Be a man. What did they tell us? Find comfort. Seek out one person who would understand. Okay, I can do that.

Besides, he couldn't wait to tell Anna about the letters and the revelation about 'Doctor' David Lane. And he needed to explain his abrupt exit from the shelter that morning.

"Anna, this is Steven," he said from the pay phone at her neighborhood market. "Any chance I could come by? I've got news about your grandfather."

"Perfect timing, Steven. There is someone here I want you to meet. Dr. Sam Robbins dropped by to see me. He is an old friend..."

"Sam...oh...uh no..." He realized it was the do-gooder doctor who had tried to help him.

Run like hell. And dropping the phone – he did.

~ ~ ~

Halfway down the block, Steven stopped mid-stride. Paralyzed with fear, he gulped air, exhausted from the terror that relentlessly overwhelmed him.

You idiot. What are you so afraid of? A little conversation? An old man who thinks he can fix you. Good luck with that! Face your demons.

Steven did a determined about-face and directed his steps back to the market where he gathered a bouquet of cheerful daisies in his arms.

"Wow, must be some special lady to deserve flowers," the store clerk chuckled.

Steven grinned, "She sure is."

Determined steps led him to Anna's modest house. She opened the door at the same moment he rang the bell. He walked through the door and shyly thrust the flowers into her hands, with an apologetic bow of his head. "I have no excuse for my flight from the shelter this morning. I'm sorry if I caused you any embarrassment. Couldn't help it – just had to leave and..."

"No explanation necessary, Steven. I appreciated your help. You weren't obligated to stay."

Wow! No recriminations. What a relief.

"Oh, please – let me introduce you to my dear, good friend Sam Robbins." Steven watched as the old man rose slowly with a sly twinkle in his eye, silent and knowing.

Steven pasted on a polite face. "Oh, we meet again. Yes, Dr. Robbins rescued me from another bout of running away today – seems this is my day for it."

He hesitantly held out his hand. Sam Robbins took it firmly in both of his.

"I'm glad to see you again – Steven is it?"

Steven nodded and eased into the kitchen to help Anna

retrieve a vase for the flowers. She gave him a warm hug and brought the flowers to the table. Anna filled the silence between the two men and explained how Sam had entered her life.

"On the very first day we were setting up the Open Heart food kitchen, we were struggling to get everything prepared to serve our first meal. A long line of hungry veterans had already gathered at the front door and it got pretty chaotic. We were still feeling our way, trying to figure out how best to serve so many people, and along came Dr. Robbins. He just showed up!"

Sure, Mr. Do-Gooder himself. Dr. Sam to the rescue.

"He walked quietly among the veterans, and explained the delay, promising food was at hand. He even organized some of the men to help. What a savior he was that day! And ever since, he's been our rock." Anna put a hand on Sam's arm.

Good luck saving me, Doctor. No fuckin' way.

"At this stage of my life, I'm glad I can still be useful," Sam said with a grin.

"Useful is an understatement, Sam. You're indispensable to us."

No way, Steven thought as he nodded in polite acknowledgement. *I've had enough of all you altruistic saviors.*

Steven nodded his head, but stayed silent, hoping for invisibility. He dreaded a conversation about their encounter when he tore down the street in terror, reliving his earlier, bizarre behavior. It was obvious to him that he was always running away from something, or someone. In a single day, he had bolted from the shelter (actually from Lindsay) and from his father, then from – what – a stupid car horn, then from

Lindsay again, and now from a confrontation with this old man.

What the hell am I running away from?

He looked up, startled. He had not realized that Tom the cat had settled into his lap, purring contentedly. Steven unconsciously stroked his silky fur.

Tom, the rescue cat. My new buddy.

Anna had been speaking to him.

"So, what's the latest with my grandfather, Steven? I'm all ears." Turning to Sam, she explained, "Steven became interested, because David Lane was a soldier in the Civil War, and well – Steven seemed to have things in common with him. What have you discovered, Steven?"

He displayed the latest letter with great formality. "This is kind of mind-blowing, Anna. Your grandfather was posing as a doctor during the Civil War and practicing medicine without t a medical degree." He held up the letter from Dr. James and read it to them.

"Incredible, huh? I wonder how he got away with it?" Anna asked.

Turning to Dr. Robbins, he added, "I did some research on what it was like to be a doctor during the Civil War – pretty awful. A lot of the doctors they recruited were simple country folk, who knew how to deliver a baby or a calf, but nothing about war wounds."

Wanting to assure Anna, he added, "So that explains why your grandfather's medical degree was dated after the war. Looks like he was covering his tracks. He was treating wounded soldiers as if he were a doctor. Have you ever heard of this, Dr. Robbins? It's pretty curious, don't you think?"

"I'm not too surprised. I don't know much about the Civil War, but I know their medical practices were primitive and their doctors were painfully ignorant. They didn't understand hygiene and the relationship between clean instruments and infections. Maybe David had a natural understanding of healing and just wanted to do his part in the war effort. Medicine was still in the Dark Ages in the mid-1800s. Medical science since then has shown great advancement in saving our injured soldiers."

"Yeah, I know. But wounds take many forms. How many come home suffering from the kinds of wounds that don't show? How many are forever tortured and in pain? Oh, never mind. We're all messed up – one way or another..."

"Steven, it's not hopeless. There are people who know how to help veterans," Sam said.

"Not the way I see it. The only true solution is to end the killing and the destruction, and...and...end war itself!" Steven shouted.

"Amen," chanted Anna.

"Yes." Sam agreed. "But right now we have to learn to help our soldiers survive their pain, their memories and their guilt."

Ahh, here we go. I can hardly wait – he's going to say, 'Just get on with their lives.' Yeah, just get over it.

"It's such a heartbreaking waste of human potential."

Steven stroked Tom vigorously.

I'll just get a cat. Warm and cuddly. Let's get off this...go to safer ground...

Turning to Anna, Steven said, "Well, there sure must be more to your mysterious grandfather. Something else went wrong. I just know it."

"All we have are those documents and letters."

"Hey," Sam said, "What about *your* father, Anna? He was

the son of that Civil War soldier. Didn't your father ever talk about your grandfather? Follow in his father's footsteps? Anything like that?"

Steven watched Anna work it out.

Anna sat stock-still. She shuddered as if in shock and said, "No, not ever. I never heard my father mention David, *his* father's name. Not ever."

They sat silently, trying to absorb the meaning of this revelation. Anna had told him about her memories of the stern, silent, angry man who was her father. What had made him that way? Steven realized this was part of the puzzle to understanding why, at the end of his life, David Lane was estranged from his family.

Sam Robbins looked up at Steven. "Looks like you have more reading to do, young man. Are there any more letters or documents?"

"Lots," Steven nodded. "Problem is, I read one letter and it sets me off on another course of research, so it's been slow-going. I get curious about what it was like for them in that war, during *that* time. I don't know why I want to understand, but I do."

"Maybe it's your nature to compare your world to theirs. Maybe by understanding their war, you can make more sense of your own."

"Maybe, but I have my doubts that it will help much. I'm never going to understand my war."

Especially the one that still lives inside me. And the constant battles with my father.

Steven stood abruptly, dumping the startled cat off his lap. "Forget it. We are not going to solve anything here. We three cannot achieve world peace, or anything close to it."

Sam stood, taking his arm. "Of course not, Steven. But we can start with us. We three. Maybe if we make some small gesture, some way to advocate for all those who suffer, maybe it's a start. Maybe you can find some measure of peace."

"Forget it, Doc. I'm out of that war. The peace I crave doesn't exist."

He turned toward the door, poised for another escape. Sam gently held his arm to pull him back. Steven whirled around out of his grasp.

"I said forget it, Doc. Find yourself another victim." As he twisted the doorknob, Steven turned with remorse and waved to Anna. He threw open the door and pounded down the steps to the front walk, wanting nothing more than to make it to his car before he humiliated himself with another outburst.

As Steven slid into the driver's seat, Anna flew down the walk after him, frantically waving both arms over her head. "Stop! Don't move, Steven! Don't start the car. Help me!"

"What now?" he yelled, trying to dispel his anger at her hysteria.

"You left the front door open. Tom ran out. I think he's under your car. Don't run over him. Please, Steven. Help me find him."

Steven jumped out and lay down in the street, stretching to see under the car. No sign of Tom.

He rolled further under, listening for any noise or cry from the cat. No noise. Anna came to stand by the car as he lay on the asphalt. "See anything?"

"Not so far. Are you sure he's under here?"

"I saw him race after you, but he never crossed to the other side of the street. He's got to be under there."

"Do you have any cat treats? He's not on the ground. He could have climbed up into the motor. We need something to entice him out."

"Okay. Now don't move." Anna chuckled. "See – he didn't want you to leave either. He's trying to keep you here, or he wants to come with you."

She ran back in the house, returning with a bag of cat treats. "Try these." She dropped some treats in his outstretched hand. "Just talk to him quietly. He must be scared. He doesn't know his way around outside."

"You've got to be kidding me. I don't cater to a cat."

"Well, you had better learn, Mister. You are not going to hurt my Tom. He's been your friend."

Anna grinned as she heard, "Here kitty, kitty." She could hear soft whispers coming from under the car, and knew Steven had given in.

"Got him!" Steven shouted. He wriggled out from under the car, held the frightened cat with both hands and lifted him into the air toward Anna. She grabbed Tom and held him tight.

"Where did you find him?"

"He had worked his way onto my wheel, between the tire and the fender. Can't believe he could get up in there so fast."

"See, I told you. Cats know. Tom senses you're in some kind of pain. He chased after you and didn't want you to leave. He wants to comfort you. Come back inside."

No more comfort, thank you.

Steven nodded to Sam who stood watching the rescue unfold. "Sorry, Anna. Not today. Gotta go."

Chapter

II

September 29, 1890

Old Soldiers & Sailors Home

My Dear Dr. James,

I reluctantly respond to your most recent letter. That I take pen to paper in this matter is most likely a grave mistake. Perhaps I will simply confess my grief and save myself from the burden of despair by burning it, as I should do with yours.

Your thoughts in my regard and your remembrance of our time at war are sorely misplaced. Perhaps you saw me as an earnest, faithful student of medicine, but it was not an accurate observation. You delude yourself, my friend. I was no more honorable than the doctors you describe. The nurses are a more accurate recipient of your admiration, as they were our true angels of mercy. They deserve your esteem, not I. For I confess that the seduction of alcohol claimed me as well and I have suffered the agony of that knowledge and the dreadful consequences of my behavior as my life has since unfolded. I assure you I have received due punishment for my sins and have lived in penance and disgrace in the years that followed.

There is nothing more I can say. I have no one else for whom I must make amends. They have left me. My evil deeds have delivered me into the life I deserve. I am rightfully alone in my grief. I thank you, my friend, but I don't deserve your generous thoughts.

With great regret,
David R. Lane

Steven found tears welling up in his eyes.

I know this guy.

Steven spoke to the letter as if he could invoke the spirit of David Lane. "You poor, broken man. I'm beginning to have some sense of what happened, and why you were abandoned by your family. You were just like the rest of us and suffered in the same way we do."

Unable to tolerate another letter with a wrenching confession, Steven reached for more distraction – his pile of research from the library's shelves. As he began thumbing through more Civil War history, it struck him that the singular difference between himself was David Lane's estrangement from his entire family. Steven's father was abusive, but at times tried to set him on the right track. Sure, his father harassed him and railed against him and demeaned him, and they butted heads constantly. But his father had taken him in. He was not living on the street. Steven looked around his room at the comforts he enjoyed. Here he was with a roof over his head, a place to study, a warm bed and a decent meal to be found in his father's house. Not that he felt welcome, but the door remained open.

It's probably because he's such a control freak, Steven thought. He wants me to be more like him. He thinks he has all the answers. What does he know? Never fought in a battle.

All I know is, he can't comprehend my world and doesn't even try.

Steven decided to change focus from the toxic nature of his father and concentrate on the good people – *The Angels of Mercy*. David had written about the Civil War nurses. *Let's see what I can find*, he thought as he reviewed David's letter.

An hour later, Steven's father pushed open his study door. "Didn't know you had come home, Steven. Nice of you to let me know. There's enough chicken for two. Want some?"

Steven kept his face buried in the book.

Don't take the bait.

He looked up and said, "Chicken sounds great. What can I do to help?"

"I've got it covered. Come on out of this cave. Take a break."

They ate dinner in blissful silence, neither man wanting to create more tension. After finishing his meal, Steven said, "Good chicken, Dad. Is this one of your new recipes?"

"No, it's actually from your mother's old assortment of experiments. She sure could cook. I miss that."

Don't you remember why she quit cooking? Why she left you? Probably couldn't tolerate your cruelty any longer.

In an even, steady tone he said, "I don't remember this one. It's good. You always were a great cook. Thanks."

"No, she was the best. I...I really screwed up."

No shit!

Steven sopped up the last of the chicken sauce with bread and didn't look up, resolving to stay silent.

"So, what have you found that's so interesting? You couldn't even lift your head out of the book. Still checking on your Civil War doctor?"

Steven took a deep breath.

So, we'll stay neutral.

"It's been a real education, Dad. I'm learning all kinds of interesting stuff about medicine and the doctors during that time. That medical degree you have in the other room has opened all kinds of issues. Did you know that during the Civil War there were nothing but country doctors who had no background related to caring for the wounded? They were sent into a battlefield and were expected to care for hundreds of wounded men right there in a field hospital with dirty instruments. Antibiotics didn't exist in those days."

"Why would they do that? Didn't they get any training?"

"It doesn't sound like they got much. Lots of lives were lost because they had no idea what they were doing. And those poor soldiers – their only salvation was the nurses. Now there's a story all by itself."

"Nurses? I didn't know they had nurses back then."

Wow, is this an actual conversation?

"From what I was reading, it wasn't easy. It says civil society in the mid-19th Century was extremely strict about the proper decorum expected of women. It wasn't acceptable for an unmarried woman to be alone with a man, much less bathe him or dress his wounds. So, women who wanted to volunteer for nursing were frowned upon and had to defy their families and society and go against all the social norms of the day."

"Sounds like the first round of women's liberation."

"Yeah, doesn't it? Can you imagine having to challenge all society's rules just to volunteer to help? And get this – one of the requirements was that only plain women were accepted. If you were young or pretty, you were rejected. You had to be middle-aged, or a widow. They had to wear brown or black clothing with no ornaments, no bows or curls, no jewelry, and definitely not the big hooped petticoats worn at that time.

"You mean they thought those poor wounded soldiers were going to make a pass at their daughters?"

"Guess so. But women volunteered anyway, and they were the ones tending to the soldiers' mutilated bodies and amputations. The soldiers called them their 'Angels of Mercy.' Over 2,000 women volunteered as nurses during the Civil War."

"Pretty impressive. How come we don't know much about them? There are lots of books about the battles and slavery."

"I guess the stigma remained and women didn't advertise their defiance against polite society. But you've heard of Louisa May Alcott. Did you know she was one of the first to volunteer as a nurse? And you probably know the name Clara Barton. She brought in food and clothing and medical supplies to the Union Army and managed to get right up to the battlefield and helped perform surgery on wounded soldiers, which was unheard of at that time. Seeing a man unclothed was considered sinful. But as more and more soldiers were wounded, the field hospitals became desperate and the lines of propriety came down. Clara Barton was the woman who started the American Red Cross."

"Amazing."

"Oh, and then there was Mary Ann Bickerdyke. Sounds like she lived up to her name. Always bickering with the doctors, arguing for better care for the soldiers. Wait, let me read this to you. Speaking of amazing..."

Steven ran to his room to get his book.

I'm having a civil conversation with my father – who knew?

He looked up. "Listen to this."

Throughout the war, 'Mother' Bickerdyke moved from one trouble-spot to another, acting on her belief that bodies healed best when they were bathed, placed in clean surroundings and fed well. She evinced a special concern for enlisted men and stopped at nothing to get supplies that would bring comfort to her 'boys.' She begged for food from any viable source, raided government supplies – often without permission – and commandeered boxes of delicacies sent from home to healthy soldiers.

His father leaned forward. "Now there's a woman for you! Don't think she would've put up with my shit any more than your mother did. Too bad I learned so late in life. What an idiot I was."

Yup!

Changing the subject, Steven said, "Have you ever heard of Harriet Tubman?" He read on without waiting for an answer.

Harriet Tubman was best known among the many blacks who rendered distinguished service as Civil War nurses. She was famous for her courageous exploits with the Underground Railroad.

She moved from one camp to another throughout the war, using her nursing skills and extensive knowledge of the healing properties of roots and herbs. Tubman rarely accepted the military rations that were offered to her, preferring to support herself by making baked goods and selling them in the camps. She gave any extra money to the freedmen who often sought refuge in the camps. Late in life, she was awarded a military pension, and when she died in 1913, she was given a military funeral.

"Now why didn't we find admirable women like that?"

Steven gave his father a sideways glance and sighed. "I think we did, Dad. We just didn't recognize it."

Chapter

12

Does the agony never leave us? Cannot our dreadful deeds be expunged from our hearts so that we can go to our Maker, forgiven of our sins? Must the fear and self-loathing haunt us forever?

The tragic sentiment kept turning over in Steven's brain. David's torment continued to boil in his mind. He knew in his gut what David meant. No explanation was necessary. His heart ached. After a fitful sleep, Steven could not block out the words.

Their suffering was so painfully similar, how could that be? The two wars were very different, fought with a dissimilar purpose. The Civil War and Vietnam. All wars caused suffering. How could he understand what David's letter was saying? And yet he did.

He not only understood, he felt the same agony. He had not discovered David's allusion to 'dreadful deeds' but he recognized his own – with complete clarity.

Nope. Don't go there.

Unable to rationally think through his unnerving reaction, Steven geared up with his standard backup plan – walking. "Time to move." Forcing his feet to negotiate the reluctance of his weary body, he headed for the front door. "Back later, Dad," he called out. Had he put on a clean shirt? Oh, well.

He decided to retrace his steps from yesterday and confront the chaos of traffic and noise on the street.

Just keep it steady and slow. One foot in front of the other. Move.

Steven breathed in the clear, crisp air, grateful to see there was little traffic so early in the morning. Turning the corner, he found himself in front of the little coffee shop where he had met Dr. Sam Robbins. Wishing to avoid another confrontation with the doctor, Steven looked through the window, saw the shop was empty and tried the door. Startled, he jumped back when it was opened from the inside by a cheerful young man, tying a white apron, wearing a contrite grin.

"Welcome," he said with a wave of his hand. "Just opening up. I'm running a bit late. I'm Joe." He chuckled. "You know...I'm your 'morning joe.' I own this place. I'm expecting a group for their weekly meeting. Should be here any minute. Have a seat. May I bring you some coffee?"

"Sure, thanks."

Steven settled back in his chair and let out a long breath, taking in the warm, sun-drenched coffee house, grateful to simply sit in wonder at the quiet, calm atmosphere. In the next moment it changed to chaos. The door tinkled its opening chime and then banged shut, as rowdy, laughing voices burst through the door to dispel his contentment. A group of disheveled, boisterous men clattered through the café and seated themselves at a large booth in the far corner. Disheartened by their disruptive behavior, Steven sprang from his seat, poised to leave.

"Steven, how did you know we were meeting today?" Dr. Sam appeared at his side and put a welcoming hand on Steven's shoulder, showing him the group of men.

"I didn't," Steven replied brusquely. Turning toward the door, he said, "Just leaving." At that moment, Joe appeared with a steaming cup of coffee.

"Sorry it took so long. First cup is on us."

Steven stood stock still – distressed by the disquieting appearance of Sam and the rowdy group of veterans.

"Come join us, Steven. Bring your cup. These guys are great, really."

"No, not now, I can't stay."

"Just for a minute, Steven. These men have been through the same..."

"No, I can't." Steven desperately wanted to get away yet plopped back down in his chair as his brain said, 'Get out.' But his legs refused to move. Sam sat down opposite him and placed a gentle hand on Steven's arm as Joe placed the cup between his hands.

Get out!

"Alright, I'm not going to push. But don't miss Joe's delicious coffee just to avoid us. Take a sip and tell me if I'm wrong. Try it."

Steven sipped the coffee and sighed contentedly, but stayed silent.

Sam gestured toward the booth as the men gathered, "We meet once a week, every Tuesday. These men are dealing with the same issues, Steven. They understand each other. They support each other. Think about it. We're always here."

Sam gave him another gentle pat and left the table to join the men in the booth. Steven slugged his coffee and bolted for the door.

~ ~ ~

Run like hell. Move!

With no destination in mind, Steven walked away from the café, putting distance between himself and Sam's group of veterans. Trying to recover his sense of calm, he forced his legs into a purposeful stride, going nowhere, as he looked for a way to escape from his anguish.

He wondered if digging into his own trauma would only make him feel worse. Did he really want to share his agony with a bunch of strangers? What good would it do? Better to keep it buried and not think about it.

No need to wallow in our own mucked up lives.

So why was he probing into someone else's life – a soldier who lived a century before? He realized it felt safer to examine another soldier's trauma.

Steven tried to empty his mind and enjoy the morning air. As he rambled along, he suddenly realized where his feet had taken him.

Oh no. The library. Not going there.

He knew Lindsay would be at her post. He needed relief.

Avoiding the entrance, he walked along the side of the building and to his delight, discovered a secluded community park behind the building with a scattering of benches, covered with a canopy of giant sycamore trees, inviting him in. Steven had lived in this town since childhood and never knew the park was behind the library, waiting to be discovered. He wandered along the path, brushing the tips of his fingers in the profusion of azaleas beginning to open. He settled onto a wooden bench, nestled among the giant sycamores and allowed his entire body to decompress. He looked up into the trees, wanting to relish the peaceful surroundings. Sunlight was peeking through the branches revealing a crystal blue sky. It enveloped Steven in its warmth. He lay on his back mesmerized by the light and shadows playing off the branches. Closing his eyes, he fell into a contented sleep.

~   ~   ~

Sensing he was being watched, Steven startled from his slumber. Feeling pressure against his shoulder, he opened one eye and looked into the face of the scruffiest dog he had ever seen. The dog didn't move. His chin leaned heavily against Steven's arm as its sad, brown eyes stared back, reflecting his own.

"What is it, boy? Are you lost? What are you trying to tell me?"

The dog lifted its head, sat back and gently placed one paw on Steven's chest, as if the dog was comforting him. Steven lay still, staring at the dog. The dog stared back. Neither moved. Steven decided he looked like one of those Benji dogs, only bigger and grubbier. Probably a golden color if he had a bath, he decided. No collar, so no tags. They stared at each other in silence.

"Hey! No dogs allowed. Get that mutt out of here." A bruising voice from beyond the trees hollered against the peaceful silence. The dog jumped away from the bench, stood alert on all fours then took off across the expanse of grass, barreling into the street in front of the oncoming traffic. Car horns blared and brakes screeched.

Steven leapt to his feet and raced to the street. Did he make it? He didn't notice that for the first time, his intense reaction to the blast of a car horn resulted from fear for the dog, not himself. He skidded to a stop at the corner and looked across as cars sped by. No dog. No smashed cars.

"Steven, what happened? Are you alright? It sounded like an accident." Lindsay raced down the stairs of the library, her stricken voice cracking with alarm.

Wouldn't you know!

"Yes, I'm fine," Steven assured her. "I found this dog in the park and someone spooked him. He took off across the street. Hell, I'd run off if someone yelled at me like that, too."

"Hmm, I do believe you would. Or should I say – I've seen you in action." She grinned.

Steven had no answer. Lindsay had him nailed. He bowed his head in agreement. "Okay, you're right, Lindsay.

How about a peace pact? You stop humiliating me and I'll stop running out on you. How's that sound?"

"I don't humiliate you!"

"That's the way I see it."

"But, I don't mean to. I was just teasing."

"To you it may be teasing and playing. To me it feels like I'm being insulted. You probably see me as some lazy bum, living on the streets. I'm more messed up than that dog, but I'm not a loser. I don't think you can understand."

"I guess I don't, Steven. But I'm willing to try. I don't mean to belittle you or humiliate you. So, help me understand. Talk to me."

He shook his head and began to walk away as she put her hand on his sleeve.

"Not now." He shrugged her off and continued to walk as Lindsay caught up with him. He looked down at her beautiful face.

"Okay, then let's just walk. Let's look for the dog. Maybe he needs your help."

She hesitantly took his arm and they silently walked together, searching each side street along the way.

Chapter

13

October 11, 1890

Old Soldiers & Sailors Home

Dear Dr. James,

I appeal to you with a heavy heart.

In our past encounters, I have made you privy to my tragic estrangement from my family. I have followed the law and kept my word. Over the years I have made no attempt to contact my children.

It has now come to my attention that my daughter Mary would wish to contact me.

I am heartened by this news, as it may

be a sign that she carries no enmity
toward me.

Have you seen or heard anything of
my family? It would lighten my heart
tenfold to know anything you can tell me
of their circumstances. Are there
avenues of communication you might find
open? I do not wish to place you in an
uncomfortable position my friend, but
I find my grief so severe, I cannot bear
enduring this heart wrenching sorrow.

In this endeavor, I must warn you,
there are those who will resist your
efforts and attempt to restrain you from
this undertaking.

With gratitude,
David Lane

Steven allowed his sadness to unfold with a deep moan.
How could he feel such compassion for a stranger, this
man who had lived and died so long ago? Why did he care
what sin David had committed? Yet he wanted to know.
He had to understand.

He wondered if he and David Lane really were related, way down the ancestry line, and maybe carried the same genes. They seemed to have suffered in the same way. He decided to make another attempt to question his father about their family's ancestry.

He knocked on the study door, determined to try a different approach.

Seated behind his massive oak desk, his father seemed half-asleep. "Dad, do you have a minute?"

His father jumped, startled from his concentration. "Sure, okay, what's up?"

"Well," Steven hesitated – *how do I begin*, he wondered. "I don't want to interrupt if you are in the middle of something."

"Spit it out."

"Well, I – maybe another time, when you're not busy."

"I'm not busy, damn it. You know what I'm doing? I'm going through menus – your mother's old collection of recipes. She didn't even want *these* when she left us."

She did not leave us, Dad – she left you.

"Yeah, she was a great cook, wasn't she?" He wanted to keep this neutral and it was already going off-track.

"Thought I'd find that other chicken recipe you always liked. I can't remember the secret sauce she concocted, but I think it's in here." Looking up at Steven, he added, "Did you want something?"

Yeah, I want an honest, non-combative conversation with my father.

"I told you about my research into David Lane, the doctor who has the medical certificate hanging on the wall behind you."

His father looked back at the old framed parchment and sat back in his chair, gathering his frown. Steven saw it coming, a new eruption of accusations. He knew his father well, how easily his anger was triggered and quickly continued before he could intervene.

"Hold on, Dad. Before you start in on me, let me remind you – in the weeks since I've been researching this man, I've calmed down a lot. I've almost become a student again – and self-motivated at that. Not the fuck-up you're used to."

His father couldn't help grinning in agreement.

"For what it's worth, I've learned a lot. These letters not only led me to questions about David Lane's life, but also the Civil War and what it was like for other soldiers, from another era – and – and a different war. And what I'm learning is that their war wasn't so different from mine – especially – most significantly the war going on inside. The pain we feel. I realize that David Lane and I are pretty much the same."

"I guess that's true. War is war," his father agreed. "So what? What's the big deal? What's it got to do with you, anyway?"

Don't take the bait. Deep breath.

"I keep going back to why you bought it. Was it random? What meaning did it have to you? I know you're interested in history, so I thought maybe you'd check to see if David Lane was some distant ancestor?"

"Who knows? I just liked it as an antique. I couldn't care

112

less who this guy was. Except he did finish medical school. Unlike...well...I don't know of any Lanes in our family."

"Well, here's what I find interesting – speaking of connections. In the last letter I found, David Lane talks about his estrangement from his family. It was tragic. He didn't see his family for years – I don't know how long. Now, doesn't that sound familiar, like history repeating itself?" He took a breath.

Oh shit, I can't help myself.

"Lack of connection, estrangement, willful refusal to have a meaningful relationship? Am I getting close? Belligerence, abuse? Remind you of anyone?

"Now wait just a minute!" His father shouted.

Steven kept going. "Maybe – maybe say – you and me? You and Mom? Me and..." He stopped himself from going further.

Damn! I did it again.

He father bolted from the chair. Steven reflexively ducked, remembering how he felt as a little boy when his father aggressively charged at him.

"Never mind, Dad, I'm out of line."

"Damn right you are. You have no idea what went on between your mother and me."

Oh, I know more than you realize, Dad. Kids know. You can't hide behind closed doors. Kids get it.

"You're right, Dad. I don't know," Steven said, as he tried to tamp down his father's outburst before it escalated into the predictable shouting match.

"I find the similarities interesting – between David

Lane's experience and mine – between our family and his. I'm beginning to understand myself better by appreciating David Lane."

Malice rose in his father's voice. "Well you just go for it, boy. But stay out of my personal affairs. It's got nothing to do with you," he bellowed.

"Oh, but it does, old man. It has everything to do with me. How do you think I learned to behave the way I do? In a vacuum? No, we learn by watching our parents." Steven stopped himself from speaking when he heard his father's venom reflected in his own voice.

We learn how to yell.

We learn how to hide our anger and our feelings and our sorrow.

We learn how to swallow it and not deal with it.

Just look at you. Hell, look at me.

You're proving my point.

"Okay, okay Dad. I won't interfere. Maybe I just want to understand *you* a little better, too. Maybe I hoped you could understand me."

"Yeah, right. How am I supposed to understand a grown man acting like a whiny baby?"

Steven turned slowly, walked away and quietly closed the door to the study, shutting out the image of his enraged father.

~   ~   ~

He left the house and walked with determined distraction until he found himself closing in on Anna's neighborhood. He called from the market and as always, she encouraged him to come right over.

114

"Do you like hamburgers?" she asked through the phone. Pick up some buns, I have everything else. I'd love the company and I'll bet you love burgers."

Revived by her openhearted nature, Steven included a cheerful bunch of flowers and continued along the familiar path to Anna's house.

When she came to the door with open arms, Steven gave her a gentle hug and said, "Hey, Anna, would you consider adopting me?"

"You bet I would, Steven," she laughed. "You're the best!"

They walked into the kitchen with Tom and Jerry trailing behind. Steven threw the empty paper bag on the floor and the cats pounced, rolling over each other as they attacked the bag, kicking with their back feet.

"Well, I think you're the only one who thinks so," he said. "Too bad we humans can't resolve our differences like these cats. Roll around on the floor until one or the other gives in."

Anna watched the cats and nodded her head. "So, what happened?"

"I had another row with my father. It's impossible to have a conversation with that man where it doesn't turn into a shouting match. Try to get a little close, develop a little understanding, and man, that curtain comes down with a thud."

"Don't give up, Steven. Keep trying. Maybe someday, with a different approach, something will stick. He can't be happy feeling so isolated and angry."

She molded the hamburgers into patties as Tom poked his nose out of the bag, smelling the meat.

"I tried talking to him about David's letter, looking for a way to have an honest conversation about families. As usual, I took it too far and Dad got furious. Since I was a little kid, I've known he was a bully."

"Don't blame it on yourself. You have no control over how people behave."

"No, this time I baited him and I knew exactly how he would react."

"Families – that can always be a powder keg waiting to explode."

"Exactly. This last letter is about your grandfather David's estrangement from his family. It's very curious – pretty sad really. I don't suppose you know any more about why he was shunned from his family. I haven't found any answers yet."

"No, we never knew the details of what happened, only rumors about his wife's fury. He must have done something horrible, but we never found what it was. Very mysterious. Polite folks simply didn't gossip or discuss people's private lives in those days."

"I don't think much has changed. We all have secrets."

She cocked her head, then looked him straight in the eye, but stayed silent.

"In those days family secrets were well hidden behind closed doors. But we knew David's wife retaliated in some way."

"Maybe *she's* the one related to my father," Steven laughed. "What happened to her?"

"She remarried. My own father George, who was David's son, was very intelligent, but wasn't allowed to attend college.

He resented his stepfather until the day he died. Talk about angry old men! That was *my* father. His resentment was not very well disguised. Even as a little girl I could feel it."

"What about David's daughter, Mary? This letter implies that Mary wanted to secretly get in contact with her father. Do you know anything about her?"

"Ah, my Aunt Mary. What a wonderful woman. She was a beauty, you know. Warmest eyes I've ever encountered – always a twinkle and a mischievous smile. Come to think of it, she was quite the rebel in her day. It wouldn't surprise me at all if she defied her mother. She would be the kind of girl to challenge tradition. If anyone in the family had the courage to disobey her mother, it would have been Mary."

"But did she actually do it? This letter suggests she wanted to."

"I don't know, Steven. I was just a little girl when I knew her. But I hope she did. Keep plowing through those letters. You'll find the answer."

"I hope so. It's kind of crazy to be digging into someone's life – a man who lived so long ago. But I've got to admit, I keep finding all these similarities between your grandfather's life and my own. My war and the Civil War. How we soldiers were ruined by our wars in very similar ways."

"Yet, there is one way your war was very different, Steven. We now have much better medical care for our soldiers. Just look at how many more were saved. As a medic, you know this. And I'm not just talking about the physical wounds. Look at people like Sam Robinson. He was comfortably retired and is now volunteering to help the veterans you saw at the shelter. He understands their agony."

"Oh, don't get me started on people like that, Anna. Those do-gooders don't have any idea what it was like. They think with a little hand-holding and a warm meal they can heal our suffering."

"But there are good people out there, Steven. I've seen them in action. They really do help."

"Maybe, but I want no part of it. I saw your Dr. Robinson this morning, holding court with a bunch of those pathetic vets. No thank you. I'm not pouring my guts out to a bunch of strangers."

"No one's forcing you, Steven."

As if he hadn't heard her, Steven continued. "People like Sam Robinson have no clue how it felt to come home and...and there were protests, against *us*. No one really understands. It's all bullshit," he croaked.

Anna stayed silent.

As she rose to serve the hamburgers, she quietly reminded him, "In the past two days, you have apologized to me three times for disappearing, or as you put it – running away. Why do you think you keep doing that, Steven? What you are running from? You don't have to answer me. But you don't seem very happy about it. Maybe it would help to understand why you're doing it." She stood facing Steven, with her feet planted firmly in front of him. "What don't you want to confront, Steven?"

He reached down and lifted Tom into his lap. Stroking the cat, he said, "I'll settle for comfort from your cats. At least I don't have to bare my soul and they don't ask for more than I can give."

Anna walked to the kitchen without a reply. As she set the plate of burgers on the table, she lifted Tom off his lap and tossed him a bit of meat. "No animals allowed while there's food on the table, Mister." Jerry poked his head out from under the chair, as if asking for his fair share.

"Okay, just a little," Anna said.

Steven pulled a piece of meat from his burger and tossed it to Jerry. They ate in comfortable silence, before Steven said, "If there's such a thing as reincarnation, I think I'd like to come back as a cat and live in a home like yours. Or maybe a dog."

Anna laughed, "I do give them a good life."

"Unlike the dog I saw today. Talk about running away. Some jerk spooked this poor stray dog and sent him running into the street, right in front of oncoming traffic. We looked all over for him, but never found him, so I guess he's safe."

"Who's 'we' Steven? Did you end up staying around with Dr. Robinson's group of vets after all?"

"Hell, no...uh, sorry. No, this was later, near the park behind the library. Lindsay, the librarian... she was headed down the front steps and saw it happen. You know her. She must be a volunteer at the shelter – I ran into her in the vegetable garden the other day."

"Oh Lindsay, sure, she's a wonderful help. Quite the green thumb. Looking at her, you would never guess she loves to get grubby and dig in the dirt. She looks like a delicate doll, and yet she can work a hoe and produce the most amazing crop of vegetables for my soup. How do you know her?"

"Long story, but I confess I don't like her, much. She rubs me the wrong way. She's the reason I left the shelter in such a hurry. She said I was looking for handouts. It was humiliating."

"That doesn't sound like her. She has a heart of gold."

"Yeah well, she's got a vicious tongue and I told her so."

"Maybe it's how we interpret what we hear, Steven."

"Yeah, that's what *she* said." He cleared the dishes from the table and picked up both Tom and Jerry, one in each arm, feeling quite at home as he sat and settled one on each leg. "I still think I prefer the company of cats."

"But they only have limited healing powers, Steven. Humans are better."

"Not from my experience."

"You know what I've learned? We humans fixate on our wounds – we keep all the hurt inside. It's all we can see. We can't get beyond it. We feel so bad that we get hooked in and find someone or some event to blame. We are consumed by the grievance and seem unable to find the resources to recover. We say to ourselves, 'look how they've harmed me,' and by believing it long enough we become the victims of our own grievance. We end up with self-inflicted wounds that are reinforced by our beliefs."

"When did you become such a wise philosopher?"

"You know what I'm saying is true."

Steven stroked the cats with determination, not wanting to contemplate Anna's ideas.

"I know what Lindsay said to me," he said with defiance.

"No Steven, you know what you *heard*. We all have this little voice in our head that interprets what we hear. Maybe this is why you were offended by Lindsay. Maybe you don't hear what she says, because you are too busy decoding what you *think* she intended."

"Yeah well, easy for you to say, Anna. Harder to put into practice."

"No, I figured it out from living with my own father. I would get so hurt by his anger, which I always felt was directed at me. Then I figured it out and I made peace with him. I realized it was coming out of *him* and I was the target of his own wounded experience with *his* father, your research subject – David. He was hurt and abandoned by his father and took it out on everyone else. Maybe that's what we do in families. We keep passing it on – the anger and the blame and the grievances."

Fathers – what a bunch of shits.

Steven sat back and continued to stroke each cat, resisting the inclination to conjure up some defensive response.

"But you can't deny the war protestors spit at us."

"Yes, they did. And what is accomplished by taking your resentment out on Lindsay?"

Chapter

14

January 13, 1891

Old Soldiers and Sailors Home
Miss Kate Simpson

Dear Girl,

I received your kind letter in due time,
and for all of this I thank you.

I did not write an answer as
promptly as I felt disposed to, because
I do not want to cause trouble for my
daughter, Mary, by too frequent
correspondence. But I did receive a
package containing paper, envelopes and

stamps, but not a word written on the paper enclosed.

On reflection I concluded that there was, in the assorted package, a gentle hint to write, and I am writing, or trying to write coherently, for to do so here is a difficult matter as there is a continual buzz of conversation, terms used in card-playing, and frequent expletives, that come in more frequently when the conversation is about this or that battle fought 21 or 28 years ago, and the relative merits of this or that general.

I am glad that Mary and George are healthy and that they get along so well with their studies. Now Kate, I beg of you to warn Mary to not unnecessarily aggravate her mother by talking about me. Tell her to not tell anyone not interested and then she, George and I will have peace, till a brief few years have passed, we may at least hope to meet unrestrainedly and live to be happy.

Next week I will enclose a letter to Mary of some importance which I ask you to address and mail to her as well as this.

My most earnest thanks are due to you and I do thank you for your kindness.

Respectfully and truly your friend,
D. R. Lane

When he entered the library the next day, Steven waved to the older woman seated at the front desk. He was relieved she was 'not Lindsey' who would have jumped up all cheery and enthusiastic. The woman gave a tentative nod and went back to her reading.

He decided to organize the letters by date. His discovery of the letter to Kate had given meaning to the secrecy around David's estrangement from his daughter, Mary, and son George. He let out a long moan, not sure how to continue his search.

"Are you alright, Steven?" Lindsay asked, carrying a stack of research papers. "I heard that sigh from two aisles away."

He backed away and plopped into the nearest chair. "Yeah, I'm just puzzled."

Do I want her involved?

He decided there would be no running this time. Just keep it neutral... maybe she could help with some research...but,...keep it strictly business.

"I guess you know Anna Lane, the lady who helps at the shelter – she does the cooking."

"Of course. We make a great team." Lindsay piled her papers on the library table and slid into a seat across from Steven.

"Anna has given me some old family letters to research from the Civil War. I'm trying to figure out what happened to her grandfather. I got interested because my father has her Grandfather's medical degree hanging in his study, and...and...I was a medic...I found evidence that David Lane was estranged from his family at some point, and don't know why, and now I've discovered that years later his daughter secretly tried to contact him."

"How delicious! This is fascinating, Steven. What's in the letter?"

"David's daughter's name was Mary. David seems to be writing to a friend of Mary's, warning her not to tell anyone of their contact, and not to 'aggravate' anyone in the family."

Lindsay said, "Well, I know young women in those times had to comply with a very strict code of conduct, and they had to obey their parents' demands, no matter how much they disagreed. It would have driven me crazy to live in the 1800's – dependent on parents."

Steven cringed. "I know. All this reading took me down

a long path of learning about women who became nurses during the Civil War, and during that time in history, people rejected the idea of women caring for wounded soldiers. Seems absurd, now. Medical care is the same, no matter who is by your side."

"Let me know if you find more, Steven. And I'd be happy to help with your research. It *is* my job, you know. Any sign of the dog that ran off?"

"Nope, no sighting so far."

"I'll keep an eye out. Where did you first see him – was it in the park?"

"Yeah, just take a look out that window once in a while," he said, pointing to the rear library window. "That's where I found him...well actually...I guess he found me. I was hanging out on a bench and next thing I knew, his chin was resting on my chest."

She laughed. "Yeah, I think he hooked you for sure. I'll watch for him. Got to go get ready for my class. See you later."

"See you, Lindsay." Steven watched her until she was out of sight and felt a new sense of loss. Denying the sensations he experienced, he picked up a book and began smoothing the cover, over and over.

Why would she be interested in me, anyway? She knows I'm jobless and probably sees me as one more crazy vet...and...I guess I am.

Steven considered Lindsay's career as a research librarian compared to the life of David's daughter Mary, 100 years earlier. From the letter, he could understand how limited Mary's life must have been. She was expected to obey her parents and adhere to the acceptable rules of society.

Defiance must have been rare. He stood and ran his hand across the spines of historical books of the Civil War era and began to explore.

~   ~   ~

He was still absorbed in his research an hour later when Lindsay popped her head around the corner after her seminar.

"Steven, you're still here. Find something interesting?"

"Do you know how lucky you are, Lindsay? I'm just starting to investigate what life was like for women during the Civil War and I can see why you're glad to be living as a woman now. They had to fight for every scrap of independence they could get. What a difference."

She slid onto the library bench. "I know. Women couldn't even vote then. Women's suffrage took years of struggle. And I don't think many women had much opportunity to go to college. Sometimes I step back and marvel at the opportunities I have."

"Ah, the random luck of the gene pool and being born in a certain era!" Steven said, "From what I've read, it was during the Civil War that so much began to change. But I don't know how much improvement may have influenced Mary's life. Women were expected to be subservient; their place was in the home. I'll bet you've heard of Mary Stanton who pushed for voting rights."

"Sure. She's one of my heroes."

"Mine too, after reading about her. She wrote what she called a 'Declaration of Independence' for women as early as 1848, detailing what she called the injuries perpetrated on women by oppressive men. Do you have time to hear this? It's great!"

"Sure, I love history." She wiggled eagerly and her eyes gave him their full attention.

Steven dropped his head to hide his attraction and looking down at his book, he began to read Mary Stanton's words. "'The history of mankind is a history of repeated injuries and usurpations on the part of man toward woman, having in direct object the establishment of an absolute tyranny over her.'" He looked up. "Her goal was to establish – and I quote – the 'rights and privileges which belong to them as citizens of the United States.'"

Lindsay leaned toward him. "And if I remember my history right, it was twelve years later when the Civil War began, that women began to take on roles traditionally reserved for men. That's when women's lives began to change. Women helped run their towns and the government while the men were off fighting."

Steven nodded. "That's when women helped in the war effort – not just making clothes for the soldiers and sewing bandages, but directly on the battlefield." He pointed to the page. "Here's a woman called Susie King Taylor who went to war with her husband's regiment. She found a way to get herself attached to his unit working as a laundress. She learned how to clean, reload, assemble and disassemble a musket, and then she learned how to shoot. She would have been viewed as decidedly unladylike in those days and frowned upon by society. I'm not sure I would have the courage."

"You'd be amazed at what you can do when you have to. Just like Susie Taylor said, you just react to the crisis and live with the horrible reality later."

Lindsay leaned forward and reached out a hand. "Isn't

that what they call war trauma? Oh, Steven. I can't imagine what it must have been like for you..."

"That's right. You can't imagine." He said. "Let's stay in the 1800s. This isn't about me."

Lindsay looked at him with a steady eye but sat silently.

He took a ragged breath.

"What about Louise May Alcott who wrote *Little Women*?" Lindsay asked. "I've studied her. Did you know she was one of the most famous nurses? She helped with the war effort in the North. She attended anti-slavery meetings and fairs and had become an Abolitionist as a young girl."

Steven looked up. "Yeah, it says here she spoke out about the mismanagement of hospitals and the indifference and callousness of the surgeons she encountered. Ah, there it is again - neglectful doctors. The more I read, the more indictments I find." He looked up from the book. "Sorry, Lindsay, am I getting carried away?"

"No, this is fascinating. Keep going."

"Women in the South couldn't legally serve on the battlefield, so they would engage in espionage. Here, it talks about a famous spy during that time, Mrs. Rose O'Neal Greenhow. She passed secret messages to a Confederate general containing critical information regarding the First Battle of Bull Run. They couldn't have known what they were getting into. Those women sure were brave," Steven agreed.

"So many people were rooted in their beliefs and convictions. Did you know Harriet Beecher Stowe continued the fight for abolition at home through her writings and speeches. You know her name."

"Sure," Lindsay agreed, "she wrote *Uncle Tom's Cabin*."

He nodded. "And I quote, '...I hope every woman who can write will not be silent.' Now that was a courageous woman."

"Hmm, I should take heed of her advice, even 100 years later. I could put all this research I do to good use," Lindsay said. She reached her hand across the table. "Maybe I can help...'

Steven focused his eyes on the history book.

"I think my favorite story is about Albert D.J. Cashier. Yes, Albert! *He* was the shortest soldier in the 95th Illinois Infantry. Here, it's documented, 'They didn't conduct physical exams in those days, the way the military does now.' They were just looking for warm bodies."

Steven continued. "Jennie Hodgers, masquerading as Albert Cashier, marched thousands of miles during the war. Her regiment took part in more than 40 skirmishes and battles. She stuck out the war from beginning to end."

He looked up at Lindsay. "Don't you wonder how she got away with it - four years? Maybe they never bathed or maybe she found a way to go off and bathe in a stream by herself."

Lindsay shuddered, "And what if she had been recognized? What would have happened if she had gotten caught? What about...well you know...what about assault? She must have lived with a lot of fear. I mean, soldiers can be pretty brutal..."

Steven looked at her sharply. "Oh, you have no idea..."

He looked back at the book. "At some point after the war they discovered she was a woman and she must have received more respect than ridicule. It says that several of her comrades rallied to Hodger's defense when officials considered taking away her veteran's pension for identity fraud. I guess, to her fellow soldiers, her status as a Union Army veteran trumped her identity as a woman."

Lindsay nodded. "I've researched this, too. A private in the Union Army made $13 a month, which was easily double what a woman would make as a laundress or a seamstress or even a maid. There's documentation of hundreds of cases of women who masqueraded as men during the war. They joined for love of country and for money. But, once they wore pants and earned more money and could spend as they liked, they seemed to greatly enjoy the freedom that came with being seen as a man."

Steven stood and stretched, then raised the book off the table so she could see the title. "And here's more; it gives you clear documentation of how life for women began to change, Lindsay. The women who went to war, who disguised themselves as men and carried a gun, were quote 'overwhelmingly working-class women, immigrant women, poor women, urban women and yeoman farm girls.' Hodgers was an immigrant from Ireland, who couldn't read or write. At the end of the war, she had to make some tough decisions about her identity.

"If she continued as Albert Cashier, it was more likely she would find work, keep the friends she had made during the war and be part of a respected community of Civil War veterans. She could have a bank account. She could vote in elections – and she did, by the way. Or, if she went back and put on a dress and told everyone she was Jennie, she would lose all the benefits of living as a male."

"Incredible," Lindsay said. "I wonder if she suffered from battle fatigue or whatever they called it back then, just like men have in other wars. Women soldiers must have suffered the same trauma as the men..."

Stephen snapped his head up and eyed her warily, then coldly said, "Drop it, Lindsay! This is about the women – not me. We're talking about another war, in a different time. It's got nothing to do with me. Let's stay on topic."

"I get it, Steven. I'm sorry. It's just...it's just that I..."

"Leave it alone. Can you let it be, Lindsay?"

He looked down at the page, avoiding her eyes, he pointed to the words. "It says here that over 250 female Civil War soldiers have been documented by historians, and there were probably more. They took part in every major battle. Like male soldiers, women were motivated by a variety of factors. In addition to the thirst for adventure and the desire to accompany their loved ones, women served out of dedication to a cause and out of the need to earn money for their families. Most female soldiers remained undetected as women unless they were wounded or killed."

"So, what does all this tell you about David Lane's daughter, Mary?" Lindsay asked, reaching across the table. "She was the daughter of a Civil War soldier. She was the next generation. Do you know when he became estranged from his family – or why? It doesn't sound like her father was any kind of role model since he doesn't seem to have been a part of her life. I wonder if this was just an act of defiance, maybe a determination to know her father and disobey her mother's commands."

"What we do know," Steven assured her, "is that she definitely had role models in the women I've read about. The door opened a crack. Did she ever say how she felt? I wonder if she had the courage to defy her family and walk through that door."

Lindsay stood, hands on hips. "It's easy to philosophize and theorize about people. How about you, Steven?" She hesitated, sat back down and lowered her voice, but kept on, "Are you ever going to open the door, even a crack? Will you *ever* let someone in?"

Steven shot up, tipping over his chair. Ready to bolt, he glared at her. "I mean it, Lindsay. Get off my case." He began shoving the history books in his bag.

He looked over at her and realized she would stand her ground, as she raised herself to her full height to face him head-on. "That's it, go ahead, run off again. Do your disappearing act. You're the master of avoidance. I've never seen anyone so adept at shutting people out. Better hurry, Steven. Better get away before someone gets to know you too well."

Steven backed away from the table, trying to avoid her words, confused by her confrontation. If nothing else, he knew how to *move*. He always won this battle, he always left first. Baffled, he realized Lindsay had gotten under his skin. He cared how she felt. He could see that she was genuinely angry.

Why do I care? Do I want her to understand?

He stood rooted in place, unable to fulfill her prophecy to run off, yet unwilling to defend himself.

He leaned into the table, defeated. "It's just – it's just – too hard to explain, Lindsay. I don't even understand *myself*. I know I keep running away, and I know it seems crazy to people. I can't help it. I don't know how..."

"*That*, I understand, Steven. And I appreciate how difficult it would be to open up to me."

He nodded in agreement.

"Then find someone who has been in the same place, someone you can talk to."

"Yeah well...I've tried that. They just criticize and try to analyze me, without really understanding or listening."

She stepped back slowly and held up her hand in a sign of peace. "Oh Steven, I can't imagine that you want to keep living like this, always running from people who might care about you." She blushed. "I can see how afraid you are, but...try, Steven, please try."

"I'm trying." He picked up the book he had been reading from. "This is how I do it, Lindsay. Maybe – I don't know – maybe by understanding David and his battles I might be able to understand my own."

"How can the life of some soldier who lived 100 years ago help you face your own demons?"

He backed away, unnerved by her awareness. Throwing the book down on the table, he said, "I – don't – have – demons, Lindsay. It's just stress." He collapsed in the chair, unwilling to continue.

"I'm so sorry. I...I...didn't mean demons exactly. I'm just curious. What is it that you find so compelling about David Lane? Have you figured out what is driving you in this quest for answers about his life?"

He looked up at her. Clear-eyed he said, "I recognize myself in him. I know this man. I understand his suffering. Maybe it was a different era and another war, but...I realize we had similar experiences. Doctor and medic. I understand his experience through my own. We all fight the same unfathomable war...and if we come out of it alive... we continue the battle that rages inside. I don't know how else to survive."

Lindsay nodded, appearing to acknowledge her understanding. Her eyes filled with tears. She put a gentle hand on his shoulder, turned and as she began to walk away said, "You need to wage this battle on your own terms. I know you can do this, Steven."

Steven watched her abrupt departure with bewilderment and dismay.

What have I done? She just walked off...this feels like shit.

He gathered his research and felt the weight increase as each book was added to the stack in his arms. Struggling to fit them all in his book bag, Steven secured the bag over his shoulder to balance the burden and lumbered down the library aisles toward the checkout desk.

Something in his head kept saying, *Change course.* He stopped suddenly and realized the old librarian woman was watching him, smiling. He swung the bag from his back, turned – reversed direction and headed back to the table by the window.

Lighten your burden. Take it slow. One letter at a time. One book at a time.

Slowly he removed each book from the bag, studied the name and returned it methodically, until each book was back in its place on the shelf.

Relieved of the weight, Steven sat quietly, trying to absorb his conversation with Lindsay.

She was right. I can't talk to her. I need someone who would understand. What a mess I've made.

Steven pulled out the letters and picked up the next one.

Keep searching...

Chapter

15

March 7, 1891

Old Soldiers and Sailors Home

My dear Dr. Stevens,

I received your letter with a glad heart. You have lightened my burden and renewed my belief in our enduring friendship. If only we could meet so that I might relieve my weeping soul. There is no one here I would dare confide in, nor for that matter, anyone I care to seek comfort with or trust, except you. If you can find some way to make the *journey, I am in sore need of your sympathetic ear.*

My heartfelt wish is that we might meet once again.

I remain your humble servant,
David Lane

Steven reread the letter with recognition. *I know how you must have felt, Old Man.*

The screeching of brakes outside the library broke Steven's reverie. He rushed to the window in time to see cars braking to a stop and the same dog from the park bounding across the street. "That's my dog!" he shouted to the glass window. No one could hear. He threw David's letters in his bag and raced down the hall and through the library doors.

He tore down the steps two at a time. A jumble of cars had stopped at various angles on the street to miss the fleeing dog. Horns honked, and drivers yelled at each other. A man hung his head out the car window and shouted to the driver he narrowly missed. "Next time I'll hit that damn dog. Or I'll hit you. He ran right back in my path. Third time I've seen him."

Steven ran into the street and pounded his fist on the hood of the man's car. "Which way did he go?"

"What the hell do I care? That damn dog nearly caused an accident. He's a menace."

Steven resisted the impulse to punch the man and walked swiftly among the maze of stopped cars. Tapping on each window, he asked, "Did you see where the dog went? Did he get hit?" A hand emerged from a car window and pointed in the direction of a narrow side street. Cars honked, and drivers shouted at him to get out of the road. Steven darted to the opposite corner, calling, "Here boy. Are you okay?"

A voice called out from a car. "He was hit by a guy riding a motorcycle, turned down that side street. I saw him hit the dog. He didn't mean to – he was avoiding another car."

"Where's the dog?"

"I don't know. He limped away down that alley."

Steven jogged up one side street and down the next, calling for the dog. He stopped to catch his breath, dropping his book bag to the ground with a thud. "Come on, you little rascal. Where are you?" Then he heard it – a quiet "woof."

"Come on, show yourself. Are you hurt?" A furry face appeared as the dog peeked around the corner of the building and slowly limped toward him.

"Hey! Come on, boy. It's okay." Steven dropped down on his haunches, as his instincts told him to stay eye level with the dog, while he spoke in a soft voice. The dog dropped down to the ground, following Steven's example. "That's it, easy now." He held out his empty hand, with nothing to offer but acceptance. The dog inched toward him, keeping his belly secured to the ground. Steven laughed, "Where did you learn the commando crawl, little guy? Have you been hit before? Are you injured? I don't see any blood. Can you walk upright?" Steven got to his knees and patted his chest. "Come on, you can do it. I know you want something. It's okay, you're safe with me."

The dog continued to limp slowly toward Steven. He was caked with dirt, his underbelly left a trail of mud and, as he reached Steven, the dog licked his chin and nuzzled his cheek. Flinging his arms around the furry neck, Steven whooped with joy. "Whew, you stink. But at least you're safe."

"What's all the commotion out here? Looks like a happy reunion," came a voice from the nearest shop.

Steven looked up and laughed. "Hey, I know you," said the shopkeeper.

"Hi, Joe. Yeah, I was here the other day."

"Oh, yeah. And who's this mangy critter? Looks like he hasn't had a bath or a decent meal in weeks."

"I don't know. He keeps showing up. He was running away in the traffic and someone said he'd been hit by a motorcycle. Look, it's his hind leg."

The dog limped over to Joe, sniffed him carefully and walked deliberately to the entrance of Joe's Café and raising one paw, pushed at the door. Both men laughed. "I do believe he smells my muffins," Joe said. "I wonder how long it's been since he was fed. Let me see what I can scrounge up for him. Poor dog must be starving. Be right back."

Minutes later Joe returned with a bowl full of stale muffins and a cup of water. The dog stumbled to the food and devoured the muffins. When the bowl was empty, he licked away every crumb and looked up at Joe.

"He's just a stray? Seems mighty well-behaved and friendly for a street dog. Where did you find him?"

"It's more like he found me. He showed up once in the library park, literally in my face, and again today. Both times he ran off into traffic, as if he'd been spooked by something. Some guy yelled at him. He's even more skittish than I am – runs off at the smallest provocation."

"Oh, yeah, I remember. Ditched Dr. Sam, didn't you?"

"Kinda," Steven admitted with a contrite grin.

"This dog almost seems to know you."

"So now what am I going to do? I've got to get him checked out. I'm worried about that leg."

"He seems to have decided he's yours. Dogs have good instincts."

"Maybe not. I was a medic in the war and can't claim to be such a great healer. It was torture when we couldn't save those dogs. We did our best to mend the wounded dogs deployed to the war zone. Man, they were brave."

"War dogs? I never knew we used dogs."

"Sure. The military had dogs trained for all kinds of skills during the war. They had tracker dogs that followed the enemy's scent, and there were scout dogs that led combat patrols with a handler and became an early warning system. The dog was kind of like a 'point man' and was given the most dangerous position in their tactical formation."

"They must have been unbelievably loyal to put themselves in so much danger."

"You're so right. And they could alert troops to booby traps, land mines and underground tunnels. Water patrol dogs even detected underwater sabotage – when the enemy was preparing for an attack."

"That's amazing. I never knew."

"Yeah. They were highly valued and saved a lot of our soldiers' lives. So, we tried to save theirs. Medics saved lots of wounded dogs. They were a tough lot – we'd patch them up and they'd be right back on the front line. Pretty admirable."

"I never saw any dogs while I was there. But then I was so doped up most of the time, it's miraculous I noticed anything," Joe said.

"Yeah, we treated lots of drugged out guys, although it was usually a tragic waste of effort – lots of soldiers got hooked on serious drugs. But it looks like you've come out the other side pretty well. How did you do it?" Steven asked.

"Well, you've met Dr. Sam. I'll tell you sometime. Right now, I think you've got your hands full. You'd better get him examined."

The dog placed his paw on Steven's foot.

Joe laughed. "Oh, you know what that means. He owns you. He's yours."

"I've patched up dogs, but I've never owned a dog or taken care of one."

"I think you'll figure it out. He seems like a nice pup."

"Do you have a rope, or something I can use for a makeshift leash? I've got to get that leg checked out."

"Let's see what I can find." Joe went inside while Steven waited, looking down at the dog.

"I guess you're mine, little guy. Or maybe, I'm yours." He patted the dog. "We'll see how it goes. No collar, no name – hey, I know – Scooter – the way you scooted in and out of traffic – very deft diversion skills for a street dog. Maybe it's in your genes or one of those war dogs was your grandfather."

Scooter sat still, looking up at Steven, listening to every word as if he understood.

Joe returned with a long piece of rope. "This should work until you can get to the pet store."

Steven cocked his head. "I need a veterinarian first, then a pet store."

"This place has both. The owner is two weeks from becoming a certified veterinarian, finishing the qualifications. He's a great guy. Name's Pete. It's two blocks down on your right. He knows all about animals. He'll help you out."

"Thanks, Joe. I appreciate the muffins and the encouragement. Don't really know what I'm doing."

"You'll be fine. Tell you what, if you're ever tempted to come to one of Dr. Sam's gab sessions..."

"Yeah, more like group therapy. Been there – done that. No thank you," Steven said.

"No, it's not like that. I listen from the kitchen and sometimes sit with them. It's just a bunch of guys with similar experiences, trying to understand what's happened to them and make their way in this world, same as you and me."

"I don't know, maybe. But I can't come in the café with this dog I seem to have adopted."

"Tell you what. If you decide to come, bring the dog. I can set up chairs out here if the weather is good. If not, we'll sneak him in the back door and make him promise not to steal any muffins."

Steven laughed. "Okay. Maybe."

"Hey, is this yours?" Joe picked up the book bag.

"Thanks. Can't lose this."

"Remember – every Tuesday at ten. You know I make a great cup of coffee."

Steven nodded and tied the rope around the dog's neck. With the book bag on his back he scooped up the dog with both hands and carried him down the street, talking to him gently to assure him he was in good hands.

"Okay, listen up, Scooter. I don't know what the hell I'm doing here, but we'll take this one step at a time. We'll get you checked out and buy you some real dog food. I think I have enough cash. I'll bet you're still hungry. Next you need a bath – badly. You are one stinky, scruffy mutt."

The street began to fill with cars as Steven held the dog tight. No more running through traffic. A motorcycle sped by with a deafening roar as Steven crouched in place. The dog wiggled and howled as he tried to leap from Steven's arms. Steven held tight and looked at him in wonder. "Sounds like the same howling that goes on in my head. Okay, easy boy. I've got you. I hate that noise, too. Shit, I wonder how Dad's going to take this. Well, one problem at a time."

Steven poked his head into the door of the pet store, calling out, "Is it okay if I bring my dog in the store?"

A voice came back, "Sure, come on in. As long as he's on a leash and doesn't steal all the dog biscuits."

As Steven walked in, he gently set the dog down and watched him limp toward the enticing scents.

The storekeeper raised a hand to say 'hello' and crouched down to greet the dog. "Hey, big guy. Looks like you need some care and feeding." Looking up at Steven he said, "I'm Pete. He looks like a stray. Where did you find him?"

"He got hit running in between cars in front of the

library. Someone said it was a motorcycle. I found him near Joe's Café. He has a definite limp."

Pete placed the dog on the counter and gently ran his hands over his body.

"I think it's just below the tibia. I'm Steven, by the way, and I just named this mutt Scooter."

As Pete moved his hand over the dog's leg, Scooter yelped and tried to jump down.

"Hold on to him. How do you know so much about canine bones?"

Steven dropped his chin and spoke to the floor. "Oh, well...you know...medic in Nam. We fixed up dogs...best we could...not...not always successful."

"I get it. Tough duty. Well, I don't feel anything that seems broken. Maybe it's a bruised bone. Here, you feel it."

Steven ran his hand carefully over the injured leg and shook his head.

"We agree, it doesn't feel like a break. Watch him for a day or so and see if he continues to limp. Bring him back if you want, but I'm not yet certified to do surgery."

"Okay, thanks Pete. Maybe you can give me some tips. I don't know anything about the actual care of dogs."

"Give him food and water...and lots of love." Pete scooped up a handful of kibble and hand-fed it to Scooter. "Poor dog is starving. We'd better make sure he takes it slow and easy. Without food for a while, the stomach will swell if you give them too much all at once."

"I sure know about that – same with m...same with humans."

"He gobbled it up. We'll let that digest. Tell you what, it's quiet in here right now. Want to give him a bath? He needs one. I don't think it'll hurt his leg. There's a tub in the back."

"That would be great. Thanks."

They lifted the dog into the deep tub. After hosing him down, they began scrubbing shampoo into his fur. The dirt turned to mud and the water turned black as it drained off his fur. Scooter stood patiently in the tub as if it felt good to be rid of the layers of grime.

Steven's heart raced and panic spread throughout his body. The tub filled with muddy water as the drain clogged with dirt and fur. Both men saw the water rising and began scooping the debris away from the drain, but the water level continued rising higher up Scooter's legs.

Steven froze. He was standing helpless again, remembering the Mekong Delta. He could see the river – torrential rain – the water rose – overflowed the banks.

Oh God, not again. The river – Jack. Murky water. Couldn't find him – the mud – couldn't get him out...

"Hurry. Get him out! The water's rising. His head will go under... He's going to drown." Steven tried to hold the dog. "We need to get him out now!"

Pete scooped at the drain. "He'll be okay."

"Do something!" Steven yelled. Frantically, he tried lifting the wet, slippery dog out of the tub. "I can't get him out. Hurry!" Scooter fell back into the water again and again, splashing with his front paws as if it were a game.

Steven stepped back, his face ashen, shaken with terror.

I can't do this.

Pete put his hand firmly on Steven's arm and turned off the water. "Don't worry. He's okay. Look, he's having fun splashing around in the water. Here, help me clean out the drain and we'll give him another scrubbing." They dug out the mud and fur that had clogged the drain and rinsed the tub.

Steven took a deep breath. "Sorry, I kind of over-reacted. It's stupid – brought back…"

Pete raised a soapy hand, as if nothing had happened. "Not a problem. He's perfectly safe. Come on, let's do it again. I don't see that it's hurting his leg."

With the final rinse, they discovered a reddish-blond, furry dog. "Now that's better," Pete said. "Dry him off with these towels, and let's see if he'll tolerate the blow dryer. We can't leave him shivering like this. Put him on the counter. That's it." Steven held on to Scooter as Pete dried him to a shiny fluff. The dog leaned his face into the warm air, ears flowing as if they were wings.

"Hey, look at you, boy! Don't you look better! You've got a nice, thick coat," Pete said.

"Is it possible that dogs smile?" Steven asked with delight.

"Sure, some do, and he's got a lot to smile about. Do you feel better, boy?" Pete carefully ran his hands over the dog's body. "I don't feel any scars or other injuries. He's in good shape for a stray, although he's malnourished. Feel how thin he is. You should contact the local animal control folks and make sure no one is looking for a lost dog."

Steven looked up at Pete with alarm.

I get attached and it's taken away?

Steven slowly nodded. "I understand – but – do I really have to give him up? We're a team now. It's – I can't do it."

Pete gently put his hand on Steven's shoulder. "I know how hard it would be. But you have to at least look into it. There might be someone out there heartbroken over his lost dog. What if it was you or some kid who raised Scooter."

"I know, I know. Okay, I'll take you up on your offer to call Animal Control. But not now, not yet. The way I see it, Scooter rescued me as much as I...well, you know. Give me a little time to, well just in case..." Steven took a breath. I can't thank you enough, Pete. I need to buy a collar and leash. Thanks for giving me a break on the cost of dog food."

"Happy to help. He seems responsive and has a nice temperament. Come back soon, before you get too attached, and I'll help you contact Animal Control. I work here every morning and I'm finishing an internship with the vet clinic in town. All I have to do is pass the state licensing exam – no easy task. I'll be a full-fledged veterinarian soon. I'm almost there. It's what I've always wanted."

"Well, I wish you good luck, Pete. From what I see, you're good with both animals and humans. That's a rare combination. We'll come back soon and maybe you can give me some lessons in dog training. Now, if you could only teach my father to be as agreeable as this dog. Not sure how he's going to react."

Pete laughed. "No, I'm better with animals. Humans – can be a problem. Family – now that can get really tricky. I suggest you let Scooter introduce himself to your father. You watch, this dog could endear himself to anyone."

"I have my doubts. You haven't met my father."

"Never know. Dogs can be a lifeline."

"Thanks for all your help, Pete. I'll let you know how it goes. We'll be back."

"See you soon. Let him walk a bit. It might just be a sore muscle. But if his limp gets worse, come on back." Pete waved as they headed out the door.

Steven smiled. Scooter smiled back. Man and dog strolled down the street as if they'd been best friends for years.

Chapter

16

If only we could meet so that I could unburden my weeping soul. There is no one here I would dare confide in ... no one to talk to...

The anguished sentiment from David's letter continued to torment Steven.

No one to talk to...

Grateful he was not alone, Steven sat with Scooter on the front steps of his father's house, planning their next move. He threw an arm around the dog. "So, what do you think, ole' boy? Shall we just march in and see what he says or sneak in the back door and hope he doesn't notice? Nah, that won't work. I think he'll notice a big fluff-ball like you. Well, it's my home too, you know, let's just go for it."

The front door flew open as Steven's father charged toward them. "What the hell is this?" he bellowed. "Get this mangy dog and his fleas off my porch. What the devil are you thinking? Get him out of here. Now!"

Steven stood and faced his father. "I rescued him, Dad. He just had a bath. He's a nice dog, really."

"Are you kidding me? You've gone and done it again, haven't you? Just react to your emotions, jump into a pile of shit without even thinking. You are one messed-up fool."

Scooter put his ears back and began to growl, inching away in a backwards crawl. Steven held fast to the leash and spoke to the dog. "It's okay, Scooter. He won't hurt you." He patted the dog and turned to his father.

"Look, you're scaring him. Just hear me out."

"Not a chance. This is it. Now you've gone too far. I've had it with you."

"What's wrong with having a dog? I'll take care of him. I could train him to be a watch dog, keep the house safe from intruders."

"Are you deaf? If you insist on keeping this dog, you're going to keep him somewhere else. Get him out of here. Now! And you can go, too."

Steven looked straight into his father's eyes, long and hard, fighting the tears burning behind his eyes. "You're sure this is the way you want it?"

"Yeah, I'm sure." His face turned red, the pitch of his voice high. "Now get the hell out of here and take that mangy mutt with you."

"Come on, Scooter. Let's go. We're not welcome here."

Steven looked evenly at his father, prepared to make one last attempt, then turned away and stomped to his car. As his father slammed the front door, Steven threw open his car door, lifted Scooter onto the car seat, then sank into the driver's seat. Shaking and bewildered, he sat numb, unable to move. He gripped the steering wheel to stop the trembling.

How could he do this?

He turned to Scooter. "He just threw me out. All I wanted was a companion – something I could be attached to – something to love. And I wanted to help you feel safe – give you a better life – get us both off the street. Is that so bad?"

He couldn't loosen his grip on the steering wheel. Resting his head on the wheel he said, "Listen to me. I'm telling my troubles to a dog. Maybe I really am crazy." As if sensing his despair, Scooter put his paw in the crook of Steven's arm and sat quietly. He leaned into the dog and was comforted. When his hands relaxed, he started the engine.

As he checked the rearview mirror before pulling into the road, he saw his father had come back outside and was standing alone on the porch watching the car. Steven kept his eyes trained on the front window of the car and drove away without looking back.

If that's the way you want it, that's what you'll have, Old Man.

"Now what are we going to do?" Steven asked. Scooter cocked his head as if trying to solve the dilemma. "Here I am, homeless again. At least I'm not alone this time. Well, let's see what we can find. It's going to be okay, ole' boy. We'll figure it out."

Steven's autopilot instincts lead him straight to Anna's house.

He parked in front of the little house and turned to the dog, talking to him as if Scooter understood. "So, now what do I do? I can't just waltz in there with you. This might be a very bad plan. How do you feel about cats, Scooter? They can be nice companions, you know. You wait here and let me talk to Anna. Her cats might be terrified of dogs, although you're sure not very scary. Stay here. I'll be right back." He tried a new command, "Stay Scooter."

Leaving the windows open a crack for air, Steven slid out of the car. Watching Scooter with every step, he bounded up the front walk and knocked on Anna's door. It was opened almost immediately. "Steven, what a nice surprise. Come on in."

"Anna, I can't. I have this new complication." He pointed to the dog sitting patiently in the car, watching Steven's every move.

"Oh, a dog! Where did it come from?" She began walking toward the car.

"Long story. He's a stray, or lost. I'm not sure. I guess he's become my rescue dog." He followed her back to the car.

"Can we let him out? What's his name? Oh Steven, he's adorable."

"Here, let me get the leash. Scooter, say hello to Anna."

Scooter hopped out of the car and circled Anna, sniffing her, backing away, then without hesitation, sat directly on her foot. Anna laughed. "Well, that's a good sign. It means he likes me." She patted the dog.

"I didn't think you would appreciate it if I just charged into your house with a dog. I don't want to scare Tom and Jerry."

"I've had lots of dogs in my day, Steven. Come on in; let's try it. Hold him close on the leash and don't let him bolt or make fast moves. Let the animals work it out. Cats and dogs can be good pals if you introduce them properly."

She led them through the front door and called to the cats. "We've got company, boys! Now Steven, just stand still right here and let the cats approach you. I'm sure Scooter can smell them, but don't let him go after them. Good, that's it." She leaned down to the dog and put up her hand, palm forward. "Scooter, stay."

Tom poked his head out from under the sofa and gave a little warning hiss as Anna talked softly to the cats, assuring them they were safe. Jerry stayed hidden somewhere in the piles of yarn. "Okay, Steven. Slowly bring Scooter into the room and sit in this chair. Good! Scooter, sit." She gently pushed her hand against Scooter's back until he sat. "That's a good boy," she said to the dog. "Now, tell me what happened. Did he just appear in your life suddenly?"

"He got hit running through traffic. He was limping but it's much better now. I've seen him before, and today I ran after him because I thought he was injured. I took him to Pete's pet store and he was pretty sure it was just a bruise. Then, stupid me, I thought my father might like the idea of having a dog in the house. Not a chance. He threw me out. No hesitation. He said the dog wasn't welcome and told me to leave if I insisted on keeping him. So, here I am. I didn't know who else to turn to, Anna."

"Oh, Steven. That must have been so hard. I'm sorry."

"Don't worry, I know we can't stay here. Poor cats would freak out. And, I refuse to give him up to the animal shelter and give in to my father. In some way, I know this dog is important in my life. I feel this bond with him. It's like he rescued me as much as I rescued him. I want to take care of him and give him a better life."

"I'm glad for you, Steven. I think you two will make a good team."

"But, where do I go? I don't know what to do."

"Hmm. I have an idea. You know the kitchen where we took the soup?"

Oh no, not again. I can't do it. I may be homeless again, but I'm no masochist.

Anna plunged forward. "No, wait. It's not what you think. Stop backing away from me. Sit down and hear me out." Steven sat with the dog by his side, realizing this was the exact same request he had made to his father.

"All right, I'm listening."

"What Open Heart Kitchen needs is more like a custodian or a watchman, someone to look after the place. It's not a shelter or a facility for housing the homeless, it's more like a soup kitchen for hungry people – families without a paycheck, people who have lost their jobs, and yes, veterans. They come for a healthy, warm meal, not to sleep at night. They've had a couple of break-ins. So, what we need is someone to look after the place. And a dog would be a bonus. He would be alert to intruders."

I think I've been there – was really hungry – don't remember. Shit. Can I do this?

"I don't know if he's any kind of watch dog." Steven said. "I've only heard him bark once, and that was a friendly greeting. He didn't even bark during my father's tirade – although he did growl at him." He smiled. "That was pretty satisfying."

She laughed. "Well, we could see how it goes. There is a small cottage next to the garden. I don't think they could pay much, but you can eat there whenever we serve meals and you know how good the food is." Before he could object, she continued. "Let me make a couple of calls. The director is a friend. Just the other day he said we needed someone in there to look after the place." She walked to the kitchen to make the call before Steven could protest.

"I plan to heat up some meatloaf if you want to stay. It's pretty good if I say so myself. It doesn't look like Scooter is going to start a war with the cats, so you two are welcome here anytime."

Steven looked under the chair. Both cats were peering out, only their noses exposed. "Thanks, Anna. He seems more curious than threatening. Maybe he's happy to find friends."

After their fill of meatloaf and mashed potatoes, they drove to the little cottage behind the soup kitchen. The organization's director had agreed to meet with Steven and Anna the next day. The cottage offered a warm, cozy feeling of well-used comfort.

Steven was hesitant. He stood rooted on the threshold.

He stood his ground. Couldn't make himself take the first step into the cottage.

But what's the alternative – back to my father's – without Scooter?

Anna said, "Try it for one night. Remember, you are not asking for a free meal or a bed. Quite the opposite. We're asking *you* for help."

"Okay, Anna. I'll try it for one night. We'll see."

She took him by the arm and led him through the front door of the cottage. As she turned on lights and showed him around, Steven absorbed the cozy atmosphere and felt immediately at home. Homemade worn quilts covered the sofa and old-fashioned rocker. He tried it out, wondering if he could fix the squeak. Next to the living area was a kitchen, leading to a small bedroom and bath.

"Here are the sheets, come help me make the bed." Before the last blanket could be spread on the bed, Scooter hopped up and made it his own. He rolled over on his back, paws in the air and settled in for the night.

"Okay, time for another lesson. Off the bed, Scooter!" Steven commanded sternly, trying not to laugh. "Good boy. At least let us finish getting the blankets on."

"There's coffee in the freezer and the coffeemaker is in this cupboard," Anna said. "Have a good night, Steven. If you two want pancakes, come on over around 9:00. We're meeting with Tony the director at 11:00. See how it feels, and remember, this isn't a handout. You could be a big help to us." She slipped out the door before he could protest, leaving him standing inside the threshold.

Steven threw off his clothes, dropped an extra blanket on the floor for Scooter and crawled under the sheets, made warm by the dog's trial run. Ignoring the blanket, Scooter hopped on the bed and cuddled up next to Steven.

Chapter

17

I can't breathe. I'm drowning.

He's wounded. They shot him and he fell in the water. I can't find him. Can't get air. It's too dark. He's drowning. I can't save him.

He's lost. I'm lost. The river's clouded with red. Oh God, it's blood, not water. Can't see. We're both going to die.

I failed him.

Steven shot up, dripping with sweat, gasping for air. He tried to catch his breath. Scooter sat watching him, with one paw on his arm, head cocked, making a soft cooing sound.

"It's okay boy. My nightmare. I lived it."

Pushing the terror from his mind, Steven put his arms around the dog for comfort. "Let's go outside and get some fresh air." He threw on a pair of jeans and walked around the cottage, wandering aimlessly in the garden, admiring the rows of vegetables, breathing in the fresh air, as Scooter hunted for the perfect bush.

I should have done more to save him.

No, the water – stop it...

After coffee for Steven and kibble for Scooter, they walked the few blocks to Anna's house. She called from the kitchen to come in. As they entered, Steven called out to the cats, "Coming in, boys. The dog is friendly, I promise." The cats scattered as Scooter pulled on the leash. "No, Scooter. Sit with me and let the cats get used to you. They'll come out when they feel safe." He sat quietly, savoring the aroma of fresh coffee brewing.

Anna came to the door of the kitchen, whipping up pancake batter. "How was your night? Sleep alright?"

"Not bad," Steven said.

She doesn't need to know.

Deflecting the question, he said, "Anything I can do to help?"

"Nope. It's all ready. Come sit in here. Is Scooter allowed to have pancakes?"

"I don't know, I guess it can't hurt him. He needs to add a little bulk. Come on, Scooter, Anna has a treat for you. Let's leave the cats in peace."

After their pancakes, they sat together as if they were a family enjoying a second cup of coffee. Anna gave him a little background on the charity that sponsored the food kitchen. "The philanthropic group is called 'Open Heart.' They have three kitchens in the state, all based on the concept of feeding anyone who is hungry and shows up. We try to provide hot meals at midday, three times a week. On holidays, we have a special meal. It's heartbreaking to realize how many people are going hungry. It's amazing how generous people are when they know it's for a good cause. The food is prepared by local residents and farmers who bring extra produce.

"You saw the vegetable garden. It used to be a big parcel of weeds. One day we all brought our shovels and dug in. We plant seasonal vegetables and volunteers, like Lindsay, keep it thriving. But what the place really needs now is a caretaker. I know they have allocated funds for someone to look after the place. We really need you."

"I don't know, Anna." Steven's voice trembled. "I have to be honest with you. I have a pretty lousy track record. That's why my father gets so infuriated with me. He thinks I've been irresponsible and reckless. He may be a jerk, but he's not wrong. My past is not one I'm very proud of. It's just...I'm just...I can't explain it. There's all this clutter going on in my head. I get angry and belligerent for stupid reasons."

"You know, Steven, I really do understand. I've seen lots of vets struggling to find their way. You're not alone. Did you ever try that group with Sam Robinson?" Steven backed his chair away from the table, poised to bolt as he held on to the arms of the chair. She appeared not to notice and kept talking. "Well, that's for another day. Your past is just that – behind you. All you can do is keep trying to set things right. For now, let's go talk to Tony. See what you think of his idea."

They walked back to the Open Heart kitchen and found Tony already there.

Anna greeted him warmly. "Tony, it's good to see you. This is my friend Steven. And *this* is his faithful watchdog Scooter. Steven, this is Tony Robinson. And yes, if he looks a bit like our Dr. Sam, it's because he's the good doctor's son." Hesitant to open his mouth, Steven stepped forward.

They shook hands and Tony crouched down to greet Scooter. "So, you're the fierce guard dog I heard about. You don't look very ferocious to me." He laughed and patted the dog. "I guess Anna has told you about our endeavor. We're proud of the help we offer. I wish we could do more. For starters, we need someone to simply be here, mostly at night. This isn't the greatest neighborhood, especially for a woman living alone." He gave Anna a look of regret. "And it's common knowledge that there is a storehouse of food in here most of the time. I haven't seen any serious theft, just hungry, desperate people. Let's go inside and talk."

They sat at the well-worn kitchen table. "So, tell me about yourself, Steven."

"Well, uh, I was a medic in Vietnam. To be honest, it has taken its toll. You would think after all this time – but I'm not the same person I was when I went into that god-awful war. I'm not sure I – I don't know what to say – I've had some bad moments."

Tony looked directly at Steven without hesitation. "Hey, man. I understand. I've had bad moments, too. I've been in your shoes. Not as a medic – I don't know how you did it, Man – stitching up bodies in that jungle. It was rough being there, and for me, painful coming back. I get it. Why do you think my father got so interested in helping veterans when he retired?" He chuckled. "Because he had *me* to contend with; so, I became his worst specimen and first test case. And I sit here now and assure you, it can get better. *We* can get better, Steven. I promise."

"I'm not sure I can guarantee anything." Steven admitted. "I've been pretty messed up. This dog is probably more reliable than I am."

"Well, that's all we really need is a good watchdog. As long as he alerts you to what's going on. Anna is a pretty good judge of character, and if she says you're okay, that's good enough for me. Look, let's try it out. I'm not even going to ask you to cut your hair. We need someone to be here at night and we need you sober. Can you do that?" Steven nodded.

"We can't pay you much, maybe $100 a week. It would at least pay for your gas and dog food. You're welcome to free meals, and don't forget you've got the best cook in town just down the street."

Anna gave a little bow.

"What do you say?"

Steven put his hand on Scooter's head and let it move down his spine.

Can I do this?

"Okay, we'll see how it goes, Tony. I don't want to mess up this time. I need to prove to myself..."

"I get it, Steven. And you can call any time, for any reason."

He wrote down his phone number, then pulled out a checkbook and wrote a check for $200.00. "This is because we have faith in you, Steven. I know you can do this."

"Thank you for your trust. I'll try my best."

What have I done?

~   ~   ~

Steven parked in front of his father's house and turned to Scooter. "You wait in the car. I'll be right back. Stay, Scooter."

Using his key, Steven slipped in the front door, hoping his father would not hear. He quietly entered his little bedroom and stopped short. His father sat at Steven's desk, his head buried in David Lyon's letters, so engrossed he seemed not to hear Steven enter.

Steven threw the house key into the pile of papers. "What the hell do you think you're doing?" Steven shouted. "You have no right to go through my stuff. Don't I have any privacy?"

His father shot up from the chair. "I – uh – was just curious. No harm done. Wanted to see what this obsess...fascination was all about."

"No, you wanted to check up on me. See what I was doing – trying to make a case for my crazy compulsion, as you call it. Well, it's none of your damn business. You're not interested – remember?"

"Well, I..."

"Never mind. It's too late. I tried to talk to you about it, but you wouldn't listen. You think this is nuts – isn't that what you said? Wouldn't let the dog in the house. Now get out! I'm here to collect my things and you can have the whole damn house to yourself."

His father made a conciliatory step toward Steven and started to speak, then head bent down, he walked out of the room.

After loading the car with his few possessions, Steven gathered the letters and documents, not realizing that the key to the house was in the stack of papers. He drove to the one bank his father didn't frequent. With a renewed sense of pride, he opened a bank account in his own name, not a joint account his father could monitor. He kept enough cash to pay for gas and dog food, along with extra money to buy groceries and supplement Anna's pantry.

The simple task of filling his car with gas, with his own money, gave him a sense of pride. *How ridiculous.* Yet he understood the significance of this event.

Okay, let's see if you can be accountable, earn their trust.

"Scooter, let's get you more dog food. We need to fatten you up a bit. You still look like a bony, starving dog, even with all the fluff." He drove to the pet store to see Pete.

~   ~   ~

"Hey, Steven. Glad to see you're back. How's it going?" Pete crouched down to greet Scooter and offered a treat.

"I think I've rescued an incredibly special dog. I never thought I could bond with any animal, much less a mutt like this."

"I think it's great. Just enjoy it. Don't question yourself. Dogs can bring us tremendous pleasure and companionship. He knows you are his savior and his loyalty is evident. Has he been limping?"

"He seems much better. I think you're right – bruised bone."

"Did you ever check with the animal shelter to make sure someone hasn't lost a dog?"

Steven felt a shiver of fear.

What if I have to give him up? Please – no.

Pete tried to assure him. "I know it would be awful. But you have to make sure. It's the right thing to do, Steven. What if someone is looking for him? What if you were the one with

169

a missing dog?"

"Okay, okay. Let's get it over with. Do you know who to call? Will you do it?" Steven began to pace, then leaned down to touch Scooter. The dog looked up and placed his head against Steven's leg.

"Sure," Pete said, as he picked up the phone and dialed the county animal shelter. Speaking into the phone he said, "Yeah, we've found a lost dog and want to make sure you don't know of anyone – well, he's kind of a mutt, mid-sized, reddish blond fluffy coat, looks like a cross between a Lab and a Cocker Spaniel. Oh, let's see." He crouched down and examined Scooter's face. "Nope, no white V on his forehead. Okay good. Yes, we have a good home for him – yes, you're welcome." Pete hung up the phone and gave Steven a grin. "He's officially yours! No lost dog fitting Scooter's description. He must have been abandoned. They're looking for a Cocker with a V on his forehead."

Tears seeped into Steven's eyes as he leaned down to hug the dog. "Scooter, I guess we belong together." Looking up at Pete, he smiled. "Thanks, Pete. I'm grateful for your help...not sure I could have done it. I didn't realize how attached I'd become."

"Yeah, I know. I'd say you both could use some love." He laughed. "The next step is to find a good woman who might appreciate the likes of either of us."

Steven grinned. "Good luck with that. I think I'll stick with my dog."

Pete nodded. "You know what, I know this great woman...my..."

"No thank you. This dog suits me just fine. He never yells, never criticizes, and he's by my side no matter what. At least I know I can count on him." Steven paid for the dog food and waved goodbye, feeling a sense of contentment for the first time in many years.

Chapter

18

(Undated)

  My dear daughter,
I am most distressed to hear that my
letter to you has been discovered. It
troubles me greatly that I have caused
you further grief and pray there will
not be repercussions against you or your
brother. As I surmise, he is not privy
to our attempt at a liaison, as he is too
young to take the risk. I fear he may
despise me forever and place consummate
blame on my abandonment and will carry
my indiscretions heavily in his heart.

Know this, my dear girl; it was never my choice to be parted from you and your brother, so many years ago. It was forced upon me against my will and my soul is forever grieved as a consequence.

Yet, I must admit the fault is mine. I do not give up hope that we will somehow, someday meet, even if in the great beyond.

This letter will be posted to your friend Kate, in hopes it will find its way to you.

Your devoted father,

"I thought my life was bad after the war, but this guy's separation from his family is downright tragic. What the hell did he do to cause this?" Steven asked, as if Scooter could answer. He patted the dog's head as he set aside the letter. "There's something else we have in common – difficult family relationships, how they must have suffered." The dog cocked his head as if in agreement.

Steven was struck by how easy it was to talk to a dog. Scooter didn't talk back or criticize or judge. Scooter listened patiently and seemed to weigh each word as if he understood. After his first cup of coffee, the man and dog were spread out

174

on the bed, Steven going through the letters with Scooter listening intently.

"Guess we better keep digging, Scooter. I'm really curious to know if David ever connected with his daughter. What horrible offense caused him to be shunned by his family? Can I learn from this man?" Scooter cocked his head.

"Yeah, I guess I could say the same. My own father can't seem to forgive me for my screw-ups and I've had plenty. Maybe I need to let it go – let *him* go. At least Anna believes in me."

Scooter suddenly popped his head up, leapt off the bed, ran to the door of the cottage and began barking in earnest. "What is it boy? I don't hear anything. Is someone out there?" He secured the leash and reassured the dog. "Good boy. Let's go do our job, Scooter."

Steven stealthily eased out the front door of the cottage, holding the leash so the dog wouldn't bolt into the garden. "Lindsay, what the hell..."

Steven emerged from the cottage, as Lindsay dropped her hoe and stood perfectly still. "Don't move. You don't want to give this fierce dog a chance to charge." He grinned.

"It's okay, Scooter. Come meet Lindsay, she's a friend."

I think.

"What the devil are you doing here, Steven?"

He allowed the dog to approach Lindsay at his own pace, slowly easing up on the leash until they were facing each other.

Lindsay crouched down so she was eye-level with the dog. "Well, look at this! You found him. Hello, boy. I'm glad to see you're safe." Looking up at Steven, she asked, "How did you find him?"

"More like he found me. After you left the library, I saw him darting through traffic and I chased after him. He was hit by someone on a motorcycle, but he seems alright now."

"What are you doing here?"

"Protecting the property, I guess. Tony hired me – well actually he hired *us* – wanted to make sure someone was keeping watch at night. I wasn't really sure how the dog would react to an intruder – and now we know!" Patting Scooter he said, "Good job, boy. You are a natural. Now you have to learn the difference between friend and foe."

Not sure about you, Lindsay.

Not sure what to say and conscious of her angry departure at the library, Steven was unwilling to provoke another confrontation.

"Well, we're off. Don't want to interfere with your gardening chores." He gave a brief wave, turned and headed back to the cottage.

"But..." Lindsay's voice trailed after him. Steven continued to walk away, creating as much distance as possible without breaking into a run.

Right back at you, Lindsay.

~   ~   ~

Picking up speed, Steven jogged down the street toward Anna's house, with the dog keeping pace. "Guess we should both get in shape, Scooter. There's that smile of yours. You like this don't you? And you've had plenty of practice running into traffic, dodging cars on the road, so I guess this jogging is for my benefit – work off a little steam."

Scooter ran straight to Anna's front door and barked his greeting. No answer. "Maybe she's out back. Let's go around to the back yard and check." Scooter would not budge. He turned his back to the front door and stood firmly on the front porch, searching the street. "What are you trying to tell me? She's not in there?" Trusting the dog's instincts, he tried the front door. "At least she had the good sense to keep it locked in this neighborhood. What if she went down those rickety stairs to the basement? Maybe she's in the backyard."

He tugged on Scooter's leash. "Come, Scooter. It's time you learned a new command. Look at me. That's it. Come, now!" Scooter obeyed, but continued to look toward the street. As they headed around the house toward the backyard, a car pulled up in front. Anna jumped out as Dr. Sam followed, hauling sacks of groceries.

"Steven, I'm so glad to see you. Hi, Scooter." Anna patted the dog. "You remember Sam? He took me on a shopping spree. Now I have to start cooking for the lunch at Open Heart tomorrow."

"Let me help you, Sam." Steven pulled grocery bags from the car, holding onto the leash.

"Here Steven, let me take Scooter and you help Sam. Come on, boy. Let's go find Tom and Jerry." The dog happily trotted by her side as she unlocked the door and called out to the cats.

"Thanks, Steven." Sam panted, as he climbed the steps to the porch. "I'm kind of in a rush. We spent too much time deciding on healthy meals, and now I'm late for the get-together at Joe's. Want to come along?"

Uh Oh! Not getting corralled into that one.

"Here, give me the groceries. Thanks for the offer, but I think I'll stay here and help Anna get started. I'm good at chopping and peeling and you never know, she might need some vegetables from the garden."

Sam gave him a knowing smile. "Okay, sure. Maybe next time." He poked his head into Anna's front hallway and called out, "I'm off to Joe's. See you soon."

"Thanks for your help Sam. I'll save leftovers for you."

"Wouldn't miss your cooking! Bye."

Steven hauled the rest of the bags into the kitchen and found Scooter sniffing under the sofa for the cats. "Good luck coaxing them out, Scooter. Try to sit quietly and maybe they'll come to you." He turned to help Anna. "What can I do to help?"

"First I want to just sit a minute. Would you bring me a glass of water?"

"Sure." As he brought her the water and plopped down opposite her, "Well, I have good news. Scooter has proven he's a competent watch dog. He did his job, Anna! He heard a noise coming from the garden and led me right to the intruder."

Anna sat wide-eyed. "Oh Steven. Good boy, Scooter. Who was out there that early?"

Steven laughed. "Only our most intrepid gardener, Lindsay."

"Oh, really!" She gave him a knowing look.

"Oh no. She's okay, but it's not going to happen, Anna. Don't encourage me. I'm bad news with women. Believe me."

"I find that hard to believe. You've been wonderfully kind to me, and I'm a woman."

Determined to change the subject Steven said, "Yeah, well we're talking about Scooter, not Lindsay, and I've got to say, I'm happy with this dog. None of us really knew if he had the protective instincts to be a good watch dog. But he sure proved himself."

"That's wonderful. I suspect he was protecting you, not the property. But it doesn't matter. He proved his loyalty to you. That's all that counts."

"So now he has to learn who is a friend and who intends to do harm. Sometimes it's hard for any of us to know."

"Trust your instincts, Steven."

"I'm not sure mine are so good, Anna. It's – it's hard to figure out. And the truth is – I'm the one who's untrustworthy."

"Stop beating yourself up, Steven. I have complete trust in you. And right now, I trust that you will help me unload these groceries and start chopping so we can get this stew going."

He gave a small bow. "As you wish, Miss Anna."

Chapter

19

May 20, 1891

Old Soldiers and Sailors Home

Dr. Jeremy Merrick
Veterans Affairs Department
Washington, D. C.

My Dear Dr. Merrick,
Your kind visit has restored my faith in
the goodness of humanity. You will never
know how much it gladdened my heart.
It was most fortunate that you arrived
in time to plead my case and convince the
authorities that my ailment was most
definitely physical and not mental.
I have seen the conditions of the

institution where they intended to send me. They are unspeakable.

I suppose my behavior could be questionable at times, but not unstable. As much as you know of my past, I am heartened by your testimony and grateful that you remain my true friend.

I recently heard about a man who came back from the horrors of our war, wandering around the town, begging and hollering. His family didn't know what was wrong with him or what to do with him. They concluded he was so ruined from the war he would never be better. They forced him into one of those dreadful mental institutions and he never recovered. I know you have saved me from a similar fate.

There is so much unknown about the effects of war on soldiers and quite impossible to diagnose. Most of us who survived are forever suffering, from more than physical wounds. No one seems to give credence to the horrifying misery of war and the toll it takes on the human soul. We have all experienced the aftermath differently, and yet I see a common thread of anguish and grief.

I call it living hell – that is what we have suffered. Do you think any of us came away unscathed? I doubt it. And the most tragic result of all is that my children are now paying a dreadful price for my mistakes.

I thank you for your visit and support, my friend. I am forever grateful.

Your friend,
David Lane

Steven was rigid, fighting back tears of grief – for David, himself and for all the soldiers who had suffered in war. After reading the letter a third time, he was convinced David Lane had suffered the same torment he had. They had even put a name to it – 'shell shocked' – same as WWI.

Don't remember. Let it go.

He closed his eyes, lying back on the bed and tried not to think, then fell into a deep sleep.

~   ~   ~

He was watching himself struggle. He was underwater, surrounded by walls of concrete, restricting his ability to move. Rule No. 1 - when under stress - move! But he couldn't. He looked around and realized he was tethered to an IV that was inserted into a permanent entry hole in his arm. The realization of confinement was unbearable. Then, as the walls turned to water and moved closer, he saw the 'Call' button. He treaded water and leaned forward, but he couldn't reach it. What was in the IV? Unreadable. Come on, you're a medic. Figure it out. Something to sedate me? Or is this why I feel crazy? Are they trying to keep me anesthetized?

Am I in a hospital? With walls made of water? Fear overwhelmed his fascination. He stretched toward the call button again but knew it was painfully out of reach. Pull out the IV? Not very smart. Maybe he could reach it with the other hand. He stretched for the alarm button and saw that he was connected to some kind of machine that was taped to his leg and tied against his arm. Was this a prison or a hospital? Felt like both.

No way out. No escape. The walls of water came closer. He was helpless to defend himself. He yelled for help.

No one came.

Shouting in vain, Steven awoke from his dream. Scooter jumped up on the bed and cuddling against him, placed one paw on his chest, as if to ease his suffering.

"Okay, that's it! I can't keep doing this. Scooter, you stay here and guard the place. I'm going for a drive to Joe's Café – maybe Dr. Sam will still be there with his band of misfits. I should fit right in."

~　　~　　~

The sentiment from David's letters haunted Steven as he drove toward town. How could a bunch of vets help? Sure, they might understand. They had all been through tough times and suffered the tortures of war. But what did they do anyway – sit around and compare war stories? See who was the most fucked up? Have a pissing contest over whose agony was the most painful? Shit, was there any point to that? What could a bunch of homeless vets offer him? How could Dr. Sam really understand what he had suffered? Was this going to do any good?

Unburden my weeping soul.

Steven stopped the car a block before reaching Joe's coffee house. Torn between years of distrust and the powerful need for human connection, he leaned his head against the steering wheel. He reached toward the passenger seat to pat his dog, searching for comfort, and realized he'd left Scooter at the cottage.

Okay, man-up you fool. Do something.

He forced himself to step out of the car, dreading the confrontation he feared lay ahead of him.

Don't be such a baby.

He walked up the street and into Joe's Café before he could second-guess himself as his flight instincts battled with his fears , and the fight he dreaded evaporated as he walked toward the welcoming aroma of freshly brewed coffee and homemade muffins.

Joe called out from behind the counter, "Hey, Steven. Glad to see you."

"Hi, Joe. Uh, well – I guess I could use a cup of coffee."

"Well, funny thing. I just happen to have plenty. Want to try my new blend? I'm taking a poll so you guys can tell me if it's too strong or maybe too bitter." He gestured toward the table where the veterans were seated. Dr. Sam waved.

"Hey, Steven. Come join us. We're having a coffee tasting. Bring a cup, we're comparing Joe's concoctions."

Steven hesitated. This is not what he expected.

Coffee tasting? What about...

He was sure he would be confronted with a bunch of hostile, low-life vets who acted out their anger while Dr. Sam consoled them. Instead, as he approached, he was surprised by their friendly faces as they welcomed him and scooted around the table to make room for him.

Not the most clean-cut – a bit disheveled, but who am I to talk?

"Hey guys. This is Steven. We only go by first names around here. I'm pretty sure he's one of us and has a lot in common with you. Steven, we're having a very serious discussion this afternoon, and any advice would be welcome. Joe needs our opinion, so join in and help us choose his most potent blend. The one you can chew will win the prize."

As Joe brought him a cup he asked, "Where's Scooter? I saved some stale biscuits that are guaranteed to fatten him up."

Steven took a gulp of coffee and gritted his teeth. "I had to leave him at the cottage. We're watching over the Open

186

Heart kitchen. He needs to do his watchdog duties and be alert to intruders." He turned to Joe. "Maybe a little lighter. This would grow hair where it doesn't belong."

One of the men laughed and said, "Hey Steven, I'm John. I've taken advantage of Open Hearts' goodwill. Got to say, they've got some great cooks. I hate to admit needing a handout sometimes, but a guy's gotta have a full belly now and then." Another vet nodded as if he agreed, but never said a word. Steven made note of his silence and understood. He'd seen men like this – mute and defeated.

Maybe just showing up is enough. It's more than I've done.

Steven looked at the lean faces around the table and said, "Yeah, I get it. I've been there. You guys are always welcome. I know they're serving a great stew tomorrow. I helped peel carrots, so I guarantee it's good for you. And they can always use help. If you have time to stay and clean up, I'm sure they could use some strong backs to haul those big pots and serve the old folks."

"Yeah, sure," said another man. "If they're going to feed us for free, the least we can do is help out."

"The whole kitchen is run by volunteers," Steven explained. "Lots of people donate food and we help wash dishes. They have a garden in back where they grow vegetables. They can always use someone who's good with a hoe. It's pretty impressive what they're doing."

Listen to me. I'm recruiting volunteers!

"Sam, they can always use more help, right? And I don't know if they have anyone helping in the garden except Lindsay."

"Thought you'd like working with her, Steven. Everyone

supports the idea of paying back by volunteering. I didn't want to put pressure on anyone," Sam said with a twinkle in his eye, "but I haven't seen you out there digging up carrots." Steven nodded in agreement and tried to ignore Sam's suggestion. "Yeah, well I'm pretty new at this. Still learning how it all works. I guess I would rather help Anna chop and peel and deliver the food."

"What can we do?" John said.

Sam answered, "If any of you want to help out, come early tomorrow and see what they need. If nothing else, you will at least get a terrific bowl of stew."

"Hi Steven, I'm Craig. I've got a truck if you need a strong back getting the food to the shelter. It's old and beat up, but it runs. I built this cover for the back, and – uh – have to sleep there sometimes."

Steven tried not to wince.

And I'm an ungrateful lout who never appreciates my father's charity. Just ask him.

"It's more than I have," Steven said. "Thanks for offering. I'll give you Anna's address and you can help take the pots of stew to the kitchen around ten tomorrow."

Joe walked over with another pot of coffee to taste. "Okay gentlemen, savor this blend."

As they all poured a cup, Steven sat back and watched the men enjoy the simple pleasure of sharing ideas about the best blend of Joe's coffee.

Maybe this won't be so bad after all.

Chapter

20

May 1, 1891

My Dear Dr. Lane,

It was a pleasure to meet with you again and be able to confirm to the Veterans Medical Board that you are of sound mind, but not so your old, tired body.

It is impossible to document the number of soldiers who continue to suffer from various illnesses after all these years, along with the long-term effects of starvation and lack of nutrition during that dreadful war. I continue to see patients who will never fully recover, many in your unfortunate circumstance and more who have already succumbed to their weaknesses.

There is so much we have learned in the years since the end of the war that will help future generations, but not for those who suffered as you have. Try to eat healthy meals and breathe fresh, clean air. If you can stand the cold, sleep outside. It may clean your scarred lungs. I will be making another trip for a second examination within the month.
Until then, be well, my friend.

Sincerely,
Dr. Jeremy Merrick
Veterans Affairs Office

From earlier research, Steven understood Dr. Merrick's letter, and knew how many Civil War soldiers had died of malnutrition. The letter had triggered his medic's curiosity, and earlier that morning he had begun searching for medical advancements in the library books strewn around the bed.

He realized that one hundred years made a significant difference in medical advances and nutritional knowledge.

Today, they served a healthy stew to the many veterans and families who had arrived at the Open Heart kitchen. Anna's little army of helpers relaxed and chatted after the meal had been served.

Craig, who had kept his promise and helped transport food from Anna's house to Open Heart, watched the needy families. "I thought I'd find a bunch of low-life vets like me," he said. "Seeing all those hungry children is enough to break a hardened heart."

"Yeah, these folks sure provide a great service to this little part of our community," Dr. Sam agreed. "And our vets deserve respect like anyone else."

"We're better off than the Civil War soldiers," Steven said.

"What the hell does the Civil War have to do with us?" Craig challenged.

"War veterans have lots in common. I got curious about Anna's grandfather who fought in the Civil War. The more I learn about it, the more I realize how much better we had it. At least the army gave us rations that were fairly nutritious. We weren't malnourished like lots of soldiers during the Civil War. It was pretty grim for them."

"Every soldier in every war suffers," Dr. Sam said.

Steven nodded. "Isn't that the truth. I read somewhere that more soldiers in the Civil War died from illnesses than from bullets. Malnutrition led to disease for not only the soldiers but their families. With men recruited off the farms, the families couldn't produce enough food. It was a deadly cycle."

"That's really tough," Craig said. "It makes you wonder how any of them survived."

"Yeah, I know. We ran out of rations once in a while, but we never starved."

"Out on patrols, we could get pretty desperate. Some brave soul would catch snakes and grill them. A few times we had to eat the food raw when the monsoons kicked up so we couldn't build a fire." Craig turned to Steven with a devilish look. "Did you ever eat rats like the locals?"

"Couldn't bring myself to," Steven said. "But when the Civil War soldiers got hungry enough, they went on 'rat patrol' and devised creative ways to cook them."

"Ugh," said Anna. "That's disgusting. How could they stomach it?"

"I guess when you're starving, you'll settle for anything that's got protein," Steven said. "And sanitation in the army camps was just plain ignored. Those guys lived with infestations of flies and rats that brought bacteria and disease into the camps. Then they got dysentery and typhoid fever. Back then they didn't understand the importance of hygiene. A simple bath was impossible. They'd wait until they came upon a pond or lake. Soldiers lived in the stench and filth of camp life and they didn't know the science of how disease spreads. It must have been barbaric for those soldiers."

"I refuse to say we had it so good," Craig said.

"Hey, I never said that," Steven said. "This research I've done has also taught me how much the two wars had in common. The more I read this man's letters the more I see how messed up he was. David Lane must have done some awful things and it seems he pretty much ruined his life and destroyed his family. And I can tell you, their suffering wasn't much different from ours. It's the same thing we've been through. And if I look hard in the mirror, I see myself going down the same path. I mean, look at us. We've been out of Vietnam for years and we still can't get our act together. What the hell's the matter with us?"

"Now wait a minute..." Craig was getting angry.

"No, I mean me, too." Steven lowered his voice. "I admit I've been a screw-up like a lot of guys. I've lived on the streets and I've taken handouts." He gestured to Anna and Doc who had risen during the rat debate to begin the cleanup. "I'm just sayin' I'm sick of it. I want to try to understand what's happened that has messed me up so much and fix it – or at least try." He leaned toward Craig. "I'm fucking sick of myself."

"I'm with you there, man."

"What I know for sure is that it feels a whole lot better to be helping people than having to ask for help."

Heading for the kitchen, Craig said, "Okay, let's start here. What can we do to help – right now?"

"Start scrubbing the pots. I'll finish clearing the tables."

As they carried dishes into the kitchen, Anna and Sam smiled. "Thanks," Anna said. "Mind if I sit for a minute? Craig, would you finish the pots? Steven, I saved some leftover stew for Scooter. Why don't you let him out of the cottage? He must be hungry."

"Thanks, Anna. I'll be right back."

Returning to the dining hall with Scooter bouncing at his side, Steven laughed. "Anna, you sure know animals." He put the bowl on the floor and watched Scooter devour the stew.

"From what I've learned from you, we feed our animals better than those soldiers were fed 100 years ago. It must have been horrible." Anna breathed a sigh of despair.

"Are you alright?" Steven asked. He looked at her with concern. "You look flushed, Anna. Here, let me take your pulse."

"Oh stop, I'm fine. Just a little tired – that's all. It's hot in the kitchen."

"No, that's not all. Your heart is racing. Do you have problems with your heart?"

"Not that I know of. Maybe I get high blood pressure once in a while."

Steven called into the kitchen, "Hey Doc. Could you come out here?"

"What is it, Steven?" Sam asked, drying his hands on a towel."

"Something's not right with Anna. She's flushed and clammy. Feel her pulse, would you? It's over 150, seems high to me. She says she isn't feeling well, her pulse is racing and she probably has undiagnosed high blood pressure."

Anna protested, "Stop fussing over me, I'm fine now. I just overdid it a little. I get a bit dizzy now and then. That's all.

"Her pulse seems okay now," Sam said, looking at Steven and called into the kitchen. "Bring a cool wet cloth, will you Craig?"

"Be right there."

"Well now, that's one way to get out of kitchen duty," Doc said, trying to make light of the crisis.

Craig rushed in with the cloth and Sam patted Anna's face. "Better now?"

Anna's eyes shone with gratitude. Her hand was tickled by Scooter's warm tongue as she caressed his furry face. "Scooter, I'm alright now. It's okay, boy. Goodness, dogs sure know when something is wrong."

"Especially this one." Steven said. "He seems to read my every thought. I swear he knows what I'm thinking."

"I think you're actually right," Sam agreed. "Dogs seem to have a sixth sense and I believe they can read our emotions better than we can ourselves."

Sam took Steven by the shoulders. "You're not so bad yourself. Very perceptive." Steven cocked his head, curious to hear how Sam could think he was good at anything.

"You said you were a medic, and you sure have retained your training. Good call with Anna."

"I was in Pre-Med when I joined. Probably the dumbest – well, it's history now. But, I sure wish I could have, that I – that I would have…"

"I know how tough it was, Steven. It's agonizing to lose wounded soldiers, to do your best and they still die."

Steven jumped to his feet and shouted, "How would you know? You were too old for Vietnam."

"But not too old for Korea."

Oh shit. What a jerk I am.

"Oh, uh, I'm sorry. I didn't mean to be disrespectful. So many people really don't understand."

"You're right," Sam said. "Few can genuinely know the hell we've lived through, and fewer still can sympathize with the hell we continue to endure."

"Well, nothing seems to change, does it? Look at this Civil War vet, David Lane - 100 years later and what has changed? We're just as messed up as they were. We're still hopeless."

"Damn straight," Craig chimed in as he returned to the kitchen.

"No," Sam said. "We're not hopeless. None of us are. We can get past the torment. I've seen it, I've lived it. People can triumph over their trauma."

Steven said. "But it feels like I still suffer – every day. Look what I've gotten from my survival."

"That doesn't mean you can't change your life, Steven. I really have seen it. And, look at you – you've done it already, whether you realize it or not."

"I haven't done a damn thing. A grown man, still dependent on my father. When I look in the mirror, I see disgusting. I leech food from Anna, who feeds me 'cause she feels sorry for me. When I lived on the streets, I begged for food. I can't hold a job 'cause I keep blowing up at people and I couldn't stay away from the bottle for long. I'd get mad for no reason, and as you have witnessed, I bolt when people try to get too close." He looked straight at Sam. "I've done things you can't imagine. I failed my friends and I've hurt good people." Steven choked on his own words, took a breath and continued quietly. "I left people behind. I – I'm not a nice guy, Sam, and all your good wishes can't make me into one. So again I ask – what good is *my* survival? I have nothing to offer."

Anna gave him a piercing look, as loving as any mother. "That is not so. You've got *us*, Steven. You've got people who care about you and will stick with you and comfort you. We're a community here and we take care of each other – we are your family."

Steven's entire body had gone rigid, not sure he could trust her words, then he crumbled onto the bench next to her. He put one arm around her shoulders and patted his dog with the other hand as his head dropped to his chest.

Sam picked up the conversation before Steven could object. "And you're wrong. You have plenty. You have a job..."

"Yeah, right! Some job."

"Okay, you have a minimal job. But you have something else, Steven. You have a skill. I just witnessed it. Have you thought about that? You don't have a medical license, but you are still a damn good medic. Your instincts were perfect. You knew exactly what to look for. You are observant and best of all, you are compassionate."

"Well, it's a little late to go back to medical school."

"So maybe you improvise. Maybe with your previous schooling and experience in the war, you could qualify for a different medical license, maybe a nursing license, or a...."

"Nursing! You're suggesting I'd want to be a nurse?"

"What? You're afraid to compete with all those cute young women?"

"Male nurses?"

"Actually – yes, there are plenty – and highly valued, I might say."

"Steven," Anna piped in, "Remember the nurses you read

about in the Civil War? Remember how much you admired them? How brave they were?"

"But me – a nurse?"

"Sure, that's an option. And the medical community today has developed a new designation called Physician's Assistant. They are becoming valuable to M.D.'s in hospitals and surgical fields. Seriously Steven, I think this could work."

"It's not realistic. I would never qualify."

"Well, you never know until you investigate," Sam said. "And here's the other thing you need to know about yourself, Steven. You are a natural. And you are needed, right here."

"What do you mean – here?"

"I'm talking about all the hungry people who walk through these doors every week. How do you think they get medical help? Do you think they can afford health insurance? Do you think they have a doctor who looks after them? No, of course not. They would be malnourished if it weren't for this place, if it weren't for the goodness of the people who volunteer to help out here."

"Who is helping them?" Steven faced Sam and knew the truth. "No – you? Are you still...?"

"If someone comes in sick, I try to help them, figure out what's wrong and get them into one of the free clinics in town. But the truth is, yes, I'm dangerously close to practicing medicine without a license. My medical license expired when I retired three years ago. But I can't stand seeing those poor folks suffer. Little children are brought to me with high fevers and illnesses I can't diagnose. If you were here Steven – if you could help – just imagine – think of the possibilities. We could really help people. You can do this, Steven. I know you can."

"Doc, you don't know me. I'm the all-pro screw-up. You shouldn't trust me."

"What I know for sure is this – when someone is determined to achieve something, they can do it. Look at how you've combed through all those letters and studied to comprehend the horrors of the Civil War. Look how you've tried to appreciate what happened to David Lane and how you relate to him and want to understand his self-destruction. Why do you think you care so much, Steven?"

"Oh, that's just a distraction. Curiosity – to keep myself occupied. And as a bonus, I get to drive my father crazy in the process."

"I'm not buyin' it," Doc said. "You're struggling with the same agony that vets in the Civil War suffered. You want to understand him so you can understand yourself."

Steven looked evenly into Sam's eyes. "Maybe you're right, Doc. But as I read his letters, I'm beginning to understand the awful truth of his reality – he failed. David Lane never recovered. Maybe it's what happens to all of us. We're just too damaged to heal."

"Hell no! I refuse to give up on you, Steven. I have seen our soldiers climb out of that dark hole and right themselves. It can be done. I know it."

"And just how does one do that, Doc?"

I happen to like dark holes in the earth.

"Only you can know what matters in your life, Steven. Only you can decide *who* matters and what you want. We all have our own moral compass, our own set of values. It's just that sometimes events happen in our lives that push us down and won't let go. We each have to decide for ourselves how to pull ourselves back up."

"Or whether we can."

"Nope, it doesn't work that way. We can – we simply need enough strength and maybe a little help from our friends."

"And you think the answer to all my troubles is to become a nurse? I don't think so." Steven stood up and turned before he backed away.

"Maybe you're right. And maybe in twenty years it will be more common. I don't even know if the pay is fair for male nurses," Doc said. But, hear me out, Steven. Not necessarily a nurse. And you don't have to do anything," Doc insisted, as Steven turned away. "Turn around and let me finish, Steven. You can continue to wallow in your own misery for the rest of your life. It's your choice. All I know is that you have an innate talent for healing people and it's a sad waste of a human being not to use one's natural abilities. There are people who need you."

As their voices grew louder, Scooter raced over to both men, pushed his front paws against Steven's chest and raised himself to his full two-legged height, as if to stop the confrontation.

"All right Scooter. It's okay." Steven gave the dog a generous hug and set him down on all-fours. "I think it's time to get Anna home to rest."

"I can take you, my dear," Sam said, offering his arm.

"Oh, for heaven's sake, I'm not an invalid. I can drive the few blocks myself."

"Not tonight, Anna. I'll drive you and make sure you're safe and settled in."

Steven chimed in, "Nurse Steven agrees, Doc. I'll drive your truck over in the morning, Anna. Maybe I can talk you into making those delicious pancakes that Scooter loves so much."

"Hah! Scooter indeed."

"Hey, did I hear pancakes?" Craig asked, coming out of the kitchen. "Can I come too? I'll bring my special maple syrup and anything else you need."

Anna laughed. "Sure, you can all come. See you in the morning."

Steven watched with envy as Anna took Sam's arm and they walked out the door like an old married couple. He thought to himself, how dense can you be? Stop with the self-absorption.

Look at what's right in front of you!

Chapter

21

He swam through the murky water, holding his breath, searching for his friend, as he followed the trail of blood. They had seen the soldier tumble into the water after the gun shot and knew he had to be down there. Steven's lungs were bursting, begging for air. He popped to the surface gasping and sputtering for oxygen.

As he jerked his eyes open with a start, his fluffy dog was licking his face.

"Scooter, it's okay boy. Same damn nightmare, over and over. Won't let me forget. I failed him – my best friend. How do I forgive myself?" As Steven moved toward the coffee pot the dog bounded off the bed and barked at the door. They both heard screaming. Scooter scratched frantically to get out. Steven grabbed his collar, attached the leash and as he opened the door, the dog raced toward the garden, dragging his master after him.

"Lindsay? What the hell...?"

"Oh God, help me Steven." Lindsay cried. "Be careful, don't get too close. Don't let Scooter come into the garden. There's a huge snake. It's slithering through the vegetables. Oh, there it goes. Look out, it's coming in your direction! Can you see it? Grab that hoe. I dropped it I was so scared. Look out, it's coming toward you!"

"Try to stay calm, Lindsay. Don't make any fast moves." Patting Scooter, he leaned down and spoke quietly to the dog. "Good boy, Scooter. He's not going to hurt you."

Steven carefully slipped among the rows of vegetables with the hoe in one hand, dog tight on the leash, sniffing the ground as they hunted for the snake.

Lindsay planted herself firmly in the soil and began shaking and sobbing. "Please help me. It's huge, it's..."

Steven pinned the snake with the hoe then lifted it into the air. "Keep still, Lindsay. It's okay. This is a king snake. They don't harm humans. In fact, we should keep him in the garden. They eat other critters, including rattlesnakes. Don't worry, it's harmless."

"Well, I'm not going to make him our pet! Get it out of here."

Steven walked to the edge of the garden and dropped the snake over the fence into the adjacent empty lot, then reached out his hand to Lindsay. "Come on inside, you're shaking. It's not going to hurt you." Still trembling, Lindsay took his hand as he led her into the safety of the little cottage.

"Here, sit in the chair and pet Scooter. You've got him all riled up and now you both have to calm down. Petting an animal is good therapy." As he poured water into the tea kettle, Steven tried to reassure her. "I learned that from Anna.

Have you met her cats? All you have to do is sit quietly with Tom or Jerry on your lap and stroke their backs, best remedy for stress. I've had both cats on my lap, one on each knee – double duty – it works! Try it with Scooter. He loves it." He grabbed a blanket off the bed and tucked it around her shoulders. "Here, maybe this will help. You're still shaking."

"Thanks Steven. That snake really scared me." With a grateful look, she brought the blanket to her face, took a deep breath and continued to stroke the dog.

He handed her a steaming cup of tea. "Here you go. Drink this. It will help calm your nerves. I know it's frightening to be confronted by such a huge snake, and he wasn't even full grown. I hope you got a good enough look to recognize the difference between a king and a rattler. And a rattlesnake does have a rattle. If they're disturbed, they will make that rattling sound as a warning."

"I don't intend to get close enough to either one to tell the difference."

"Good girl. That's the best policy. Now – pet the dog and drink your tea. We have a date with the best pancake maker in town. Want to come?"

"I don't know if I can eat. Let me just sit here a minute. Your experience as a medic sure comes in handy. I can see you know about shock, but how do you know so much about snakes?"

"Vietnam is not a place you want to go if you're afraid of snakes. Of course, most of the snakes there are poisonous. There's a weird symbiotic relationship – it goes like this – rats were abundant in the area and will gravitate to food sources. American soldiers had the most food and were on patrol in the jungle and they had rations, so the rats tagged along. Along came the snakes, who ate the rats. And in your garden, that's a good thing."

"Oh great! Now you're telling me there are rats in the garden?"

"I've never seen evidence, but I don't think snakes like vegetables much, so..."

"So, soldiers would have this invisible parade following them? The rats were after your food, and the snakes trailed along after the rats?"

"Something like that. Only those were very dangerous snakes – cobras, who love to hunt rats, and vipers that are very poisonous. And then there was the two-step Vietnamese viper. Two steps and you fall. We definitely learned to stay clear of them."

"How dreadful."

"Did I ever tell you about the starving Civil War soldiers and their rat patrols..."

"Never mind. I can guess – oh no, did they eat them?"

Steven nodded his head. "Disgusting!" Lindsay said.

"You never know what you'll do when you're starving, Lindsay."

"I'm sure you're right. I can't imagine." They sipped tea in silence until she asked, "Didn't you have any protection from the snakes? Did you shoot them?"

"Not very often. When they were on patrol, soldiers had to be careful not to announce their location in the jungle."

"So, what did they do?"

"We had trained dogs in the patrols."

206

"Were they trained to kill snakes?"

"No, that was their natural instinct. But our Armed Forces employed dogs to perform lots of jobs. They were trained to detect mines, track enemy patrols and they even served as sentries at basecamps and as scouts to help troops in the bush."

"That's amazing! They must have been in as much danger as any soldier."

"That's true. I took my share of bullets out of many a brave dog. You know, I wonder if the soldiers had dogs during the Civil War. I'm going to have to look that up."

"How's your research going?"

"I'm learning a lot about the war but can't figure out much about David Lane. There's more digging to be done. Maybe you can help me, since you're so good at – you know – digging."

"Ha, very clever. I'll stick to digging in the dirt and leave you to dig into that awful war."

"All wars are awful, Lindsay."

She nodded. They silently sipped their tea as Steven took over the task of petting the dog.

Take a deep breath. My war is over...let it be over.

"Okay, next best cure for stress? Moving. It's my own secret remedy. Let's stroll on over to Anna's and walk off that stress. Come on, Scooter. Ready for pancakes?"

Scooter raced to the door and led them down the street toward Anna's house.

~   ~   ~

Scooter bounced up the steps to Anna's front porch and

barked to be allowed entrance. As she opened the door, Anna laughed as he sped by her, searching for Tom and Jerry. "Well, hello to you too, Scooter. Make yourself right at home. You'll find the cats hiding under the sofa." She held out her arms to Lindsay. "I'm so glad to see you. I thought it would take you hours to finish harvesting the carrots."

"Oh, I'm not finished by a long shot. I had a major interruption and a huge fright. There was a snake in the garden and..."

"How dreadful," Anna said. "Come on in and tell me all about it." Leading them into the living room, she continued. "First let me bring you some coffee. Steven, will you help?"

As she returned with steaming cups of coffee, Lindsay sat and continued her tale.

"It was a gigantic snake and I was sure it would slither toward me. I screamed and cried and finally Scooter heard me. But I don't know what I would have done if Steven hadn't been there." Turning to Anna she said, "He knows all about snakes and assured me this one wasn't dangerous. What would I have done? You're my hero."

"Don't call me a hero. Not even close."

"But..."

"Forget it, Lindsay," Steven said harshly. "Stop trying to be my cheerleader."

Anna gently put her hand on Lindsay's knee and looked at her steadily. "Never mind. Okay, who's hungry?"

"I'm starving," Craig said – walking through the open door. "Hope I'm still invited."

"Always," said Anna. "And since you've arrived late, you get to help me flip the pancakes. Come on in."

They headed toward the kitchen, leaving Steven and Lindsay sitting silently and separately. Scooter nuzzled his nose under Steven's clenched fist and looked up at him as if to say, 'Time to practice that stress-reducing, pet-the-dog trick.' Steven looked down at his devoted pup, and began rubbing his ears. "You're the best, Scooter." As if on cue, Tom peeked out from under the sofa and seeing Scooter getting all the attention, hopped into Steven's lap and pushed his head under his free hand.

Steven's face relaxed and he said, "Okay, I've got two hands. I can manage this."

"Not when Jerry gets into the mix," said Lindsay. "Come over here, kitty." She patted her lap, and invited Jerry to join her. "Come on up. I've got plenty of good lap, too."

Anna called from the kitchen, "Pancakes are ready. Come and get 'em." Everyone scattered – the cats raced back under the sofa, the dog stuck his nose under too, trying to follow, and the humans settled into the warmth of Anna's kitchen.

As they dug into stacks of buttermilk pancakes, Scooter reversed direction and smelling the sausage, produced his starving dog routine – nose on the table, eyebrows arching, sad eyes looking forlorn and forgotten.

Steven said sternly, "No Scooter, no begging at the table. Anna has a bowl for you. Here, she has special pancakes and one sausage just for you. See? There you go."

As the dog happily devoured his meal, Craig said, "He's a great dog, Steven. Really well behaved. We sure could have used him in Nam. How are his hunting skills?"

"I'm not sure. He's only been with me a couple of weeks.

I know he's street savvy. I watched him weave his way in and out of moving cars and saw him evade some guy trying to catch him. And this morning he did exactly what I commanded him to do. There was a snake in the garden and I didn't want him going after it until I knew what it was. I told him to stay by my side and he did! It was amazing. I haven't really trained him much, but he obeys me most of the time."

"They were both so brave," Lindsay said. "Steven knew just what to do and..."

"Lindsay, let it go. Besides, Craig would have done the same thing."

"Hell, no! Oops, sorry Anna...not a chance. I would have run like hell – uh – heck – well, I wouldn't have gotten anywhere near those slimy critters. You would have been on your own, Lindsay. You could scream your head off and I'd be running in the opposite direction. I'm a big baby when it comes to snakes."

"What did you do on patrol?" Steven asked. "We used to run into them all the time."

"Like I said, I'd run like hell."

"Well, Mr. Medic here knew just what to do." Lindsay said, pointing to Steven.

"Hey, that's it!" Craig said. "I've got the solution, Steven. Train to be an EMT. You know – like the fire departments use, emergency medical technicians. You already know what to do in war – and how to care for soldiers, so why not..."

"And I don't want any part of it. No more pain, no more death, can't do it anymore."

"But this isn't a war zone, Steven."

"It feels that way to me."

"But you could be there for the people coming into the kitchen who need help."

"Yea, but there's this one critical ingredient – it requires someone who can be responsible and I don't qualify."

"You sure were responsible this morning," Lindsay chimed in. "Craig, you would have been worthless."

He laughed. "I'd be insulted if it weren't the truth."

She turned to Steven. "I'm glad it was you and Scooter who came to my rescue...and don't look at me like that, Steven. I can be grateful if I want and I have the right to say so if I want. So just take it graciously and accept my thanks and hush up."

"Okay, you're welcome." Steven said shyly. "Now, drop it."

Craig stood and put his hand up. "Okay, go back to your corners and take a break. Uh, are there any more pancakes?"

Anna gave him a smile and piled more on his plate. "Anyone else?"

Scooter sat attentively next to his bowl, tail wagging vigorously.

Chapter

22

June 17, 1891

Dr. Jeremy Merrick
Veterans Affairs Office

Dear Dr. Lane,
Upon fulfilling my obligation to attend to you with a second visit, I regret to inform you that I found no substantial improvement in your health. We discussed your symptoms at our first examination, and I find little has changed. However, of equal significance, I recognized during my visit, a certain melancholia emerge during our conversation. Despondency can

develop with soldiers during times of war and continue for years after. I sense your deep anguish and can only suggest you attempt to heal your heart as you convalesce. Find an understanding friend with whom you can relate, someone who might have had similar circumstances. I wish you the best, Dr. Lane. May you find peace in your heart and rise above your sins.

Most sincerely,
Jeremy Merrick, M. D.

"So," Steven said to Scooter, "We only need to 'heal our hearts' and everything will be A-Okay. What a crock. Like this doctor could understand. No better than my father who tells me to just get over it."

The dog cocked his head as Steven scooped up the letters. "I wonder what 'Veterans Affairs' was like in those days. Doesn't sound any better than the help we get from them today. They don't know how to help us. And they sure as hell don't know what to do with us. I guess in fairness the good doctor did give David a bit of helpful advice. Let's go for a walk, Scooter. Find your leash. Today is Tuesday. We'll take that advice. Let's go meet with Dr. Sam's group of down-and-out warriors and maybe find some understanding comrades.

Isn't that what they say they're doing?"

Scooter wagged his tail.

"Okay! Let's go."

~   ~   ~

The soothing scent of freshly brewed coffee greeted them as they arrived at Joe's Café. Steven stood in the doorway, reluctant to enter without an invitation. He held Scooter tight on the leash, so he wouldn't race toward the scent trailing from a pile of muffins on the counter.

"Glad to see you, Steven, your timing is perfect," Joe greeted him. "It's alright, the dog is welcome. He sure cleaned up nicely. Take a seat on the far side of the table and Scooter will be out of sight. The gang's all here. Okay Scooter, two stale muffins comin' up."

Steven gave Joe a little salute and walked to the back of the café. He was greeted by a chorus of, "Hey Steven. Glad to see you, man."

"Great dog," said one man. "My name is Jeff. What's his name?"

"This is Scooter, and I have to keep him under wraps. Under the table boy. That's it, now lie down and be still. Muffins are on their way."

"Glad you gave us another chance, Steven." Doc said. "Pour some coffee and help yourself to the muffins." They all dug in as Steven slipped one under the table.

"What brought you here today?"

"What the hell? You've gotta be kidding me," Steven said with disdain. "Gimme a break, Doc. If that isn't the standard leading question to a therapy session, I don't know what is. I didn't come here to be analyzed. Maybe I should reply with,

'Hi, my name is Steven and I'm a...what...an alcoholic...all around disgusting guy'? I'm so sick of all the do-gooders with all the answers."

"That's not what I meant Steven. It was more curiosity – I meant why today?"

"None of your damn business."

The other men gathered at the table began to slide lower in their chairs.

"Okay. Let's start over," Doc said with an even voice. "Regroup – I'm glad to see *all* of you today and hope we can *all* try to lighten up instead of getting so damn defensive. I'm on your side, remember? I'm one of you – different age, different war – same despair to cope with. We're all the same, you know – just different triggers set off our anger and our suffering."

"Damn, I'm really sorry Doc." Steven dropped his chin to his chest. "You hit a nerve.'

"Don't stress over it," said Craig. "We can all get pretty obnoxious. Don't you see? It's the easiest way to build walls. We need some way to protect ourselves – I've learned that much. Sit back and relax. You're one of us." Craig set his cup on the bench and slipped a bottle out of his pocket then poured some of the contents into his coffee.

Steven noticed, smelled the alcohol, but said nothing.

"So, let me rephrase the question," Doc said. "What happened that led you here today, not last week or the week before."

"Yeah, dumb shit," Craig sneered. "Why are you here?"

Steven dropped his shoulders, took a deep breath and a

sip of coffee. "You know those Civil War letters I've been reading?"

"I don't," Jeff said.

"I've been reading letters from a Civil War soldier and I've discovered he wrecked his life and abandoned his children...not much different from any of us." He paused, reddened and looked around the table. "Sorry guys, I don't know any of you that well. I can only speak for myself."

Craig squirmed. "We're right there with you, man."

"At the time he wrote the letters he had to be old and sick, alone and convalescing in some old soldier's home. Talk about misery. So today, I read a letter from a doctor who had examined him. The doctor couldn't help him with his illness but used the word melancholia. Is that an old-fashioned word for depression, Doc? What did he mean?"

"You're close, Steven. It's a word that goes back to the ancient Greeks, and was used more often in the 18th and 19th century. More accurately, melancholy is an old word that means to be despondent or to mourn."

"Wow! Probably fits all of us, couldn't it Doc?" Jeff asked.

"Well, not all the time, but I'm sure we all have moments of despondency. And it's not just soldiers. Most people experience trauma sometime in their lives and suffer the same as we do. That's how we feel like we're mourning."

"But for what?" Craig asked. "I get really angry and mean sometimes and I don't know where it comes from. It's not like I'm in mourning for anyone. I've got this new girl who is so cute and good to me. Patient too. And then I fly off the handle for no reason or go into some awful funk. I think I scare her –

I can see it in her eyes – she's ready to bolt – and I can't blame her. I don't like *me* either. I don't deserve her anyway."

"Be patient with yourself," Doc implored. "She's still around, isn't she?" He looked around the table. "Truth is, we're all still in mourning, and it's genuine. It's about loss and sadness and despair." He turned to Steven. "Yes, war can kill our souls and break our hearts. It crushes our spirits. That's why we mourn. We've lost the happy young men we used to be, and we don't know how to come home from war or how to find him. We don't know how to live normal lives. So, we get angry. We take it out on the very people we care about most."

"After all these years? What's wrong with us that we can't pull it together?" Jeff asked.

"My father's favorite saying is 'Just get over it.'" Steven said. "I guess I don't know how. I feel stuck in this muck of anger, and I can't dig myself out of it."

"My family finally threw me out. I've been living in that truck. Why do you think I like Anna's pancakes so much? She not only feeds us, she forgives us and makes us feel welcome, makes us feel useful," Craig said.

"No one has to go hungry with the soup kitchen. Pitch in and help sometime. There's always enough food," Doc assured them. "If you want to show your appreciation to Anna, help her around the house. Offer to trim her bushes, mow the lawn, clean out the gutters. There's lots you could do to help."

"Yeah, and we could help Lindsay in the garden." Steven said. "She had a snake encounter the other day and now she's a little reluctant to start digging again. The carrots need harvesting."

218

"Count me out," Craig said. "You know how I feel about snakes. I'll haul stuff in the truck and do dishes and scrub pans, but no fucking snakes."

"Yeah, we know." Steven grinned. "There's plenty of ways to contribute. Someday I'll tell you about my nightmares and swimming in bloody water. I couldn't even give Scooter a bath without getting hysterical – that's how crazy I am."

Am I really telling them all this?

"We all have irrational fears, Steven." Doc said. "The worst thing you can do is beat yourself up about it. The next worst thing is to use alcohol and drugs to cover up your fears." He took a long look at Craig but said nothing more.

Steven sat silently, remembering his last encounter with the bottom of a bottle.

"Okay, so why don't we divide up the labor. I'm glad to help Lindsay in the garden."

"I'll bet you are!" Craig teased.

"No, uh uh, no way. Not my type. She's way too good for me. Besides, we always find something to argue about. Nope, she's not for me." Steven said.

"Yeah, sure."

"Stick to the topic – and that's helping out at the Open Heart kitchen. So, Craig you have the truck. The market near Anna donates day-old stuff like bread and produce. Can you help Anna haul the food she prepares? I can walk down and lend a hand. Jeff, what do you want to do?" Steven asked.

"Peel potatoes. That's my skill level."

"Not true," Doc said. "I've seen you cook some mean chili and corn bread to go with it. We're not letting you off the hook that easily."

"Okay," Jeff said. "I can help cook."

Sam raised his hand. "So gentlemen...yeah, yeah...I know there aren't any gentlemen at this table." He grinned. "Let me start over. So guys – who feels despair at this very moment? Anyone?"

Silence.

"I thought not. Do you know why?"

Silence. Sipping of coffee. Munching on muffins.

"Think about it."

Chapter

23

... my children are now paying the dreadful price for my mistakes ...

The walk home from Joe's Café gave Steven the opportunity to digest Doc's question. Why *did* they feel better?

Steven marveled to himself. The idea of contributing to a good cause sure felt great. We've all needed a handout now and then. Now we get to give back.

For once he didn't feel compelled to move for the sake of working off anxiety. He walked along, heading to the cottage with a lighter step as Scooter hopped along beside him.

As they approached the Open Heart Kitchen property, Scooter stopped abruptly and sniffed the air. Moving forward cautiously, he began to growl. "What is it, boy? What's wrong? Okay, slow down – show me." He dropped the leash as Scooter bounded down the street and followed the scent, leading Steven around the cottage. The dog burst into the vegetable garden barking ferociously.

Digging into the dirt was a boy on his hands and knees, frantically pulling up carrots and shoving them in his mouth as fast as he could chew. "Hey!" Steven yelled, "You're stealing food for hungry people. Stop!"

"I'm hungry, too," the boy shouted back, as he shoved more carrots in his pockets and began to back away, then turned and broke into a run.

"Go after him, Scooter. Go get him!"

Scooter raced after the boy and grabbed his worn pant leg with his teeth and pulled him to the ground. Standing over the boy, Scooter looked up at Steven as if to say, "Look what I caught. Aren't you proud of me?"

"Good hunting, Scooter. Now let him go." He pulled the boy from the ground as the kid tried to wriggle out of his grasp. It was hard to guess his age because he was so thin and his mouth was covered with dirt. "Stay still, kid. You're not going anywhere. What are you doing back here?" The boy faced Steven, raised his chin in the air and said nothing.

"You'd better tell me who you are, kid. What's your name?" Silence. Steven dragged him toward the cottage, as the boy wiped garden dirt from the corners of his mouth.

Wonder when he had a decent meal, Steven thought. Amazing how strong he is for a kid who is clearly malnourished – like the villagers in Nam.

He pushed the boy through the open door to the cottage. "Now sit." The boy ground his heels into the door frame, refusing to move. "I said sit." Scooter, who was following close behind abruptly sat at attention. Steven started to laugh. "Well, at least someone minds my words. Good dog, Scooter." Without warning he lifted the boy off the floor with one arm, carried him toward the kitchen table, and lowered him firmly into the chair. "Now, stay there!"

Other than being painfully thin and grubby, Steven assessed the boy, who seemed to be in good health. Feisty was better than subdued. His hair was filthy, and his nails were black from digging in the soil. His mouth matched his nails. His clothes were grimy and Steven recognized the condition of 'homelessness.' He recognized the boy as if it were himself. "What's your name?" Steven asked. "I can tell you haven't eaten in a while and I see you haven't had a bath either." With a defiant cock of his head the boy stayed silent.

"Okay, have it your way. I'm calling Child Services. Let them deal with you."

The boy leapt up. "No, please," he begged. "My name is Richie. I'm sorry I stole your carrots. I was starving."

"Yeah, we all get hungry sometimes, but that doesn't give you the right to steal, especially from people worse off than you."

"I didn't know I was taking food from poor people. I haven't eaten for a while."

"Where's your family?"

"I don't know. I'm lost. No – they're lost. I can't find them." The boy dug into his pocket and pulled out a carrot. Soil from the garden filtered to the floor. "I'm really hungry, Mister, can I eat this one?"

"I think I can fix that problem. Go ahead, eat the carrot. Wipe the dirt off first. And stay put." Turning to the dog,

Steven said, "Scooter, don't let him move." Turning to Richie he said, "I can take you for a good meal, but you have to promise not to bolt. Sit in that chair and don't move." Richie nodded, suddenly more eager to please.

Steven walked over to the phone, turned his back to the boy and called the one place he knew he could find a quick meal. "Hey, Anna, it's Steven. I have a strange situation here." Quietly he explained, "I think I've got a runaway. He was pulling up carrots from the garden. Looks like he's malnourished. Sure hasn't eaten much in a while. Could I bring him over? Do you have some hamburger? I'll buy more for you and promise to do dishes."

"You know I do," Anna said. "If you think he's stable, not violent or anything, bring him down, I'll start cooking hamburgers. How many do you want, two for you, two for the boy and how many for Scooter?" He could hear her chuckling as she hung up the phone.

Steven turned. "Okay, Richie. We're going to take a walk and I don't want to have to put a leash on you, too. If you try to run away from me, you'll miss the best burgers in town."

As they walked down the street, Richie looked carefully at each house they passed along the way.

"Any of those houses look familiar?" Steven asked. The boy shook his head.

When they approached Anna's house, Scooter pulled on the leash, eager to find his feline friends.

Steven stopped and looked down at the boy. "I expect you to be polite, Richie. I hope you have retained some manners. This is my friend Anna's house. She is a very kind, generous lady and does a lot of the cooking for the soup kitchen – using the vegetables you were trying to steal, by the way."

The boy looked down, then back up into Steven's stern eyes. "When I was a little kid my family taught me manners and how to be polite. I'll try to remember."

"You'd better, kid. It won't take much for me to throw you out of here and call Juvenile Hall. Let's go get some food in you."

They walked to the porch with Scooter leading the way, barking his greeting as the cats watched from behind the sheer curtains. Anna opened the door before there was time to knock. "Come on in." The dog flew toward the sofa as Tom and Jerry dove underneath. "Hi Steven, who's your friend?"

"This is Richie. Say hello to Anna."

"Thank you for letting me come to your house. The burgers smell really good."

"Well, come into the kitchen, I'm just finishing up. Richie, you had better come over to the sink and wash your hands. I understand you've been digging in the dirt. Are you the one responsible for vegetables disappearing from our garden?"

Richie blushed, and gave Steven a contrite look that said – busted!

"I'm really sorry, Mrs. Anna. I didn't know..."

"I've been hungry enough to steal, too." Steven put a hand on Richie's shoulder. "Just don't do it again. We'll get some food in you and see how we can help you out. Go wash your hands."

Anna slipped the juicy, simmering burgers into buns and set them on the table. Richie's eyes glistened as he walked from the sink and sat across from Steven. "Go ahead and take one, Richie. I know you're hungry, but don't eat too fast. It will make you sick when your stomach is so empty."

Steven watched as the boy ate greedily, shoveling the food into his mouth. Finishing the first, he looked up at Anna and asked for a second helping. "Go ahead, help yourself. How about some milk?" Richie happily nodded his head.

"Ahem!" Steven cautioned.

"Oh...yes please, Mrs. Anna. I love milk."

As Anna poured, she looked across at Steven with sympathetic eyes. "When did you last eat, Richie?"

He took a long gulp of the milk and thought a moment. "There's a restaurant downtown that throws food in their trash bins. And there's a coffee place where the guy leaves day-old donuts outside his back door sometimes."

"Whoa!" Steven said. "That must be Joe."

"Yeah? Joe's Café."

"Well now, aren't you resourceful?" Steven said. "How long have you been on the streets?"

"No, that's not it," the boy protested. "I'm looking for someone."

"Oh yeah. Who?"

Richie hesitated, looking down at his second hamburger.

"Uh, could I finish my burger?" He took a bite and chewed, pointing to his mouth as if to say he knew he shouldn't talk with food in his mouth.

Steven folded his arms and waited.

Anna looked into the living room. "Scooter, I made a burger for you too. Come here." She crumbled the meat into a bowl and set it on the floor as Richie finished his meal.

Steven leaned toward the boy. "I guess we don't have to worry about a balanced meal today. We know you've had your vegetables."

"I'm really sorry." Richie said. "I'll go back and help you, if you want me to."

"We just might do that. First, I want to understand what's going on. Who are you looking for? Don't you have a family somewhere looking for you? Maybe we can help. Anna knows just about everyone in town."

"I, uh – no one is looking for me."

"Don't you have parents?"

"My mom is in jail. She's probably too stoned to care if I'm gone."

"Where do you live?"

"Oregon."

"How did you get here from Oregon?"

"Hitchhiked."

"Are you kidding me? That's not safe."

"It was okay. There are some pretty nice truck drivers on the roads. I waited at the truck stops next to a big rig and sometimes they let me ride along. I just get kind of hungry. Since they're nice enough to give me a ride, I don't ask for food."

"How old are you, Richie?"

"Uh – fifteen."

"I don't think so. I'll ask again. How old are you, Richie?"

"Twelve."

Steven took a deep breath. "So why here?"

"I told you, I'm looking for someone."

"Who?"

"My dad."

"Why *here*?"

"I think my grandparents live in this area and I thought maybe he'd be here looking for a handout from them. He's kind of a bum. I walked around the neighborhoods, but don't know where they live. I hoped I would see my dad on the street or something. I went to the market around the corner a few times, scouting out the food they leave on the sidewalk in bins." Anna nodded in recognition. "It was really tempting, but I think the guy got suspicious. He stood there watching me and asked me if I was hungry and when I said yes, he gave me a banana and a bag of cookies. He told me about the soup kitchen down the street. I thought that would be just the kind of place my dad would go. The last time I saw him, he was as messed up as my mom and might be living on the street if he's not at my grandpa's."

"Gee, I'm sorry, kid." Steven's body slumped into despair as he looked at Anna, shrugging his shoulders as if to say, 'So now what do we do?'

Anna reached out and took the boy's hand. "Let's see if we can help. What is your father's name?"

"But, I don't want to get him in trouble."

"Well, maybe he has been to the kitchen and we might be able to find him."

"Uh – his name is Craig."

"Craig? Craig!" Steven paused, not wanting to push too hard. "And what is his last name?"

"Johnson."

"Craig Johnson!"

Anna looked from Richie to Steven and raised a hand to silence him. "Richie, why don't you take Scooter into the living room and help him look for the cats. Their names are Tom and Jerry – they're probably hiding under the sofa."

"Sure, I like cats. Come on, Scooter. We're friends now, okay?" He hugged the dog then ran to the sofa where the cats hid. Scooter followed after the boy, leaving Anna and Steven to sort out the mystery of Richie's father.

"Could it be the same Craig?" Anna wondered aloud.

"Sounds like it. Do you know how to find him?" Steven asked.

"I don't know him too well. I doubt if there's a way to call him. Didn't he say his parents kicked him out and he's living in his truck?"

Steven paused, disturbed by his own self-awareness.

This could be me. It isn't what this kid deserves. Man, what shits we are.

Anna reached up and took Steven by the shoulders. "Are you alright?"

"Just thinking about – we're all so wrapped up in our own misery – we don't realize – the pain we cause our own families."

"This isn't the time for a guilt trip on yourself, Steven. Right now, let's worry about Richie. He needs our help."

"You're right. We know Craig said he would be here

tomorrow to help deliver your soup to Open Heart. And if he flakes on us, I'm pretty sure he'll still be at Joe's next Tuesday for a free donut and coffee."

"We don't even know if it's the same Craig. In the meantime, what do I do with the kid?"

"He can stay here until..."

"No, no. I don't think that's a good idea. You don't need that burden. Besides, you've got cooking to do. I'll take him back to the cottage. He can sleep on the floor with Scooter. The kid won't mind, as long as he's warm. Who knows where he's been sleeping. I can keep an eye on him."

What am I doing?

"Steven, stay focused. I was saying – I'll give you some blankets to use."

"Sorry. Thanks. Hey, I have an idea! What are you cooking for tomorrow's meal at Open Heart?"

"Vegetable soup. I was waiting for Lindsay to bring the carrots to me."

"You may be waiting all week for her to get up the nerve to dig in that garden again. Who knows if the snake came back for a visit. She's afraid to go through the gate. Tell you what...I'm going to take Richie back to the cottage. He's going to learn what it means to volunteer. He can finish harvesting the carrots; we'll bring them back here and help you prepare the soup. We'll turn him into a little farmer, or maybe a chef or a dishwasher for sure. How does that sound?"

"Brilliant. Thanks Steven."

The rest of the day was spent harvesting carrots, hauling them to Anna's, peeling and chopping vegetables, scrubbing pots, playing with cats and performing a final taste test on the soup. That night Richie slept safely and soundly, snuggled against a furry warm dog. Steven looked down as the boy cuddled his dog with a mixture of unfamiliar pride and unbearable regret.

Chapter

24

September 16, 1891

Old Sailors and Soldiers Home

Dear Dr. Merrick,

I wish to express my gratitude for your assessment of my condition and your kind advice of how I might diminish my apparent despondency. I have made many dreadful mistakes in my life, for which I am now paying a high price.

I do not know of any person in this facility who might qualify as a confidante, nor does it seem likely it would improve my despair, for I know

I have brought this misery upon myself and fear it is too late to make amends.

My only hope is that my daughter...

Daughter? What about his daughter? Steven pushed himself upright.

"Whatcha readin'?" Richie asked, jumping onto the bed.

"Some old letters I'm trying to understand. This one is from Anna's grandfather, way back a long time ago."

"Wow! Those letters look really old." Richie examined the letter. "See, look at all the squiggles, I've never seen such fancy handwriting. I guess they didn't have typewriters. The paper is kinda yellow, it must be older than my grandpa."

"Have you heard anything from your grandpa lately? Maybe if we could find him, we'll find your dad."

"Naw, we never heard from him. I don't think he knew how messed up my mom was, and I remember he used to get really mad at my dad. I just figured if I came down here I might find someone in my family. This is where my dad would come, I know it. If I stayed up there, they would've put me in a foster home. So, after my mom was sent to jail, I took off before they could find me. I don't think she even knows I'm gone."

Steven stayed silent, aching for the boy, allowing him to reveal his circumstances without judgment.

"If your dad's in the area, I'm sure we'll find him. Anna knows lots of people."

"Maybe I could just stay with you. It's nice here and I sure wouldn't go hungry anymore. You've got Anna and the garden and..."

How could I take care of a kid?

"Let's see if we can find your family, Richie. I won't let you go hungry ever again. No more carrots and dirt. Although there's plenty of nutrition in carrots, I'm not sure about the dirt." Richie laughed. "We'll make sure you are cared for properly. And speaking of hungry, how about some pancakes? I think Anna will feed us if we help her take the food we fixed for the Open Heart lunch."

"You mean all that soup has to be carried from Anna's house to that big kitchen? Those pots are too heavy to carry all that way."

"No, we use a truck. We'll get help. Now let's get you cleaned up. You've got the smell of a street kid."

I recognize that smell.

He pointed toward the bathroom. Go take a shower while I make some coffee."

"I don't have any clean clothes to put on."

"Do you have any other clothes?"

"Nope. I got out of there as fast as I could. All I brought was my toothbrush, but I wasn't going to brush my teeth with soap from a public bathroom! I had a little money my mom had stashed in the cookie jar – but it's all gone now. I used it to buy food until the money ran out."

"I'll find a tee-shirt you can wear. It'll be too big, but at least it's clean."

As Richie headed for the bathroom he asked, "Can I take

Scooter in with me? He kinda needs a bath too."

"Not a bad idea," Steven laughed. "Maybe another time."

As soon as he heard the water running, he called Anna. "Mind if we come over a little early? I don't have any food here. You know, it feels like I'm starting to be a real mooch. I promise I'll make up for it. If you get the batter ready, I'll make the pancakes."

"Sounds like a deal, Steven. How was your night?"

"Richie crashed. He and Scooter snuggled on the floor under your blankets. It was pretty sweet to see."

"Oh, good. Now what are we going to do about Craig? I have no idea how to reach him."

"What if he just shows up – or – what if he doesn't show up?"

"I think we're going to have to let this play out, Steven. We don't even know if Craig is indeed Richie's father – and if he is, whether he's capable of caring for him. If his parents kicked him out, he sure isn't very responsible."

Who am I to judge? My father kicked me out plenty of times.

Anna broke into his thoughts. "Maybe Richie should be with his grandparents...if these are his grandparents. As I said, we're going to have to wait and see. I'll get the batter ready and we can at least feed that boy."

"Okay. See you in a bit."

"Oh, guess what else. Richie has no other clothes. Any chance you have anything that would fit him?"

"Let me look. I'm sure I do."

"Why would you have boys' clothes?"

"Maybe I have family secrets, too."

236

"Hmm. Now you've got me curious."

"Another time, Steven. Come on over."

~   ~   ~

Steven let Richie hold Scooter's leash as they headed toward Anna's house.

Steven walked alongside, watching the dog lead the boy.

"Looks like you've got a new buddy, Richie. And you're on the right end of the leash!"

"Very funny. Hey, don't you think I'm proving to you how good I can be. I'll betcha I'm more responsible than either of my parents. I got myself to school, and cooked up eggs and beans, and I did laundry. I can do lots of stuff."

"So, you've been going to school?"

"Well, sort of – sometimes I had to stay home to take care of my mom. She forgot to get up sometimes. Some days I couldn't wake her up. It was kinda scary. They had me in some advanced classes and I heard my teacher tell my mom how smart I was, but I don't know if it mattered much to her. She didn't always remember to take me to school – but when she did...she...uh...she made sure I got there on time."

"Well, we need to get you back in school. You don't want to get behind in your classes."

"I guess – but the first thing I want is to find my dad."

As they climbed the steps to Anna's front porch, Steven patted Richie's back, trying to reassure him. The boy turned toward him, and Steven's pat became a comforting hug as Richie wrapped his arms around Steven's waist. They stood together for a moment, with Steven's arms around the boy until Scooter pushed between them, forcing them apart.

Turning his back to Richie, Steven wiped his eyes, brimming with tears.

When was the last time I was given such affection?

Richie leaned down and patted the dog. "Are you jealous? It's okay boy. I like you, too."

"Look, there are the guard cats watching for intruders," Steven said, rubbing his eyes. "We'd better watch our step."

Richie giggled.

The door flew open as Anna welcomed them in. Richie dropped the leash as Scooter made a mad dash for the sofa. Too late.

"Don't you think he'd learn by now?" Steven laughed. "Come on, Richie. Let's make pancakes."

"Not yet," Anna said. "I have something for you, Richie." She handed a bag to the boy. He rummaged around in the bag and pulled out a handful of clean, worn clothes.

"Where did the clothes come from?" Steven asked.

"The basement..."

"What! You went down there..."

"I'm back up in one piece, aren't I?"

"But...boy's...You've got boy's clothes?"

"A story for another day. Richie, go change into these clothes. They're old and worn, but at least they're clean." Anna led him into the bedroom.

When he came out with clean clothes, she said. "Well, look at you! That's better. Come on, let's make those pancakes." They all raced to the kitchen.

Richie said, "Oh boy! Can I make some?"

"Sure. I promised Anna we would do the work if she made the batter."

"Okay. How do we do it?"

"Use this soup spoon and scoop out the batter – about the size of a little plate."

Richie concentrated on his skills as Steven guided his hand over the griddle.

"Wait until you see the batter bubble a little – there – now take the spatula and flip it over."

How do I know this? Who taught me?

"I did it!" Richie crowed as he jumped up and down.

"Good job. Go ahead and put that one on a plate and I'll make you more. How many do you think you can eat?"

"Lots. I'm really hungry."

"Yeah well, you have to save some for us."

Anna stood at the edge of the kitchen watching the pancakes pile up. She leaned in to take the spoon from Steven.

"Oh, no," he said. "You sit down and I'll cook for *you* this time. Isn't that what I promised? I can do pancakes. May I pour you more coffee, madam?"

She hesitated, "I'm not accustomed to being waited on in my own kitchen."

"Come on, Anna, sit down. How many pancakes do you want?" Holding up two fingers and smiling gratefully she dutifully sat at the table.

Richie finished his pile and jumped up. "Can I make some for you and Anna?"

Steven moved and gave the boy room to scoop and flip.

"Can I make some for Scooter?"

"Sure. But first finish making those for Anna."

With all the gallantry he could muster, Richie served pancakes to Anna as Steven sat and waited for more.

"How about the cats?" he asked. "I'm getting pretty good at this. I could make little bitty ones."

Anna laughed. "I don't think they would like pancakes. Make some for Scooter. He likes them. Put them on top of his dog food. I bought special food for him, it's in the bowl."

"Come and eat, Scooter," he hollered. The dog raced into the kitchen, skidding over the kitchen tile as the doorbell rang. Reversing course, he raced to the door, barking furiously as he achieved his best guard dog stance.

Steven and Anna looked warily at each other. Nobody moved. The dog barked at the closed door, looking back at Steven for approval. Richie gobbled his last pancake and asked, "Do you want me to get the door?"

"No!" Steven and Anna shouted in unison over the dog's barking.

Anna recovered first. "Go ahead and give Scooter his pancakes, Richie. Call him to you. I'll answer the door."

"Come and get it, Scooter," Richie hollered.

Anna walked to the front of the house, pulled back the sheer curtain and peeked out the front window. Steven followed close behind.

"Oh my! It's Craig," she said softly. "He saw me when I pulled back the curtain. What are we going to do?"

"Let me go out and talk to him – give him some warning."

"He might not even be…"

Steven opened the door, intending to slip quickly onto the front porch but Craig pushed past him into the house. "Hey, Anna. I could smell coffee from the sidewalk. Could I have some before we load up the tru...oh...Richie! Oh my g...Richie is that you?"

The boy looked up at his father's face as he dropped the pancakes into the dog bowl and ran to Craig, throwing his arms around his waist.

"Dad! I found you! I found you!" Richie buried his face in his father's chest as his shoulders shook.

"What's going on? How did you get here?" Craig looked up. "What the hell, Steven."

Richie stepped back from his father's embrace. "No Dad. It's not his fault. I came here looking for you. He found me in the garden."

"What garden – with the snakes?"

"No, the one with the vegetables. I was kinda hungry." He grinned.

"Let's all sit down for a few minutes," Anna suggested. "Come to the table, Craig. I'll make you some pancakes and Richie can explain why he's here."

"But..."

"Just sit down – here – next to your son."

As Anna moved to the stove she shot a look at Steven as if to say, 'Sit with them. Help them work this out.'

"My son!" Craig said, turning the boy gently by the shoulders to face him. "Just look at you. Wow, how you've grown."

Richie glowed, grinning as if his face would split. "I'm

almost eleven now, Dad. I'm not a little kid anymore."

"Almost eleven. I thought you said twelve." Steven asked.

"Well, real close."

Craig looked at his son. "But how did you get here? Why did you come? Where's your mother?"

Steven interceded for Richie as Anna slipped a plate of pancakes in front of Craig, slowing down the torrent of questions. "Evidently, he hitchhiked here to find you."

Richie nodded. "It's been two years, Dad. I haven't seen you in two years!"

Craig had the look of a wounded animal. "You hitchhiked? Why didn't you just ask your mother to..."

"Mom's in jail. She doesn't know I left. She..." Tears welled up. Steven could see that the trauma finally hit him. "She's in pretty bad shape, Dad." His body shook. "They...they sent her to jail and I ran away before they could get me and put me in one of those foster homes, like they did before."

Craig dropped his head with a look of disgrace, as he threw an arm around Richie and tried to comfort him. "A foster home? I don't remember a foster home. Where was I?"

"I don't know. Maybe...maybe there was no way to reach you. Cause I know you'd have come..." Richie straightened, and wiped his tears with the back of his hand. "It's okay Dad, I'm fine. Steven took care of me and Anna fed me and...and she's been so nice."

Gratitude mixed with guilt filled Craig's face as he mouthed, 'Thank you' to his friends.

"Hurry up and eat, Dad. We made soup yesterday and

there's lots of hungry people waiting to be fed."

"We've got plenty of time," Anna assured him. "Let's just sit here for a bit, help your dad understand. This must be quite a shock, Craig."

"You've got that right! What the heck am I..."

"Careful, Craig," Steven cautioned.

"Don't worry, Dad. I told you I'm grown up now. I can – do you have a place to stay?"

"Uh...well not right now." A look of shame fell across his face as he looked up at Anna for guidance.

Steven silently watched father and son.

What shits we are.

"I know. Let's decide that later, we don't have to solve everything right this minute," Anna volunteered. "You're right, Richie. We've got hungry people to feed."

"Now I get it," Craig said warily. "You thought you would find me at the soup kitchen, didn't you?" Choking on his words he continued quietly. "And you were right."

"Wait a minute." Steven said. "That's not the way it went. You came because you wanted to help out at Open Heart, you weren't looking for a handout. Let's start over. Right now, this is about Richie. Tell your son how courageous and resilient he's been."

Craig looked down at his son. "He's right, you know. You are one clever boy. I'm just glad you're safe."

"Amen," Anna agreed. Then taking on a commanding voice she said, "Okay troops, put your dishes in the sink. Let's start loading up the food and we'll see what unfolds after lunch is finished. Richie, show your dad where the soup is stored and you two start loading up the truck. Steven, we'll bring the rest. Come on Scooter, we'll take you back to the cottage. Let's go."

Taking his father's hand, Richie led him to the oversized refrigerator. "In here, Dad. I can help carry the pots, too. And I learned to cook soup yesterday. But I had to peel a lot of carrots!"

Chapter

25

September 30, 1891

David R. Lane, M. D.
Old Sailors and Soldiers Home
Sandusky, Ohio

My Beloved Daughter,
Word has come that you have been searching for me. How could I be so fortunate? If only I could see you one more time.

I am heartened by your persistence and wish I could, in good conscience, applaud your defiance and encourage you to visit, before it is too late. With great regret, I insist you must abandon *all thought of me. I implore you, it is not worth the risk.*

My dear Mary, you must not defy your mother, nor endanger the security of your home and the embrace of your family.

I beseech you, my dear. Stay home and live a good life. Do this for me.

Your loving Father,
David Lane

Steven wondered what David Lane had done to deserve such isolation?

Steven watched Richie proudly help his father carry the pots of vegetable soup into Open Heart's kitchen.

Could they be a family again? Is it too late?

He understood what Craig must be feeling.

What have we done? Do we clutch at our own pain so intensely, we cannot see someone else's? What wounds we cause by heartless abandonment.

After the soup was served, Richie made friends with a young boy named Johnny who frequented the soup kitchen with his parents. Richie whispered to Steven that the boy's family spent most nights sleeping in their car and had been living on the streets for the past month. Steven realized

Richie's experience on the street gave him a stark understanding of what it must be like for his new friend.

After lunch, Johnny's parents allowed the boys to play together. They raced among the tables, grabbing the napkins, rolling them into balls, shooting baskets into the paper bins. A cheering squad spontaneously erupted, encouraging each boy to make a basket. Today, they could just be boys. The two ran outside and raced through the garden searching for the scary snake. Craig hollered, "Be careful! No telling what you'll find out there."

Doc arrived as they finished serving soup and salad to the veterans and families. Steven and Craig waved to him and Anna filled their bowls with the last of the meal. "Have a seat, Doc. We've got quite a tale to tell you," Anna said, with a twinkle in her eye. Without a word, Craig ducked his head and concentrated on his soup. "So, what's the news?" Sam asked.

"Did you see that boy who raced past you when you came in? The one playing with Johnny?"

"Yeah, I haven't seen him here before."

"Because he's never been here before. Steven found him in the garden yesterday – so hungry he was pulling up carrots and stuffing them in his mouth, dirt and all."

"Where did he come from? Any idea who he is?"

"Yup," Steven said.

Doc looked at Anna, then Steven.

"Well, what's the big news?"

"It appears he's Craig's son. His name is Richie."

Sam dropped his spoon and looked across the table. "Craig, is this true?"

"Yeah, it's true, Doc. I don't know what the hell I'm going to do. Here I am, living in my truck. My parents won't let me near their house anymore. Said I'd have to get a job and pay rent if I want to live there." He hung his head and continued quietly, "They think I drink too much. Nice role model I've turned into."

Steven looked at Craig with disgust. "Ya know? Right now, this isn't about you and your troubles. This is about Richie. We found your kid – your kid – starving – so hungry he was stealing carrots out of the ground. Do you get that?" Turning to Sam, he said, "We'll tell you the long version when Richie's not around. For now, we're going to find a place for him to stay. Last night he slept with Scooter on my floor at the cottage."

Craig whipped around in his chair, facing Steven. "Well, you seem to have taken charge pretty well. Nice work, taking on my fatherly duties," he said. "What makes you so qualified to care for my son?"

"Hey, back off. What can you offer him? It was pretty obvious the boy was starving, so I took him to Anna's and got him fed. We didn't know who he was. I probably should have taken him to child protective services, but...well...when he told us his story and gave us his last name, we thought it might be you he was looking for."

Craig dropped his head. "Shit. And now it's not just my life I've ruined, it's Richie's. I'm sorry, man. I just don't know what to do. I've made such a mess of things."

"Be a man, you jerk. Try being a supportive father." Steven said.

Craig jumped out of his chair and leaned into Steven's face.

Doc grabbed Craig by the shoulders. "Alright, let's take it down a notch. Sit down," he commanded. Craig sank into the chair.

Anna stepped in. "So, let's see if we can fix your mess, at least for now. Who are your parents, Craig? Maybe I know them."

"They're so furious with me; I don't think they would let me through the door – even to explain."

"This is their grandson we're talking about."

"They've wiped their hands of me. They're going to think he's a loser, just like me – or worse, like his mother."

"This isn't about you, Craig. Let's get past the self-pity for now." Anna flashed a look of disgust.

Steven looked at her with shock.

Who was this woman? What happened to her kind words and gentle demeanor?

"Don't look at me like that." Anna shot back. "This is about taking care of Richie. This is about being a parent. Right now, the only thing that matters is that boy. Now tell us how we can reach your parents, Craig. If they won't talk to you, maybe they'll talk to Doc or me."

"Name's Johnson, Marge and Ben. They live on Chestnut Street."

"Sure, I know them," Sam said. "Maybe Anna and I should take a trip over to see them while you 'gentlemen' clean up the kitchen."

"I don't know. This is kind of awkward, Doc. I mean, here I am, a grown man...." He turned red. "Here I am, letting you fight my battles and plead my case. I feel like a complete failure."

"Just cut it out, Craig." Anna said. "Believe me when I say I know a thing or two about bad parenting." The three men looked at her as if she were speaking in a foreign tongue.

Anna – a bad parent? Not possible!

She glared back at all their disbelieving eyes, took a breath and continued. "Remember, this is about Richie and what's best for him. One thing at a time. Okay?"

"Yeah, okay." Craig agreed. "And thanks. I just – hell I don't know. This is..."

Steven interrupted. "You know Craig, I really get it. But try to think of it this way – you get another chance. We don't all get that opportunity. I've got this letter that goes back to the Civil War. The man who wrote that letter lost his chance to make amends. Don't do that to yourself. You can still make this right."

"Good advice," Anna said as she grabbed her purse. Sam took a last spoonful of soup and ushered her toward the door. "Just stay here and get the place cleaned up," she said. "And it wouldn't hurt to ask Richie to pitch in too. He's a good little helper."

"But, he's having so much fun out there. How many chances has he had to play lately? What's his life been like – caring for his mother, trying to hitch rides to find his no-good father and scrounging for food? I feel so guilty."

"He's your son, Craig. You're going to have to start being a father," Anna said with a wave.

"Shit, I don't know how to be a father," Craig said, turning to Steven for support. "You're lucky you don't have this problem."

Oh yay! Lucky me...

Steven spooned the last bit of soup, noting the carrot at the bottom of the bowl. "You know? Richie was a champ at helping out yesterday. He peeled all those carrots without one complaint. Maybe we need to learn from him. No self-pity with that kid, he just did what he had to do to get here. And he knew how to stay safe. His only goal was to find you."

"And look what he found. The truth is I'm a damn pathetic loser. He comes down here and where's the first place he thinks to look for me? Thought he'd find me begging at a soup kitchen. That's pretty fucked up."

"What was he supposed to do? He was afraid they would put him in a foster home. Can't blame him for running away. Where was he supposed to go?"

"I feel like such a fuckin' failure." Craig slumped in the chair, looking as if he wanted to disappear.

"Well, maybe you were yesterday. But today you've got a second chance. Make up your mind, Craig."

The boys hollered as they tore through the kitchen door, giving a quick high-five, then chased each other around every table and ran back out the same door.

Steven smiled as if he had been given a brief glimpse of what his own childhood might have been.

"Guess we'd better get this place cleaned up before Anna comes back," Craig said. "She's on my case, big-time." Picking up bowls and plates, both men headed for the kitchen.

"You want to wash this time? I'll dry."

"Sure."

Richie burst into the kitchen, threw himself against his father's chest, encircling his arms around his father and held on tight. Craig gasped as tears filled his eyes.

Steven looked at the pair as they held each other.

I wish you well, he prayed silently.

Chapter

26

October 2, 1891

Old Soldiers and Sailors Home

My dearest daughter,
My joy at the thought that you might
come to visit is desperately overshadowed
by my fear for you. I am elated and
devastated all in the same moment.
Under no circumstances must you
forsake your family or defy your mother.
I do not wish your life to end up as
mine, abandoned by your family.

Remember that I have been justly
shunned for my evil ways. That is how
your mother views our estrangement.

She does not want you to behave as I have or become a plague on society as I have become, but to grow into a proper, upstanding lady. Defiance is not possible for a young woman today, if she wishes to keep her family gathered around her.

I fear for you, my dear. While my selfish nature desires your company, if only this once, the father I remain, begs you to retreat from this folly.

Your loving father,
David R. Lane

Steven finished reading David's letter aloud to Dr. Sam. "See, I told you, Doc! What did this guy do? I can't wait to find out."

They had arranged to meet early at Joe's Café before the rest of the veterans arrived. Sam wanted to give Steven a heads-up about Richie before Craig showed up. Instead, Steven had bolted through the door waving the letter hollering, "This is dynamite. I've got the next installment of the David Lane saga. Wait till you hear this, Doc!"

Sam listened to the letter and leaned forward in his chair, his arms stretched across the table until his hands

Invisible

Wounds

Invisible

Wounds

Lyn Roberts

reached out to touch Steven's. Sam faced him squarely and said, "It sure makes you stop and wonder. Do you see the connection? Families. Suffering. Abandonment."

"It's just this guy's life. I've become a – what do you call it – I feel like a sleuth."

"No, it's more than that."

"I'm just curious about this guy. We have things in common."

"Exactly." Sam slapped his hand against the table.

"So, what are you saying?"

"Why did you bring this today?" Sam said.

"Because it's pretty amazing. I just read it this morning for the first time."

"Ah! Yes, it's truly serendipitous."

"What do you mean?"

"I find it pretty interesting that you have come across this particular letter at this particular time. It's not a coincidence."

"That's crazy." Steven stood up and paced around the table.

"Steven, I'm not sure there's such a thing as coincidence. All your sorrows, all Craig's troubles, and along comes this letter, written 100 years ago, expressing the same suffering about families. Estrangement. Separation."

"So what? How does it help us now?" Steven flopped back into the chair.

"I don't know that it will. But it sure introduces an interesting dynamic."

"I don't understand."

"I don't think you're ready to understand. Let's put it aside right now."

"No, I want to figure this out. I'm sick of hating my own father. I dread every confrontation. Why can't he understand me?"

"Maybe he can't. Maybe he never will? Then what? Can you forgive him – no matter what he has done to you? Can you accept him for who he is – with all his flaws?"

"But *he's* the father. He's supposed to love me and accept *me*, no matter what."

"Think about David's letter that you just read to me. Does his daughter, Mary, know what he has done? Is she accusing him of being a lousy father? She could certainly blame him for abandonment and a whole lot more. It sounds as if she only wants to be with him. She only wants her father. No judgment."

"I don't think he was abusive to her – like... It's not the same. He wasn't even in her life."

"Exactly!"

"So why isn't she resentful? Is that what you're saying?"

"I'm saying there's a correlation – I'm saying all humanity is connected," Doc said.

"I guess you've got a point. I keep seeing similarities between my life and David's."

"Think about it."

"And then there's Richie. I don't want him to feel the same way about Craig that I do about my father."

"As I said, I believe we all have connections and should try to understand each other. Most everyone has had trauma

256

of one kind or another. We empathize because we've had similar experiences."

"But…"

"Let's continue this another time. How did it go last night after we left?" Doc asked, changing the subject.

Steven turned to Sam. "Craig and I kinda got into it again last night. He stalked off and left. Nice fatherly conduct. He's got to learn to stop walking out on that kid."

"We don't know what happened the first time Craig left his family. Let's be fair."

"Yeah, okay. But it's painful to watch this poor boy. He was so hurt when he realized his father had left last night. I didn't have a chance to tell you. He was racing around with this other boy, then out of the blue he ran in and gave his father a giant hug. It was so nice to see. Then I guess, to be honest, I got jealous. I felt like he didn't deserve this great kid and I told him so. He needs to straighten out, get a job and learn to be a responsible father. Richie deserves better."

"Ouch!"

"Yeah, I know. None of my business, really."

Who am I to judge?

"So, he yelled in my face, stalked off, jumped in his truck and roared away. Then you and Anna came back with the Johnsons and Richie was so happy and they were so confused, and then furious with Craig for leaving – damn, what a mess."

"Not really. The Johnsons are thrilled to have Richie live with them. And I think the kid was relieved to know he didn't have to keep foraging in the streets. They seem to be nice folks and I think they'll do right by him. I can't blame them for being frustrated with Craig."

257

"Truth is, I'm going to miss that kid. And I know Scooter will."

"We'll make plenty of opportunities to see him, don't worry."

"Good, that's great. But it's not the same."

"Steven, he's not your son."

"I know, but..."

The door flew open as Craig staggered into the café. "So, is anyone speaking to me this morning?" Craig hollered, as he squeezed into a chair. Steven backed away in disgust.

"You damn fool. Where have you been? Drinking all night? You stink. What did you say about fatherly duties? Looks like you could learn a few."

Sam pushed a cup toward Craig. "Alright, let it go. Settle down and have some coffee. Hey, Joe. Could you throw some biscuits on a plate – my treat. I think these men need some food in their bellies."

"Comin' right up," said Joe, offering a little bow. "But I get to join in and watch the fireworks."

"Sure, more the merrier. Place your bet. Who's going to crack first?"

Craig silently slurped his coffee and glared at Steven.

Steven glared back.

You're not getting any information out of me, you ass. You don't even know where your kid is and you're too messed up to ask.

"You two are acting like a couple of eight-year-olds." Doc said. "Let's put on our big-boy pants and stop antagonizing each other."

Neither eight-year-old spoke as the glaring and slurping continued.

Sam tried a different tack. "Seems to me you both want the same thing – what's best for Richie. Right? So, man up and let's talk this out. What's your beef, Craig?"

"He just wants to criticize me. Can't see the shit I'm going through."

"The shit *you're* going through?" Steven howled. "To hell with what you're going through. What about your son? What do you think *he's* been going through? I know how he feels. I've been there. My father was the same...Maybe you should think about someone else's pain for once. Try a little sympathy, asshole."

Sam sat back as he watched the exchange and grinned.

Joe set the steaming biscuits down and silently slipped into a chair.

"Okay, I'm a screw-up. Is that what you want to hear? I confess," Craig voice rose an octave. "That fucking war chewed me up and spit me out. I love to drink till I'm numb. I don't want to remember. All the horror I..."

Sam raised a hand. "Take it down a notch. Let's start over."

"Okay. I get it." Steven leaned forward. "I feel the same way. But this is about your son. It's simple. Richie deserves your support. He's a great kid and he needs his father."

"Well, maybe you're right about me. I'm just a miserable loser, a screw-up and I can't be responsible."

"Nonsense," said Doc. "I watched you last night. I saw a

wonderful parent."

Craig's tormented eyes looked into Sam's. "Do you really think so?"

Sam nodded.

"Sure, I saw it too," Steven agreed, trying a different tact. "You can do it. First you quit drinking, then you get a job. It's easy!"

"Drop the sarcasm," Doc said. "Of course, it's not easy. It's agonizing, I understand that. But I've seen lots of guys do it – some were a whole lot worse off than you."

Joe tentatively sat taller. "Yeah, just look at me. You remember, Doc." He turned to the other men. "First time I saw Sam, was through blurry eyes. I was lying in the street and woke up in my own vomit – one of my better moments."

Sam nodded his head in agreement. "Not exactly the nicest way to meet someone, but look at you now, Joe."

Beaming at the compliment, Joe added, "If I can do it, anyone can."

"No way! I don't believe it," Steven protested.

"Believe it. Not so very long ago, I was living on the street, begging for food and only cared where my next drink was coming from. Obsessing over all the shit I saw in Nam and the drugs I got hooked on. It was ugly, man. I think what finally turned me around was when Doc reached for my hand and pulled me up from that sidewalk. Even in my drunken stupor I knew I had found a good guy."

"No, no. You did it, Joe. Ultimately, it has to come from inside you."

Here we go with Saint Sam again. Nobody's that perfect.

260

"With a lot of support and understanding," he said, bowing his head in deference to Sam. "Now I have this little café and I'm actually supporting myself. I even have a chance to give back and help other vets who..."

"Hey," Steven interrupted. "You're going to love this. Your latest 'good deed' went to Richie! He told us he found a plate of old muffins behind your shop. It kept him from going hungry one night."

"That's great. Glad to know folks are finding my little treats."

"Yeah. Really great," Craig said. "Your handouts kept my kid from starving."

"Then do something about it, you fool." Steven slammed his hand down on the table.

"Fuck off."

Rather than punch Craig in the face, Steven jumped to his feet, kicked the chair away and headed for the door, determined to leave. He looked back, returned to the table, and with his face inches from Craig's said in disgust, "You haven't even asked where he is, you shit. Don't you want to know what happened to your kid last night, Craig?"

Craig's head fell to his chest in defeat.

Nice going, Stevie boy. Who am I to make accusations?

Unsure if he felt more revulsion for himself or his friend, Steven shoved his chair back to the table, pushed his way through the door and stomped out of the café. He stood outside the door and took deep breaths, trying to tamp down his rage.

Great friend I am. Drunks – what shits we are.

Doing a soldier's about-face, he marched back through the door. Craig sprang from his chair and took a crouched stance as if he were about to be punched. Steven put his hands up in a sign of peace, took Craig gently by the shoulders, pulled him upright, straightened his spine and wrapped his arms around the stunned man.

"I'm sorry, Craig. I have no right to judge you. Forgive me."

Steven turned, and with a little salute and a lighter step, walked out the café door and into the clear morning air.

We're all a bunch of lunatics.

Chapter

27

... She does not want you to behave as I have, or become a plague on society as I have become ...

"Is that what I've done?" Steven wondered aloud. The words from David's letter to his daughter hit him in the gut. "Is it why I feel so connected to this old Civil War soldier? A plague on society. Is that what I am? My father thinks so."

Before picking up Scooter at Anna's, he called her and explained he needed to make a quick trip to the library for some research.

Walking through the heavy glass doors of the library never failed to captivate him. The sunlight created a kaleidoscope of rainbows, always a promise of new insight. He was counting on it. He slipped past the research desk, grateful that Lindsay was not at her post. He nodded at the old woman always seated behind the main desk.

Good. Stay out of my way, Lindsay.

Instead of heading to his usual table in the history section, Steven went in search of books on psychology. He needed to know how they had become a 'plague on society' as David called it – from war heroes to a bunch of useless misfits. Could history repeat itself, over and over?

What happened to us? Are we all so broken?

He searched through every stack of books that might give him answers and came up empty. Maybe he needed medical history. Overwhelmed, but not yet ready to give up on his quest, he headed back to the entrance and found the same librarian he had greeted when he arrived. With her sensible shoes, dowdy clothes and hair pulled back in a bun, he might almost describe her as a typical spinster, except for the tendrils of hair that had loosened and tumbled to her shoulders. He could almost read her mind as he approached her desk. 'Who is this low-life?'

"Hello ma'am. I wonder if you might help me," Steven began. "I'm looking for information about the history of abnormal conduct – well not exactly – more about people's understanding of weird behavior – or – well..."

"Young man, please be clear. I have no idea what you are looking for, and I don't think you do either."

With a contrite smile, Steven agreed. "Yes ma'am. I think you're right. Let's see..." He hesitated. "I guess I'm trying to understand the psychological effects of war on soldiers, but I want to know if there are any studies or research, way back a long time ago."

"Oh, do you mean like shell shock in World War I?"

264

"Yes, ma'am. And other wars, and if there is any research or understanding of the causes."

"Well, I think the cause is pretty obvious. What those poor soldiers must have endured...the trauma...and I bet you understand that very well, don't you, son?"

Steven dropped his head. "Yes, Ma'am," he answered quietly.

"Would you stop calling me ma'am, it makes me feel old. *My* name is Gladys. And you're apparently not a soldier anymore, from the looks of you. When's the last time you had a haircut?"

Steven looked up red-faced, "Well, uh..."

"And you are in sorry need of a shave. If you want to see the effects of war, take a look in the mirror, son...saddest eyes I've ever seen."

Steven flushed with shame. He had no response.

Gladys continued. "Oh well, I'm sorry to be so crabby, but I see you in here almost every day and you've never even had the courtesy to say hello, just a cursory wave. I've watched you, young man, it's almost like you're looking for solitude rather than answers."

"I guess you're right. I'm just...it's just that, I'm kind of struggling."

"Oh, for heaven's sake. We're all struggling to make our way in this world, aren't we? At least you haven't given up, I can see that. Now look at you. I can tell you'd clean up real nice. I bet you're hiding a nice-looking face if you'd allow it."

Steven stood stock-still, waiting for the next assault. How many years ago was it? The army recruiter said he could be their 'poster boy.'

"Are you just going to stand there? Do something –
anything!"

He grinned, "Got a pair of scissors?"

Gladys laughed. "Tell you what. Let's try an experiment
– all in the name of your research." She fumbled around in her
purse and handed him a $20 bill. "Go out the front door, turn
left at the bottom of the library steps, walk one block and
you'll find a barber shop. Get a haircut and a shave – then
come back and we'll talk about your request. While you're
gone, I'll see what books I can find for your research."

Steven's feet stayed rooted to the floor as he looked
down at the twenty-dollar bill.

"Now go! Don't you respond to orders anymore? Let's
see what we can uncover."

He rushed to the front doors before she could humiliate
him again.

~   ~   ~

When Steven returned, all polished and spiffed, Gladys
was not at her desk. He wandered the stacks, taking peeks at
his new self in the old lead mirrors along the corridor, not sure
who was looking back at him. He found her trying to pull
down a book out of her reach.

"Excuse me, ma'am. May I be of assistance?" He said in
his most formal voice.

She turned around and smiled broadly. "Ah ha! I
wouldn't have recognized you. Not bad – not bad at all."

"I hardly recognized myself when the barber finished
with me."

"Now, don't you clean up nicely? I knew it."

266

He handed her the change. "Thank you, Gladys. I promise to repay you when I can."

"You're most welcome, uh – now I need to know *your* name, so I can greet you when you arrive."

"Steven, my name is Steven."

"Ah, do you know what Steven stands for? It's of Greek origin, from the name Stephen, and means 'garland, or crown.' So you must be quite princely – regal."

"Hardly."

"Oh, yes. Somewhere hidden beneath all that scruffiness is a prince of a man."

Steven blushed, deciding not to argue with her.

Changing the subject, he asked, "Is this the book you were trying to reach? *The Struggles of Soldiers in War*."

"And the one next to it."

He held both books against his chest and gave a little bow of gratitude. "Thank you, Gladys."

"Don't you want to know what *my* name means? You should be able to guess by now."

"Uh, cranky and bossy?"

She threw her hands on her hips and glared.

He grinned. "Okay, sure. I'll bite."

"I looked it up a long time ago. Ready? I am prophetic, philosophical, and soul-searching – ah ha – see? But it also means analytical, critical and opinionated." She laughed and handed him two more books. "Best get back to my post. You're lookin' mighty fine, young man."

He shook his head in amusement and headed for his table by the window.

~   ~   ~

Steven's intent was to find research relating to the history of war trauma. His findings took him back 3,000 years to the first recorded reference, where an Egyptian combat veteran wrote about the feelings he experienced during battle, "...Shuddering seizes you, the hair on your head stands on end, your soul lies in your hand." Steven gasped.

Your soul lies in your hand and you don't know how to put it back.

In 1678 Swiss military physicians were among the first to identify behaviors that define acute combat reaction. They called it "nostalgia" and characterized the condition by melancholy, incessant thinking of home, disturbed sleep or insomnia, weakness, loss of appetite, anxiety, cardiac palpitations, stupor and fever.

Steven found that in the American Civil War, military physicians diagnosed many cases of functional disability as the result of fear of battle and the stresses of military life. This included a wide range of illnesses known to be caused by emotional turbulence, including paralysis, tremors, self-inflicted wounds, nostalgia, and severe palpitations – also called "soldier's heart" and "exhausted heart."

Exhausted heart – that pretty much sums it up.

Steven discovered that by 1863, two years into the Civil War, the number of insane soldiers wandering around in a fog was so great, there was a public outcry. Because of this, and at the urging of physicians, the first military hospital for the insane was established. The most common diagnosis was nostalgia. The government made no effort to deal with the mentally wounded after the war.

Steven realized this must have been the kind of hospital David had feared so much.

In a more current book he discovered that after the Vietnam War, the attitude prevailed that combat veterans with psychological problems were considered malingerers, trying to gain economically. He understood this was exactly how his father would characterize him and why he had never wavered from disparaging the son he couldn't understand.

They gave it a name and called it Post-Traumatic Stress Disorder. It was marked by a re-experiencing of the trauma in thought, feeling, or dream content. The research described PTSD as characterized by depression, loss of interest in work or activities, psychic and emotional numbing, anger, anxiety, cynicism and distrust, memory loss and alienation.

And there we are, David. Feels brutally familiar, doesn't it?

Steven slouched back in his chair, realizing he felt both comforted and agitated by the information he had found. At least he wasn't alone.

All those soldiers – all those wars.

He breathed deeply and released as much tension as he could, then stood up and began to pace the room. He stopped at the window looking out onto the front steps of the library and watched all the people blithely going about their day.

Steven felt a tap on his shoulder. "Excuse me, Sir. May I be of help?" He swung around at the sound of Lindsay's voice.

She grinned. "Well, look at you! Aren't you all polished and preppy? Very nice, Steven. I wouldn't have recognized you, except for that scowl on your face."

"You're right, Lindsay, you don't know me. Keep it that way."

No more. Get away from her.

As Steven turned away and rushed toward the entrance Lindsay looked down at the books left on the library table. She examined the titles and spoke to the empty hallway. "Oh yes, Steven. I *will* know you. Like it or not, I want to understand who you really are. I want to understand you."

She sat down to read.

Chapter

28

I do not wish your life to end up as mine, abandoned by your family and a stranger to your children.

The tragic words in David's letter continued to reverberate in Steven's head, competing with Lindsay's rebuke.

Always a scowl on my face. What the hell!

Was he overreacting? He picked up speed, eager to read David's letter to Anna and not let Scooter overstay his welcome. Perhaps this letter would explain why Anna's father, David Lane's son, was such an angry man. David had admitted in the letter that he was at fault and the estrangement from his children was caused by his own actions. But what did he do that was so horrible? This was the mystery Steven had been unable to solve. There was more to explore.

As he walked up the front steps he heard Scooter barking his welcome. The door flew open and the dog joyfully danced around his master. Steven patted his chest, giving Scooter permission to jump up and greet him.

Anna laughed. "Well now, look at you! Nice haircut. And I can actually see your face. You clean up real nice, young man."

"Uh thanks. Have you ever met Gladys at the library? She sits at the front desk. She bullied me into it."

"Good for her! She's great. You now look civilized, Steven. I should stop being so nice to you and add to her motherly advice."

"Hold on, I didn't say I wanted more abuse. You should've heard Lindsay. Do I always have a scowl on my face? That's what she said."

"Do you want the truth?"

"Uh oh. Well, I guess so."

"Then yes. Most of the time you look pretty glum, walking around like the world is against you."

"It feels that way, Anna."

"Tell you what I believe – I'm certain that what we put into the universe is exactly what we get back. Kind of a karmic debt fulfilled."

"I don't understand."

"I know. You're still in protection mode, Steven – waiting for the next bomb to drop, or the next insult to be hurled at you. It'll get better. Leave it for now. Come on, show me the letter. Let's figure out my grandfather, David. We'll get to you next." Anna walked into the kitchen to fill her cup. "I made a fresh pot of coffee. Do you want some?"

"No, I had plenty at Joe's. Man, what an uproar that was."

"Oh, no. What happened? Did you ever track down Craig?"

"Oh, yeah! Actually, he found us. I think he came directly from some all-night bar to Joe's. He smelled like a brewery. Here we all are, trying to stay sober, walk the walk, you know – do the right thing. It was maddening to see him like that. He didn't even ask where Richie was, just kept saying he didn't know how to be a father."

"Oh my dear. What a shame."

"Truth is – I didn't handle it very well. We got into a shouting match and I walked out. Then guess what happened? I had one of those 'ah ha' moments – you know – when you have some sort of revelation? Funny thing – I realized I was being a jerk, too. I'm just as messed up as he is. So I went back in and apologized. I mean, who am I to criticize – like I've been such a saint? What's that saying, 'until you walk in my shoes...'"

"I'm proud of you. I hope Craig can get himself straightened out. It worries me to think he might abandon his son. We don't want Richie to end up like *my* father, resentful and angry for an entire lifetime."

And how different is that from my life?

"Steven, are you listening?"

"Sure, I get it – more than you might realize. So guess what? I have interesting news. The letter I read from David today was written to his daughter, Mary, and says the same thing. He didn't want her life to end up like his, 'Abandoned by your family and a stranger to your children.' That's pretty heavy stuff."

"That poor man."

"Well, I'm not so sure. The letter also said he had been justly shunned for his evil ways. Those were his exact words – evil ways."

"What could he possibly mean?"

"No idea, but I'm going to find out. Could we check back in the basement? There has to be more – maybe we missed something. Is it possible there's more down there with your documents and certificates?"

"Sure, we can look, but I doubt it."

Squealing brakes and a deafening crash interrupted their conversation. Steven ran to the front window. "Call 911," he commanded. "Stay inside. It's a car crash. I'm going to see if I can help." Anna picked up the phone as Steven raced to the street.

He found two cars that looked as if giant hands had crushed them together. Windshields were shattered and Steven smelled gasoline. As he ran toward the cars he was heartened to hear screaming. At least someone was alive.

A woman in the front seat cried out, "Help, get him out. My baby! He's in the back seat."

"Are you hurt?" Steven asked.

"I don't know. The steering wheel is pushing against my chest and I'm trapped. Help me! First get my baby out. Is he there? Is he alright?"

Steven peered through the window, forced the back door open and found a child in a car seat. He seemed to be unhurt. The baby began to scream as Steven yanked at the straps to release him.

"I know how you feel, little guy. Scream all you want. It proves you're alive."

He looked toward the house and saw Anna watching through the screen door. "I need your help. Hurry! There's a baby in here." By the time he had reached in and extracted the baby from the car, the smell of gasoline became stronger. Anna rushed to his side and took the screaming infant in her arms.

"Get him into the house. I smell gas. No wait. Show him to his mother." He leaned his head in and spoke to the mother. "We've got your baby. See! He's safe." Tears ran down her cheeks, mixing with the blood that streamed down her forehead. "Now, let's get you out of here."

Steven raced to the second car and saw a body slumped over the steering wheel. The smell of gasoline wasn't as strong, but as he thrust his head into the open window, the smell of alcohol was overpowering. The unconscious man was still clutching an empty bottle of vodka.

And this is how we ruin lives.

A hole in the windshield had been made by the man's forehead. Steven spoke to him and getting no response, he ran back to the woman trapped in her car. She was now unconscious, but breathing. Reaching inside, he forced the door open and spoke to the woman.

"Can you hear me? What's your name? Talk to me!"

The woman opened her eyes and mouthed, 'Help.'

The strong smell of gas propelled Steven to risk moving the woman. He reached in and pushed the seat back to get the steering wheel off her chest, cradled her in his arms, and lifted her out of the car. He carried her onto the lawn and gently placed her on the grass. She had stopped breathing. CPR was second nature to Steven and although he hadn't performed it in many years, muscle memory brought it back. He began pressing air into her lungs, and heard sirens blaring as a fire truck rounded the corner.

Several firemen jumped out and began assessing the crash.

One of them ran toward Steven, "What's the status?"

"There's a man in the other car. Not sure if he's alive. I pulled a baby out of this woman's car and we took him in the house – I think he's okay. The mother has stopped breathing. I'll continue CPR until you get help." The fireman raced back to the cars.

Steven called after him. "Hey, wait. Be careful, there's a strong gas smell. Those cars could blow anytime."

"Thanks, man. We'll get more help. The ambulance should be right behind us."

Steven continued CPR another minute and the woman began coughing and choking, then screamed, "My baby. Where're my boy?"

"He's fine. He's in the house. Lie still. What's your name?"

"Janice," she sobbed.

"Okay, Janice. We're going to get you into a neck brace and slide you onto a back board, then get you to the hospital. Does anything hurt?"

"I don't know. I want my baby. Let me see him."

Steven called to Anna through the screen door. "Can you bring the baby out here? His mother needs to see that he's alright."

"We're coming," Anna called back.

A medical technician rushed to the woman and asked Steven. "What's her condition?"

"She had stopped breathing, but after a minute of CPR she's breathing well, but groggy. My friend is bringing her baby out so his mother can be reassured."

"Can you tell me anything more about the woman?"

"Her name is Janice. You can talk to her. She seems pretty lucid now. Her chest was crushed against the steering wheel. Check her spine when you get her to the hospital. Right now she's hysterical because she needs assurance that her baby is okay."

"Nice job. Who are you?"

"Just a guy who happened to be in the right place..." Steven said, evading the question.

Anna gently cradled the baby as she approached the lawn, and the mother tried to stand up to take her boy. "Hey, hey, stay still, Ma'am. We don't want you to move around until we've checked you out." The paramedic gently ran his hands along the infant's spine and body, then set him beside his mother on the grass.

"We'll get you both checked out at the hospital." Turning to Steven he said, "Hey, man. Good work! Thanks for your help. Could you help me get this woman on a gurney? My guys are with the other driver."

"Can they get him out? Is he alive?"

"He's still breathing. That's all I know right now."

"What about the gas leak?"

"My guys stopped the leak, it's no longer dangerous."

They carried the woman and her child to the waiting

ambulance. As they lifted the gurney, Janice grabbed Steven's hand and said, 'Thank you.'

"Glad I could help, Ma'am. You're going to be fine." He squeezed her hand and they slid her into the ambulance, strapping the baby next to her. Steven stepped away from the smashed cars and walked slowly toward the house as the police officers began examining the accident scene.

"Hey," the officer called after him, "we need your statement."

Get me out of here.

"I didn't see the accident, only heard it. If you need any more information, I'll be in the house."

"Okay, gotcha."

As he walked in the front door, Scooter trotted quietly to his side, as if he sensed the serious mood of his master.

"Come sit down." Anna said. "You were amazing out there."

"Times like this – I dread the most. Now that it's over I can't stop shaking."

She nodded. "The coffee's still hot; I'll get you some."

He collapsed into the overstuffed easy chair, leaned his head back and took a deep breath. Anna handed him a cup of coffee, which he gratefully sipped with shaking hands. Scooter lay by his side, and slowly inched forward so his paws rested on top of Steven's feet.

"I think he's trying to comfort you," Anna said. "Maybe he's learning from the cats." As if he'd been called to service, Tom slipped out from under the sofa and jumped into Steven's lap. Scooter didn't move. He seemed to know he had first dibs on ownership. Tom curled against Steven's chest as if he too was trying to offer comfort.

278

"There, I told you. Cats have an instinct when you're hurting or anxious. Look at this. It's wonderful. One time, I had surgery on my leg and this cat lay next to the wound all night without moving, trying to comfort me. They know."

"Too bad the poor people in that accident can't benefit from all this consolation. It's frustrating to watch them being driven away and not know if they're alright."

"They'll be well cared for."

"I know. You'd think I'd get used to it – the not-knowing – same as having a helicopter swoop down and pick up the injured. We did as much as we could, but most of the time we never knew if they made it – if we had done a good job."

"Must have been hard. You sure were amazing out there. You knew exactly what to do. It's evident you've had lots of experience in crisis situations."

I guess I have, more than I'd like to remember.

Scooter began barking as the doorbell rang. Anna peeked out the front window and opened the door to a police officer.

"Come on in. Anything we can do to help?"

"Just checking in, ma'am."

"Have a seat." She waved him toward Steven. Did you two meet outside?"

"Yes ma'am. Just a couple of questions, if I may."

"Sure, but as I said, we didn't see the accident happen – only the results. We were back here in the living room when we heard the crash."

"Yes, I understand you didn't see the initial collision. My question is whether you have any sense of the cause, since you were the first on-scene."

"I'm sure you saw the bottle of vodka in that guy's car. There's the cause as far as I can tell."

And not long ago it could have been me. Steven shivered.

"Nice work."

"Well, uh – thank you, sir."

"Don't be so modest." He cocked his head. "Okay, let me guess. From your age and expertise, my bet goes toward medic – Vietnam?"

"Yeah. You got it."

"You should talk to Alan at the firehouse and consider working with the firefighters. I think they're setting up a paramedic unit in his station. They could really use more men like you."

"I'm not sure I can stomach it anymore. I've seen enough suffering to last two lifetimes. I still get nightmares. I'm working hard to forget all the agony those people went through, civilians and soldiers, pain and injuries. Don't think I want to see more."

"I understand, but it's an honorable profession, I assure you. With your background, you're a natural and badly needed."

"Thanks for saying so, but I don't think I can. I'm still messed up from Nam. To be honest, it's made me a different person."

The police officer nodded his head as he stood to leave. "Just think about it."

Leading him to the door, Steven said, "I appreciate your confidence in me, Officer, let me talk to my wise advisor here." He gave a little bow to Anna and led the officer out the door.

"Steven!" Anna said, as soon as the door had closed.

"Don't even start." He flopped back in the chair. "I just said that to get him to leave. I'm not competent to be an EMT. I was lucky – today I managed to keep it together. You haven't seen me fall apart in emergencies or go ballistic over the smallest thing."

"Okay Steven, one more time. People have the ability to change, to be better. I've already watched you become a better person. Look what you've done for Open Heart and Richie."

He raised a hand that said 'Stop.'

Can't do it.

Anna stood over him, hands on her hips, eyes flashing.

"You are one tough cookie," he said. She continued to glare at him.

"So far two professionals have said you are more than competent. Just look into it."

"Okay, okay. I'll look into it – I'll find out what kind of training is required. Will that satisfy you?"

"This is your calling, Steven. Recognize this about yourself and step up. You can do this."

The hell I can...you don't know me.

Chapter

29

... I have made many dreadful mistakes in my life, for which I am now paying a high price ...

Steven was reminded of his own faults as David's letter swirled through his head. He tried to divert Anna away from medical competence and back to Civil War documents.

"Can we not talk about my future right now? The reason I came here was to tell you about the latest letter I found. Your grandfather, David Lane, talked about 'dreadful mistakes, being abandoned by his family and a stranger to his children' – those were his exact words. And he said, in writing, that it was his own fault."

"But we can't seem to discover what he did that was so dreadful and that's the key to everything." Anna said.

"I haven't found the answer yet. It's a good thing I decided to read the letters in sequence, one day at a time. It takes a while to absorb the information and do the research."

"Maybe there's nothing more to find."

"I think there might be more, maybe some documents we've missed, or letters that got misplaced."

"If you want to take your chances on my rickety stairs again, I'm happy to go exploring. The family lineage stored in the basement is the only possibility. Maybe you're right. Papers and documents could have gotten mixed up with other stuff."

"It's worth a try."

"Okay by me."

"Happy to oblige. I happen to find comfort in places that resemble tunnels and bunkers."

"What can be so enticing about dusky and dank?"

He answered without considering the consequences of an honest response. "I guess it feels safe to me. Dark, quiet, can't hear anyone screaming, no one to make demands. It's my shelter, my security."

"But I read somewhere that the bunkers were used by the Viet Cong to hide bombs and ammunition."

"And booby traps against the U.S. – you're right. And I was the one – well there were lots of medics – who tried to put the injured 'Tunnel Rats' back together. It was ugly. Not many survived – it was pretty grim."

"Tunnel Rats – it must have been treacherous for them."

"But once the tunnels were cleared and no longer dangerous, they were the perfect place to hide, to feel safe –

at least for me."

"Well Steven, if it makes you feel better, you're welcome to descend into my basement any ole' time. Make yourself at home." Anna held on to his arm. "I'm in your capable hands."

He looked down at her with gratitude. A weight had been lifted. He had taken a chance and confessed his secret, knowing how irrational and weird he probably seemed to the rest of the world. She had accepted him.

"Okay, let's go," he said light-heartedly. "Scooter, you stay up here and guard the cats. We'll be right back." The dog followed them to the top of the steep staircase and watched as they descended.

Steven held Anna firmly, making sure they didn't trip over the piles of books and newspapers along the stairway. He stopped to let their eyes adjust to the darkness. "Do you really need to keep all this stuff on the stairs? It's kind of dangerous."

"And it's the reason I never come down here by myself," she answered. "I'm willing to accept any offers to help dispose of this mess."

He laughed. "Sure, glad to do it." They reached the basement floor and Anna turned on the lights.

"And you also need a light at the top of the stairs."

"I know, I know. I just don't want to pay an electrician."

"I can't help you there."

"But if I fell, you could carry me upstairs and stitch me up, huh!"

"Yeah, I guess I could." He laughed, "You just won't let up on me, will you? Okay, change of subject. Where will we find more clues to David Lane in all these piles of papers?"

"Hold the flashlight." She rummaged through the cabinets, searching the files that held the Lane family lineage.

Steven directed the light toward the papers, watching in wonder.

"It's incredible to have this amazing family history, Anna. You are fortunate."

She whirled around, dropping the pile of papers in her hand. "And just what is it that makes me so lucky, Steven?" He stepped back, confused by her reaction.

"Well, I – I just thought..."

"You think because I have this long family pedigree, I'm so blessed? It doesn't make me a happier person, and certainly not a wealthy person. You can look around and see that. My heritage doesn't make me a better person, or any more important than anyone else."

Steven was shocked at her unexpected antagonism. "Well, I just thought..."

"You don't know anything about me, young man. You see this sweet little old lady and don't consider what my life might have been – what suffering I might have experienced."

"I apologize. You're right. I'm so self-involved with my own problems, it never occurred to me...so selfish of me...so...will you tell me?"

She took a deep breath. "I happened to have fallen in love and married a dear, wonderful man who never made much money. My family would have considered him 'common' if I had cared to ask their opinion. I loved him so much and we had a wonderful marriage. He died young and I miss him every minute of every day. He wasn't part of that grand ancestry, but he's the one who made me happy." Anna hesitated, then continued with a catch in her voice, "I have two sons, Jerome and Thomas – yeah, don't look so surprised – you didn't know that did you?"

He was startled by her outburst. "You've never mentioned them. I'm sorry. I didn't mean lucky, exactly. Just...I don't know. It seems to me, a family with such an impressive history would have some sort of advantage."

"This is America, Steven. Equality – remember? There's no aristocracy here. And even with my so-called illustrious ancestry, there's no guarantee of happiness. That's up to each of us to create for ourselves."

"But your family. Look at this genealogy." He pointed to the drawers filled with documents.

"Do you know why I'm so involved with Open Heart? Because I am closer to those people than I am to my own sons. That's right – my own sons. They never offer to help me out. The only time they come around is to borrow money. And here's the biggest irony – one is an electrician. He grew up in this house. He knows this old building intimately. Do you think it has ever occurred to him that his mother might not be safe?" She dropped her head. "Not a chance."

Steven reached out to calm her trembling hand. "I'm so sorry."

She held tight to his hand. "Never mind. I didn't mean to complain. It's just – so disheartening. I thought I raised them right, but along the way they became very self-centered. Somewhere I went wrong. That's one reason I'm so concerned about Craig. Richie needs a supportive father."

He yanked open two folding chairs, dusted them off and gestured for her to sit as he sat facing her. "Sit for a minute.

It's your turn to listen to me. Don't do this to yourself. You are a kind, good woman. Why do you blame yourself? Do you think parents have complete control over how their children turn out?"

"No, but..."

"Is my father to blame because I'm so messed up? Sure, I'd like to blame him. He's a lousy father. But if I were honest with myself and had to pinpoint where I went off the rails, I'd blame a lot on the war – and it's not just my war, it's every soldier in every war. It destroys our souls, not just our bodies."

"But we humans can also heal from our wounds, Steven. I know it is painful and takes work."

"Yeah, yeah, I know – what really matters is how we respond to the things that happen in our lives – easy to say – hard to do."

"So how can you make it better?"

"Right now, we're not talking about me; it's about you and your family."

"Boy, you are masterful at deflecting the subject away from yourself."

"It's just – it's too painful. I know it sounds weird, but I keep thinking maybe your grandfather, David, can help me heal."

"You know what you said about Doc, well, maybe he's on to something – could there be some connection between you and David? Maybe we're all connected in ways we don't understand."

"Tell me about your sons."

"Not now. See, I can deflect too!"

"But why do you blame yourself?"

"I think I must have been so devastated when my husband died that I ignored my boys. I forgot they were hurting, too," she confessed.

"It's not too late, Anna. Reach out to them. At least you didn't abandon them like..."

"What? Who are you talking about?"

He hung his head, regretting he had blurted out his painful memory. "While I was in the swamps of Vietnam, my mother walked out on my father. She never came back. I don't know where she is and I can't blame her. My father was one abusive SOB – sorry, but it's the truth."

"Oh Steven, I'm so sorry."

"When we came home, we were all a bunch of screwed-up soldiers. Remember our reception? We were scum in the eyes of most American civilians. They picketed against us. It was excruciating."

"I can't imagine how awful it must have been for you."

"Yeah, it was. So, like a little kid, all I wanted was my mother and she wasn't there. My father didn't qualify. He thought I was nuts. And I guess I was. So many of the guys I knew couldn't adjust to civilian life, especially because of the overwhelming prejudice against the war and the way we were treated."

"Oh, Steven!"

He raised a hand as if to dismiss the pity in her voice. "So, yeah." He choked out his words. "I needed my mother. Someone to believe in me. I have no idea where she is now, or how to find her. She hasn't tried to contact me. I keep telling myself she didn't abandon me – she actually left my father, not me, but I still wonder. I don't even know if she's still alive."

"There are ways to look for her," Anna said. "You've learned how to do the research. You found me, didn't you? Lindsay can help you. Maybe it was meant to be this way. Who knows?"

"That's what Doc was saying, that he believes we're all tied together, that humanity is all connected. I'd been telling him about my father refusing to allow Scooter in the house and Craig bailing on Richie. I had just read that letter from your grandfather about all David's regrets and agony. Maybe we all have to learn how to be a family and care about each other enough to do what's right."

"So what we've got is your mother and my sons to figure out." She stood and continued her search through the files. "Alright, let's get to work. Let's see if we can find some answers. How can my grandfather help you understand?" She flipped through each file as Steven picked up the papers she had dropped.

"Where do these go in your files? Were they in the desk?"

"No they were loose, in front of the other files."

"Let me see." He shone the flashlight on the pile of documents. "Here! There's more! Look, this has David's name on it. This may be it. We found it!"

"What does it say?"

"It looks like a legal document. But it's hand-written, dated 1883, certification from the State of Ohio." He skimmed through the document and read aloud.

> *"Having failed to appear, the court finds him in default...and that the allegations thereof are confessed by him to be true."*

"What allegations? What did he do?"

"I think this is it! Let's take it upstairs so we can read it in better light. I think we found the answer. Let's read it together," Steven said.

Anna struggled up the stairs with Steven behind her for support, they rushed to the kitchen table. Sitting side-by-side, Anna squeezed close to Steven, placed her glasses on the end of her nose and looked with fascination at the document. "It says the Plaintiff is Florence Lane, that's my grandmother, filing claim against David Lane." She gently ran her fingers over the fragile paper. "The whole document is handwritten. See? Look at this seal. This is the original, Steven."

"So, this is it." He shivered.

"Florence was my grandmother, David's wife. Does it say what he did?"

"The first part affirms they were residents and legally married, and – oh here it is."

> *"...and that during their marriage there were born to them two children, Mary Lane and George Lane."*

"That's your father, George and his sister, Mary. Remember the letter that said Mary wanted to secretly visit her father?" He continued reading aloud.

> *"The Court does further find upon the evidence*

> *adduced that the said defendant David R. Lane has been guilty of habitual drunkenness, gross neglect of duty and extreme cruelty toward the said Plaintiff in manner and form as is charged in her said petition..."*

Anna gasped. "Can this be true?"

Steven shook his head. "There's no way to know for sure. It says at the top of the petition that he didn't show up for the hearing. I looks as if he never had a chance to defend himself. Or, worst case, he was guilty of all those accusations, he gave in and confessed. But it doesn't say he was abusive to his children. That's important."

> *"...and that by reason thereof, the said Plaintiff is entitled to a divorce from said Defendant as prayed for by her. It is therefore ordered and judged by the court that the marriage contract be hereby dissolved and that each are released from all obligations of the same.*
>
> *It is further ordered by the court that the custody of care, education and control of the said children of the parties hereby be confined and given to the said Florence Lane exclusively and the said David R. Lane is..."*

Oh, shit!

He looked up and saw tears in Anna's eyes. "Oh, man. Here it is. Here's why he was estranged from his family."

> *"...is hereby forbidden and enjoined from in any way interfering with or disturbing the said*

children in her custody, care or charge of them,
and from visiting them in any way."

Anna gulped in air, and cried out, "Oh, how awful. It's so cruel, so punitive. This is like a permanent restraining order. Could he have been such a horrible man?"

"We can't know for sure. He wasn't there to defend himself. Remember David talked about a 'vindictive woman' in one of his letters? It must have been his wife. No wonder he said he was a stranger to his children."

"Oh Steven, this is devastating. 'Forbidden from visiting his children in any way.' Now I understand why my poor father was so desolate his whole life. David Lane was never allowed to see his children again. It might be that his son never again saw his father and never understood why. It sounds like his mother made sure of it. What a tragedy!"

Steven covered her trembling hand with his. "But look – it wasn't actual desertion. The tragedy seems to be that he didn't intentionally abandon his children – he was forced to."

And he suffered the rest of his life.

"We all make bad decisions sometimes. But to deny access to your children forever? No chance to make amends? That seems pretty heartless to me."

"That's just plain cruel, especially to the children." Steven agreed.

"Think of how he must have suffered."

Steven sat back, absorbed in memories he had tried so hard to ignore.

Not me – I'm fuckin' sick of suffering.

Chapter

30

I have been justly shunned for my evil ways ...

The divorce decree had shaken Steven to his core. David's letter to his daughter that said he had been 'justly shunned' hit too close to home. The letter reflected his own life, too. What 'evil' had *he* committed when he returned from that stinking war? He could barely remember. He was drunk most of the time. And what he remembered put him to shame. Abandonment. Cruelty.

What a disgusting excuse for a human being...

Steven had come home with good intentions – struggled to fit in. He tried to be domestic – quickly disconnected. Ran like hell. To live a normal, civilian life felt more insane than the crazy war he had left behind. People seemed to be able to spot you right away, as if they knew you were some low-life

Vietnam vet. In his drug-induced fog he felt judged by the entire town. His attempt to climb out of that haze seemed to be an impossible feat. He couldn't relate to anyone. He wanted to be left alone to wallow in his own misery and live up to his own despicable image of himself. His father tried to change him by berating him relentlessly.

And then he discovered David's letters. He still didn't understand why he felt so connected to this man, but it had finally led him to an understanding of the agony David had inflicted on himself. He felt a kinship. He was not alone. He felt he and David had a connection that spoke of the consequences of war, the suffering and trauma inherited from war.

But now I understand his agony was self-inflicted. David did this to himself. So have I.

He now understood there had always been choices. They had both made bad ones.

Steven felt something shift inside himself after reading the divorce decree.

Do it differently. It's not about how we've suffered in similar ways; it's about finding my own path.

He could not allow himself to descend into the life of despair David had suffered. It was all about decisions. Making choices.

My choices have been self-destructive and abusive. Is it too late to take a different path?

~   ~   ~

Steven found himself sitting on a bench outside the ER facility of the local hospital.

What the hell? Why here?

Scooter needed to be exercised and he needed to clear his head. They had walked from Anna's house to the center of town. For whatever reason, he had ended up on this particular bench, and realized he was glad to be outside looking in for once. But what had led him to this spot?

He vaguely remembered being brought into this very facility – remembered a nurse shaking her head, and saying, "Another one." What had he done? Why had they chained him to the bed? Had he been out of control? High on...what? Were they afraid he would flee?

Bet your ass I would...

Maybe he had tried to strangle his father – it wouldn't surprise him. He had never asked what he had done to end up in the psych ward. It was enough to know the torture. The memories started to surface. He remembered the rage. He wasn't sure who he loathed more – himself or everyone around him. The hospital dried him out and the police locked him up. His father refused to come up with bail money. In his muddled brain he remembered some judge in a courtroom looking at him with disgust and saying, "Is this really how you want to live your life, young man? I will give you a one-year probation – one more chance. If I see you in this courtroom again, you'll go to jail. Your choice. Your life."

And here he was, back at the same hospital. What led him here?

He noticed a shift change as the medical staff began to leave the building, chatting and enjoying the fresh air. As they passed him they nodded to Steven and spoke to Scooter. A man in green scrubs stretched his hands over his head and took a deep breath. A young nurse ran to catch a bus rounding the corner.

"What a great dog," a man said. "May I pet him?"

"Sure, he loves all the attention he can get. Say hello to the man, Scooter."

Scooter sat. "Now that's impressive," the man said. "I can't get my dog to obey commands. Maybe I should take lessons from you."

Steven laughed. "Not from me. Go to the pet store on Main Street. The guy in there is brilliant with dogs. He'll teach you."

"I'm Jerry. Just got off work."

"I saw you come out of the Emergency Department. How do you like it?"

"It's tough work, but can be satisfying. We help lots of folks. Once I get my degree, I'll feel like I can really make a difference. Right now my work is pretty much like an orderly."

"How can you go to med school and hold down a full time job?"

"Oh – no – I'm getting my nursing degree. I'm in a residency program, so the work here is part of my schooling."

"Sounds like a tough haul."

"Naw – not really."

"So there really are male nurses now, huh?"

"Yeah, it's great. And I get to work with all these cute women, do good work, help people out – what more could a guy ask for? I considered becoming a physician's assistant, but it takes longer. The school that offers all the degrees and certifications is great."

"I don't think I could afford it. Probably too old, anyway."

"What's your background?"

"I, uh – I was a medic in Vietnam. I – I don't know if I really want to get back into..."

"A medic, huh! You'd be a cinch. If you're interested, you should look into it. I think they even offer special grants to veterans."

"Really?"

"Yeah. I met a guy the other day, about your age, he was going for his M.D. degree."

"No, I don't think that's for me. I've seen all the dead and wounded I can stand in this lifetime."

"I get it. But there's lots of other options."

"Maybe I'll check it out. Where do I go?"

"There's a community college that offers all kinds of medical disciplines. They can answer all your questions."

Steven grinned. "Oh, if they only could."

"Well, maybe not the big questions," Jerry laughed. "But they're really supportive. If you were a medic for four years..."

"Yea, thanks, I'll check into it. Thanks Jerry. Maybe I'll see you around."

Jerry patted Scooter and shook hands with Steven. "See ya."

Steven sat very still, watching the activity around the ER, as he absorbed the atmosphere. An ambulance roared in and an unconscious woman was wheeled through the emergency doors. As the gurney disappeared from sight a car screeched to a stop in the last open parking spot. A young woman jumped out, looking frantically into the ambulance. As she turned to Steven, he pointed in the direction of the doors they had entered.

Do I want this way of life? More suffering and anxiety?

His question was answered by a sense of dread. He shivered and reached down to stroke Scooter's soft fur.

A car pulled up behind the ambulance; a man jumped out, ran to the passenger side, picked up a screaming child and carried her into the emergency entrance.

What if I couldn't save her either?

Steven saw that the car doors had been left open. He walked over to the car, made sure the keys had not been left in the ignition and cringed at the pool of blood on the passenger seat. Shutting the car doors, he resolutely turned and walked away.

Not this. No more blood.

"Come on, Scooter. Let's pay a visit to Alan at the fire station. Maybe that's more my speed."

Back on Main Street, Steven changed pace, walking as fast as he could without breaking into a run. Scooter trotted beside him with his loopy smile, revealing pleasure in the outing.

"Let's stop by the pet store and say hello to Pete," Steven said to Scooter, amused with himself for talking to his dog, as if Scooter could answer back. To his surprise, Scooter gave a cheerful 'woof' and pulled Steven and the leash to the left, turning the corner in the direction of the pet store.

Opening the door, Steven called out, "Hey Pete, Scooter wanted to come by for a visit. Anyone here?"

An elderly woman popped her head up from behind a pile of boxes.

"He's not here," she said. "I'm his mother, Grace. I'm filling in for him today. Pete is taking his final exams to qualify to become a veterinarian. I'm so proud of him. It's nerve wracking, but exciting too."

"Hey, that's great. I'm Steven and this is Scooter."

"Well aren't you a handsome mutt – the dog, not you." She chuckled at her own humor.

"No, you've probably got it right," Steven grinned. "Scooter is better behaved."

"Have you learned to shake?" Facing the dog she raised her arm, palm up and said, "Okay, sit Scooter." The dog sat and cocked his head. "Shake, Scooter," Grace commanded, as she gently picked up Scooter's paw and shook it. "There you go, that's it. Good boy."

Steven laughed. "That's great. We'll have to practice. Teach you some manners, Scooter. I could probably learn a few, too."

"Peter will finish the licensing exams this afternoon. You'll find him back here tomorrow. You know Pete. This is so important to him; it was the only goal that turned him around. That boy was a mighty mess."

Steven didn't tell her he had only just met Pete. "Sounds like he found purpose in his life. He had a goal and best of all, he had you for support."

"It's nice of you to say, but his wish to be a veterinarian was his salvation. It's kind of ironic, going from a vet to a Vet. Guess he just loves animals."

"Tell him we came by and wish him luck. We'll stop in soon to see how he did on the exams. Say, do you know where the new firehouse is?"

"Two blocks down, then turn right."

"Thanks. Nice to meet you, Grace."

"Thanks, Steven."

Although Steven had lived in Crystal Springs most of his life, he had never seen the new fire station – the police station – yes – and the courthouse – definitely, yes. "Very impressive," he said to Scooter as they approached the building. "We'll just check it out. See how they operate. They said they needed someone like 'me' – just not sure it should be – *me*."

Am I ready for this?

He stood at the door, hesitant to ring the bell. All the fire trucks were lined up, ready to roll, which told him the crew was inside. He hesitated, stopped short of ringing the bell.

"Nope, not ready," he said. "Let's go, Scooter."

He turned and was halfway up the driveway when a voice called out, "Anything we can do? Need some help?"

Steven was reluctant to turn around. Did he recognize that voice? Would they remember him from the accident in front of Anna's? Without turning he raised his hand to wave him off, "No, just taking a walk. Hadn't seen your new building, so..."

"Hey, I know you."

Steven turned to face the man. It was Alan, the fire chief, who beckoned him in. "Glad to see you, man. Come on in. I'll show you around."

"Well, I – I don't want you to get the wrong idea."

"Just come take a look. We're in the middle of a serious gin rummy match. Once the trucks are ready to roll, we need time to relax. It's important to learn how to cope in this world."

"That's just it. I guess I haven't learned how."

"Never mind. Come on in." Alan chattered away as he showed him the new building and introduced him to some of the crew.

"So, I heard about you," said a man stirring spaghetti sauce. "Steven, right? We sure could use an EMT in the station. Alan told us about your heroics."

"No, really, I'm no hero – and definitely not qualified to be an EMT."

"Sounds to me like you knew what you were doing. Emergency Medical Technician – you definitely fit the requirements if you were a medic in Vietnam."

"Not sure I can do it anymore."

Change the subject, you fool.

"Say, that spaghetti sauce smells mighty good."

"If you join up with us, you can have as much as you like. We cook our own meals around here."

Shit.

"Well that disqualifies me right away. I have no cooking skills." Steven grinned, thinking he was off the hook.

"Not a problem. You'll learn. In the meantime, you can do dishes."

"Sounds real enticing."

An alarm blasted throughout the firehouse. Everyone scattered, preparing to respond to the emergency. The men threw on their safety gear, ran to the trucks – engines roared, sirens blared. Alan shouted over the noise, "Gotta go, Steven – really want to talk to you. Come back tomorrow."

Steven rushed out the door, turning to watch, fascinated by the organized scramble. "Let's go, Scooter. We don't want to get in the way."

As they started up the driveway, Steven turned and saw the firehouse door had been left open as the last trucks stormed past them. "Hey," he called out. "Is anyone still here?"

"Yeah," a voice called back. "Someone has to stay and man the store. Is that you Steven? Want some spaghetti?"

Steven stepped across the threshold.

"Come on in. Hey, do you know how to play gin?"

Chapter

31

... I was no more honorable than the doctors you describe... For I confess that the seduction of alcohol claimed me as well and I have suffered the agony of that knowledge and the dreadful consequences of my behavior as my life has since unfolded ...

David's words pounded through Steven's head. He tried to imagine what it must have been like to treat soldiers in the open air, laid out on the fields, as the army tents overflowed with the wounded. How could you amputate by candlelight? No anesthesia, no way to clean instruments? They must have lost so many lives, simply because they couldn't see. They anesthetized themselves right along with their patients.

David had admitted he didn't have a medical degree. And yet, in those days most doctors were ignorant of ways to treat wounds. Civil War doctors must have agonized over their losses, not understanding how infection contributed to their enormous death count. It was no wonder they turned to alcohol for solace.

Did they use morphine and opium, too? Did the doctors become addicted? Was that David's downfall?

The stresses of war and frustration over their inadequacies must have been unbearable. Were they worse than Vietnam? He couldn't know. Steven had even read of Civil War doctors who took that one slug of alcohol intended for their surgical patients. When they ran out of the chloroform used as anesthesia, they resorted to alcohol, poured it straight down the soldier's throat. Steven cringed at his own judgmental attitudes.

He paced the room, trying to make sense of David's life as well as his own.

Who am I to place blame?

He had often found himself in similar circumstances, not knowing how to treat a wounded soldier and not sure the decision to amputate was the best procedure.

Stop their agony, stop their suffering, stop the screaming.

The majority of Vietnam soldiers also had their favorite antidotes to numb the suffering – alcohol, hash, heroin – anything to obliterate the torment. Drugs had been rampant, easily accessible in Vietnam. Many had come home already addicted to drugs and alcohol and were expected to pick up where they left off – settle into normal, civilian lives. When veterans returned home, they discovered nothing was normal

– not for them.

And here he was, trying to qualify to become a paramedic.

He wondered how he could measure up to a younger generation. He felt old, inadequate and tired. Did his war experience have such great value in a civilian world? The fire chief seemed to think so. He was encouraged by his visit to the firehouse yet doubted his abilities. Alan didn't know what a mess Steven had made of his life after the war. Steven couldn't count the number of soldiers he had lost. He still agonized over how many more he could have saved with better skills or a clear head. How many times had he been drunk or stoned when confronted with an injured soldier?

With a jolt, he realized David Lane would have identified with that same agony. Their paths had taken a similar course – until now. Steven continued to pace. He was determined to reject the self-destructive path David had followed. David's divorce decree had shaken Steven into action. He would find a different way. Would the school accept a messed up medic?

~   ~   ~

Steven was still shaking when he drove from the medical school into the fire station's parking lot. The door opened after the first bell. "By god, you actually took me at my word," Alan cheered. "Come on in."

Steven grinned. "Uh, no, I've just come to get that spaghetti sauce recipe from Jeremy. It was the best."

"Huh? Don't mess with me, man. Why are you here?"

Steven hesitated.

What the hell.

"I just came from the medical school to find out whether I have any chance of qualifying to be a paramedic," Steven said. His broad smile silently spoke of relief and pride.

"And?"

"And when I told them my background, they said I probably qualified already!"

"Man, that is so great!"

"Well, it's not quite that simple, Alan. They want me to take a preliminary test to see how much I've retained from my medic training; it's been a while you know. They probably need to make sure I haven't turned my brain to mush."

I wonder myself.

Steven dropped his head. "I don't think they have any illusions about the vets who came out of Vietnam. So, I have to take a mental health exam. If that goes okay, I have to study the new techniques and protocol used by fire fighters. Then I have to take a physical test, to make sure I'm fit enough – which might be questionable. And last, I have to take a drug test."

"That doesn't sound so bad. Should be a slam-dunk."

Steven turned to face him squarely. "Listen to me Alan, listen carefully. I was in Vietnam. Do you get it? That's where I was a medic. You know how messed up we got? We all came out of that war with a new battle to fight. It's been rough. Lots of us are still struggling, waging the war that's inside of us." Steven looked away, ashamed of his admission.

"So I've heard. We still see those poor guys on the streets."

"Alan, you need to know…I was one of those guys on the street. I'm still pretty messed up – not sure I'll ever get past it. It rips your heart out."

"It doesn't mean you can't be a competent paramedic."

"No guarantees. I've been known to be pretty irresponsible and that's the least of my flaws."

"I promise not to be one of those people who say, 'just get over it' – I know it's more than that. And you'll have a great support group right here, helping you through the rough spots."

"Thanks. You know, when I think about my life with some objectivity, I guess maybe I've made some progress climbing out of my own personal hell. I've met some great people. I'm helping at the Open Heart Kitchen, Scooter and I live in the cottage and guard the place at night."

"Well, with that fierce watchdog of yours, it's a slam-dunk!"

"You're right about that," Steven laughed. "I'm meeting with the organization's director this afternoon. We'll see if he's happy with our services. So far, we've scared off a snake, a starving boy and a woman who tends to the garden. I'm thinking he's going to figure out we're not so necessary."

"You know I was just kidding about Scooter, and a dog can be invaluable," Alan said. "And you know what you can do? You could train him to be a service dog. Help the veterans who come to the kitchen. Give them something to love and soft fur to pet. They've found service dogs to be very comforting."

"Scooter would love the attention."

"We could use him here, too. I'd like to teach him to detect the source of smoke and find fire victims."

"Let's take first things first. Find out if I even qualify."

"I've watched you in action – you qualify."

"We'll see. Gotta run, Alan. Thanks for being so encouraging." Steven resisted the urge to dance up the driveway to his car.

~   ~   ~

As he drove toward the cottage entrance, he found three cars parked in front of the Open Heart building.

He wondered what was going on as he pulled in next to the old Dodge and recognized it as Doc's car. He rolled over the possibilities in his mind, wondering if he had somehow failed in his job and they had come to tell him it wasn't going to work out. Or they didn't need him. Rescuing carrots from a starving boy wasn't exactly a heroic recommendation. He could just hear it now – 'and what have you done to keep the place safe, Steven?'

'Oh, I manhandled a little boy and terrified the gardener.'

How's that for heroics?

He sat forward, trying to inspect himself in the rear-view mirror. Did he remember to shave this morning? He rubbed his cheek. At least he was getting better at paying attention to his grooming. His hair was clean. He looked down at his shirt. No dirty paw prints. Guess he looked presentable.

He got out of the car and rubbed the top of his shoe against the back of the opposite calf and then realized he was wearing tennis shoes – dirty ones at that. They would just have to settle for his work-in-progress rehabilitation.

What if that wasn't enough? Maybe they had found someone else. What if they asked him to leave? Where would he go? The thought of moving back into his father's house was unbearable. He always felt like a vagrant invading his father's house. The cottage was beginning to feel like home, a place he could call home, where he returned with gratitude at the end of each day. David's divorce decree had given Steven a determination to turn his life around.

~   ~   ~

In retrospect, he realized his worries had been needless. Tony, the Director of Open Heart kitchen, was there with Sam and Anna, who had come along for moral support. As he walked in to greet them, they seemed friendly enough. After taking a deep breath, he told them, "What I learned from the college gave me the encouragement that I could become a certified paramedic and work at the fire department." He explained he might qualify for financial aid to pay for the classes, so they wouldn't assume he was asking for more money. He tried to show them he was an okay guy. Anna hollered with glee and danced around him as Doc shook his hand. They offered to testify on his behalf to assure whoever needed to know that he was a stand-up guy. Steven stood dumbstruck by their support and praise.

When Tony found an opening in the celebration, he explained they had come to ask him to stay in the cottage as a caretaker and a night watchman.

"We're glad you're here, Steven. I'm going to talk to the Board of Directors about raising your pay. You've been a big help to Anna. We thought you might continue to take up the slack and help with the heavy lifting."

"Sure can." He nodded to Anna. "We need to lighten your load. And I've gotten pretty good at scrubbing pans."

Sam added, "When you're certified, you'll be able to help me care for our little community of families and veterans. By then you'll be qualified to actually treat them. I need your expertise."

Steven looked at him quizzically, as if Sam were speaking a foreign language.

Me – with expertise?

"You've become a valuable asset to our team," Tony said.

Me? No shit!

Chapter

32

... There is so much unknown about the effects of war on soldiers and quite impossible to diagnose. Most of us who survived are forever suffering from more than physical wounds. No one seems to give credence to the horrifying misery of war and the toll it takes on the human soul. We have all experienced the aftermath of war differently, and yet I see a common thread of anguish and grief.

Do you think any of us come away unscathed?

David's words reverberated in his heart as Steven walked with Scooter toward Anna's house. After reading the letter a second time, he realized again how much he had in common with the Civil War soldier.

Yet, after discovering the divorce decree, Steven felt compelled to change course. He would make a conscious decision to transform his life. He wondered if it was simply a difference in temperament, or personality, or tolerance. Why had David been unable to take a more positive path? Why would he destroy his life by betraying his family?

The old bunker mentality may have helped Steven feel safe, but it also kept him isolated, unable to connect with people. He could see what he was doing to himself. He needed to learn to trust. He was determined to change his path and make a better life. Something had shifted in Steven.

Not me. Not like David. I will not become some pathetic old man.

As they stepped onto the porch at Anna's house, Scooter raced to the window to touch noses with her guard-cat Tom. Although there was a pane of glass between them, the dog hopped about with joy. Two wet spots were left on the window. Scooter quivered as he waited at the door, anticipating another race to see who could make it to the sofa first. Sure enough, as Anna opened the door, Scooter tore through the entrance in hot pursuit of his feline friend, Tom.

"Hi, Steven."

"Sorry. He loves this game."

"Not to worry. Look, I have a surprise for you."

Richie popped up from behind the sofa. "Steven, Steven. I'm so happy..."

The boy ran toward Steven and threw both arms around his waist, squeezing as hard as he could. Tears sprang to Steven's eyes as he looked down at the boy.

"Hey, little man. I'm happy to see you, too. Whatcha doing here?"

"I've come to help you and Anna get ready for today's lunch at the kitchen. And – and I – I miss you."

"I miss you too, buddy. And Scooter doesn't have anyone to snuggle with on the floor. So, he comes up on the bed and pushes me toward the edge of the bed, trying to hog it all."

Richie giggled. Hearing his name, Scooter broke his focus on the sofa and bounced around the boy until Richie gave him a big hug. Tears welled up in Anna's eyes as she slipped into the kitchen.

"Looks like you've put on a few pounds." Steven said.

Richie looked down and happily patted his belly. "They feed me all the time. Grams is a pretty good cook – but not as good as Anna. She says she's trying to fatten me up."

"How did you get here?"

"My grandpa dropped me off. They're going to meet us at the kitchen. I asked my grandparents to help out, too."

"Hey, that's great. Sounds like they're treating you right. Do you like it there?"

"Yeah, it's okay. I have my own room. It's kinda cool. They said I could have it any way I wanted. And I start school next week."

"That's great, Richie. I'm glad you like being with your grandparents. Hey, let's go see what we can do to help Anna."

Richie pulled at Steven's sleeve. "Wait," he whispered. "Have you seen my dad anywhere?"

"No. But I know he loves you kid. Maybe he just needs some time to..."

"Don'tcha think he's had enough time? Is he ever coming back? I need my dad."

Steven didn't know what to say to comfort the boy. He knew plenty about needing a father. "I know you do, Richie. I know."

Anna called from the kitchen, "Hey, you two. I'm making peanut butter and jelly sandwiches. You need your energy to get the pots loaded into the truck. Come and get it!"

Steven gave Richie a quick hug and they raced to the kitchen. Richie won.

~   ~   ~

"Hey," Richie hollered. "Isn't that my dad's truck?" They had begun loading the pots of stew. Craig drove up and hopped out before he saw Richie and Steven. Richie raced to his father, arms outstretched.

"How's my boy?" Craig said, looking quizzically at Steven and gave Richie a bear hug. "Where have you been?"

Richie leaned away, looking carefully at his father. "What do you mean, 'where have I been?' Where have *you* been? You just disappear, like Mom used to do. I've been right here – with Grampa and Gramma. I've been waiting for you."

"Sorry, kid. It's...it's complicated."

"Don't treat me like a kid. I know more than you think I do. I know why you haven't come around. You're not welcome at their house." He started to walk toward Anna and turned back. "You only come to borrow money, looking for handouts."

"Well, uh – that's not…"

"I know how to listen, Dad. I hear them talk when they don't know I'm listening. They're really sad about you. Do you know that?"

With a slight nod of acknowledgement, Craig hung his head.

"Hey, you guys. Let's get going," Anna said, breaking the silence. "There's a bunch of people waiting for this stew. Let's get it to them. You can talk later."

Craig took a deep breath and turned to Steven. "Let's get these pots onto the trucks. It's why I'm here."

"Thanks." Steven said gratefully. "Richie, go get Scooter. We'll take him back to the cottage in the truck. He's not allowed in the kitchen. Find his leash, okay."

"Sure."

As Richie ran into the house, Craig turned to Steven. "What the hell, man."

"Let it go, Craig. I haven't seen him since you took off and Doc drove Richie to your parents. Leave this for now. You want him to feel worse than he does already?"

"Yeah, okay."

Steven leaned forward to take the other pot handle and recoiled. "Oh shit. Don't tell me you've been drinking. Damn you!"

"I haven't – really."

"Then what do I smell? Anna's not brewing beer in these pots."

"It's – well – it was just one beer. Hell, I didn't know Richie would be here."

"What difference does *that* make? You're either a drunk or you're not."

"It was just one beer."

"At nine in the morning? You shit."

Anna called to the men. "Ready to roll, you two? Richie and Scooter are riding with me. Let's go."

Steven hopped into Craig's truck and swept empty beer cans off the seat. They clattered to the floor. They rode to Open Heart Kitchen in strained silence. The clang of metal hitting Steven's foot echoed through the truck as he kicked the beer cans rolling around his feet.

~   ~   ~

They found the usual veterans and families waiting at the front entrance, ready to help haul the pots into the kitchen. As the two men jumped out of the truck, Steven saw an elderly couple waiting inside the front door.

"Could that be your parents, Craig?" Steven ran back toward Anna's truck as she pulled up behind him. He looked at her evenly. "Would you drive around to the cottage and put Scooter inside? Take Richie with you. I'll help with the pots." Turning to Richie, he said, "Help Anna and make sure Scooter's water bowl is full, would you?" Anna looked over at the front entrance and nodded, then drove away from the building to the cottage as Steven walked back to Craig's truck.

Craig hadn't moved. Steven called from the behind truck. "Come on, open up the back and let the men help with the pots."

As Craig reached for the door handle, he looked into the building. "Is that really my parents? What the hell are they doing here?"

"They came to help – with Richie. Let's get the pots unloaded and you can figure out how to deal with this. Stay and apologize or leave and be a shit. Your choice."

Several men grabbed the pots and carried them into the building. Craig stood next to the truck staring at the front door. As soon as the truck was empty, he jumped in the driver's seat and sped off. Steven stared in disbelief as he watched Craig drive away.

Turn around, you shit! Please come back, Craig.

When Steven could no longer see the truck, he walked through the front door to introduce himself to the Johnsons, just as Richie ran into the building from the back door. The boy raced through the dining hall to the front door and out into the driveway. His shoulders drooped when he saw the empty curb, then looked up and down the empty street. Seeing Richie's shoulders begin to shake, Steven hurried toward him, but retreated when he saw Mrs. Johnson rush to the sobbing boy. His body slumped. He turned and headed to the kitchen.

Inside, Anna looked up at Steven. He silently shook his head. Anna dropped her head, then moved along the large industrial stove, stirring each pot, instructing the volunteers to slice the bread. She showed them how to start an assembly line to pass the bowls into the dining hall. "Is it my imagination, or is our family of needy folks growing each week?" She watched as hungry people lined up in the hall.

~   ~   ~

After everyone had been served, Steven began filling bowls of stew for the volunteers, encouraging Anna and the Johnsons to sit and relax. Richie returned to the table but kept a vigilant eye on the front door as he plopped down onto the bench.

"He's not coming back, is he Steven?" Richie asked, tears spilling down his cheeks.

"Maybe not today, pal, but I know he'll be back. How could he not come back to a great kid like you?"

"I'm going to check at the front door one more time, just in case he's afraid to come in," Richie whispered.

Steven didn't try to stop him. The boy needed to work this out for himself. Richie raced toward the front door while Steven joined Anna and the Johnsons.

"Thanks again for taking such good care of our grandson," Mr. Johnson said to Steven.

"Most of the credit goes to Anna and her homemade hamburgers and pancakes. I didn't have much food in my little cottage. One of these days, I'm going to get some cooking lessons from the pro here." He smiled at Anna in appreciation.

"May I join the class?" Mrs. Johnson asked. "I'm not accustomed to feeding a growing boy. I swear I've never seen anyone put away so much food."

"Well, he's got some catching up to do. No telling how long he was hiding out in town trying to find you and – and his father. He went hungry, I'm sure. You should have seen him devour those carrots, dirt and all. Smart though. He knew where to come. He was pretty sure this was the right town."

"We are grateful," Mrs. Johnson said.

Richie raced back to their table and tugged on Steven's sleeve. "There's an old guy at the front door asking for you."

Steven looked up, shocked to see his father standing in

the doorway, eyeing the down-and-out people at all the tables. His face flushed as he looked at Anna and silently mouthed, 'It's my father.'

"Excuse me," he said.

He steeled himself, squared his shoulders and strode to the entrance.

As Steven approached, his father bellowed, "Ha, I knew I'd find you here. Still looking for a handout, huh? Best place to get a free meal, is that it?"

"You've got it wrong, Father. I work..."

"Yeah, sure. You are one pathetic loser. Can't believe this is where you ended up – a place like this."

"Did you come here just to tell me that? I already know what you think of me." Steven gave up trying to explain. His father's image of him was not going to change. He spun around, away from his father.

"Hey, don't walk away from me." His father grabbed him by the shoulder. Steven resisted the urge to punch him as he whirled around to face him.

"I'm done being insulted by you, old man."

"Tough shit. You deserve it. Stand still. I just came to deliver a message."

"Yeah? Well, you've been giving me that message for years. 'Loser,' that's been your message for years. But this time you've got it all wrong."

"Yeah, yeah. Not buyin' it." He leaned toward Steven as if he were deaf and spoke as he would to a child. "Now, listen to me, you idiot. Stand still."

Steven stood in front of his father, hands clenched in

fists, jaw set, silently waiting.

"It's your mother. She's looking for you."

"My mother?" His body didn't know whether to release the tension or increase it.

"Are you going deaf, too? Yeah, I said your mother – she wants to talk to you."

"Me?"

"She wouldn't even talk to me, only you. I have a number for you to call." His hand shook as he handed Steven a piece of paper.

"Are you sure? Is something wrong?"

"How would I know? Call your mother."

The old man turned away, took a ragged breath and pushed through the doors into the street.

Chapter

33

I do not wish your life to end up as mine, abandoned by your family and a stranger to your children.

Was David speaking to him directly from the grave? Steven shivered, took a deep breath and tried to shake it off. It was his mother. *She* had abandoned them.

She was looking for him. How could this be? She wanted him to call. Steven didn't know what to make of it. Should he be furious or worried? All these years – why now? At least he could be sure she was still alive. He had always set his mind to the belief that she had left because of his father – it was his fault – he was an abusive bully. Yet Steven had to face the fact that she had left him, too. His mother had never returned. She had never reached out to him. Before this, she had never called. There were no letters – no phone calls He had decided long ago that she must have learned about his nosedive into a life of alcohol and had given up on him. She would be ashamed of him. Here he was, a 30-year-old, grown man, yearning for his mother. He couldn't blame her for not wanting any part of him.

But how could she leave me? She was my mother.

She had left while Steven was stitching up soldiers in Vietnam. His father rarely wrote to him and hadn't revealed that she was gone. Steven had written to his mother, confessing his suffering to no one else. He didn't know she had left. She never answered.

He returned home to a desolate house, and an angry father, who stoked the flames of hatred when anti-war protests were at their peak. The rage against returning soldiers was painful and demoralizing, but the news of his mother's desertion had completely derailed him. He had come home believing she could help him reset his compass. His torment during the war had knocked him to his knees and he had hoped she could help him be a better man. She had been his center of gravity and she was gone. Steven had descended into a life of despair, aching to find whatever alcohol was available or bottle he could empty. It guaranteed him a restless state of oblivion – a way to forget and retreat to the safety of his beloved bunker.

After several years, he had met Sharon. She would be his salvation. He had been sure of it. For one blissful month he had sobered up, stayed straight and fallen in love. He did his very best to obliterate the loss of his mother by believing he had found the perfect replacement. He was too old to need a mother anyway. Sharon was warm, understanding and loving – his ability to be intimate returned and he was grateful to

324

know he was still capable of having a love life. The war had done its damage, but Sharon was sympathetic and struggled to keep him straight. She stuck by him. It was perfect, until the excesses took priority over his lover. That was the moment it all fell apart.

He tried to remember what he had done to cause the breakup, but after she disappeared, he was too drunk to remember much of anything. Sharon was suddenly and permanently gone. Steven fell into despair – the only two women who had loved him had vanished and he was to blame. He crawled back into his emotional bunker and lived on the streets as he spiraled into his own private hell, sampling the accommodations of every homeless shelter, street corner and soup kitchen in the area. At some point his father had found him and brought him home, where he was confronted with a revelation that would upend his world.

He had a child.

Without warning, his father had brusquely informed him that after Steven's disappearance, there had been a call from Sharon to inform Steven that there was a child. She said it was definitely his baby.

Steven's father, ignited by his dormant fury, had callously given Sharon all the sordid details of Steven's ruined life since she had left. His father had lied to Steven, saying how Sharon swore that Steven would never see his child. The lie was magnified. His father said that Sharon insisted Steven wasn't worthy of being a father. She would not say where she was living nor reveal how to locate them. He had lost any chance of reconciliation.

Steven's devastation sent him back to the streets. When

he finally ended up chained to a hospital bed and then in jail, he couldn't remember the reason for his infraction. His father bailed him out, dragged him home, dried him out, and berated him until Steven couldn't stand the abuse and returned to the streets. The agonizing pattern continued – living in shelters or under his father's roof, trying to blot out the relentless criticism and self-loathing. He came to believe he deserved every insult.

I don't deserve to be a father.

And then one day he looked in the mirror and didn't recognize the man staring back at him. Disheveled, filthy uncut hair, dark circles under eyes that stared back at him with pain and misery. He was sure his skin had turned a permanent shade of gray, as if he had been hiding away in some dank bunker for years. Something snapped. He couldn't bear to look at the repulsive man in the mirror a moment longer. He couldn't stand himself or what he had become. He resolved to change course. As an antidote he paced the house, then rushed down the front steps to the street and walked block after block to ease the tension and tried to find the courage to climb out of his despair.

He had a child but was forbidden from being a father. The suffering was unbearable. He tried to forget. He managed to keep busy by developing a regimen. He walked the streets, hour after hour, then fell into fitful sleep, making every effort not to think.

Then he remembered David Lane's medical certificate, and the letter he had discovered as a boy, hidden in plain sight in his father's study – and everything changed. His father was right – he had become obsessed – didn't understand why and didn't care. The old parchment became his splendid distraction. The more he learned about David's Civil War, the more he understood the suffering of all soldiers. The trauma of war was universal. Through David's letters, Steven discovered a profound connection to this other father who had become estranged from his children. He came to know another soldier, struggling through another war in another time. The two soldiers, separated by 100 years, had much in common.

When he found the divorce decree it gave him the insight to understand David's mistakes and Steven resolved he would not repeat them.

I will find a way to do this differently.

Each of David's offences was documented in the divorce papers, disallowing any opportunity to make amends. Steven ached for him. He developed a deep understanding of what became of David as he aged into a lonely old man. Steven was determined to choose a different course.

This will not be me. I will not forsake my child.

He set upon the belief that he needed to find a purpose, an honorable way to make a living and a path forward to redeem himself.

I will find a way to my child.

Steven realized he was not yet prepared to face his mother, even by phone. He wanted to assure her he was on the road to recovery and he needed to believe he could make a better life for himself.

I need to believe in myself – heal myself.

He carefully tucked the paper with her phone number into his wallet and grabbed his jacket. "Scooter, time to do your watchdog duties. I'll be back soon." The dog hopped up on the bench and looked out the window as if to stand sentry over the garden. Steven jumped into his car and with new determination headed for the paramedic training registration offices.

~   ~   ~

Two hours later, Steven called Anna from the hospital pay phone. "I've done it, Anna. I wanted you to be the first to know. I applied for certification to become a paramedic. Thank you for believing in me."

"Oh Steven, I'm so proud of you. I knew you could do it. Congratulations."

"I'll tell you all about it when I see you. There's a new class session starting soon and with my experience as a medic, they said I might advance quickly."

"Wonderful."

Steven's voice quivered. "I'm scared. What if I can't cut it?"

"I've seen you step up in a crisis. You'll be fine."

"Hope you're right."

"Of course, I'm right. I'm always right – you know that." The sound of her laughter gave him hope.

"Yeah, I know! My next phone call will be to Sam. I want to tell him myself, okay?"

"Absolutely. I understand. It's none of my business, but why was your father looking for you last night. Is everything alright?"

"I'll tell you when I see you."

"I can't stand the suspense. Can I bribe you with meatloaf tonight? I'll see if Sam can join us, if you want to talk

328

with him, too."

"Sure, that would be great."

"Come when you can."

~   ~   ~

When Steven returned to the cottage, he could hear Scooter barking before he had one foot out the car door. He raced around to the side yard and into the garden. He found someone sitting on the ground at the edge of the garden with his head between his knees. He couldn't tell who it was until he rushed to the man.

"Craig, what the hell? Have you been drinking?"

Craig looked up, his eyes bloodshot, his hands trembling.

"Wait, let me get Scooter. He won't stop barking until he sees you."

As soon as Steven opened the door, the dog raced to Craig's side and snuggling against him, licked his shaking hands.

Craig looked up, patting the dog. "I know it sounds stupid, but I thought if I could face my fears, I could beat this miserable addiction."

"What are you doing in the garden?"

"Waiting to confront the snake."

"You really are crazy!"

Steven bit his tongue and tried not laugh. "Hey man, you could sit here for weeks and never see another snake." He sat down next to his friend. "If you want to overcome your fear of snakes, go to the library and study up on them. Learn which ones are dangerous. Didn't you learn about snakes in Nam?"

"Hell, no. I just ran away as fast as I could."

Steven couldn't contain himself and busted up. He doubled over and laughed so hard his stomach hurt. It was contagious. Craig saw the absurdity and started laughing too. Steven stood up, reached out his hand and pulled his friend off the ground. "Come on in, I'll make a pot of coffee."

As he set a cup in front of Craig, Steven said, "Okay, what's this really about?"

"It's fear, I guess. I'm afraid I'll never be able to quit drinking. I'm afraid I've ruined my life. I'm afraid I'll lose my son – that my parents will never let me see him. I've been a screw-up for so long, I – I don't know where to start."

"I understand, man."

"What should I do?"

"Are you asking my opinion?"

Craig nodded. "It looks like you're on the road to recovery. Unless I'm imagining things, you seem to have managed to stay sober for a while. How did you do it?"

"One day I looked in the mirror and saw a piece of shit staring back at me. I was so disgusted, I had to do something. It was agonizing, but I couldn't stand the person I saw."

"I'm afraid to look – maybe that's the problem."

"Try it – and as hard as it will be, imagine how your son sees you. That should motivate you."

"I don't know if I can do it, but I've got to try to be better. I'm determined to go apologize to my folks..."

"Yeah, and Richie too."

"Especially Richie. I don't want to lose that boy."

"Mind if I make a suggestion?"

"Yeah, sure."

330

"Show up at your parents' door and ask for forgiveness. Tell them what you said to me. Tell them you need their help to be better. Promise to find a job, even it's making deliveries in your truck. Commit to stop drinking. Promise them you will try and will keep trying. Apologize to your son and ask your family not to give up on you."

Craig winced. His chin dropped to his chest.

"And stop feeling sorry for yourself. Be grateful you have a family who cares about you."

"Thanks, Steven." Craig stood up unsteadily and headed for the door.

"Hey, wait. Do you have any clean clothes in your truck? First go take a shower and clean up."

Steven put his hands on Craig's shoulders. "Don't give up on yourself. You can do this."

"Shit, I hope so."

"Listen, at least you have a family you can go to. Be grateful for that – I'd give anything if..."

"But your father..."

"Keeps throwing me out. He has every right to question my sanity and my sobriety. I haven't been exactly trustworthy over the years either. Now go do it, before you lose your nerve. Get your family back while you still have one."

After his shower, Craig emerged looking almost human.

The second Craig closed the door, Steven dropped onto the bed and fell into a fitful sleep.

The bodies were lined up in their coffins – all in a tidy row – his patients – his comrades – the soldiers he couldn't save. The corpses rose up from their coffins and slowly walked toward him, pointing their fingers, their wounds still dripping with blood. One soldier was carrying the arm he had lost, aiming it at Steven as if it were a gun.

"You failed us," they shouted. "We didn't need to die."

A soldier – his friend who had drowned in the swamp, was covered with slime. He never spoke, just glared at Steven with hatred. The venom directed at him was unbearable.

The corpses continued toward him, confronting him with each injury – each death.

He raised himself to a sitting position, screaming for help. Scooter jumped onto the bed and hovered over his master, licking his face as Steven recovered from his nightmare.

...all the people I failed...

He put his arms around his dog and held on. Steven dropped his head onto his dog, struggling to deny the dream.

Don't let this derail me.

Chapter

34

... We have all experienced the aftermath of war differently, and yet I see a common thread of anguish and grief.

Do you think any of us came away unscathed?

The dog seemed to be walking the man. Lost in thought, Steven allowed himself to be led along the street. His evening with Anna and Sam had been heartening. He had shared every event, his lost love, the child he was forbidden to see and his mother, who was asking for a phone call. His friends were by his side and would help to support his resolve.

He reflected on the awful truth Dr. James, David Lane's friend, had expressed with such eloquence – the common thread of anguish and grief. He was writing about the Civil

War, yet how many men had he met from *his* war who could relate to those words?

Steven had to remind himself there were those who had the determination to find a better way – Joe, who rose out of the gutter and sustained himself by owning a coffee shop; Tony, Doc's son, who could now credit himself with managing all three Open Heart Kitchens throughout the state; and Pete, whose salvation rested on his ability to become a veterinarian.

Did any of us come away unscathed? Not really, and yet some have had the courage to say 'enough' – I am fucking sick of suffering.

Scooter trotted along the sidewalk, sniffing each shop and doorway as he led Steven toward the pet store, unaware that he was headed toward his second bath and Steven's effort to tamp down his fear of rising water.

How can a grown man be afraid of a tubful of water?

Although he keenly understood his nightmares and fear of water, he still felt like an idiot. Why couldn't he get past that visceral reaction? They walked into the pet shop and Steven stopped short when he saw Pete's mother, Grace, standing behind the counter. Where was Pete? Did this mean he hadn't passed his final tests?

Grace waved with a cheerful, "Hey, I remember you – Steven is it? So glad you came by. And Scooter, what a handsome mutt, I definitely remember you."

"Tell me quick, Grace. How'd he do?"

"Oh, I'm sorry. I thought you knew. He passed with excellent grades – top of his class."

"Fantastic."

"Yeah, isn't it great?" Pete hollered from the back room.

"Congratulations, my friend. You deserve it," Steven yelled back.

"Yes, I do."

"Come on out. We want to see the new veterinarian in person."

Steven almost dropped to his knees as Pete proudly marched from the storage room with his arm draped around Lindsay's shoulders.

My Lindsay? What the...

"Isn't this the best news?" Lindsay said as she turned toward Pete and gave him a big hug.

Steven's face turned to chalk, as he stammered, "Yeah, it's – it's great."

Elation bubbling over, Pete kissed Lindsay on the cheek and danced around the room to his mother and Steven. "Come on Scooter, I want a hug from you, too."

Why am I so shocked? I have no claim on her – I'm not even sure I like her.

Steven tried to recover as he looked from Pete to Lindsay to Grace. "So, what now? Are you going to open up a vet hospital somewhere? I want the honor of being your first customer." He tried to smile. "Scooter can be your first patient. He needs a checkup. What do you think?"

"As a matter of fact, that's what we were planning when you came in. My partner and I..." he danced back to Lindsay and kissed her again, "...have permission from the owner of the shop to turn the storeroom into a clinic. I should be able to hang a shingle out front in about a month."

"What a generous owner," Steven said.

"Aren't I, though!" Grace clapped her hands together with glee.

"What? So, you're the owner of the store?" Steven asked.

"Better than that," Grace puffed out her chest proudly. "I'm the owner of the building."

"Now, that's just plain impressive," Steven said.

"Yes, indeed it is. When my Pete came back from that horrible war, I could tell right away he was one big mess. He was racing down the road to self-destruction." She looked over at her son as he nodded in agreement. "And I knew the only thing he'd ever wanted to do in life was to be a veterinarian. So, in case you're thinking how manipulative I was, you're right. I took out all my savings and bought this building, turned it into a pet store and cajoled Pete into running it for me. The man loves animals, what can I say? It kept him out of the bars and kept me from sleepless nights of worrying."

Pete let go of Lindsay and embraced his mother. "She really did save me," he said simply.

"And if it hadn't been for my little sister, here..." bowing to Lindsay, "supporting our mother..."

"Your sister? Your sister!" The tension drained out of Steven's body. Color returned to his face.

"Lindsay is my sister, you knew that, didn't you?"

"How would I know?"

"Well, she's the best sister a guy could have. While I was struggling to stay sober and run the shop, Lindsay supported Mom, and helped in the shop when she could.

Lindsay gave her brother a gentle shove. "It's not a big deal, Pete. That's what families do for each other."

336

Steven felt his body go cold. "Not my family," he said with a hint of sarcasm.

"Oh, I'm sorry, Steven. What would I know – you're so open and forthcoming. And – damn – I did it again, didn't I? So, uh – well – I need to shut my mouth and get out of here. I'm giving a genealogy seminar in an hour. Better get going."

"Thanks for your ideas, Lindsay." Pete gave her another hug. I'll call your contractor friend tomorrow and we'll get going on plans for the clinic."

"Okay, good. Bye Mom, see you at home." She put an arm around her mother and turned to Steven. "And the other thing our mother did for us was to keep our family together, under one roof. She fed us and cared for us. We supported each other. So, you see..." Grace raised her hand as if to say 'stop' and gave her daughter a look that said, 'enough.'

"Okay, I'm done. See ya, Steven." Lindsay zeroed in on the exit, then stopped and looked up at Pete. "I can already see your clinic sign over the doorway. Way to go, big brother." She waved goodbye.

Steven turned to Pete. "You are one lucky guy, my friend. I hope you appreciate these two women. I mean – man – what they have done for you. Mighty righteous."

Hands on her hips, Grace added, "Well, Peter did his part, too. Don't forget, he stayed straight, studied hard and had this store earning a profit in less than a year. Pretty admirable if you ask me."

"Yeah, I agree. It's great to see a family that..." He took a deep breath. "What I wouldn't give... but the truth is, it's up to me, isn't it? Seems like I haven't done much of anything but slouch around and feel sorry for myself."

"Nope – don't go there, man." Pete put both hands on Steven's shoulders. "We *all* had a rough time over there and a worse time when we came home. We all heal differently. But look at me – I'm a walking testament – we *can* heal, I promise."

Steven stepped back and showed him respect with a deep bow. "You will be my role model, Pete. If you can find a path to success, so can I."

But what do I do with all the corpses that show up in my dreams?

"So, I have a great distraction for you."

Steven cocked his head. "Okay, let me guess. You want help building the clinic."

Pete vigorously nodded his head.

"Well, it just so happens I'm good with a hammer, but you'll have to catch me in between classes – I've been accepted to paramedic school. I've been accepted for classes to get certification!"

"Hey, that's terrific. I'm happy for you," Pete said. " And for your generosity, I'll offer free baths for Scooter for a full year."

"Thanks. But this is one hurdle I need to get over by myself. I know you must think I'm a bit crazy...I mean, the rising water...leads to a panic attack..."

"It's okay. We're all a little whacked. Anything you want."

"Okay then – let's do it."

The two men led Scooter to the tub where the dog happily jumped onto the counter, tail wagging, ready for a scrubbing.

Grace called to the men. "Hellooo, I'm still here. Shall I hold down the fort out here?"

"Oops! Uh, thanks, Mom." He turned to Steven. "Don't want to ever take advantage of her good will. She's been so good to me."

"Lucky man."

As the tub began to fill, Pete poured in soap and lifted the dog into the water. Steven held his breath as the water began rising over Scooter's feet and up his legs. Steven started to shake.

"Talk to me," Pete said. "Remember, there is no way a dog can drown in this tub. Keep watching the water rise and understand that Scooter is safe. Do you want to tell me what happened? Your fear is about something else."

"I still have nightmares..."

"Okay, I'm listening. Take the hose and pour water over him. That's it. You won't hurt him. Get some soap on your hands and scrub his fur. That's it; now talk to me while you're washing Scooter."

Steven took a deep breath and scrubbed Scooter down to his skin. He tensed as the water rose. Memories flooded back.

"In Nam – our guys were ambushed and got themselves into a firefight near this village that was spread out next to a muddy inlet of the Mekong Delta. I'll never forget that river. It was so polluted you couldn't see down into it – filled with mud and debris. The stuff floating on top that – well – it was foul. During the fight, the Viet Cong used the villagers as shields. It was a brutal, ugly battle. Our guys dragged the wounded into the brush where the medical staff tried to keep the soldiers dry enough to examine. Working in the jungle was miserable - hot and damp. That's how infection latches on. Couldn't keep anything dry. Couldn't use water from that putrid river to clean a wound. We could remove superficial bullets, but we weren't set up for major injuries or surgeries, not in those conditions.

"Then it started to pour – sheets of rain – one of those monsoons that suddenly explodes, where torrents of rain can create six inches of water in minutes. The battle stopped. No one could see through the downpour. We slid the wounded under the bushes sort of like a triage, as more were brought in.

"Someone called my name. 'Steven, we need you! Jack's been shot. He landed in the river. Help us look for him.' It was dangerous to go in those rivers. Like our swamps in the South, no telling what might be down there. Poisonous snakes for sure. I handed my patient off to another medic and raced to the edge of the river. The river looked like it had risen a foot. The rain pelted down. The shooting had stopped, but the villagers were too frightened to move. One old man looked straight at me and pointed to a spot in the water."

Steven scrubbed Scooter furiously. "As the pounding rain pelted down on us, I turned and saw Jack's head sink under the water. Everything else melted away. I saw nothing but the water as it rose higher. I dove down to search for him, desperately looking for my friend. When you opened your eyes in that murky water it was torture – burned your eyes, you could barely see. The water kept rising as I continued to dive. It was agonizing searching for him, it seemed like forever, but we never found Jack."

He paused, trying to get his bearings. "I've never forgiven myself. I'm a good swimmer. I should have found him. The water rose too fast. If I had found him, I might have saved him. I could perform CPR with the best of them."

He choked and scrubbed the dog harder. "I can still taste that putrid water. It was like rancid mold. I can't bear the sight of rising water. I've never told anyone. I'm to blame."

"I get it," Pete said. He put his hand on Steven's wet arm to stop his constant scrubbing motion. "It's easy for me to stand here and say you're not to blame. Doesn't sound like there was any way to find your friend. Try to forgive yourself. You'll get a chance to save people in other ways, maybe as a paramedic, and you'll know you've done everything you could to help someone else. You can't change what happened, but you still have a chance to make a difference in the future."

"Yeah, I know. But, damn it Pete, I still feel like a failure." He dropped his head as his arms went limp. His body shuddered.

Pete took over and rinsed off the dog. "Okay, now *you* lift him out of the tub. Get him out of the water. There, that's it. Here, use these towels. Dry him off. Okay, good. You did it!"

Steven lifted the dog to the floor, knelt down and began rubbing him dry. In one motion, he draped the towel around Scooter as if it were a baby blanket, wrapped his arms around his dog and wept.

Chapter

35

February 18, 1892

Old Soldiers and Sailors Home
Sandusky, Ohio

My Dear Daughter,
I now begin the letter I should have
written days ago but hesitated and
thought a good deal about propriety and
what I would wish to say if we could
have been together. I write with a heavy
heart and I conclude that any visit you
might wish to make will be unrealized.
I suppose it is for the best, my dear,
although I admit to being heartbroken.

Of greatest import, I do not wish you to be alienated from your mother.

Mary, we should always try and think well of those about us and give credit for good qualities and not imagine that one person has only evil qualities. I pray you do not follow in your father's footsteps but find an inner path of goodness.

I am now an old man and have seen some hard times and many results of sinning against the laws of God and nature. I have not been all bad I assure you; and I do not blame 'hereditary tendency' for my past wrongdoing, and pray you will do the same. With good decisions and the right choices, we can determine our own fate and live virtuous lives. With great regret, I learned this lesson much too late. Take heart and live a good life, my dear daughter.

With kindest wishes for you,
I remain truly your loving father

Steven read David's sorrowful letter with deep sadness.

'With good decisions and the right choices...'

Too late for that. The best I can do is make amends.

He was struck by David's expression, 'hereditary tendency.' What did he mean – that his children would not inherit his own bad behavior? Was there any scientific basis for this theory or was it old-fashioned thinking?

This might be a question Lindsay could answer. Nature vs. Nurture. Did it make a difference – what people had experienced? Not every soldier came away from war damaged and broken – did they? Not all people inherited their parents' psychological traits. Was he anything like his father? He hoped not. Was his disposition more like his mother's? Time to find out.

Was reconciliation possible? His mother wanted him to call. Time to face up to it. Steven's hands began to shake as he reached for the phone. His fingers went numb as he tried to dial the number. He dropped the handset.

Maybe she won't answer. What should I say?

He tried again. He started to hang up.

A voice on the line said, "Hello? Is someone there?"

"This is..." He lowered the phone away from his ear and took a ragged breath, then started again. "This is Steven. You asked that I call." His voice echoed in his ear – dead – hard.

"Oh, Steven." He could hear a sob rise up from her

throat. "I – I'm so glad you called."

Her voice felt like home. As his knees went weak, he sat down on the bed.

Both lines sat silent.

"It's been awful without you here." His voice croaked. He felt like a little boy, needing comfort from his mother. Just as quickly, resentment rose up as he realized the awful truth.

"I owe you my deepest apology. I'm sure you felt abandoned. I am so, so sorry Steven. Forgive me. You came back from that awful war and you were confronted with an abusive, bully of a father. I never thought..."

He jumped to his feet as anger overcame sorrow.

"Tell me why – just – explain to me how you could leave me like that."

"I never thought you would stay shackled to that man as long as you have. I thought..."

"No, that's not good enough. When you left him, you left me, too."

"I – alright let me try to help you understand."

"Good idea. I'm not sure there's any excuse you could give..." Steven stopped, before regretting what he was about to say.

"Please try to hear me out, Steven. Just listen. After you left for Vietnam, my buffer was gone. You. Yes, you had been my reason to stay – for years. With you gone, your father became unbearable, cruel, and I – and I started to drink – a lot."

She kept talking. "It was so easy to use it as an escape. I drank every night until I passed out. I kept drinking during the day to block out his relentless abuse. There came a point when I couldn't stand it any longer, I couldn't stand myself or him. I left – I simply walked away."

"But..." His hand went numb from gripping the phone.

"I wasn't thinking about anything except getting away from him. I packed a bag, took all the kitchen money, grabbed the last bottle of scotch and walked to the bus depot. I didn't even care where I was going – I got on the first bus and let it take me as far away as possible."

"Where did you go?"

"I didn't end up far away. I'm in a small town near the Oregon border."

"But you never tried to contact me – in all that time – I figured you didn't care, or worse. I thought maybe you found out what a screwup I'd become after the war and – and didn't want any part of me."

"No, Steven. Listen to me. I wrote letters. Hundreds of letters – for ten years. Believe me."

"It's hard to believe. I didn't get any. Not one. I'm..."

"Please believe me. I think your father..."

"Are we going to blame everything on him? Listen. This has got me all twisted up. I don't know what to think. I need to take a break. Give me some time to absorb all this. I'll call you back."

"But..."

Steven hung up the phone and wrapped his arms around Scooter and said, "What if – what if there weren't any letters?"

~   ~   ~

It was time for a serious walk-about. "Scooter, I'll be back."

347

Steven jogged into town and sprinted up the library steps. He decided this was the perfect time to open up to Lindsay. He would tell her about his mother. He would share his worries. He needed her understanding.

What if...

Barely pausing to appreciate the entrance, he headed straight for Lindsay's research desk. Empty. Where could she be? It was too early for her seminars. He turned around, searching for her, then walked around the stacks of books and back to the entrance. Gladys gave a friendly wave and motioned him to her massive desk.

"Hi, Steven." The old woman stood and patted the chair in front of her desk. "Come have a seat."

"Hey, Gladys. I'm looking for Lindsay. Any idea where she's gone?"

"I think Pete needed her help today. She took a day off."

"Oh, well..."

"Anything I can do to help? You look so forlorn."

"Maybe. It's kind of personal, Gladys. I know you give good advice."

"Of course, I do. Then, out with it, young man."

Steven told Gladys about his mother's disappearance from his life and their conversation.

"My goodness, what a dilemma. She sure was in a tough spot."

"The letters, Gladys. How do I believe her? She was drinking." He dropped his head. "I know how a person's memory gets messed up when you spend most of your waking hours drunk."

348

She looked straight at Steven without flinching.

He leaned forward. "How do I believe her? I never saw a letter. Not one."

"But you were drinking, too. How can you be sure?"

"Damn!"

"I know how tough this must be, Steven. Why don't you sleep on it. Go home and try to remember if you ever saw mail at your father's house that was addressed to you. Give it a day, then call her back."

"Good plan, thanks Gladys."

She nodded as he stood to leave. "She's not the kind of person who would lie about such a thing."

Steven whipped around. "What? Did you..."

Gladys shooed him away. "Go forth and ponder, young man."

Steven shrugged and headed down the library's stairs.

Chapter

36

... we should always try and think well of those about us and give credit for good qualities and not imagine that one person has only evil qualities ...

Steven opened his eyes the next morning, patted his sleeping dog and rose to make a pot of coffee. As it brewed, he picked up the letter that David Lane had written to his daughter. He considered what David was trying to say. People aren't all bad. Human beings are complicated. We've all experienced trauma. As Steven finished the letter, Scooter popped his head up and growled, then leapt to the floor as someone pounded on the door.

"What the hell," Steven said. "Who is it?" He called out.

"Message for you, Sir."

Steven opened the door a slit.

"Please allow me in, Sir. I have a large package for you."

Mystified, Steven opened the door, and held Scooter back. A burly young man walked to the bed and turned the package upside down. Hundreds of letters tumbled on to the bed.

The young man looked at Steven with a satisfied smile. "I am delivering this package precisely in the manner requested, Sir." He turned and walked out of the cottage.

Steven called after him, "Thank you!" The guy must have driven all night.

An envelope slid off the top of the pile. Steven caught it before it hit the floor, turned it over and recognized his mother's handwriting. It hadn't changed since he was a kid. He scooped up the piles of letters, set them gently on the old rocking chair and began to read the letter that landed on top.

He picked up the phone.

~   ~   ~

"Steven! You got the delivery?"

"I'm no longer confused. I'm sorry I doubted you. Forgive me."

"These are all the letters I wrote to you, Steven. The ones that came back to me. I began to think your father had given me the wrong address. I didn't know how to write directly to you in Vietnam, so I hoped he would have the decency...I didn't know when you returned, but I kept writing. I hoped one would get through to you. By then, I'd been drinking a long time. I was in pretty bad shape."

"Okay, I can relate to that."

"I know."

352

"What! How do you know?"

"I'll explain. Let me finish. It's important that you hear it all."

Steven stopped shaking and held on to the phone, wanting to know, yet fearing what he was about to hear.

"Are you still there?"

"I'm not so sure I want to hear this." He paced the room as far as the phone cord would reach. Back and forth, he created a path of anguish.

"You must. What I have to say...it's important that you know..."

He stopped dead in his tracks and lay on the bed as the phone became his lifeline.

"Okay, let's do this."

"I ended up in a small hospital where I was cared for, making every effort to dry out and stay sober. Steven, I am so ashamed. I got caught trying to steal drugs from the hospital pharmacy."

He took a breath.

"They were going to arrest me until a wonderful young nurse helped me get into a rehab clinic, with a promise to be my guardian. It was crazy. I was the adult and she was some pretty young thing who happened to believe in me."

He stopped pacing.

"You were lucky. When I'm honest with myself, I have to admit Dad tried his best to get me straight. I couldn't stand his badgering every time he took me in, so I'd split."

"Oh, my dear boy. I understand completely."

"So, you went into rehab?"

"And I promise, I've been clean and sober all these years. I don't know what I'd have done without...so Steven...here's the amazing part..."

He sat back on the bed, alert to the joy resonating in her voice.

"Do you believe in miracles, Steven? Maybe a little magic that could change your life?"

"No – not so far. What are you trying to tell me?"

"Here's my miracle, Steven. My nurse – my guardian angel – the young woman who saved me – it's Sharon!"

"The Sharon who left me? What the hell?" He flopped back against the mattress and started to shake again. He could barely remember her face.

"When she left you, this is where she settled."

"But – but then – I was told there was a child."

"Yes, Steven. There *is* a child. You have a daughter – her name is Kate. She'll be seven years old next week."

"His heart ached. The blood drained from his face. He didn't know whether to feel grateful to know the truth or to be despondent over the wasted years.

"Are you there? I know this is a shock, but I felt it was time to tell you. Ever since I left, I felt I had failed you. This was my chance to make up for my mistakes...for abandoning you. If I couldn't be there for you, I could at least be there for your daughter. Don't you see?"

"I don't know what to say. Years ago, Dad told me that Sharon said I could never see my child, that – that I didn't deserve to be a father."

"No! Oh no. She never said that. I promise."

354

"But, why..."

"I don't know. He lied to you. Cruel – he can be heartless."

"How do you know what she said to him? How can you be sure?"

"I know because she told me."

"She told you? Do you still see her?"

"Steven, that's what I'm trying to tell you. It's a blessing. I live with her. I'm helping care for Katie. After all – *your* daughter is *my* granddaughter."

He sat up straight on the bed. His body began to shake as he sobbed, his face wet with tears. He had found his family.

Chapter

37

March 1, 1892

Old Soldiers and Sailors Home

My Dear Daughter,

I am heartened by your reply and most especially your persistence. I wish I could, in good conscience, applaud your defiance and encourage you to visit — if only just once. With great regret I insist again that you must not risk it, my dear. I admit my health is tenuous, but your Uncle William should not have put this worry into your head.

My dear Mary, you must not defy your mother, nor endanger the comfort *of your home and family. It is difficult for a young woman to safely travel alone, without a companion or chaperone.*

I implore you, my dear, stay home and continue to be a good daughter.

Your devoted father,
David Lane

As he read the letter, Steven began to lose patience with David, when he usually felt sympathy. First, David had encouraged Mary to come to him and the last two letters discouraged her from taking the risk. He had always felt so connected to this man. Not with this letter.

But who am I to judge? What have I done to find my child?

He had begun to see the series of letters as a cautionary tale. Was he making the same mistakes? Was it too late? If he didn't change course, would he end up a lonely, angry old recluse, exactly like David?

The night before, he had told Anna and Sam about the amazing discovery of his mother and Katie. He made a little ceremony of thanking them, taking them to the local diner and treating them to a steak dinner as a thank you for their kindness and support. He shared the emotional conversation he had had with his mother and revealed the story of his daughter, Katie. He told them about David's daughter, Mary, and the letters he had found, her persistent defiance and quest to visit her father.

"Maybe she did go to him," Anna said. "Remember, I told you what an angry man my own father, George, became? He was David's son, and surely felt neglected and abandoned. George was much younger than Mary, and probably didn't know about his sister's schemes. It's curious how these tendencies are carried through generations in families."

Doc swallowed his last bite and agreed. "I've learned over my many years that people who are always angry, take it out on other people. They can't look inside, at their own rage, so they take it out on the very people who would love them most."

What shits we humans can be.

Steven sat straight in his chair as he made the connection. "All the fathers..." he looked at Anna. "Look at what we've done or failed to do...and I'm at the top of the list. Did I ever, in all this time try to find my daughter? No. Just sat around wallowing in self-pity."

Anna put a hand on his arm. "Steven, you were barely aware she existed and had been told..."

He looked at Sam who was quiet as a stone, observing the conversation without saying a word.

I need to try harder. Reach out to my daughter.

"Yeah, I know, but did I try? And look at *my* father – an abusive, belligerent coward. And then there's Craig. Can't manage to get off booze long enough to find a job and take responsibility for his own son. I ache for Richie. He deserves better. And look at David, who ruined any chance of being a loving father. I guess I'm looking at all these fathers I know who seem to have failed at their most important job. And I don't mean you, Sam. Seems you worked through your troubles after Korea, and came out stronger at the other end."

Sam gave a slight nod of appreciation, "It can be done." He looked directly into Steven's eyes. "So, you're simply going to declare yourself a martyr and leave it there? Poor me, I failed? I'm challenging you – what would you have done differently? What can you still do?"

"What I did was put my tail between my legs and felt sorry for myself. I guess I didn't have the courage to do anything about it. I gave up." Steven said with a catch in his voice.

"Well, it's time to drop the self-pity, Steven. It's not too late. What are you going to do about it now?"

Steven grabbed the arms of his chair and resisted his inclination to bolt from the room. "But..."

Sam responded to the gesture. "No excuses. What are you going to do?"

"Well I..."

"Come on, Steven. Stop complaining and take charge of your life."

"Damn." Steven said.

"Okay. So, what does that mean – taking charge of your life?" Doc asked.

"You're starting to sound like a shrink, Doc."

Sam laughed. "Maybe I missed my calling. It's just that we care about you, Steven. I know you have great potential. You're a natural healer."

"That's pretty ironic. I see my failings by the number of people I couldn't save. All those soldiers I couldn't heal. More like a natural screw-up, if you ask me."

Anna chimed in. "So, let your mother be your guide. What was she doing all these years? She found a way to help the woman who saved *her*. As a bonus she was able to help raise her granddaughter. You can find ways to help others – to make up for those you couldn't save, whether it was your fellow soldiers or your family. Isn't that what your mother did?"

"So, she got her fairy tale. How does that allow me to be better?"

Anna slapped her hand on the table. "Don't you see? It's your choice. Your decision. Your life."

Steven sat bolt upright. "That's exactly what Pete said to me. We can't rewrite history and we can't go back and fix our mistakes. We can only go forward and find ways to be better."

"That's it. Pay it forward...ever thought about that?" Anna said.

"Man, we can be pretty dense sometimes."

"I hope you realize the door has already been opened – now all you have to do is step through it." Doc said.

Steven resisted, straightened his spine, and said, "Stop talking in symbols. What door? What are you talking about?"

"You're right, you *can* be pretty dense sometimes. You take the training to become a paramedic, that's the door you need to walk through. And by doing that, you'll learn the latest in emergency medicine and crisis skills."

Anna jumped to her feet almost knocking over her chair. "And with your skills you'll be able to build on them and help Doc at the Open Heart Kitchen. Think of all those people who need your help, Steven."

He shivered. "I'm not sure I'm ready for the responsibility." Steven gripped the chair and stood. "Okay, one thing at a time. First, I have to get the training, learn the skills."

She beamed. "And there it is. I think they're called 'your Marching Orders,' Steven.

Chapter

38

... With good decisions and the right choices, we can determine our own fate and live virtuous lives.   With great regret,

I learned this lesson much too late. Take heart and live a good life, my dear daughter.

With kindest wishes for you, I remain truly your loving father.

Steven gently placed the letter David had written to his daughter, Mary, in the stack he had recently read.

Do our choices define our destiny? Can we change course?

It was difficult to make the transition from David's world to his, except for his complete understanding of the trauma of war that had affected them both with such force.

How do we become better fathers to our daughters, David?

He set aside the stack of letters and picked up the textbook he should have been studying for his paramedic certification. He was gratified to realize his medic training in the army had given him an advantage. The most important things he needed to review were recent developments in the emergency medical field.

As he found his place in the book, Scooter leapt off the bed and sniffed at the door, then began his friendly bark of greeting. "Who is it boy? What are you trying to tell me?" He walked to the door and looked through the side window without being seen. Lindsay! She was pacing the little porch, then stood in front of the door, put out her hand as if to knock, then turned and began to walk away. Scooter looked from the door to Steven as if to say, "Come on you dope, open the door!"

"Okay boy, you can be our official greeter" As he opened the door, Scooter bounded down the walk, barking happily as he danced around Lindsay. She crouched down and gave the dog a hug as Steven watched from the porch.

Keep your distance.

"I didn't think you were home until I heard Scooter bark." She walked hesitantly toward the house.

"Anything I can do?" He closed the front door behind him to hide the mess of papers and books.

"Steven, I need your help. I – I need to harvest some potatoes and take them to Anna for the stew she's making for tomorrow's lunch. I think she's still got plenty of carrots, thanks to you and Richie."

"Need some help? I'll get the bushel basket and we'll load them up in no time."

"No, that's not it. I – I'm afraid to go back in the garden. I know it's stupid to be so afraid, but maybe if I could take Scooter with me, he could be my point guard and alert me to anything crawling in the dirt. I keep seeing that thing slithering toward me."

"It's not stupid, Lindsay. I understand, I really do. Irrational fear can be paralyzing. Believe me, I know."

"Doesn't sound like you're afraid of anything. You've healed wounded men, you've been shot at, poisonous snakes..."

"Fear is different for all of us. What's easy for you might be daunting for me. The thought of getting up in front of a bunch of people to teach them genealogy or history – whew – that terrifies me. You're not alone, believe me."

"But that's easy. You just have to know stuff and be informed. It's not like being shot at or spit at by a poisonous..."

"Oh, yes we *were* spit at, Lindsay. Even worse, by *people*. They picketed us when we came home. You *know* that. Poison comes in different forms. You know your history, you remember what it was like for veterans when we came back from that godforsaken war. Facing that hate felt like confronting poisonous minds. Most civilians thought we were murderers, killers of children and drug addicts. They weren't so wrong either." He paused and swallowed to get control of his voice. "We learned to drown it out – got so soused we didn't care."

"It's hard to share our fears, isn't it? I feel like such a fool.

My fear of snakes is probably irrational."

"No, we all have groundless fears. I'll tell you one of my fears, one of my secrets." He sat on the porch steps and motioned for her to join him. He patted the wood steps and Scooter hopped between them. "Maybe you won't feel so foolish, or at least you'll know you're not the only one who feels that way."

What am I doing?

He took a deep breath. "Sometimes, I try hard to keep my eyes propped open at night so I won't fall asleep, for fear I'll have more nightmares about the war."

Lindsay reached out to touch his arm as he instinctively backed away. Palm forward, he stretched out his arm, keeping her at a distance.

"Okay, I get it, Steven. No sympathy, no acceptance, no understanding allowed."

"It's not that, it's just – it's just so hard to set it right."

"Never mind. I came here to ask for help, not to argue."

She stood and patted Scooter. "It always seems to turn out that way, doesn't it?"

As he stood beside her, Lindsay looked up at him with sadness. "I'll leave you be. May I borrow Scooter for a few minutes? He'll keep me safe, won't he?"

"Not sure. He seems to be friendly with all the animals he's been around. I don't think he would hurt anyone or any other animal. He's a good alert dog, but not an attack dog. Come on – I'll take you out to the garden. We'll do it together."

"Really? That's – thanks Steven."

They grabbed the shovels leaning against the fence and walked along the rows of vegetables, as Lindsay led him to the plot of potatoes. "Here they are. We should be able to get them out easily." As she leaned over to pick the potatoes, the pile of leaves moved and a snake appeared along the path. Scooter began to bark and the snake moved into the underbrush. Lindsay screamed and grabbed Steven's arm, dragging him away from the snake.

"See, it came back. Get me out of here." She tried to run, but Steven held her hand tight and forced her to stay.

He took her by the shoulders and turned her back to him to face the snake, holding on so she couldn't run. "Now, look. What do you see? It's the same snake we saw the other day, same size, same coloring. He's harmless, I promise. He's not venomous and he isn't interested in making a meal of you. Snakes are generally very shy and they don't attack unless they're provoked. This is a benign king snake. He won't hurt you." The snake changed direction and headed toward them.

"Look out!" She cried, as she turned toward Steven and pushing her face into his chest she started to shake. He tried to turn her around to confront the snake, but she refused to move, digging her nose into his shoulder.

"Lindsay look, he won't hurt you." She cautiously turned and watched the snake slither away, seemingly oblivious to their existence. She turned her head and took a deep breath of air, peeked out from the comfort of his chest and looked up at Steven. Their eyes met – he saw passion in hers, as his reflected sorrow. As she began to move her face toward his,

Steven took her gently by the shoulders and created distance between them.

As he let go, he said, "I – I can't. I don't know if I can... It's – I'm not ready. Too much baggage, too messed up. I – I'm sorry, Lindsay."

He turned his back, picked up the shovel and began to dig.

Lindsay remained rooted where she stood and spoke to his back. "No, Steven, not this time. You're not going to run off, or turn away from me anymore. You must have a pretty good idea of how I feel about you – God knows why, since you've been so obvious in your rejection..."

Steven whirled around and faced her. "This has nothing to do with you, Lindsay. It's me – it's *my* pile of baggage, it's *my* messed up life, the mistakes I've made, people who died on my watch and the people I've hurt – you included. I can't get past the memories."

"So why can't you share any of your worries. I can be a good listener, I promise. I'm a good sounding board."

"If you only knew..."

"What? Knew what?" She reached out to touch his hand as he backed away.

"Not now. I can't."

"Can't what – be close – to anyone? Can't share your fears and sorrows with me? Is that it?"

"I said, not now, Lindsay."

"Okay, I give up – for now. I have loads of patience. I'll wait...for a bit.

"It's just that...I'm afraid that...if you really knew me, you'd be the one running like hell...away from me and my messed-up life. And I wouldn't blame you."

"No Steven. Don't say that." Lindsay stepped closer. "Try me – tell me something that you think will drive me away. Come on – try me."

"No, I...said not now."

"I'm not giving up on you, Steven. Don't ask me why. You sure don't make it easy to lo...to care about you." As she looked up at him, her eyes pooled with tears. She grabbed the shovel from him, turned away and started digging.

Steven took her gently by the shoulders and turned her toward him. He pulled her into an embrace and her arms dove around his waist as she held on tight, not letting go.

Looking up at him, she said, "I could be your comfort, Steven. Let me in your life."

He looked down at her sorrowful face and stepped back. "I...I can't begin to tell you how much those words mean to me, but you don't know me. I'm so afraid...if you knew me...I don't deserve you."

"Give me a chance, Steven."

He took a deep breath, stepped back from the warmth of her embrace, took both her hands in his and said, "Give me some time. I've got to finish what I started. I'm taking the paramedic exams next week; I've got to concentrate and pass the test. And I've got a family mess to clean up and apologies to make."

Lindsay started to speak as he pressed one finger gently to her lips.

"Let me start with you. I apologize for the way I've treated you. I'm sorry I keep arguing with you and running off to avoid confrontation, or closeness or whatever the hell I'm afraid of. There are things you need to know about me. You need to know I am not a good guy. I've hurt people and can't guarantee I won't hurt you. Use that good brain of yours to realize I'm not the best person for...Lindsay, listen to me – you deserve better."

"And I'll say it again, Steven. I'm volunteering...my choice...let me be your comfort."

"I'm not worthy of you, Lindsay." He turned away, reaching for the other shovel.

Lindsay grabbed him by the shoulder, forcing him to face her. "I won't believe that until you let me see who you are."

He gave her a doubtful smile. "Okay...well maybe. You'll see and you'll run like hell."

She threw up her hands in a gesture of surrender. "Okay, fair enough. Hand me the shovel and I'll start digging...for potatoes..."

He laughed. "It's about time."

Chapter

39

March 25, 1892
Soldiers and Sailors Home
Sandusky, Ohio

My Dear Daughter,
It is with great trepidation that I
answer the questions you have asked
about my life. Please understand, my
dear Mary, that I make no claim to
your pity and have no right to ask for
forgiveness. The dreadful deeds your
mother would accuse of me are true.

The War took a terrible toll on us
all. I know of no man who did not
suffer greatly and no soldier who would

not have preferred an early grave to the agony endured during and after that atrocious war. This is the awful truth you have begged to know: most of the medical staff on the battlefields had easy access to alcohol, because it was often the solution for anesthesia when we ran out of chloroform; and morphine was the most common painkiller. We craved the means to deaden our own pain as well.

We did not realize how addictive morphine could be, nor how easily alcohol calmed our suffering. Many of us quickly found ourselves dependent on the very analgesic meant to help the wounded soldiers.

Yes, I admit, the War was barely behind me when I began medical school. I could not have explained my impulsive decision at the time, yet naively believed I would learn new methods to cure disease and live a noble, useful life. I deluded myself into believing I could become a healer of men, when my true, *unconscious goal was to gain continued access to the drugs we provided to our patients.*

Your mother is not lying to you. I was a despicable man and she had every right to throw me out and deny my rights as a husband and a father.

I have no right to forgiveness, yet I now ask for your mercy. I have failed as a father and will go to my grave praying for redemption.

Your sorrowful father,
David Lane

Steven sat completely still, sickened by the revelations divulged in the letter. He realized this was the explanation he had been waiting for: the answer to David Lane's cruel separation from his children. He was the architect of his own downfall.

We create our own disgrace.

Steven ached for the broken man with whom he felt so much in common.

The wounds of war. Not so different after all.

The revelation brought Steven full circle – to the consequences of David Lane's ruin. The rejection from his family was followed by the inevitable isolation and inability to receive forgiveness or support.

David's permanent estrangement from his family, as declared in the divorce decree, brought secrets and suffering to his children, Mary and George. Steven realized Anna's father, George, never knew what had happened to his father. It would have been considered a family disgrace. He probably heard whisperings but was too young to understand. The family may have hoped, with the mother's remarriage, that George would forget about his loss. Yet, it seemed he continued to grieve over the parent he had lost and lived out his life as an angry, resentful man. This is what Anna had sensed about her father and why the suffering continued to the next generation.

From the many letters Steven had discovered, it was clear that George's sister Mary had desperately tried to reconcile with her father. This letter proved that she had persisted in a yearning to understand what had happened to her father. Was the confession in the letter ever delivered? Did Mary ever learn the full extent of her father's disgrace?

Steven patted his breast pocket as he carried the letter to Joe's Café to meet with Sam. He needed a wise sounding board. He was determined to be different from David Lane. As he approached the café, Steven was knocked aside as Craig crashed out the door. The smell of stale alcohol overpowered the aroma of fresh coffee beans.

"There you are, you asshole!" Craig lunged at Steven and lost his footing.

Steven stepped back, unwilling to replay their last ugly encounter. "Don't..."

"Where's my son? What have you done with Richie?"

"What are you talking about, Craig? I haven't seen him since he started school."

Craig turned into the wall of the building and began pounding his head against the bricks. Steven twisted him by the shoulders, forcing Craig to face him.

Dr. Sam rushed around the corner and appeared by their side.

"What happened?"

"I...well I..."

"Talk to us, Craig," Doc insisted.

"Well, I got pissed. My parents wouldn't let me see Richie until I...until I...well, you know."

"No, we don't know. Tell us." Doc approached him gently, then placed his hand on Craig's shoulder.

"My parents refused to let me near my boy until I stopped drinking and got a job. So far, that hasn't happened. So...so I got mad and went to Richie's school anyway and waited till he came out. I tried to talk to him, make him understand how much I..." Craig's voice cracked as he continued. "When I ran up to him and gave him a hug, he backed away and started hollering at me – told me I stunk of booze and he hated me and didn't want another parent who smelled like his mother." Craig sobbed as he slid down the wall until he collapsed on the sidewalk.

"There's more, isn't there?" Doc said. "Tell us the rest."

"He…said he wished Steven was his father, and he never wanted to see me again. He…he said this time *he* was going to abandon *me*. He twisted out of my arms and ran away."

"I'm sorry, Craig," Steven said. "You know I wouldn't encourage Richie to do that." He took hold of Craig's arms and helped him rise until he was standing.

"So, he's not at your place?"

"It's a small cottage, Craig. No, I promise you…"

"Where would he go?"

"Anna's?"

"No," Doc said. "I talked to her last night. She would have told me."

Steven gave Sam a knowing look, turned back to Craig and said, "He must have gone back to his grandparent's house."

"Exactly, otherwise the Johnsons would have contacted me if he hadn't come home from school," Doc said.

Joe cracked the door open and poked his head out. "Stay out of my place, Craig. You were way out of line, stomping around, accusing me of hiding Richie. Steven, get him out of here. I've got customers, man. Do you think they're going to come back with some crazy guy on the loose?"

"Okay, I'll go." Craig turned to leave, as Joe went back inside.

"Wait one second," Steven said. He grabbed Craig by the shoulder. "How did you get here, in your truck?"

"Well, duh!"

"Cut the hostility, Craig. Let's see, you've had – how much to drink? And you're driving around town in your truck? What the hell, man!"

376

"So – what's it to you?"

"You shit. Remember that accident I told you about in front of Anna's? The guy who caused the crash and died was still holding a bottle of vodka. The car he hit had a mother and baby! If that was you, who do you think would raise your son?"

Craig flipped up his arm in a gesture of disgust and began to walk off.

"Come back here you jerk. Listen to me."

Craig turned around – red-faced and belligerent. "What?"

"How would you feel if Richie had been in that car? You're driving drunk, Craig. How close are you to causing an accident that might kill someone's child?"

"I'm...but it's where I *live*. My truck, it's my only bed. How can I give it up?"

"That's not the point."

Doc chimed in. "Think about it, Craig. What if you're stopped when you've been drinking? What if you get a DUI? The odd jobs you still manage to get will be gone, because you'll be in jail. Is that really what you want? Then you'll lose your son forever."

"What the hell am I supposed to do?"

"The answer is obvious," Doc said. "Make a commitment to stop drinking – now – this minute. Find the nearest AA meeting and promise yourself you'll go – every day. Then, you'd be driving sober."

"I don't know if I can do it."

Steven said, "I didn't know if I could either. But I did. You have to try."

"How did you do it?"

"I'm not saying it's easy. It's not. I got to a place where I hated the face looking back at me in the mirror. I couldn't stand myself. I knew something had to change."

"Pretty much how I feel now. And when I realize how much Richie hates me, it's...it's..."

"I really do understand," Steven assured him. "And I know how tough it is. Hey, remember Joe's story about Doc pulling him out of the gutter – literally? I know he could help. Go in there and talk to Joe. Ask him for help."

"He's not going to let me in. You heard him." He gestured to Sam. "I've got Doc right here. He can tell me." He leaned toward Sam. "You can help me, can't you Doc?"

Sam put both hands on Craig's chest and pushed him in the direction of the café. "This is one thing you have to do for yourself, Craig. I didn't do anything for Joe. At the end of the day, he saved himself."

"But how?"

"Go ask him," Steven said. "You don't know, till you try. Ask him how he did it. He's accomplished a lot. He found a purpose. Look at this café. This is his. Go ask him how he did it."

"He's really mad at me. I don't think he'll let me in."

"Joe will ply you full of coffee until you're sober enough to safely drive to AA."

"Not funny."

"It wasn't meant to be."

Steven put a gentle hand on Craig's shoulder. "Come on, I'll go with you." Steven turned and mouthed a 'thank you' to

Doc, then turned Craig around so he faced away from the truck and toward the door to Joe's Café.

They walked in together.

Chapter

40

(Undated)

Soldiers and Sailors Home
Sandusky, Ohio

   To my family,
How do I tell you how truly sorry
I am for the sins I have committed
and the pain I have caused?

   It is with deep regret that I write
with heart in hand to sincerely apologize
to you, my beloved family. I have failed
as a soldier, as a doctor, a husband and
most tragically, I have failed as a

father. I have caused the suffering of so many.

I would give up most anything to have you in my life as I reach the end...

Steven bolted upright. Papers scattered as Scooter yelped.

A letter of apology. Steven wondered if David had ever mailed it. He realized it was unfinished. The letter had no date.

What had he said to Craig during their latest row? "And while you're at it, why don't you apologize to your family."

Listen to your own advice, you hypocrite.

Steven paced the room. Five long strides and he reached the opposite wall. An apology. *Shouldn't I be doing the same?*

"Come on, Scooter. Let's find your favorite bush. I'll take you for a walk later, I've got business to take care of." They walked along the rows of vegetables, heading for the bushes and trees at the back of the property. Steven noted the straight, clean lines, ready for the next planting of carrot seeds. He could see Lindsay had been working in the garden, preparing for the next harvest. When had she been here? He had been in EMT classes for a month. He'd been so focused on learning protocol for paramedics, he had barely noticed the back of the cottage.

"Scooter, has Lindsay been to visit?" The dog popped his head up. He never locked the door when he was gone, or when his oh-so vicious guard dog was in attendance. Maybe she realized Scooter was alone and let him out for a little run. He could tell she'd been working. The garden reflected Lindsay's skill with a shovel and care for the harvest.

~ ~ ~

Steven gave a wave as Gladys looked up from her work at the library's front desk. She beckoned to him. He knew better than to deny this shrewd woman.

"Well, look who's back. Glad to see you, Steven. You're looking good – even combed your hair this morning. Got a hot date?"

Steven blushed. "No, not exactly."

"You look a little lost, young man. Can I help? I'm good with directions and advice, and nagging, of course."

"Lost is a good description, Gladys. I'm in need of advice. Solemn advice. No nagging," Steven said.

"My, my – this sounds serious." She patted the chair next to the desk.

Steven flopped down and leaned forward to speak softly.

"I don't know what to do. If I follow my instincts, and am completely honest with..."

"With?"

"Honesty can come back to haunt you. Maybe this isn't the best time. Right now, I think it would be better to take a flying leap toward the door and get out of here while I still can."

"But then you aren't following your best instincts, are you Steven? Have you heard that expression – from the Civil War – I think Lincoln said it – 'The better angels of our nature' – do what's right. I think that's what he meant."

"Not so easy."

"Of course not. But you can't go wrong when you do what's right. And guess who said that?" She laughed and raised her hand straight into the air. "Me! I just said it. Pretty clever, aren't I."

Steven jumped up from his seat. "Don't make this into a joke, Gladys. Please, I'm..."

"Okay. I'm sorry. Just trying to lighten your load, Steven. I've known plenty of men trying to get Vietnam out of their heads." She patted the desk. "Come on. Tell me why you're worried."

Steven sat back down and hesitated. He looked into her eyes and took a ragged breath. "Here's my dilemma. How do you give someone information that – uh – if you tell them, there's a pretty good chance you'll lose their friendship, even worse, their respect."

"I don't understand. Are you asking if it's better to be honest, no matter what?"

"I guess that's what I mean."

"Well, I don't know about the rest of the world, but I'd take honest any day. It's worth the risk because you also must be honest with yourself. You still have to face yourself in the mirror. Remember those better angels?"

"But what if I risk being honest, admit what an awful person I am and..."

"Really? You're an awful person? Hard to imagine."

"This is serious, Gladys."

"I know, and I guarantee you – it's worth the risk. Now

hurry on up to Lindsay's office before her seminar starts."

Steven's mouth dropped open.

Gladys stood up and took him by the shoulders. "Go. Risk it, Steven. I believe in you. And I know you're a good person, no matter what you think – I *know*." Steven gave her a quick hug and hurried to the stairs.

~   ~   ~

Without thinking or knocking, Steven walked into Lindsay's office. He thought he might drop to the floor his knees felt so weak. He stood in the doorway and clung to the frame.

"Steven! What? Come on in."

"Look Lindsay, I've got to talk to you. There's things you need to know, and..."

He quickly slipped into the chair in front of her desk before she could see him shaking.

Oh, what I'd give for a shot of vodka – just one shot.

"Steven, what's the matter..."

"Don't talk, Lindsay. I need to..."

"But..."

"I need to tell you..."

Lindsay leaned across the desk and reached for Steven, as if she could help him get the words out.

"Oh, Steven..."

"Don't say a word." He held on to her hand. "It's – I have to be honest with you. You need to know who I really am, what kind of man – I've tried to tell you, Lindsay. I'm not a good person. You need to know..."

"But..."

He let go, put his hand out, palm forward. "Stop. Just listen."

Lindsay stayed silent as her hands continued to stretch toward him.

Steven's hand started to shake. He brought it down below the desk and held his hands together, as if in prayer. He began to speak.

"I have a child. I didn't know it for a long time and when I found out, I didn't try to find them, never tried to help them. I ignored them, as if they didn't exist. Just kept doing what I do – sat around hating what I had become – who I am. The mother of my child told me I didn't deserve to be a father. She was right." Lindsay looked straight into his eyes and didn't flinch.

"There's more." He paused and took a deep breath. "I've let men die. I was a medic. I was supposed to be saving people but was out getting roaring drunk instead. Who knows how many soldiers were lost because I wasn't there to help them. My best friend drowned. I'm a good swimmer and I couldn't save him. I can't get all their suffering out of my head – all those soldiers. I can't forgive myself."

Lindsay stayed silent as tears spilled down her face.

"And there's my father. I could have killed him – so many times. He's a hateful, cruel person. I think I'm brutal enough to kill him. My mother left him – left us. I can't blame her. I must be more like him – damaged – hateful."

Lindsay leapt from her chair and pulled him to his feet. "No, Steven. No, no, no! You're not. You are a good man, filled with kindness. I see you. I know you." She took him by the shoulders and held him to her.

They stood together, holding each other – shaking.

She stepped back, took both his hands and looked up at Steven. "Thank you for telling me. I'm truly grateful you have trusted me."

She reached up, held his head in both her hands and kissed him gently. "There is nothing you can say that will make me love you less."

Chapter

41

... I have failed as a soldier, as a doctor, a husband and most tragically, I have failed as a father. I have caused the suffering of so many ...

David's grief continued to haunt Steven, distracting him as he hauled the pots of minestrone off Craig's truck in front of the Open Heart Kitchen. He studied Craig who seemed to have shed the hostility that usually enveloped him. Did he reconcile with his parents? Can we stay sober so easily? Steven wondered. Unlikely.

He leaned in closer to identify the scent of beer. No alcohol today. "Thanks, Craig. Leave your truck here for now. Could you help me get the pots to the kitchen so we can start heating up the soup?"

"Right behind you, man."

Steven watched his friend, who lifted the pots with ease and realized how different Craig was when he wasn't working on his third beer.

"I'll help Anna unload her car. She was following right behind us with the bread and cheese. Let me show you how to turn on the stove and start the soup."

"Give me a little credit, Steven. I'm not a complete idiot."

"Sorry, didn't mean to be insulting. I can't tell you how many guys I know who are lost in a kitchen."

"Ya know? I'm lost in a lot of ways, but I know how to turn on a stove. Didn't I tell you what my job was in Nam?"

"No..."

"I worked in the mess. That's why it's so funny that you had Richie peeling carrots. I've bloodied a few knuckles, myself."

"No way!"

"Remember when I told you about being on patrol and my fear of snakes. That was the beginning of my downfall in the U.S. Army. It got so bad they demoted me and stuck me with KP duty from then on."

"How'd that happen?"

"The last time I came face-to-face with this giant Python, I screamed bloody hell. The platoon leader was furious that I'd put our guys in danger, making so much noise, and wanted to send me home with a dishonorable discharge. I was terrified of the Viet Cong and terrified of being in Vietnam, so sending me home sounded fine to me. Instead they demoted me to the kitchen and it wasn't all that bad. I felt safe with four walls around me instead of fighting out in the jungle."

"I had all the food I wanted, and it gave me access to guys who supplied all kinds of illegal booze and drugs. You wouldn't believe how much stuff came in, hidden in with the food deliveries." They unloaded the pots.

"Oh, yes I would."

"But none of that stash numbed me enough to sooth my fears. I've been terrified of snakes ever since. I'll settle for being the kitchen guy."

"And now we've got an expert, someone who knows how to prepare food for large numbers. We've got the perfect person to help us. We just need to keep you clean, away from the booze," Steven said. "Hope Joe can help you."

"He's a good guy. Man, it's lousy what he's been through."

Anna walked in with an armload of bread. "Let's go, gentlemen. I thought someone was going to come out and help me. No dawdling. We've got a lunch to serve."

Steven saluted. "Yes, Ma'am. I'll get the rest out of your car."

They hauled the last pot onto the stove.

"Wouldn't those Civil War soldiers have been grateful. All this food," Steven said.

"Right now," Anna said, "let's concentrate on the families and children right here."

Steven looked at her with disbelief. "You sure are cranky today."

"Sorry. I had unpleasant visitors this morning. They made me angry and late."

"Never thought you could be bad-tempered, Anna."

"Oh, I'm just full of surprises. I never claimed to be

perfect. Now, let's get the show on the road."

Steven cocked his head, then dropped the inquiry as Doctor Sam walked in with hunks of cheese and distributed them around the tables. Steven leaned toward Sam as they set the table. "Hey Doc, you're never going to believe this. Our boy Craig learned how to be a cook in the army's mess. I think I know just the place for him," Steven said, cocking his head toward the kitchen.

"Perfect solution," Doc chuckled. "We'll keep him so busy, he won't have a chance to get himself in trouble. Let's see if he can take some of the load off Anna." They distributed the silverware. "I got close enough for a quick sniff. He smells like soap – he must have showered. Did you stay with him last week? Where did he go after he talked to Joe?"

"I tried to stay out of it, but I think Joe convinced him to talk to his parents and beg for forgiveness. He promised to start AA meetings. When he left the café, he was stone-cold sober. Probably didn't sleep for days considering the amount of coffee we plied him with."

Sam laughed. "Craig needs a place to call home and a family who cares about him. So does Richie. Maybe they can finally learn to be a family."

Steven blinked and took in a breath. "Oh, don't we all."

Sam looked up and jabbed him with the end of a fork. "Hey, in case you haven't noticed, you've already got a family, Steven. We're just not blood-related."

Steven reached out and put his hand on Sam's shoulder. "It means a lot to hear you say that. Thanks, my friend."

"Just tellin' it like it is."

"Let's add Anna to our little clan. I know she's got sons, but they're no support."

"Of course," Sam said. "She and I have been 'family' for years."

"Oh, really?"

"Yes, really. I'll tell you all about it someday. Let's go, folks are starting to line up at the door."

~　　~　　~

After everyone had been served, Steven dished up the remaining soup for the volunteers. He looked out at the rows of tables, filled with families and veterans, children with single mothers. For the first time he saw there were shopping carts lined up outside, five - filled with the meager belongings of the homeless. Steven wondered how far they had walked to find food.

This was me not so long ago. How did I manage to find my way to the other side of it?

As he set a bowl of soup in front of Anna, he suddenly felt a presence behind him and a tender touch on his shoulder. He whipped around and found Lindsay wearing a crooked grin and dirty overalls. She wiped her hands on the back of her dungarees, examined them front and back, and shrugged.

"Hi everyone," she called out. "Any chance there's enough soup left to feed your local gardener?"

"Comin' right up," Craig said.

"Everyone squeeze left and make room on the bench," Steven commanded as he patted the space next to him. Lindsay leaned toward Steven with her hands raised for examination then headed for the kitchen to wash off the dirt.

Steven grinned when Sam's eyes widened as he nudged Anna.

She looked up and smiled at Steven. "It's about time, Mister."

Steven blushed and ran his fingers along his mouth as if it were a zipper.

"Okay, I'm filling the awkward silence," Sam said. As Lindsay slipped into the space on the bench, he asked, "Need any help in the garden? We've got a couple of very able-bodied men here."

"Not today," she said. "As you know, Richie helped harvest the carrots, and a couple of weeks ago Steven and Scooter helped me when our resident snake showed up. I get hysterical around snakes. Steven seemed to want to make him a pet, said he was good for the garden."

"It's true, they are." Steven said.

Now it was Anna's turn to nudge Sam. She gave him a look as if to say, 'How come you haven't told me about these two?' He shrugged and changed the subject again.

"Hey, Steven. How are the EMT classes?"

"Going well, thanks. It's amazing how much my time in 'Nam counts, even when half of it was spent passed out."

"Steven!" Anna cautioned in a sharp tone.

"Never mind, Anna. You can't protect me from myself. It's time to be up front and honest. They're never going to pass me at school unless they know my true war background. Evidently, there are some men who are beyond redemption. Their brains are pickled and they can't be helped."

"But surely not you," Anna protested.

"Strange as it may seem – no – not me. The EMT system

requires a battery of neurological tests. We have to show we can sustain stress and keep our head straight in emergencies."

Craig stood, raised both hands and clapped them in the air. "Mighty fine, brother. I salute you." And he did.

"I've still got a way to go, so no cheering yet. I've got to pass a written test and a physical test. Then we become paramedics-in-training."

Lindsay asked, "But you've already spent four years as a medic, after two years of med school. Doesn't that count?"

"I'm sure it does, but that was years ago. Lots of new stuff to learn, and..." Steven went rigid as he stared at the entry door. His father had shown up and was slowly walking among the table of veterans, examining each face.

Steven put his hand over Lindsay's. "Something I have to deal with. Be right back." She looked toward the door, squeezed his hand, then let him go.

~   ~   ~

His father had turned to leave. "Well, looky here. Haven't you cleaned up so pretty. Doubt it will help your prospects, but hey, it's a start."

A group of veterans who sat at the front table turned to watch the exchange.

"What are you doing here?"

"Well, I – I thought I'd come find you – give you another chance. Maybe let you come back home. You know, get you off the streets."

"I don't need your charity. I'm doing very well, thank you."

"Oh yeah? So which shopping cart is yours, Steven? Who

do you think you're kidding?"

"Fuck you, Mister," said a vet who stood up to face Steven's father. "Let's show him."

Four men wearily raised themselves from their seats at the table. Each one walked outside and stood by a cart.

The veteran said, "That empty shopping cart is mine. Steven doesn't need one. He works here. He helps us and feeds us."

"Yeah, sure," snapped his father.

"It's true, you jerk," said the veteran, who then turned toward Steven. "One word from you and I'd be happy to hurt him, if you want me to."

Steven suppressed a grin and held up his hand in a signal to cease. He moved directly in front of his father, then took his arm and led him to the door. "You are not welcome here. Please leave."

"But..."

"If the day ever comes when you're able to see me through a different lens, we could use more support around here. A volunteer dishwasher would be helpful."

Several men raised their hands and hollered, "I'll do it, I'll help!"

Steven leaned into his father to make sure he was heard over the shouting. "I am no longer willing to take your shit. See yourself out."

Chapter

42

It is with deep regret that I write with heart in hand to sincerely apologize to you ...

Steven set down the letter. He looked reverently at the words and realized this must be a letter of apology David Lane had written to his family, or his children – it wasn't addressed to anyone. It seemed like a draft.

This is the letter I should write. My apology. Sharon deserves at least that much.

He continued reading David's draft.

I have wronged you mightily, and confess I am completely at fault for our troubles and estrangement. The divorce, which was forced upon me, might never have happened if I had found the courage to be honest with those I loved. Had I not been forgiven, I would at least have gone to my grave knowing I had told you everything. Instead I kept silent — until now. The cruel consequence of divorce and years of rejection, of losing my children, has been more than I can bear.

It is time for truth-telling, while there is still time.

As I have confessed, while serving in the army, I became addicted to a craving for alcohol and it has shadowed me throughout my life. After the war, I was determined to turn my life around, be a better man, and so I entered medical school. I wanted to heal people, not watch soldiers die on my table. I wished to be an authentic doctor.

After I received my degree, the fear of making mistakes sent me back to the embrace of the bottle. I was terrified of losing one more patient after so many soldiers had died by what I believed to be my neglect.

I recognize this sad irony, and yet it is the truth.

I was told by many of my fellow doctors that I was a gifted surgeon, yet inside I shuddered with terror. They thought I was exceptional. I knew otherwise. As if fulfilling my own dreadful prophesy, the unimaginable happened. I caused a spinal injury to a young man. I reduced him to a cripple. I have never forgiven myself.

When it became clear he would never walk again, I put down my scalpel and was determined to never harm another soul or perform another surgical procedure. I gave up the practice of medicine. I gave up on myself. As penance for my sins, I supported this *man throughout his painful life until the day he died.*

I alone caused his misery, but I was never able to confess this sin to a living soul.

Because I had no other means of income, I began siphoning off enough from our family estate to support this poor man and tried my best to make amends. Eventually the thefts were discovered, and I was banished from the family and shunned for the remainder of my life, never to see my children again. I was so ashamed, I couldn't bear to show up at court.

I have never known how to confess...

Steven let go of his tight grip on the letter and watched it float to the floor. He ached for this broken man and wished he could comfort him. He searched for a second sheet of paper and realized he had been through most of the letters – only a few were left. The confession was incomplete. The letter had never been sent.

The phone by his little desk began to ring. He wasn't

prepared to talk with anyone, least of all Anna. Should he tell her about her grandfather, or just burn the letter? Which was worse? What would she want? The phone continued to ring and Steven reluctantly picked it up.

"Yes, hello."

"Yes, indeed. That's the right answer. Yes!"

"Excuse me, who is this?" Steven asked.

"Oh, sorry. I thought you'd recognize my voice. It's your paramedic instructor, Jim. Remember me?"

"Oh, sure. Sorry. I was so involved in..."

"No problem. I wanted to call you myself and give you the good news. You passed, Steven. You passed with flying, sparkling colors. Congratulations."

"Oh – wow – I'm a little surprised. I've had so much crazy stuff going on..."

"Never mind, I understand. Despite your distractions, you're on your way, Steven."

"Thanks. So, what do I do next?"

"Ordinarily, you'd apply to various firehouses for internships, you know – on-the-job training, and you'd wait till one of them hired you. But you've already been selected by the firehouse here in town. I guess they've been clamoring for you and they requested you by name before you even took the test."

"That's great. They're a good bunch of guys."

"You're slated to start next Monday. So, you might want to stop by before then and have them show you the ropes. You'll be going 'live' when you officially begin next week."

"Okay. Will do. And thanks for calling. It means a lot."

What the hell, I did it!

Steven flopped down on the bed and smiled at the ceiling.

"Hey, Scooter. You're going to be a firehouse dog. We're going to help save people. Sound good to you?" The dog opened one eye, curled into a ball and continued his slumber.

Steven jumped up and retrieved the letter. He was struck by the vast difference between John's phone call and David's letter. He realized how lucky he was – he had managed to get beyond the grip of addiction and maybe he could be on the other end of healing. And helping. And saving.

What am I waiting for? I will not be like David. No holding back.

"Hey, Scooter. Wake up! Let's go. We've got to start now."

Scooter scrambled to his feet and ran to the door. "Okay, that's more like it. And no more walking. All this studying and we're both getting lazy. I think we'd better start running, I know you can run – and you're best at racing through traffic. Let's see what kind of shape we're in – maybe we'll start by jogging. Okay?" Scooter gave a happy "woof, woof" – his signature bark.

"Let's go."

~   ~   ~

Automatic pilot landed them at Anna's driveway. Steven hesitated as they approached the house. There were two cars in front. He recognized one as Doc's but the other was a mystery. "Come on, Scooter. Maybe this isn't a good time. Let's keep going." He tugged on the leash as the dog tried to lead him to the front door.

402

Steven slowed their pace and reluctantly walked past the house that had become his second home. Suddenly, he heard shouting as the front door slammed and two men raced down the walkway. The door flew open again and Sam raced down the porch shaking his fist at the men running to their car.

Sam yelled, "Your mother doesn't deserve this cruel treatment from you two. How can you walk out on the best woman I know? Never mind, go ahead and leave – I'll take good care of her." The two men jumped into the car, which shot down the street and out of sight. As Sam turned toward the front door, he looked in Steven's direction, raised an arm in the air as if to wave, then grabbed the railing and pulled himself up the steps to the front door.

"Come on, Scooter." Steven led the dog back to the house and ran up the steps. "What the hell, Sam?"

"Come on in," Sam said, his voice a whisper of despair. "Anna could use our support right about now." They eased into the living room and found Anna rocking back and forth, holding onto her cat, Tom, weeping into his fur as if her heart would break. The two men slipped onto the sofa and sat on either side of her, looked at each other with dismay, unsure how to comfort her. Scooter began to howl in sympathy. Tom leapt from her arms and scurried under the sofa. The howling hit a new pitch. "AuOuuuu!" The two men looked at one another and began to giggle as the dog continued his sympathetic cry. Before long they were all in tears of laughter.

"This is ridiculous," Steven said. "Scooter, hush." The minute Anna stopped crying, the dog stopped howling. They looked at each other as if they'd declared an unspoken truce. "I didn't mean to intrude, Anna. Sam said to come in."

She dried her wet face with the flat of her hand. "I'm glad to have you here, Steven. Right now, what I need most is my two best men, and I don't mean my sons.

Steven went to the kitchen and brought her a glass of water. "Want something stronger?"

She smiled. "Maybe later. I think I have a bottle of sherry in there somewhere – for emergencies like this."

"What happened?" Steven asked. "Or maybe you don't want to talk about it."

"You tell him, Sam."

"Are you sure?"

She nodded.

"Anna and I have decided to get married."

"Well, what do you know! So that *was* your car I saw in the driveway the other night." Steven gave Sam a knowing nod. "It was dark, and I wasn't sure. You devil! That's wonderful."

"Well, my sons don't think so," Anna said.

Sam took up the charge. "They were downright hostile to the idea. They seem to think Anna has a stash of cash somewhere in this old house and she's hiding it from them."

"Would I be living in this ole' house if I had money?"

Sam turned toward Anna and took her hand, as Tom and Jerry together hopped back onto her lap. Scooter put his chin on Anna's knee. Sam laughed. "I think Scooter wants to cuddle on your lap, too. And all this time I thought my competition was going to be your sons!" He turned to Steven. "I've been courting this good woman forever. We've become

404

our own private support system. We're good together and good *to* each other."

Anna blushed and continued. "We thought it would be a good idea to invite my sons over for a nice dinner and give them the news together. I kept hoping this time they might see how we could be a family and they'd be grateful of how good Sam has been to me."

"Right! One big happy family. Well, you saw what they thought of that idea," Sam said.

"It's my own fault," Anna said. "First I spoiled them when they were little and when their father died, I went into such a terrible time of grief – they must have felt so neglected."

Steven took her other hand and said shyly, "I would be proud to be your family. You've been the best..." Anna hung her head and the tears flowed.

Sam jumped up and dug into the pantry for the sherry. "Who's ready for some?" He called from the kitchen.

"Oh, yes please," Anna said between sobs.

"Not for me," Steven called back. "Although I must admit, a beer sounds good."

Sam returned with the sherry. "Do you drink alcohol, Steven? I've never seen you touch a drop."

"Occasionally. I'm trying to be a good role model for Craig. I was lucky. I can drink in moderation and not feel compelled to go back for more. Unlike my poor mother who became addicted and, I guess, should never have another sip."

"Well, be careful. Those inherited addictions can be tricky. If your mother has a problem, pay attention to your own cravings."

"I know. Especially now that I'll have all this new responsibility at the firehouse. Don't worry, Sam. I'm aware."

Anna took a slow, grateful sip of the sherry, followed by a deep sigh. "I realize it doesn't solve problems, but it smooths the rough edges sometimes."

"Then you'd better keep drinking, Anna. I've got news. You might as well get it all at once. You know this digging I've been doing - into your grandfather's past? I have more answers. I think I've finally discovered the truth to it all."

Anna jumped to her feet and both cats leapt to the floor. Scooter chased after them as they dove under the sofa.

"Oh, my! Do I need to finish the bottle?"

"Not quite. But another sip wouldn't hurt. Be warned – this is heartbreaking."

Sam trotted back to the kitchen. "I saw a bottle of scotch in there. I think I'll join you, my dear."

Steven pulled out the letter, as Sam returned and settled in next to Anna. "Okay, brace yourself." He read the letter and came to the last lines.

Because I had no other means of income, I began siphoning off enough from our family annuity to support this poor man and try my best to make amends. Eventually the theft was discovered, and I was banished from the family and shunned for the remainder of my life, never to see my children again.

I was so ashamed, I couldn't bear to show up at court.

"And that's how it ends. Looks as if he never finished it or mailed it anywhere."

"Oh, that poor, dear man. What a tragedy." Anna said as she buried her face in her hands. Sam held her against his body. She leaned into him and let the tears flow.

"At least now we know why he was stealing money from the family and why my grandmother divorced him. And now we know why there wasn't any left when he died."

"I still think his punishment was unjustly harsh. Why couldn't he tell his wife what had happened? Shame? Pride? What do you think, Sam? You're a doctor."

"But not a surgeon."

"They knew so little in those days."

"I was never directly responsible for another man's death during my years of practice. And the word fits perfectly – 'practice.' Remember your research, Steven. After the Civil War, during David's time as a surgeon, it was experimentation most of the time. Practice indeed!"

Chapter

43

It is with deep regret that I write with heart in hand to sincerely apologize to you ...

Steven stared at David's words.

They're good words. That's the way I feel – maybe I could borrow them.

~   ~   ~

He gripped the pen tightly to keep his hand from shaking.

September 8, 1989

Dear Sharon,
It is with deep regret that I write with heart in hand to sincerely apologize to you.

I'm afraid I have ruined your life and I can't bear the thought of doing the same to Katie. I'm so glad my mother reached out. I am grateful you had the kindness to help her out of her dark troubles and she found the courage to call me.

May I phone you, Sharon? I would love to hear the remarkable story of how you saved my mother and discovered her connection to Katie. I would also like to give you my good news, in my own voice, and tell you how my life has changed. I'm slowly learning to be a better man, and with your help, I want to learn to be a good father. Perhaps you can teach me, as I have no role model.

I hope to hear from you soon.
Steven

Steven carefully placed the envelope in the mailbox and raised both hands in the air with silent elation. He took a deep breath and patted the box. He was certain he was on the right path – to where, he wasn't sure. He had decided to visit the fire station and deliver a bag of Joe's homemade muffins to the men who would become part of his second family. He continued their stroll, allowing Scooter to lead him along the 'sidewalk from hell' where he had experienced the extreme panic that led him into the capable hands of Dr. Sam. He realized with delight that they had reached the wooded park by the library where the dog had found his master.

"Look at you, Scooter. Did you intend to come here? Let's search for our special bench – can you find it?"

The dog hopped along the path, sniffing each bench until he stopped abruptly in front of the very one where he had found Steven napping. "Well, aren't you a smart dog. I think you're right, this is the one." Scooter responded with a single bark, circled the wooden bench, then hopped on it. Steven laughed as he threw his arms around his beloved dog and held on.

He looked up into the sky at the light coming through the trees and into the library's third-story window where he saw Lindsay looking down at them intently. She gave a little wave, then turned and moved out of his line of vision.

Seeing her face forced Steven to realize he would have to tell Lindsay about Sharon. He had confessed to her that he had a child but had avoided telling her the details. He didn't know if Sharon had a boyfriend, or maybe a husband...a built-in father for Katie.

He sat buried in confusion until he felt a gentle hand on his shoulder. He looked up. "Hi, Lindsay. How'd your class go?"

She sat beside him and wound her arm through his. Steven leaned into her, realizing she felt like home.

"More important, how did *your* class go, Steven?"

He grinned. "I passed, Lindsay. It feels like I've gotten over this huge hurdle. It's...I'm so..."

"Proud? It's okay, you can say it. You're allowed to be proud of yourself. Look at what you've achieved. When we first met, you saw yourself as some kind of vet-bum, and so did everyone else – except me, of course."

"And Anna. She believed in me from the start. Never criticized my dirty hair and beard."

"She's used to people showing up in her neighborhood who are down on their luck, but not at her front door. She was awfully trusting with you from the beginning."

Lindsay caressed his clean-shaven face. "I can still see your expression when I popped up from under the desk at the library."

"My expression? What about yours? You must have been thinking – who is this street bum who says he wants to research the Civil War?"

"Actually, I thought...I'll bet there's a mighty fine face hidden under all that hair. It was in your eyes. I wondered – what he's trying to hide?"

"How right you were. And I'm still working to understand all the stuff I've been trying to hide – from myself and everyone else. But I'm getting there. Self-awareness is hard to accept, you know?"

She nodded. "Denial is even harder. It's exhausting – takes a lot of energy to refuse to know."

"Uh oh – you're getting philosophical again." Steven grinned. "Let me just enjoy this moment. No thinking allowed. Scooter and I are taking the slow route to the firehouse. Want to join us?"

"I'll go as far as the pet store. Pete needs me to take over so he can pick up his permits for the extension on the building. He's excited to build his animal hospital. Talk about proud."

"He deserves to be, and he's worked hard. Earning your veterinary degree is as long and grueling as getting a medical degree. You and your mom are pretty amazing too, supporting him all those years."

"Yup, we're all so amazing!"

"And Scooter's the most amazing of all." He patted the bench. "He found our old park bench right off the bat. He's going to be the most terrific firehouse dog. What a nose!" He took Lindsay's hand as if he'd been holding on to her for his entire life.

"Okay, Scooter. Let's see how good you really are. Lead the way to Pete. Where's the pet store, Scooter? Can you find the treats?"

Scooter jumped off the bench and pulled on the leash, turned toward Steven and Lindsay, then barked, as if to say, 'Okay, my humans. Let's get going. I know where to find the treats...and a bath if I'm really good.'

~ ~ ~

Scooter barked his 'hello' and raced through the door as a voice from inside called out, "Who's on the other end of the leash, Scooter – is it Steven? Hey, there you are. Congratulations, man. I heard the good news." He waved to Lindsay. "Thanks for helping out, Sis."

"When do we bring the hammers?" Steven asked.

"I'll call you. Do you have a schedule at the firehouse for next week?"

"Not yet. I'll let you know."

"Sounds good."

Scooter raced to the back room and leapt onto the counter next to the bathtub.

Steven laughed and set him back on the floor. "Creatures of habit. Not today, Scooter."

"He remembers my promise," Pete said. He offered the dog a handful of treats and headed for the door. "Thanks for holding down the fort, Sis. I'll be back in an hour. Uh, you're welcome to stay and keep her company, Steven."

"I'm on an important mission. Going to the firehouse – for the first time as a member of their team. These are Joe's special mini-muffins."

Pete grabbed the bag. "Hmm - I could smell it coming through the door."

"Go ahead, take one."

Pete popped a muffin in his mouth, tossed the bag to Steven and headed for the door. "Back in an hour."

"Right behind you," Steven said.

He offered the bag to Lindsay. As she shook her head 'no' he took her hand and said, "Let's get together, soon. We need to talk."

Her eyes widened. "I'm free tomorrow from five to seven-thirty."

He nodded and led Scooter out the door.

~   ~   ~

As Steven and Scooter rounded the corner into the wide driveway leading to the firehouse, the large engine doors burst open and firemen in dress uniform spilled out onto the drive. Fifteen men began hooting and cheering, hollering their congratulations to Steven. He stood mute, unable to comprehend that he was the recipient of their celebration.

They're doing this for me?

Scooter barked and hopped around his master as if he understood.

Alan approached Steven and gave him a big bear hug. "You did it! I knew you could – congratulations." The men roared their approval and led Steven into the firehouse.

"I tried to tell you how much we needed a paramedic," Alan said. "Didn't want to put more pressure on you before your tests. But man, we're so happy to have you with us, Steven. That's what the guys are trying to say to you. We're all here to celebrate."

"I have no words. Thank you."

Oh God, what if I can't do this?

"It's been a long, difficult program. So tonight we're making..."

"Hey, what's this *we* stuff?" came a voice from the back of the kitchen.

"Okay – *we* decided – and Jeremy fulfilled our wish to consume piles of his special spaghetti. He even made a batch for Scooter, because he'll be part of the team, too."

"Sounds great. And I brought muffins from Joe's Café.

"Terrific. Okay, men. Out of your dress uniforms. Be ready to roll," Alan commanded.

"Is this the whole crew? Last time I was here, there were only five or six guys."

"That's how many are on duty in the station. We alternate – on 48 hours, off 24. The whole team's here tonight because of

Jeremy's spaghetti – and because of you, of course."

"I'm, I – don't know what to say."

"No need." He stood on one of the benches and hollered to his men. "Okay, gentlemen. Take a seat at the table. Jeremy's almost ready to serve his gourmet spaghetti." The men cheered.

"Come sit with me a minute and let's talk about what the next two weeks look like." They settled onto a bench at the battered community table and Steven wondered how many dice games they could teach him. He watched as the men joined them around the table, politely introducing themselves. Each firefighter told Steven, in various ways, how grateful they were for his experience and training.

Steven turned to Alan. "Give me an idea of what you expect from me."

"Come in every day at 9:00, get acquainted with both teams, get accustomed to our regulations and systems. It's likely we'll take you along on every ride next week, just to get you involved in how we operate. A month ago, we put in a request to the city for a fire and rescue vehicle with equipment for medical emergencies, smoke inhalation and burn injuries. These requests can take forever to get approved, so in the meantime, we want you to help us outfit one of the regular rigs with emergency equipment that you anticipate needing."

Steven nodded.

"I want you to get acquainted with each of our men." Alan continued, "Find out how much they know and get each firefighter up to speed on the latest emergency medical protocol, so they can help you and we aren't caught short in the middle of a crisis. They all expect to get assessed and trained by you. Let's ask them..." he banged his glass with a fork. "Hey men, give Steven some idea of what you want to learn from him and what we need for medical emergencies."

"You know, we've been trained to save a burning building, and we're glad we've now got someone with us who can help the people in the building."

Steven gave him a nod. "I appreciate your confidence in me. It means a lot."

He looked around the table at the earnest faces and as they leaned toward him, he felt comforted by their aspiration to learn new skills.

Another man asked, "Is there anything we can do to ease the pain of a burn patient before we can get them to the hospital?"

The questions continued.

"Tell us what special medical equipment we should have in each rig?"

"What should we be doing to educate the town to maintain safety from brush fires that can spread to houses and whole communities."

"And forest fires."

"Give me an idea of what you mean," Steven said.

"For starters, we've had two very dry years, back-to-back. I'd say, we're in a drought and we need to stay vigilant. A wildfire in this area would be deadly."

"So, the first thing I'll do is make sure every man is skilled in helping burn victims." Steven said.

"Good," said Alan. "There's been a noticeable increase in

our homeless population – veterans and families."

Steven looked around the table and inwardly cringed.

"It's not unusual to get emergency calls because an illegal campfire has spread or a homeless kid gets hurt or sick," said a man named Jerry. "Instead of calling 911 and asking for an ambulance, these poor people call the fire department. They can't afford an ambulance, and feel they'll get sympathy from a firefighter, along with getting bandaged up. They're afraid of the hospital system or can't afford the costs."

"So, without making too many waves, we often send them to Open Heart and hope they get help from your friend, Doctor Sam," Alan said.

"Just the other day, our organizer, Anna, noticed the increase in people showing up for a free meal. Now I see why," Steven said.

"We've got to do something," Alan said. "We can't have them starting campfires in the middle of empty fields. We can't let little kids get sick with no one to help them."

"I agree."

"We know you're involved with Open Heart, Steven, and we hope you can balance the two organizations so people get fed and children can get treated. Ideally, I'd like to see your schedule eventually set up so you're at the firehouse part time and Open Heart part time. We're going to get set up with two-way radios, so we can reach you if there's an emergency that needs immediate medical care."

"Good plan. And there may be times when I need to reach you with an emergency. It goes both ways."

Steven looked around the table with gratitude. He was

awed by this team of men who had each other's back, who wanted to learn new methods and help their community.

These are my new teammates, my new tribe. I've found a place where I belong.

Without thinking, Steven asked, "So who can teach me some new dice games? I can tell this table has had lots of activity."

The men around the table laughed, their shoulders relaxed as someone leapt up to grab the dice cup.

Jeremey hollered from the kitchen. "Spaghetti's hot! Come and get it!"

Alan grinned at Steven. "I guess in the meantime, yelling at each other still works."

Chapter

44

Hello Steven,

Thanks for your letter. I'm glad to know you have taken a new path to recovery. It sounds as though your life has gotten better since we were together.

Your mother and I have formed a great bond and we've created our own little family. We support each other. I assure you, we're doing fine, but it's your daughter who needs you. The apology you want to offer should be directed at your daughter, not me.

Please know this, Steven, I never said to anyone that you didn't deserve to be a father to your child. Never. Katie is our connection, and she will always be your daughter. I can't tell you how to be a good father, Steven. You will have to work that out on your own.

Katie has begun to ask about you. I have given her limited information and feel that it is now up to you. I will never keep Katie from her father. But be careful not to sabotage yourself with excuses. She is old enough to understand honesty. It doesn't seem possible that she has already turned seven-years-old.

And so, Steven, your most important task is to call your daughter — soon.

My best to you,
Sharon

Steven read Sharon's letter with a mixture of joy and despair. He was elated that Sharon wouldn't stand in his way to be part of his daughter's life yet saddened with the knowledge that he had already caused so much heartache. The thought of calling Katie put him in a state of impossible trepidation. What would he say? How would he explain? He'd have to wait.

And then there was Lindsay. It was time to tell her the

whole truth – take his chances – be honest and hope she understood. He could finally admit it to himself that he loved her. It seemed inconceivable that she could feel the same about him – she said she did – and yet she didn't know him, not completely. Could he ever have a loving, honest relationship?

It was time to face his demons and the consequences of his failures. He walked along the familiar route to Anna's house, still enveloped in the euphoria of the firemen's welcome. Scooter pulled at his leash, as they headed for his feline pals. He needed his friend, Anna.

As they turned the corner, he stopped dead. Scooter pulled at the leash. Craig's truck sat in front of Anna's house. What could it mean? Maybe she was letting him use her driveway to park and sleep in his truck. Maybe he had brought Richie to visit. As they walked around the truck and up the walk, Scooter bounded up the stairs, barking to gain entry and begin the merry chase with Tom and Jerry. The front windows were open and the sheer curtains blew cheerfully. Steven could hear the banging of pots and pans, as Anna laughed happily and Craig chattered away. Not bothering to ring the bell, he cracked the door enough for Scooter to slip through and called out to them.

"Hello in there. It's Steven and Scooter."

"Hey, Steven. Glad to see you, man. Wait till you see what we're doing."

What the hell are you doing? I'm the one who helps Anna.

"Steven, your timing is perfect. I'm just showing Craig..."

"Yeah, I can see that."

She put her hands on her hips. "He's helping me."

"When did he take over my job?"

Craig watched the back and forth silently.

"But – what was I to do? Think about it. You're not going to be so available anymore – to just hop over to help me haul the food." She wiped her hands on a kitchen towel. "You're the one who encouraged us to give him a chance. You're the one who discovered Craig had all these cooking skills from the army. Aren't you the one who thought this would be the perfect way for him to find his footing? Isn't that how you put it?"

"Well, yeah but..."

"But nothing. Don't you see? It's the perfect solution."

"First he has to prove he's reliable," Steven said.

Craig raised his arm. "I'm still in the room, people! I hear you!"

"So, let's give him a chance," Anna said, turning to Craig.

"Yeah, give me a chance. Can you do that, Steven?" He walked to Anna's side. "You convinced me to start going to AA meetings. I've even got a sponsor now."

"When was your last drink?"

"Uh, last week. But, it was only one beer. Honest."

"It doesn't work that way, Craig. With you, it's all or nothing. You've got to choose 'nothing.'"

"Okay, I promise."

"Well, it's not that simple. If you commit to help Anna at Open Heart, you can't let her down. You can't drink – ever."

"Yeah, yeah, I know."

"No, you don't. It wasn't so long ago that you took off and left your son stranded at Open Heart. He was heartbroken. No way, I'm not buyin' it. You can't do that to Anna. There's too many empty stomachs depending on her – and now on you too."

"But..."

"You aren't trustworthy, Craig."

Anna walked toward Steven until she was toe-to-toe with him. She looked up at him and said, "Don't you think this is for me to decide?"

He looked down at her and took a deep breath. "Alright then. You've decided. If you prefer Craig's help – so be it." Anna reached for Steven as he pulled away. He turned to Scooter who was half under the sofa playing with the cats. "Let's go." Scooter pulled his head around and ran to the opposite end of the sofa. "Come on, it's time to go." The dog ducked his head and hid behind the sofa.

"Okay, fine. Stay."

"Come on, Man. Don't do this. Give me a chance," Craig pleaded.

"I'm not stopping you. I'm getting out of the way. It seems to be Anna's preference, too."

Steven stalked out of the house and picked up speed, then ran down the street.

~ ~ ~

When he reached the cottage, he flopped down on the bed, wondering how he could have been such a fool. Anna was right. She needed help and was convinced Craig would stay straight if he had purpose in his life – a job to make him feel useful.

Purpose. It's what I need. It's what we all need.

425

Steven examined his own motives. Jealousy, that's all it was – along with some over-protective macho genes. As he had put physical distance between himself and Anna's kitchen, Steven had seen the wisdom of Anna's idea. Let Craig learn the Open Heart system of food donations and charity, give him responsibility and a chance to stay clean. Let him cook to his heart's content, keep him so busy, make him so tired he wouldn't have time to drink.

Steven jumped up, ready to apologize and headed for the door, intent on jogging back to Anna's. He threw open the door and crashed into Lindsay.

"Whoa! Slow down, Mister. Where're you headed in such a rush?"

"Lindsay. You okay? I almost knocked you off your feet."

She grinned. "I think you've already done that, Steven."

He smiled and gave her a long, even look – took both shoulders and pulled her to him. She raised her head from the comfort of his chest and said, "Is this as far as we're ever going to go?"

He held her tighter, reluctant to let her go. "It is today. Right now, I'm on a mission. Want to walk with me to Anna's? I'll give you another example of what an idiot I am."

"I doubt you'll convince me, but sure. You can help me carry the sack of potatoes."

"Where'd they come from...wait...I know, you bought them at the store. No way you got them from the garden."

"Well thanks a lot! Actually, I did. Harvested them myself, see the dirt? I did it all on my own. You can do soil samples is you don't believe me."

426

"Congratulations!" He gave her a deep bow.

"Only because I didn't think you and Scooter were here. That's why I did it. Anna called and asked me to bring potatoes to her. She's making stew for the Open Heart lunch tomorrow."

"Yeah, I know."

"Hey, where's Scooter? I figured I'd have heard him barking if you were inside."

"Well, that's part of the story. I'll tell you on the way. Give me one of the handles. We can carry this between us."

"Why don't we just drive?"

"Because I need to walk off a little steam, and a little...well...you know."

"You mean passion?"

He blushed.

"You do, don't you!"

"Naw. Come on, let's go. Anna's waiting for you."

"Then I'll tell you what. You walk off your 'whatever' and I'm driving the potatoes to Anna's. Help me get them in the trunk."

"Don't you want to know why I'm here without Scooter?"

She jumped in the driver's seat and leaned out the window. "Tell me when you get there."

Steven threw the bushel of potatoes into the car and hollered, "You'll figure it out when you get there." He watched as Lindsay sped off.

He was struck by the realization that bravery comes in many forms. Steven was in awe of all the courageous people he had encountered on this singular, memorable day: Craig, who was finding his way out of the bottom of a bottle; Anna, who gave him a chance to right himself; Lindsay, who faced the possible encounter with their resident snake, and a crew of valiant firemen who faced danger every day.

Chapter

45

... determined to never harm another soul
or perform another surgical procedure.
I gave up the practice of medicine.
I gave up on myself.

David's words returned to Steven's memory with the fleeting realization that he was doing the exact opposite. He found himself saving the life of another human being. He reached for the suffocating baby as smoke blew out of the single-story bungalow. The fireman handed off the infant through the window of the burning building to their new paramedic. Steven checked the baby's breathing pathways as she shrieked in terror and studied every inch of her skin for burns. Satisfied she was unharmed, he cradled her in his arms to quiet her screams, then seeing the frantic mother rush to him, gently carried the baby to her.

Gratitude was the word that first came to Steven's mind. He had helped save a child. He would not fall into David's morass. Steven had begun to right himself. He could feel it. He would not give up on himself as David had. The proof came from the screaming, frightened baby he held in his arms. He had returned the child to her mother. He had helped save the infant from the fire. And as he would later understand, he had saved himself as well.

Steven heard his name and ran toward the burning building. Alan called to him, "Check with the mother, let's make sure there's no one else in the house." He raced down the walk where the ambulances were parked. All he had to do was follow the voice of the crying infant.

There she was, snuggled against her mother's breast. He ran up to her. "Are there other children, anyone else in the house?"

"No, it was just my baby and me. My husband is at work."

He called Alan on the two-way radio. "We're clear. No one else in the house."

He turned back to the mother and asked if she knew how the fire had started.

"It started in the oven, flames and smoke. I tried to put it out with baking soda, isn't that what you're supposed to do? It didn't work. The smoke got thicker – I tried to call 911. The line was dead, so I ran outside to yell for help. I was so scared! By the time I turned back around, the front door was on fire and I couldn't get back inside to find my baby." She grabbed Steven's hand. "You saved us, you saved Maddie. I didn't know...I never realized...you...you'd help folks like me. I am so grateful."

430

"It was all of us, ma'am. We're a team."

She started to sob as she clutched her baby. "Please tell them, tell your men thank you."

"You did everything right, ma'am." He knelt in front of her, wanting to comfort her. "It doesn't look like there's any structural damage, just scorched walls, the front door and the oven. Maybe it was faulty. You should check into it."

"I will. I scrub that oven every week. It couldn't have been grease piling up."

"The inspectors will let you know how it happened."

"Good." She looked around at the chaotic street. "I wonder who called the fire department. My neighbors aren't too friendly – not too happy having us living here."

"Well, there's someone who cares. That's for sure. Someone called." He stood up and gently placed his hand on her shoulder. "Give the inspector your name and number. We'll call as soon as we know anything."

~ ~ ~

Steven looked down the street. When he was still a kid he'd ride his bike in this neighborhood, one block from his home. He returned to the truck and watched his fellow firemen put out the last of the flames. Had he followed protocol? He decided to ask Alan for a debriefing when they returned to the firehouse. He needed to make sure he had done everything right.

~ ~ ~

As the men climbed into the truck, the alarms on every radio squawked. Alan held up his arm as they all listened intently. Man lying lifeless in the street, just around the corner in the next block. "This one's for you, Steven."

"Yes, sir. I've got it. Call for an ambulance." He hesitated for only a moment. What if he didn't know what was wrong? What if he didn't know what to do?

Don't give up on yourself.

The fire truck barreled around the corner and stopped near a man lying face down in the street. Neighbors had gathered around as the firemen moved the crowd back. Steven hollered instructions. "Move back. Give him air." He pushed through the crowd, and knelt next to the man, turned him onto his back and gasped. His father! It was his father.

What irony!

Steven began CPR, pressing on the inert chest of his father. He raised his arm to send the message – Get Help! He continued CPR as two firemen raced to his side with a stretcher and his medical bag. The old man began to cough and sputter. His eyes went wide when he saw Steven leaning over him, pressing on his chest.

"Get off me!" His father raised himself on one arm and tried to sit up.

Steven pushed him back down and signaled for the stretcher. "Quiet down. Now lie still." He grabbed the stethoscope from his bag and listened to his father's heartbeat.

"What do you think you're doing? Playing doctor? Get off me, you idiot."

On Steven's command, the firemen lifted the old man onto the stretcher as he struggled to jump off. They moved him toward the ambulance. Steven followed next to the moving stretcher as his father kept trying to sit up and Steven continued to push him down.

"Get away from me," his father shouted. "Let me go." He grabbed the sleeve of the fireman. "Those people need to be taught a lesson...gotta get them out of the neighborhood ... could have burned down the whole block. Get those coloreds out of our town. They tried to burn us down..."

Steven looked down in disgust at the despicable man who claimed to be his father. He shook his head and turned to the paramedic from the hospital. "Get him to Emergency as fast as you can. My guess is a heart attack. If you can't manage to shut him up, put a muzzle on him. Stop the garbage coming out of his mouth. He needs to lie still." The ambulance raced away.

Steven stood mute, shoulders slumped, head raised to the heavens, looking for insight. His father – not only a disgraceful man, but a cruel bigot besides. Under the circumstances, it was hard to follow David's advice to 'never harm another soul.' He found Alan and explained that the man was his father, then walked back to his specially rigged medical truck, shoved the key into the ignition and headed for the hospital.

Before he searched for his father, Steven walked along the rows of cribs looking for the baby girl, Maddie. The ER nurse explained she had already been discharged, mother and child had been picked up by the woman's husband. Did they have a place to stay? She didn't know. Steven smiled, enlightened by his simple plan. It was the best of all solutions. He knew where there was a large empty house in their neighborhood, just around the corner from the family's scorched home. It would be available for a while...and free. He was sorry he had missed them.

Steven reluctantly walked through the Emergency

Department, checking each bed, asking at each station. He eventually found a doctor who recognized the man he described.

"They took him to the ER for further examination. He kept yelling about someone trying to burn down his neighborhood, so we sedated him."

"Can't tell you how many times I wished I'd had a supply of whatever you gave him," Steven said, only half joking. "Glad you quieted that foul mouth." He waved goodbye and said he'd be back in the morning.

Before heading back to the fire station, Steven drove by the house that had burned, hoping he might find the baby girl and her parents. And there they were, gazing at their scorched house, lost in sorrow.

He reminded them everyone was safe, and that's what mattered most.

"Do you have a place to stay?" He asked.

"Yes, there was a motel on the edge of town."

He made sure he knew how to contact them. They would need a place to live until their house was repaired and he had the perfect place for them – "Close by – right around the corner in this very same neighborhood," he said. "And it wouldn't cost them a dime."

~   ~   ~

Two weeks later, Steven drove his father home from the rehab hospital. As they walked in the door his father said, "When did you say the home health nurse will be coming? You sure I'm okay to be by myself?"

"That's what the doctor said."

"Maybe you should...you know...come back home...take care of me."

As they reached the porch, Steven unlocked the door and handed his father the key. "The doctor said you are fine, completely recovered. Minor heart attack. No lasting damage."

I wonder if they even found a heart.

"But..."

"You heard him. All you have to do is call 911, if you have even a twinge. Besides, since you think I'm such an incompetent..."

"I don't know. Seems to me I need someone here with me. Should I be alone?" He whimpered."

Who would put up with your shit?

The old man shuffled into the house and sniffed the air as if a skunk had slipped in the front door.

"What's that I smell?" He asked.

"Don't know," said Steven, deadpan. "Smell's nice."

Did they leave something behind?

"It smells like lemon oil." He walked along the hallway and poked his head into the door of his office. "Look at the bookshelves. They've been dusted. I'm sure of it. Books are out of place. Have you been in here messing with my private papers?"

"Not interested in your private stuff. Only David Lane's medical certificate. Besides, I've been busy. Still have my internship to finish."

"For what? Oh yeah, still trying to convince me you're a doctor or something. I know damn well you never finished medical school. Had to go play hero in that godforsaken war."

"Hardly a hero. No, I'm training to become a paramedic with the Fire Department."

"Oh – sure."

"I no longer care what you think."

"So now they hire homeless drunks off the street to save people in fires?"

"And unlike you, they give some people a second chance when they prove themselves capable. That's what I'm working to become – competent and capable."

"Ha! Hard to believe." His father smirked.

"Believe it."

"Naw. Worthless to the core."

"I hope you live long enough to realize just how wrong you are. Now come in the kitchen and I'll make you a pot of tea. I've put some frozen dinners in the freezer and restocked your refrigerator. The doctor gave you a list of the food you shouldn't eat.

They continued down the hall, his father sniffing into each room.

"There's that smell again." They turned into the kitchen. "Did someone polish the floors? And look, there, that's it! The kitchen cabinets look brand new. That's the smell all right – lemon oil." Steven stopped dead. The kitchen had been thoroughly scrubbed. The cabinets had been polished to a mirror-bright shine and looked as if they were brand new.

"And a plate of brownies. I wonder who left these? Are they from...? No, not from you. We both heard what the doctor said. No sweets, no food with sugar or fat."

Steven kept his voice steady, trying not to crack a smile.

Good thing they didn't leave a 'Thank You' note.

"Well, then they must be for me. I'll take them to Open Heart for the kids tomorrow."

"You're still wasting time with those homeless bums?"

"You bet I am. They deserve our support – families with little kids. The working poor, the folks who never got a fair start in life.

"Yeah, and those worthless vets...looking for a handout, just like you. If it weren't for me, you'd still be on the street."

Steven whirled around and looked long and hard into his father's eyes. "Is this really how you want it? Don't you wonder how you've ended up so alone and completely isolated?"

"But..."

"Your heart may have healed, but you remain without a soul. Live with it. This is exactly what you deserve. Although I don't recommend facing yourself in the mirror."

Steven grabbed the plate of brownies, charged down the hall and gave a respectful salute to David's medical degree as he headed for the door.

Chapter

46

May 10, 1892

Soldiers and Sailors Home
Sandusky, Ohio

My Dear Dr. Merrick,
I do not wish to make my condition
sound desperate, but my insight as a
physician tells me the end is near.
I have suffered much with the lung
disease, which results in coughing spasms
and blood expulsion.

While I am still able, I want to
express my gratitude for your continued
care and kindness. You, my dear
friend, have given me the one gift

I wished for before leaving this world. Of course, I cannot reveal your charity in writing, yet. I assure you the meeting you arranged was of great consequence. My only regret was that only one came, not both.

I would be most happy to see you again if you have reason to be in the area. Regarding the other matter, it appears that my pension will not arrive to be of any help to me. When the time is right, please contact the War Department and if you have the legal ability to transfer my war pension to my children, Mary and George, I would be eternally grateful. Knowing this, would allow me to leave this life a peaceful man.

With gratitude,
David R. Lane

"There, he did it! He met with Mary. Don't you think that's what he meant?" Steven pointed to the words in David's letter, "See, he wrote 'our meeting was of great consequence.'

He meant his meeting with his daughter, Mary. Don't you think?"

Anna nodded, tears brimming against her eyelids as she took the letter gently in her hands and read it a second time. "It also appears that his death was imminent. It is so heartening. And, he seems to be hinting that he regrets not having George there. I wonder what actually happened at that meeting." She leaned her head against Sam's shoulder as they sat quietly contemplating the letter.

"I brought another letter to read," Steven said. "This one is current – from Sharon. Remember Sharon?"

"Of course, you told us all about her," Anna said, sitting up straighter. "You ended up treating her very badly, Steven. Isn't that what you said?"

"More than you imagine. I...there's...um..."

Sam squirmed impatiently. "Come on, out with it, young man. You can be honest with us. We know there's no such thing as a perfect person. Certainly not anyone in this room. Tell us what happened?"

Steven hesitated and then blurted out, "She got pregnant. I didn't know. We had broken off any communication. I was already back on the streets, so she left. At least I think that's how it happened. I was in an alcoholic haze and didn't even know she'd left."

"Oh Steven," Anna said. "That means..."

"I have a child, a girl who's seven-years-old. Seven! Her name is Katie. Think of it! The worst part of this is my father knew. Sharon had called and when he told her the condition I was in, she asked him to tell me. He waited until two years later to tell me."

"Despicable," Anna said.

"When he finally told me, he had no idea where they'd gone. He said...oh, this feels awful...he told me that Sharon had said I didn't deserve to be a father, and I would never be allowed to see my child."

"It's a cruel punishment, Steven. Your father had no right..."

"I've given up hope for any kind of understanding or reconciliation with him. It was vindictive...he's...he's a mean-spirited, cold man. When he had his heart attack, I had a hard time caring if he lived or died. It's awful to feel that way about your own father, but I do. I cared more about the mother and her baby in the burning house. Isn't that sad?"

"Be grateful you have a more compassionate heart, Steven."

"At least you now know Sharon wants you in Katie's life," Sam said.

"I don't want to be my father, to do to Katie what he did to me. And look at David, how he abandoned his children. I want to be better than that."

"And now, well...priorities, Steven. What are you going to do?" asked Sam.

"My priority is to have a loving relationship with my daughter. Learn to be a father. Oh! And one more thing. By some miracle, my mother and Sharon found each other and discovered Katie is my daughter, so that makes her my mother's..."

"Granddaughter!" hollered Anna. "Isn't that the best! Now that's a good old-fashioned fairy tale."

"I'd call it justified karma," said Sam.

442

"You believe in karma?" David asked.

"I believe there's such a thing as karmic debt."

"Gives me the shivers." Anna snuggled closer to Sam.

"Could be," Steven said. These coincidences make me wonder."

"One earns good karma," Anna said.

"Well, we'll see, won't we?" He hesitated. "And here's the other letter I brought to show you. I wrote to Sharon and here's what she wrote back." Steven read the letter that ended with...*your most important task is to call your daughter, soon.*

"The thought of calling Katie scares me to death. What do I say? How do I explain where I've been for the last five years? And I can't go to visit until I've completed my training, and..."

"Slow down, Steven. You can still call her. Come on, we'll support you."

"But...I don't know what's the best way to handle this. And then there's Lindsay..."

"Oh Steven, don't tell me you haven't told her." Anna said.

"I told her I have a child, but we haven't talked about it. I just blurted it out and got all snarled up in my own words, and...left."

"Oh, perfect. I can't imagine why that woman cares so much about you." Anna gave Steven a little punch in the shoulder.

"Cuz...I save her from snakes."

"Well, it's not because you've allowed her into your life," Anna said.

443

Steven began pacing. He moved back and forth along the well-worn path in front of the sofa that doubled for a feline hiding place. Tom poked his nose out.

Walk it out...

"I did tell her who I was. I'm not sure I said it in a very effective way. I was honestly trying to warn her off – tell her I'm not a good person."

"But you are, Steven."

He settled back into the chair. "I'm not too proud of who I am, Anna. I have no reason to be."

She cocked her head and reached out to touch his hand.

Sam asked the obvious, "She knows you have a child, nothing else? And knows nothing about Sharon?"

"And she hasn't asked?" Anna wondered.

"Now there's a rare woman," quipped Sam. "Hang on to that one, Steven."

"Well, she has to assume there's a mother – that Katie has a mother – that she and I – that we..."

"Okay, I get it. So, Steven, I think your priority is to talk to Lindsay. I mean tell her everything."

"Everything? I don't even remember every..."

"Come on, get serious." Sam said. "You know what she meant. I think the word is honesty."

"Don't get ahead of yourself, Steven," said Anna. "First, you need a heart-to-heart with yourself. What do you want? How do you feel about Lindsay?"

Steven started to answer, and Anna continued. "You've been trying to adjust to so many life changes in the last several months, I don't know if you're ready to take on a daughter and a wife..."

"A wife?"

"Okay, a serious relationship."

"I like that idea. It would be so nice to have a loving companion. Someone to trust, where there's mutual respect."

"And that goes both ways. You have to be willing to commit to her, be there for her, too." Anna continued. "You've got decisions to make, Steven. You said it was so important to have purpose. But, have you taken on more than you can handle? Does your father need care?" Are you going to continue as caretaker at Open Heart? Between your paramedic responsibilities and Open Heart, will you have much time for Lindsay? You can't just casually 'take up' with her and never have time to see her."

"I wouldn't do that. I love her." He blushed.

"Good! Then go tell her."

Okay, I'll tell her.

~   ~   ~

Steven found Lindsay behind her desk at the library, buried in a book. He didn't know where to start.

What do I say?

She looked up and responded with the loving smile he hoped she reserved only for him.

Am I reading this all wrong?

"Steven!"

"How's my timing? You look busy."

"I've got to finish this one section on the Irish Rebellion

for my seminar tonight. Could we meet somewhere in an hour?"

Another hour to wait? He tried to stay calm.

"Sure, I've got to pick up Scooter, he's due for a good run. We'll make our way to the park bench behind the library and I'll wait for you there. You know which one I mean? It's the bench where I found Scooter and...and you know...we connected."

"Of course, I remember."

"So, it should be our bench."

Her head whipped up in surprise, paused, then dipped back into her book. "Okay, I'll meet you at *our* bench. See you in about an hour."

~ ~ ~

Scooter had begun specialized training to become a service dog. The county's fire service felt his first task, after basic obedience training, should be smoke detection and tracking. Steven picked up Scooter and drove him back to the library for a jog around the park. He decided to practice the skills they would both need to learn.

With a gentle tightening on the leash, Steven commanded, "Walk." The dog immediately came to 'heel' – walking in step and keeping stride with his master. "Good job, Scooter. You learn fast."

"Hey, get that mutt outta here. Dogs aren't allowed," came a voice from beyond the trees.

Steven recognized the same voice, then saw a disheveled man without a uniform. "Who put you in charge of this park? And he's not a mutt, he's a service dog in-training. I don't see any signs saying dogs aren't allowed."

446

"Well, uh, keep him on that leash – hear me?"

"You've scared this dog enough, mister." He turned his back on the man's voice and said, "Come on, Scooter, let's have a proper jog." He loosened the leash and they picked up speed in unison, heading for the most important park bench in town.

~   ~   ~

The bench was empty. Had she changed her mind? His heart dropped to his stomach. No special bench for them? Would she understand if he explained?

"Well, damn. She's not here. You're a great dog, Scooter, but I'm sorry to tell you, there's someone else in my life. Lindsay comes first. I've been such a fool. Hope it's not too late." He squatted down to be at eye level with the dog. "But I've learned my lesson. It's about what's important in life – a commitment to someone you love, someone to spend the rest of your life with. And for me – Lindsay is it." The dog wagged his tail as if he agreed whole heartedly, and gave a friendly little bark, looking over Steven's shoulder...

"Oh boy, she's right behind me, isn't she – and heard everything I said."

"I sure did, Steven." He rose and turned to face her, as Lindsay threw herself into his arms, almost knocking him to the ground. She leaned away and looked up at him. "What's that stupid grin on your face? Oh, I know, you're glad to see me!"

"You bet I am." He patted the bench. "Come sit with me." Lindsay cocked her head and sat primly with her hands in her lap as if she were expecting a lecture.

"This sounds awfully serious."

447

"It is – it really is."

Lindsay sat back and began stroking Scooter's head. "I'm listening."

"Remember that time I came to your office?"

"When you were acting like a crazy man?"

"And I still am."

"What are you trying to tell me, Steven?"

"Do you remember I told you I had a child?"

"Hard to forget."

"It meant a lot to me that you didn't ask a bunch of questions – you waited until I was ready."

"I figured you'd tell me when the time was right. Besides, I assumed you had a child in Vietnam, and...I thought you might have lost touch...the distance was so great.

"Oh! Well, that's not quite accurate." Steven squirmed.

Oh, no.

"I can tell how important this is to you. Please trust me."

He took both her hands in his. "I've been afraid it would ruin everything – we're so close to..."

"Trust me."

He breathed deeply. "My child is a seven-year-old girl. She's not Vietnamese. Her name is Katie. She lives in Oregon. I only found out about her existence a few months ago...my father, in his vengeance, kept the information from me. I didn't know how to tell you. I'm afraid it will change how you feel about me. I feel as if I've neglected her and at the same time, I've distanced myself from you, because...I've made such a mess of this, I was sure you wouldn't want any part of me if you knew."

Lindsay's eyes widened and a smile spread across her face. "Well, you've got it all backwards. The fact is that you're telling me now, that you're not trying to keep secrets from me. This is wonderful, Steven. When can I meet her?"

His body decompressed. "I haven't even met her. I wanted to tell you right away. And, maybe it sounds stupid, but I sure haven't got much of a role model. Look at my father. I may never know what made him into such a coward. And look at David Lane, who ruined his chances to redeem himself. He betrayed his family and lost both his children." He leaned toward her. "Oh, Lindsay, it's so important for me to be a good father."

"I wouldn't want you to feel any other way. In genealogy we see it as changing the dynamic, reasserting family patterns. From an ethical standpoint, I'd say you've figured out what you value – what matters to you."

"Do you really mean it?"

"Of course. How could I respect you if you didn't want to be a part of your child's life? Here's the way I see it – I want to be in your life." She held onto his hands. "And so, I want to be part of whatever is important to you. I know you would feel the same for me. This is what gives life meaning. Connecting. Caring."

Steven sat in a daze.

"You can never know how much this means to me, Lindsay." He pulled her gently to him and kissed her softly on the mouth. She smiled under his kiss, then pulled away as she looked into his eyes, brimming with tears.

"Okay, now tell me all about Katie, I love the name Katie."

Chapter

47

... and most tragically, I have failed as a father. I have caused the suffering of so many.

Steven walked toward the cottage with Scooter by his side, contemplating Sharon's letter and David's sentiment, determined to find a different path to fatherhood. How could he find a loving way into Katie's life? Seven years old. Was she old enough to understand? Did she already resent him?

I'm so afraid. What can I say to her?

How could he tell her why so many years had gone by? He could never reveal that she had a grandfather who was so vindictive. What good would it do to tell her about him?

'Failed as a father.' The phrase kept running through his head. He wondered what had happened to the father who had raised him, the man who had dragged him in from the streets during his worst moments after Vietnam, then berated him and antagonized him, driving Steven back to the streets, again to a life as one of the homeless.

His father had been so abusive to his mother, she had left the family, risking alienation from Steven rather than tolerate his father. Who was this man? To simply say he was cruel, solved nothing.

Would it help me be a better father if I understood my own?

Steven decided he had to try.

As he walked through the cottage door, he said, "Scooter, I'm putting you in charge, time to be a guard dog. I'm on a mission, wish me luck." He hopped in the car and headed to the confrontation he knew had always been inevitable. On the way, he stopped at the market and selected a bag full of heart-healthy food.

As he stood at the front door to his father's house and reached into his pocket, he realized he had never given back the house key. He no longer wanted to enter his father's house without an invitation. He unlocked the door and dropped the key on the table in the entry hall.

Steven called out, "Hello, anyone home?" He knew his father was not allowed to drive after the heart attack, so the question was irrelevant. He had to be home. He had no choice. Yet, there was no reply. Where was he? Had his father ignored doctor's orders and taken the car for a drive or had he fallen somewhere in the house? Steven rushed down the hall and continued to call out. He stepped into every room, ran into his father's office and checked behind the desk. He continued to the back of the house, dropped the groceries in the kitchen and began to panic. He pushed open

452

the kitchen door, ran down the steps and across the grass to the garage. As he threw open the door he shouted to the sky, "Damn you, old man. Where have you gone?" As if on cue, the car turned into the driveway with his father at the wheel. He raced along beside the driver-side door, as his father parked the car and Steven threw open the door.

"What the hell! What do you think you're trying to prove? You're not allowed to drive yet, don't you remember?"

"What do you care? Haven't heard a word from you, just up and deserted me, so I thought I'd just take a little drive. It's too quiet..."

Steven took his father's arm and directed him back to the house.

"Your loneliness is your own doing."

His father pulled away and charged ahead on his own. As they entered the kitchen, Steven realized they were headed toward the same arguments, and was determined not to get hooked this time. He looked around at the neglected kitchen. Except for the newly polished cabinets that still made him smile, it was unchanged from his childhood days.

No memories. Not now.

Paint peeled from the walls and he was sure the appliances hadn't been cleaned since his mother fled the house. At least the counter was clean. He emptied the bag of groceries and sat at the kitchen table.

"Come sit down. I want to talk to you."

"You're not going to tell me what to do. I'm still in charge. I'll sit when I want to."

Steven took a deep breath.

"Sit...please." His father plopped down in the opposite chair.

"I have a question. Please hear me out. I'm trying to understand you."

His father shoved the table forward, pushed his chair back, and took a step toward the door.

"Sit down. This is important."

His father sat, folded his arms across his chest and glowered at his son.

Steven looked into his father's eyes, then reached both hands across the table. "Why do I feel you're always trying to hurt me? It's as if you want to punish me. I don't even know what I've done."

"What the hell are you talking about?"

Steven raised his forearms off the table and from tight fists, he opened one hand and showed five fingers. "Five years! It took you five years to tell me about Sharon's phone call – to tell me I had a child. I was deprived of knowing I had a daughter. She must have been two at the time Sharon called and told you. And now she's seven? In all that time I wasn't part of her life." He looked at his father, slammed both hands on the table. "Why would you do that? You intentionally didn't tell me."

His father began peeling candle wax from the table. "You didn't deserve to know. You were still a messed-up druggy – incapable of being a father."

"So, it's not that you forgot. You deliberately didn't tell me. In all that time I might have been motivated to change course. It would have given me a reason to be better. Cruel –

it was so damn cruel to keep my child from me...to not even... not even have a..."

His father looked down and continued to peel layers of wax. "Sharon said you didn't deserve to be a father. And she was right."

"No! You're lying. She never said that."

"Well...well...that's what I remember."

"Do you remember where that wax you're peeling came from? Do you?"

His father stopped peeling and looked up at Steven, raised his hands, palms in the air, in a gesture of denial.

"I was just a little kid. Mom had lit Christmas candles around the house. I knocked this one over. You grabbed me and hit me, knocked me to the floor – called me an idiot and made me watch as the wax spread all over the table. You wouldn't let Mom clean it up."

His father repeated the gesture and said, "So what."

Steven grabbed the edge of the table, arms spread wide.? He leaned into his father. "Why would you want to hurt me? Your son!"

"You're not..."

"Not what?"

"You're...I don't..."

"Come on, talk to me. What are you trying to say?"

His father shook his head and pushed the wax around.

"Please, I want to..."

"No. It's...I can't..."

"You can't talk to your son? You can't explain why you...You enjoyed it...hitting me."

His father's head shot up. He was sweating. "No, I..."

Steven pounded the table. "Talk to me, damnit!"

His father leapt out of his chair and hollered, "You're not my son."

Steven jumped from the chair and threw his arms in the air. "What? What do you mean?"

His father slumped back and stared at the table. Silent.

Steven sat, reached across the table and grabbed his father's shoulders. "Talk to me, what are you saying? Have you disowned me?"

"No. I said you're not my son. Biologically..."

Steven looked straight at him. "How do you know? Was I adopted or something?"

"No, it's..."

"Tell me."

"Your mother...she...betrayed me. She...she had an affair."

"The hell you say. You're lying again. She wouldn't – she wasn't..."

"Oh yeah? I saw it with my own eyes."

"I don't believe you." Steven whirled around to face his father. "I'm done with you and your deceitful accusations." He pushed through the screen door without looking back.

~   ~   ~

Steven stomped along the sidewalk.

This is crazy...okay, a little fear won't kill you.

He picked up speed.

Try again – head up, shoulders square, spine straight. That's it.

He began to jog.

Keep moving.

And he did.

~ ~ ~

After keeping pace around the block, Steven slammed back through the kitchen door. His father hadn't moved. The wax had disappeared.

"Come on, start from the beginning."

"It's – I can't."

"You can't lie to me anymore, or you don't know the truth?"

His father covered his head with his arms.

"I never wanted..." He looked up and swallowed. "It's too...repulsive."

"But it keeps seeping out in the way you treat me. Talk to me. Just start at the beginning."

His father let his arms fall, drew in a deep breath and looked at Steven. "By the time the war began, your mother was unable to get pregnant. I was drafted and sent overseas, then I was sent back to the states to conduct flight training. I hadn't seen her for three years and I kept getting letters saying how lonely she was. Then the letters stopped. I didn't know what had happened. I was stationed at a flight school in Arizona – not that far away. We had a little place near here in Northern California. D-Day planning had begun and I knew it was only a matter of time before the war would be over and I was sure most of us would be discharged.

Steven held on the edges of the table but stayed silent.

"I left. I couldn't get permission to formally take leave so I just hopped on a bus and headed home. I had to see her. I got a taxi that drove me to our street and I had him stop a block away. I wanted to surprise her and walk in the front door. And then...it was revolting."

"Tell me."

"Your mother came out on the front porch with a man. He had his arms around her and gave her a big hug before driving away in his snazzy car."

"What did you do?"

He looked up with fury in his eyes. "I lost control! I ran toward the house as he drove off. Your mother saw me. I was screaming at her. She ran to the front door, but I caught her before she could lock me out."

"Tell me."

"I grabbed her and threw her on the floor. I hit her hard, knocked her down. I kicked her over and over. She was crying, yelling that nothing had happened. I was in a rage and I...forced myself on her. I wanted to punish her. Then, I was so furious, I left. I guess she was scared after...what I had done...she must have called the police." He was red-faced, panting.

"My god! She must have been terrified."

"What the hell. She...was my wife...I could do whatever I wanted."

Steven shot out of his chair, whirled around, stopped himself and paced the kitchen.

His father kept talking. "They turned me over to the military police who threw me in prison for desertion. I tried to explain. I told them it was her fault. She made me mad. She cheated on me."

He looked at Steven with disdain. "I was given a dishonorable discharge. When I walked out of prison, your mother stood there waiting for me. She was pregnant. I accused her of infidelity as strongly as she insisted the child was mine. She said it was a baby growing out of my rage and violence. We never spoke of it again, but I didn't believe her, not ever." He hung his head.

"But, my mother is not a liar. How can you know for sure?"

"Well, it's pretty obvious, isn't it? Your and I aren't alike at all – we don't even look alike."

"But, you don't know, do you? You've been living with this...assumption...and this hatred...and you've taken it out on me my whole life."

"Yeah. You were always a big baby. The way I see it – if you really were my son you wouldn't have been so destroyed by the war. You'd have been stronger, more like me."

"So, you're disappointed that I haven't lived my life like you, as some tough, abusive..." His father jumped to his feet. Steven raised himself to meet his stance. "You see me as lacking some kind of combat gene that you would have passed on to me. Is that what you're saying?"

"Yeah, I guess."

Steven sat back, stunned into silence.

His father continued. "You're just so..."

"I realized you were incapable of understanding..."

"You were always so sensitive, like a little girl. Not like

me at all. Vietnam ruined you. That's not how I would have reacted. Soldiers are tough. If one civilian had spit at me, I'd have..."

That's the whole point, isn't it? We're very different people. And I can't say I'm very sorry about that."

"Now that you know the truth, are you going to abandon me with this bad heart? I need you to take care of me."

"I don't know the truth – and neither do you. Eventually we'll have answers. And I'm told your heart has healed very nicely. Wish it were true."

"I'm not such a bad guy, you know. What about all the times I tried to help you after the war? You'd wallow in your misery; a soldier would never do that. You'd go out and get stoned..."

"I never took drugs when I got back. Not once."

"Well, whatever it was..."

"Vodka."

"I'd bring you home, get you off the streets, clean you up, get some decent food in you..."

"And why did you do that? If I'm not your son...if you hated me so much...why?"

His father shrugged, then said, "And what would you do? You'd bolt again."

"Why did you care if I left?" Steven turned to go, ready to end the fight, then spun back. "Oh, I know! I see it now. You didn't want to be alone. No one around to abuse. That's it, isn't it. You needed me to be your scapegoat. Someone to blame for your miserable life."

"I took good care of you and you'd didn't appreciate..."

460

"You're right, I didn't. I finally realized I had to get away from *you*. I had to save myself. I left because you constantly berated me and criticized me. You called me a low life so many times, I grew to believe it. You gave up on me."

"You're damn right I gave up on you. Sharon said you didn't deserve to be a father. And she was right."

"No! You're lying." Steven grabbed his father's arm. "I have a letter from her. She never said that or believed it."

Steven said quietly, yet firmly, "I am sad to say, you're the one who should never have been a father. I will no longer allow your abuse. I have friends who care about me and believe in me – people who support me and each other – they are the family I want. They believe I can be a better man, and so do I."

"Well, I hate to break it to you. I don't believe you *are* capable of being better. The war ruined you, and there's no coming back from that."

Steven sucked in his breath, unable to believe his father's words. "Do you mean that, or are you just taking it out on me – resenting me if I'm not your 'real' son and hating me if I am, because either way..."

His father turned away. "Hell, I've seen you fail so many times..."

Steven looked at his father as if for the first time. "Yes, I have failed. But I know how to change course. You don't know me at all. Listen carefully – I've become a certified paramedic. I'm a health professional and plan to live the rest of my life helping other people. I'm proud of what I've accomplished."

His father shrugged his shoulders. "Who cares?"

Steven walked toward the front door.

Can I really do this?

He turned as his father followed him down the hall. "I've left the key on the front hall table. I don't need it anymore."

"But, what about getting answers?"

"I found the answers I needed in that old medical certificate. Truth is, I'm still your son...either way...and you will resent me...either way. You are not the father I would have chosen, nor the kind of father I would want to be."

Can I walk away for good?

He whirled around, walked toward his father, then stopped. "You know where to find me. If you need me, I'll be there for you. But I don't need a key to the house anymore. This is not my home."

As he drove away, Steven saw his father in the rearview, standing on the front porch, isolated and alone. He continued driving.

Chapter

48

June 12, 1892

Old Soldiers and Sailors Home
Sandusky, Ohio

Hon. John Sherman,
It appears, Sir, that the pension
which I have requested for over a year,
has come too late. I will not live many
more days to make good use of it.
I would beg of you to reassign this sum
to my two children, Mary and George
Lane, and especially to their mother,
Elizabeth. It is the right and just
conclusion to rectify the tragic
circumstances I have made of their lives.

With my deepest gratitude,
David R. Lane

Steven lay on his bed, slumped over Scooter's warm body. He knew Scooter sensed the sadness he felt after reading this final letter. And it *was* the last letter. There were no more in the satchel. Yet, in the end, David had the foresight to make the honorable decision. His intent to pay back the money he had stolen from his family might somehow offer him redemption, even in death.

It's time for me to learn from this man's mistakes.

Time to call my daughter.

No, not yet. She'll hate me. First, call your mother.

No, not yet. I need advice from Sam. He'll help me sort this out.

~   ~   ~

He stood at the door to Joe's Café with Scooter straining against the leash. "Smell the biscuits, don't you boy. We'll wait till Sam gets here. I'm not sure Joe wants you inside."

"Right behind you, Steven," Sam said.

"Hey, glad to see you. Thanks for coming down on my day off. I don't have much time to talk these days." Steven looked through the glass door. "I'm not sure we should go in."

"I'll check. Be right back." Sam went inside and came back out with Joe beckoning to come in.

"Isn't he a service dog-in-training? Of course, he's wearing his training vest, so he's allowed inside." He leaned

464

down to face Scooter. "Come on in. Let's see what you've learned so far."

"He's learning to follow directions," Steven said. "But, what he's told to do should be specific, and only from me. He has to get used to responding to my commands." He looked at Scooter. "Sit, Scooter." Scooter sat. "Now come." The dog followed his master into the café, tail wagging vigorously. Steven grinned. "Good dog."

He suggested they sit at a quiet corner in the back, in case anyone complained about a dog in a restaurant. Steven told Sam about David Lane's last letter. "It's the perfect ending – he had the foresight to pay back his family when he was so ill and knew he was going to die. I can learn from David." Steven said.

"Oh, my Annie's going to be so happy to know this," Sam said. "We've got to go see her."

"Okay, yes. First, I want to...First – I need to tell you – I had another ugly row with my father, and...he...he..." Steven thought it would be easy to tell Sam about his father's accusations, but he found himself stopping, then his anger took over and in the end, after telling Sam about the confrontation he felt better by simply talking it out.

"What should I do? I feel so twisted up inside."

"This is unbelievable. I suppose you don't have any reason to doubt his words."

"I think he was telling me his version – his truth. In a way, it was kind of a relief. At least I understand his belligerence and why I've felt this antagonism from him, especially when I came back from Vietnam. He lacks compassion, Sam. And he's disgusted with me for being so messed up and he really believes I can't possibly be his son."

"You said it right the first time, Steven. This is *his* truth – what he believes to be fact – only without any evidence to back up his reality."

"Yeah, I know. It's impossible to look at this dispassionately. And as I said to him, it doesn't matter either way. He hates who I am. I guess because we're so different. But I do intend to find a test that will give us answers."

"Good. But first you've got to call your mother...find out *her* truth. You need her version of what happened."

"Shit. I know I should. But I'm not sure I want to do that to her. The way he told it, about his *own* violence, was brutal. Should I put my mother through that – make her resurrect all those ugly memories again?"

"To be fair to her – and you – yes – I think you should. But I've got to commend you. Here you are, more concerned about your mother and what this will do to her, than yourself. That's real compassion, son. I'm proud of you."

"But, remember Sam, I haven't even seen my mother for years. Look at me – I start shaking, just thinking about it. Maybe I should meet her somewhere and talk with her in person, not on the phone."

"Good idea."

"Okay, enough with the shrink talk. Let's go tell Anna."

~   ~   ~

As they turned the corner onto Anna's street, Steven saw two men turn to wave as they walked out of her house with Anna calling after them. Steven stepped on the accelerator. "What the hell! Who is that?"

466

He slammed on the brakes and prepared to leap out of the car as Sam pushed his arm against Steven's chest. "Wait! Stop!" Sam said. "Don't get out. See who it is? It's Anna's sons. Let's not interfere." They watched as Anna ran up to them and gave each a hug.

"Well, I'll be damned." Steven said. "Would you look at that. Looks like there's been some kind of reconciliation. Maybe Anna finally worked up the nerve to tell them how she felt," Sam said.

"That we should all be so fortunate," Steven agreed.

"Oh, yeah."

They watched the car drive away and Anna waved goodbye. Steven drove further up to the curb where Anna was smiling broadly. Scooter began barking happily when he spotted her. Sam jumped out of the car, ran up to her and held her as she wept.

She waved to Steven. "It's tears of joy, I promise."

Sam put his arm around Anna and guided her up the walkway to the house. Steven opened the car door as Scooter raced to the front porch. Tom and Jerry leapt from their post at the windowsill and as the door was opened the cats began their favorite game of 'Catch-me-if-you-can.'

Anna plopped down on the sofa, emotional exhaustion visibly draining from every pore. She put her face to her knees and began shivering until Sam sat next to her and held on to stop the shaking. "Do you want to tell us?" Sam asked.

"They showed up out of nowhere. My older son was carrying his toolbox. When I opened the door, he said, 'I've come to apologize. I've been a jerk.' Then he lifted the toolbox to eye-level and said, 'This is my way of making amends. My little brother is going to help, whether he likes it or not.' I stood shaking my head in disbelief. I told them to come in and asked them to sit a minute so I could make sense of it. Then I asked why – what had happened? It was simple – their best friend's mother had died and he had this huge regret that he had never reconciled with her. He had been estranged from his mother for years, and then she died and it was too late."

Steven sat rigid, listening to every word. Sam said, "What a lesson to learn. I'm so glad for you, Anna."

"I'm so happy. Now, maybe we can communicate, figure out what went wrong and why they had all this resentment. We didn't get into it today, because my son wanted to make good on his promise to help with repairs. You're going to love this, Steven. Guess, what I asked him to do?"

"Fix the lighting on the basement stairs!"

"You've got it. Go look. It's great. Now, I can see the stairs. Boy, have I made a mess down there. So, with a nudge from his brother, my younger son said he'd help clean up the stairs and work his way down to the basement. I am so grateful."

Sam laughed. "There must be something magical about this day, Anna. Or you're getting a double dose of good karma. Wait till Steven tells you about your grandfather's last letter. He turned to Steven. "Go on, tell her."

"From what he said in his letter, your grandfather knew he was going to die. He wrote to John Sherman about his pension and asked him to reassign the money to his wife and children, since he wasn't going to live long enough to use it. Talk about redemption, this was just the best. David finally did the decent thing. I sure wish we had some way of knowing what his family had to say when they started receiving the money."

Anna said, "Well, now that I've got light in the basement, I'll keep sorting through all those papers. Maybe I'll find something."

Steven eased closer to Anna and looked across at Sam. "There's more that has happened on this redemptive, karmic day to tell you about. I took some groceries to my father this morning..."

Scooter suddenly left his post guarding the cats as the bell rang and ran to the door, barking joyously. "Stay put, I'll get it," Steven said. He threw open the door, thinking it might be Anna's sons returning and there stood Lindsay. He was so happy, he threw his arms around her and held her close.

"Wow, look who's here."

Steven guided her to the living room and snuggled next to Lindsay on the sofa. She smiled broadly, but said, "Hold on, Steven. I've got vegetables in the car, freshly picked for the stew." She turned to Anna, "Didn't you ask me to bring them to you?"

"Yes, of course. We'll help you get them out of the car in a minute. First, we're waiting for Steven's story."

They all settled into their seats, leaned forward and listened to Steven as he explained why he might not be who he thought he was. "So, what do I do? Is this man my father or not?"

"Go see your mother. I agree, you should talk to her in person. Get her version of this," Lindsay said.

"But think about how painful that will be for her. Do you want to put her through that, Steven?" Anna said.

Sam chimed in, "I think Steven needs to hear this event from his mother's perspective. Maybe there's a perfectly reasonable explanation. He has to hear it from her, in person."

Anna stood up and tried to pull Steven to his feet. "We all agree. The phone's in the kitchen. Call your mother. Don't wait."

Steven shook his head. "No, I think it's time to see her in person."

Chapter

49

He held on with longing and tenderness. Had he been blind, he would have recognized her scent – as if she spent most of her time in the garden – crisp, clean scent of fresh air and pine needles.

Lindsay will love her.

As Steven comforted his mother, she stopped shaking and began to weep. She pulled away and apologized for what he had been through – for the painful confrontation with his father, for the battles he might have avoided, for abandoning him to the mean spirit of a man who would not accept him. He took her shoulders and held her against his heart.

"It will be all right."

She shook her head in disbelief.

"I promise – I will make it right."

"I don't think you can. I tried for so many painful years."

"Tell me."

"I'm so afraid he'll come after me."

"He's old and sick. He doesn't know where to find you."

"He never believed me."

"I know."

She shuddered.

"Come, sit down. You're shaking."

She set herself away. "I can't sit too close. Now that you're here, all I want to do is cling to you."

Steven reached across the table and took her hand.

She smiled. "Before I say anything else, I want you to know – you are my son – without question."

Steven smiled. "I would never think otherwise. Look at us. We have the same eyes. Yours are that deep blue that can look ominous, full of so much sadness."

She nodded.

"But I look nothing like my father. He made a point of saying so, especially that we have very different characters. In so many ways, we're opposites."

"Oh Steven, I promise, you are your father's son – whether he wants to believe it or not. You are undeniably his son, his biological son."

He put his other hand over hers. "Tell me what happened."

She dropped her head. "It's...awful to tell."

"I need to hear this from your side. I want to understand your point of view. Tell me. No more secrets."

She leaned forward and looked straight at Steven.

"He was so excited to become a soldier. He learned to fly and he envisioned himself blasting over Germany and fighting the enemy. They discovered he had somehow cheated on his vision test, and they sent him home, out of the war zone to teach younger soldiers how to fly. He was devastated. Hated being in the States. He believed he was destined to shoot down Nazi planes, kill Germans, and here he was, living a cushy Army life in Arizona."

Steven nodded. "He said they wouldn't give him a pass to go home – to leave the base to see you."

"From what I understand, the invasion at Normandy was in the final stages. They needed pilots to fly our soldiers over France and parachute them behind enemy lines before the beach landings. So, those conducting the training were working double-duty."

"He said you wrote to him, saying how lonely you were."

"I was miserable for a while and begged him to come home. He was so close. Arizona – he could have made it home in a day. But then I realized I was putting him in an impossible situation and I stopped asking. I volunteered at the hospital in town and stopped missing him." She looked shyly at Steven.

"Then...and then I met this doctor...his name was Tom...this incredibly talented man who performed medical miracles. I admired him greatly. We became friends. He started coming by at the end of a long day and I'd cook simple dinners for us."

Steven sat quietly, unsure of where her story was going.

"I admit to finding him very attractive, but I wasn't in love with him." She smiled. "And I truly was devoted to your father."

"One evening, after our dinner, Tom gave me a big bear hug. He gently sat me back into the dining chair and thanked me for being so kind to him. Then he said the most unexpected thing. He told me he was a homosexual and the armed forces refused his effort to enlist. When they told him, he was inconsolable. He felt he could have made an important contribution and might have saved many lives. I had never met a homosexual before, but it explained why he had never made a pass at me – he wasn't interested in women. I was so heartbroken for him I pulled him from the chair and gave him a big hug in return and as he left I gave him another hug outside on the porch. I doubted I would see him again and told him we would always be friends."

"That's it?"

"That is what your father saw – a hug – nothing more."

"What did he do?"

"He...he waited until Tom had driven away, then he charged at me as if he were going to kill me. I thought he would. He...started hitting me and kicking me. He knocked me to the ground and kicked me some more."

Steven put his head in his hands and covered his ears. She reached across the table and pulled them away.

"You said you had to hear this. So, you must." She hesitated. "He raped me. And then he ran off. I think you know what happened after that."

"I am so, so sorry."

"And yet, from that brutal moment came you...and from you, came Katie. And so, I can never fully regret what he did."

Steven nodded and slid from his chair. He paced the room, then walked to his mother, lifted her from the chair, gently placed his arms around her and rubbed her back as if to warm her.

She turned her head and tenderly looked up at him.

He sat back down.

"How do I make this right with Katie? Tell me about her."

"She's loving and sweet." His mother smiled. "Sometimes she can be quite willful. Always asking questions. Lately, questions about you."

"Oh man. What a lousy father I've been. Just like... how can I..."

"She needs you, Steven. She needs her father."

He dropped his head, then looked back into her eyes.

"I don't know what to do. Help me. I need to understand the best way to go at this. I can't just show up and say, 'Hi there. I'm your father.' How do I do this?"

"Do what feels right, Steven. Don't listen to anything but your own heart.

"She must hate me. Seven years. She's been in this world for seven years. How do I explain that to her? How do I tell her that her grandfather withheld the secret of her birth because he thought I wasn't worthy? He thought I would fail as a father, like I've failed at everything else."

"No, not anymore, Steven. Look at what you've accomplished. You've overcome so much. And you've become a professional, a paramedic. You save people. You're a healer."

"So what? To a kid, seven years is a lifetime – it's *her* lifetime. How do I explain? I know she must hate me."

"I'm sure she doesn't."

"What should I do?"

"Call her, Steven. Call your daughter."

Chapter

50

It is the right and just conclusion ...

Steven entered the Open Heart dining hall after setting his tired puppy in the cottage. He had come off a firefighter's 24-hour shift with Scooter, who was in training to become a fire rescue service dog.

He scanned the room looking for Lindsay. He heard a commotion at the entrance and headed toward the group of veterans who always sat at the large table near the front door. The reflection through the windows played tricks with the light. He thought he saw his father glaring at the vets. They had shoved back their chairs with more force than seemed necessary, but as he approached, the image of his father disappeared as they quietly sat and greeted Steven respectfully. He looked out toward the street and there he was. It was his father's car as it raced away from the building through the quiet neighborhood.

So much for not being allowed to drive.

He turned back to the vets.

"What was that all about?" Steven asked.

Red-faced and angry, one vet leapt up and said, "That was the old man who was so mean to you before. What a loudmouth. We told him to shove off if he wasn't here to help out. He called us a bunch of free-loaders and when he started yelling, we chased him off."

Steven smiled. "Yes, I can identify with the yelling."

Barely able to contain the laugh about to burst from his mouth, Steven was suddenly grabbed from behind and small hands squeezed him around his middle. He whirled around and there stood Richie, ready to give him a big bear hug.

"Hey, little man, I'm glad to see you." Steven stepped back, examining the boy. "Well, well. Look at you! I see you've been well-fed since the last time I saw you. Put on some weight, did you?"

Richie patted his belly and grinned. "Oh Steven. I'm so happy you're here."

"Me too! Did you come with your grandparents?"

"Yup. They're in the kitchen helping Anna." Richie tugged at Steven's sleeve. "And guess who else is here!"

"I don't know. Who?"

"My dad!"

Good for him. Now he's got a purpose.

"Hey, that's great! Maybe I can back off a bit. So, he's helping Anna with the planning and cooking?"

"Yup. And...and guess what else?" Richie didn't wait for an answer. "He's living with us – at my grandparent's house.

478

We're all a family now." Richie produced a wider grin. "I'm so happy! And he's got a part-time job delivering food to restaurants in town. It started with Joe and his café. He did such a good job, more people hired him for deliveries." He did a little dance.

"That's so great, Richie. I'm glad for him and happy for you."

Richie tugged on his sleeve again and pulled Steven down to his level. The boy beckoned to come closer, and whispered in his ear, "Don't turn around, but those men behind you look like my dad used to – kind of scruffy and hungry."

Steven flinched.

And me too.

Steven whispered back. "Richie, those men were brave soldiers who fought in the Vietnam War like I did. They came home kinda messed up. So, we show them respect and always make sure they're well-fed. It might be the only meal they get today."

"I remember what that feels like, your belly aches cuz you're so hungry."

Never forget that hollow feeling. Keep perspective.

"You're so right. And there's something you could do for them. Go to each vet, shake his hand and say, 'Thank you for your service, sir.' It would mean a lot to them."

Without hesitating, Richie stood tall, approached each man and used the exact words Steven had suggested. Steven stood back, savoring the moment of respect given to his fellow veterans. Then Richie said to the group, "Your food's coming up. I'll bring it myself." He scampered off to the kitchen.

Steven headed back to the veterans, seeing each face expressing amazement, looking at each other as if they had just witnessed a miracle. Suddenly he felt warm arms around him again, this time connected to a soft, slender body. He turned and gave Lindsay a long kiss, as the men behind him whistled and clapped. His eyes twinkled as he gave them a nod, placed his arm around her shoulders and guided her toward the kitchen.

He leaned down to her. "I've got to protect my lady from the hooligans."

She laughed and said, "It feels like days since I've seen you. How's my heroic paramedic? Tell me about your visit to see your mother. What did she say? I can't wait to hear." She stopped and laced her arm through his. "Come on, Steven. Did you get answers?" He grinned and stayed silent. "Out with it," she insisted.

"Later. It's a long story," he said and stepped into the chaos of the Open Heart kitchen. "Hi everybody. What can we do to help?" Lindsay gave him a loving swat on his bottom and joined the volunteers.

Anna quickly dried her hands and encircled Steven with her arms. "Glad to see you, Mister. Look who's taken over your job." She motioned to Craig, who was beginning to dish pasta into bowls.

"Hey, Steven. Didn't think you'd mind if I took over some of the heavy lifting. There's still plenty to do."

~ ~ ~

"It's great, Craig. I know this is your expertise, so get us organized. Tell us what to do." Craig beamed.

"Okay. Steven and Lindsay, Richie and..." he looked around the kitchen... "Dad and Mom, take the pasta to the tables, serve the food starting from the inside-out – less confusion. Richie, start with the vets."

"Okay, Dad." But first, Richie walked up his father, grabbed his hand, shook it and said, "Thank you for your service, Sir." Then he took a bowl from Anna, gave Steven a high-five and headed to the veterans' table. Craig remained still, eyes bright with tears, anchored to the floor as he watched his son deliver nourishment – and respect – to the veterans.

"Well, I'll be..." said Anna, as she watched Richie head out. She held up serving spoons with both hands and said, "Okay, everyone. Grab a spoon and start filling the bowls... like Craig said."

Sam arrived, followed by Pete and his mother Grace. "Well, look who's late," Anna said, as she gave Sam a warm hug. "Glad to see you brought reinforcements," she said to him. "We've got a crowd today. Pete, could you help Craig bring in the extra tables? Look at the people standing at the door with nowhere to sit."

Anna handed silverware to Grace. "Could you take this out to the tables?"

Grace whispered to Anna, "The truth is, we all want to hear about Steven's trip to visit his mother. Does anyone know? Do you have an answer to Steven's parentage?" she asked quietly.

Steven turned and gave her a grin. "Uh, there's nothing wrong with my hearing, Grace."

"I'm glad you asked," Lindsay said, as she gave Steven an affectionate nudge. "I guess he'll tell us when he's ready."

"And I'll be ready after we serve these folks their lunch and we have a chance to sit."

"Okay, let's get this show on the road," Anna said to her troops.

~   ~   ~

The volunteers at Open Heart began to dish up the leftover pasta and settled around an empty table as the families walked up to offer their thanks before leaving. The veterans had begun clearing the tables and washing up.

"Will you look at that?" Anna said. "Did you ask them to help, Steven? I saw you talking to them."

"Nope. I think they want to contribute and are just grateful...and I know exactly how they feel."

"Me too!" Craig agreed. "And I gotta tell you, I am so glad to be on the other side of it."

"Amen," said his mother.

"It's humbling to see what you all have accomplished," Grace said. "I wonder how many you fed today? And families with little children. Count me in. From now on, I expect a call when you need help."

"Thanks, Mom." Lindsay gave her mother a hug.

"I don't know how you do it," Craig chimed in. "How did you grow all those herbs for the pasta?"

Lindsay grinned.

"Oh, I know how she did it," said Grace. "You should see our kitchen window at home. Filled with pots and pots of herbs. My brilliant daughter."

482

"Do you think your brilliant daughter could coerce her stubborn boyfriend over there into telling us his mother's side of the story?" Sam turned to Steven. "Come on, give it up. Tell us who you believe. Who are you, anyway?"

"Yeah," Craig agreed. "We want the straight skinny on your parentage. Do you know yet?"

Steven looked around to make sure Richie was out of earshot and saw him helping the vets clear the tables. "You have an amazing son, Craig. Appreciate what you've got there."

"Yeah, I know. He's something, isn't he? Now don't try to change the subject. You're avoiding the question, Steven. What did your mother have to say?"

"What is this? Does everyone know about what my father said to me?" All heads nodded. "What the hell! Are there no secrets from you all?"

"We care about you," Anna said tenderly. "We're family."

Steven looked at her with gratitude and began to tell his story.

"Okay. Here's my mother's side of this story. And I believe her – every word..."

~   ~   ~

After Steven finished telling his friends about his meeting with his mother, Sam pushed himself into the back of the chair and folded his arms. "So now what are you going to do, Steven?"

Anna leaned forward and gently placed her hand on Steven's arm. "Your mother asked you to call Katie. She was very clear."

Steven laced his hands behind his neck, ducked his head to hide his face. "I can't. Don't you see?" He slid off the bench and stood, leaning on the table for support. "I failed her. It's as if I deserted my daughter. She's old enough to get the fact that it took me all those years to contact her. Don't you think she'd be awfully resentful?" He plopped back down on the corner of the bench – defeated.

"Well then, explain it to her. Tell her the truth," Sam said.

"She doesn't need to know about her vile grandfather."

"Why not," Anna asked? "He doesn't deserve your protection. She's going to find out eventually. Besides, this isn't what matters."

Sam jumped in. "Steven, listen to me. Do you remember how you felt when you found that first letter from David's daughter, Mary? You were so happy for him. He's been dead 100 years and you're still cheering for him. He got his redemption. So should you. Call your daughter, Steven. David Lane couldn't make a phone call, but *you* can. You can do this."

Steven shook his head and sat anchored to the bench.

Lindsay shoved herself sideways against Steven's inert frame. "You're really starting to infuriate me, Steven. Why is it so difficult? Just call her."

Steven turned toward Lindsay and in a rasping whisper said, "You of all people. You don't understand?"

"Of course I understand. I simply don't agree with you. Look – I'm the genealogy expert. Can we agree on that fact?"

"Okay, so?"

Their friends at the table leaned toward Lindsay and nodded.

"So, I've studied lots of family histories, stories about how people pulled apart, became estranged, scattered away from each other. It's so easy to let it happen. And I've researched other families who found value in each other, supported each other, accepted each other and stuck together." Lindsay twisted around so she was facing Steven fully and placed her hands in his. "You've got to decide, Steven. What do you value? No matter how afraid you are, what are you unwilling to lose? What are you willing to fight for – to hold on to?"

People at the table looked toward each other.

Anna rose and spoke directly to Steven, "Only you can decide. What do you cherish? What matters?"

"I know what matters. All of you matter. You are my family." Steven stood and faced his friends. "I realize that David Lane made a huge mistake. He didn't have to let this tragedy happen to him. All he had to do was *show up*. All he had to do was go to that hearing and refute the accusations and indictment. All he had to do was tell the truth. He failed because he didn't show up. We'll never know why. He didn't speak up for himself. But do you know what he did very well? He wrote letters."

And I became the beneficiary.

Lindsay smiled and squeezed his hands. "Yes, I see. All this time, you've been learning from David."

"Yes, I have. I finally get it!" Steven jumped to his feet and faced his loyal, extended family. "First, I'll write a letter to Katie. It worked for David, maybe it'll work for me."

Dear Katie,

I have found you! How could I be so lucky?

Your Grammy has told me all about you.
I am mighty proud to be your father.

The good news is that I've started a new
job. The not-so-good news is that I can't leave
my work right now. It's a great job, I can't
wait to tell you all about it when we meet.

It's breaking my heart that I can't jump
in the car and drive to you. Please understand.
I'll be there as soon as I can.

Love from your Dad.

Why don't you call me Daddy -
I like the sound of that better.

486

Dear Daddy,

I was so excited to get your letter. My very first letter! See, I'm calling you Daddy.

Grammy helped me write back to you and told me about your new job and how important it is. I think you're a hero. I know why you can't come to see me - not yet, anyway.

She also told me about your dog, Scooter. Can you bring him when you come? I want to meet him too. I'm not allowed to have a dog until I'm eight.

Maybe you can call me until you can come in person. can you, please? I'd really like that!

I love you, Daddy,

Katie

Steven gently set down the letter and placed one hand over it, as if to bless it.

His eyes brimming with tears and bright with joy, Steven reached for the phone.

A Word
About the Type

Cormorant is a contemporary
typeface developed by Christian Thalmann
in Zurich, Switzerland. Inspired by the heart and feel
of Garamond, Cormorant is characterized by strikingly
small counters, sharp serifs, elegant curves,
and accents that reach high
for attention.

*Cormorant was
selected to emphasize
Steven's tactile and emotional
connection to the letters he found.*

Made in the USA
Middletown, DE
02 September 2021

47443885R00300